Beyond The Shield

A Novel by

Nachman Kataczinsky

Beyond the Shield

This is a work of fiction. Any references to historical events, real people, real locales, businesses and incidents are the products of the author's imagination or used in a fictitious manner.

First printing: September 2016

Second edition: October 2016

Library of Congress Control Number: 2016915878
CreateSpace Independent Publishing Platform, North Charleston, SC

BISAC: Fiction / Science Fiction / Time Travel

ISBN-13: 978-1537705620
ISBN-10: 1537705628

Rank Armor Publishing
www.TheShield.RankArmor.com

This is a work of fiction dedicated to my parents,
who survived the real horrors, and in memory of those who did not –

my Uncle Ze'ev (Wolf) Frumin, aunt Sheina Kataczinsky,
grandparents on both sides of the family, and millions of others.

Introduction

This novel is the second in a series taking place in an alternate universe. In the previous book, ***The Shield***, 21st century Israel was accidentally transported into the past – specifically, 1941, days before Germany attacked the Soviet Union and started systematic mass killings of Jews. By stealth and force, Israel stopped the Holocaust and brought the endangered people home, greatly increasing the population and creating confusing family relations. So that the reader will not be confused, here are the members of the newly-expanded Hirshson family featured in this book:

From the 21st century:

Ze'ev, 64 years old, founder and CEO of Consolidated Industries, graduate of the Technion, and an MIT Ph.D.

Linda, Ze'ev's wife, 60 years old.

Chaim, Ze'ev's and Linda's eldest son and a manager at Consolidated Industries, in his late 30s.

Ephraim, their second son. IDF Brigadier General, in his mid 30s.

Shoshana, their daughter. A nurse and head of a nursing school, in her early 30s. Married to Noam Shaviv, an architect.

Benjamin, the youngest son. A clothing designer, in his late 20s.

From the 1940s or saved from the Holocaust:

Jacob Hirshson, Ze'ev's father, in his early 20s.

Sara Hirshson, Jacob's mother - saved from murder, in her forties.

Sheina Hirshson, Jacob's sister – saved from murder, in her late teens.

Esther Frumin, Ze'ev's mother, in her late teens.

Nachman and Tzila, Esther's parents – saved from murder, in their forties.

Wolf, Esther's brother – saved from murder, in his early twenties.

Historical figures appear in this novel completely fictionalized, although I tried to make them as true as possible. Historical events are mostly fictional but weapons, both historical and modern, are as close to reality as I could make them.

Beyond the Shield can be read on its own, although I do hope you will read ***The Shield*** as well. Enjoy!

Chapter 1
February 1942

The weather was lousy, but what can one expect in London in February? At least the embassy was warm. Most of the damage done to the building by a German bomb in 1940 had been repaired and the structure was actually better than new; parts were newly constructed of thick, reinforced concrete to withstand a direct hit.

The Israeli Ambassador to the Court of St. James, Avigdor Mizrahi, decided he had enough time to relax before his afternoon meeting with Winston Churchill. He was satisfied that everything was in order, including the outline of his presentation.

He left shortly after lunch and arrived at his destination with no incident and on time. No mean achievement taking into account the traffic. England had definitely recovered from the German U-boat blockade and fuel was plentiful.

✡✡✡

“Good afternoon ambassador. How are you?” Churchill greeted Mizrahi cheerfully.

“Fine, Prime Minister. And I hear that the news from Africa is good.”

“Yes. The Germans seem to have lost their desire to fight. Montgomery tells me that he may be done with them within the next month or so.” Churchill started clipping a cigar. “We also have a proposal from the French to attack the Germans from bases in Morocco. What do you think?”

“I’m sure that my government will approve. Since it seems that your forces will be free to decamp from North Africa fairly soon I was asked by my government to discuss the Italian project.”

“Ah,” Churchill puffed on his cigar to get it going. “I agree. We need to get ready. But it will take time. As you know, we’re still gathering forces and doing our best to equip them.”

"Mr. Prime Minister, one reason I requested a personal meeting is the issue of equipment. Britain isn't as stressed as it was a few months ago and this may be a good time for a technological jump.

"You may recall our concerns about giving you advanced technology. At the time our opinion was that it might cause damage by diverting your development and manufacturing efforts, thus reducing the number of weapons you were producing." Mizrahi paused and unrolled some drawings. "One of our engineers came up with an idea that will both give you a significant advantage and is within your current capabilities."

He spread the top drawing on Churchill's desk; it took up most of the surface. "This is the full manufacturing file for the Centurion tank. It would have been designed by Britain in 1943 and entered service in 1945, just as the war in Europe ended. We tweaked the design to improve reliability. This tank design was the mainstay of our armored forces for several decades."

The Prime Minister got up from his chair to take a closer look at the large drawings. "Mr. Ambassador, I am grateful, but did your government really think us so stupid and untrustworthy? They didn't trust us – me - to make the right decision several months ago?"

Mizrahi expected a response along these lines and was prepared. "Mr. Prime Minister, it wasn't a question of trustworthiness or stupidity. May I remind you of the near catastrophe at Al Alamein? Your commanders got overconfident with the intelligence and weapons we gave you. If it wasn't for our intervention Rommel would likely now be on the south bank of the Suez Canal. The temptation to switch to making the new tanks several months earlier would have been irresistible and my government decided to avoid the risk. Do you think that the Germans would have been beaten as quickly if Britain decided to switch tank models before the end of the African campaign? My government assessed the possibility of you going with the new tank prematurely at about 20% and it didn't dare take that chance. Millions of our people's lives depended on a prompt German defeat in North Africa."

Churchill sat down and revived his cigar. "Twenty percent? That low?" He smiled. "I would have estimated it at 50, but I do resent your government sitting in judgment on my possible decisions and depriving me of making my own choices. Can you let them know in the most forceful way that this is not acceptable to me?"

"I will do that," Mizrahi responded, "but I have to point out that we are allies and as such free to do what we think best for our own nation. I assure you that this is highly unlikely to happen again. History has been changed in massive ways and our clear crystal ball is now as cloudy as yours.

"In any case, let me continue since I have several more pieces of technology to share."

Churchill nodded.

Mizrahi removed the next bundle of drawings from his briefcase. "Here are all the plans and manufacturing data for what we call an assault rifle. This particular model is the AK-47. It would have been designed by a Russian, one Michael Kalashnikov, in 1947. In our estimation this weapon will greatly improve the firepower of your infantry. If you decide to manufacture it, we will be more than happy to assist. I also have several samples and boxes of ammunition at my office for General Wilson.

"The next weapon we would like to offer for your use is a fuel-air bomb or, as it's also known, a thermobaric bomb. This is a formidable weapon if designed and implemented properly. Your experts would have one designed and tested by 1944 but that design is not optimal. I have brought drawings and a design handbook. We have not used these bombs very frequently – they are basically block busters and city destroyers. The bomb in these drawings will easily destroy a typical European city block and cause widespread fires.

"The last but by no means the least weapon I would like to present to you is what we call an RPG, Rocket Propelled Grenade. The name is a bit misleading. In fact it's an anti-tank weapon that can also be used against fortifications. I will leave these drawings, specifications and photographs with you.

"Here is another list. Your 'Tube alloys' project and the American 'Manhattan District' or 'Manhattan Project' are riddled with spies. Soviet spies. Any advance you or the Americans make is being reported to Stalin almost as soon as it happens. This list includes all of the spies and some outside the projects that serve as conduits. I hope you'll deal with them soon."

Churchill puffed on his cigar without saying anything. Finally he put the cigar down. "I'm curious, Mr. Ambassador. You said that you didn't use the fuel air bombs very frequently. Might I ask why?"

Mizrahi nodded with a smile. "I guess I invited the question. There are a number of reasons we don't use them. The most important one is that these are imprecise weapons that cause destruction on a wide scale and we Israelis always try to do as little harm as possible to civilians."

"Yet you give the technology to us. Why?" Churchill was again puffing on the cigar.

Mizrahi smiled a predatory smile. "We learn from our past mistakes and don't want to repeat them. An enemy has to know when it's defeated and one sure way to impart this knowledge is to make the civilian population realize that an armed conflict is lost. Without such realization the next war is only a question of time.

"I believe that you will agree with me, Prime Minister, that the Nazis couldn't have started the current war if their population believed that Germany lost the previous war fair and square and wasn't 'stabbed in the back'. Such belief has to be visceral: If your neighborhood and city is mostly in ruins, you will be wary of anyone proposing a war.

"We give you the tools to convince the enemy that they lost the war. These bombs will not necessarily win the war for us but they might prevent the next one."

✡✡✡

Mizrahi's next stop was the Soviet embassy. Ivan Mikhailovich Maisky, the Soviet ambassador to the court of St. James, appeared to be a simple and straightforward man. Mizrahi knew it was just a façade. Still, it was easier to work with people who were smart. The two ambassadors had met the previous month at a cocktail party organized by the British Foreign Office. Churchill had personally introduced Mizrahi to Maisky as "the honorable Ambassador from Palestine". If Maisky was puzzled he never showed it. Since then the two had a short, private discussion in which Mizrahi clarified what Churchill meant without disclosing the full truth. No hint was given of coming from the future with advanced knowledge. Mizrahi intended to lay the ground for formal diplomatic relations at this meeting.

"Would you like a drink? Tea? Coffee?" the Soviet ambassador asked.

"Tea would be nice. Hot and no milk please," Mizrahi responded.

Maisky smiled. "No milk? You may not be as British as I assumed."

"Oh, I'm not British at all," Mizrahi responded. "I represent the independent state of Israel that is located in what used to be called Palestine. We are allies with Britain in the war against the Nazis."

"I know," Maisky said. "We heard from the British and our own sources how helpful you have been to them."

"We would also like to be of assistance to the Soviet Union. After all, we're fighting a common enemy."

"What can such a small country do for us?" Maisky looked genuinely puzzled.

Mizrahi relaxed a bit. It was clear to him that whatever information the Soviets had was very fragmentary and inaccurate.

"We have superb information gathering and analysis capabilities. Let me show you an example."

Mizrahi pulled a photograph from his briefcase. "This is an aerial image from yesterday of the front near Moscow. It suggests that the salient anchored by Demyansk and Rzhev is vulnerable to being cut off. But if you look closely, the Germans have concentrated large forces near Rzhev. According to other information, they will try to attack in the direction of Mozhaisk and Moscow, leaving the northern forces near Demyansk where they are. They're also ready for your counterattack on Rzhev."

Maisky studied the satellite photo. "This must have been taken from a very high altitude. Interesting. How do you know what the Fascists are planning?"

Mizrahi smiled. "This is something I'm not free to tell you. You'll have to trust us on the reliability of our sources." He pulled out several additional photographs.

"This is the general area around Voroshilovgrad, also yesterday. As you see, the Germans are almost up against the Don and we know that they plan to attack in two directions: primary attack across the Don in the direction of Stalingrad and a secondary attack to the south on Rostov. The Stalingrad attack will be by General von Paulus and his sixth army. His orders are to take Stalingrad, cross the Volga, and move north on Moscow."

Maisky carefully examined the photographs and asked, somewhat skeptically, "Do you have advice for our generals on how to counter this?"

"We would not presume to give you advice of that sort. The Red Army knows what it's doing. We only hope that this information will help. Please do not hesitate to call me if your High Command needs more information."

Maisky nodded. "Assuming your information is good, which I have no way of judging, what would you want in the future for information like this?"

"It's a little too early to discuss. I suggest that you transfer this information as soon as possible and after it proves useful we will meet again.

✡✡✡

The South European Desk Manager at the Mossad (the Israeli intelligence service) handed a file to the good-looking woman in her mid-twenties sitting in front of him.

"I think you'll like this job."

The agent, Michella Stern, looked at the first page. "Interesting assignment. You know that my family is still living in Milan in 1942? Maybe I'll visit them. How long do I have to consider this assignment?"

"You have until the beginning of April, but the file isn't complete, so you'll have to do some research."

✡✡✡

General Ephraim Hirshson, the commander of the Israeli base in Brindisi, had been busy planning, observing the fighting in North Africa, and then more planning. He felt tired and thought that a walk outdoors might do him good.

The weather was on the cold side but not too bad. His army issue coat was warm and the slight sea breeze was invigorating. The part of the base used for housing Jewish refugees from Europe was almost empty, with several hundred people waiting until there were enough to fill a ship. Hirshson expected more to arrive this week, a far cry from several months ago when the base was processing forty-thousand refugees every day.

Ephraim himself was the grandson of Holocaust survivors. Most of his father's family had been murdered by the Germans. In this new reality they were rescued and in Israel. This was both confusing and uplifting. Ephraim suddenly had a large extended family, with his grandfather, Jacob, younger than him.

He walked through the gate built into the tall concrete wall separating the refugee part of the base from the much larger military part. Today no transport aircraft were parked on the runway. His jeep was waiting. The driver started the engine and they rolled across the wide field to the south, where elements of the Seventh Armor Brigade were setting up their encampment.

The brigade had arrived only two days ago on an Israeli cargo ship, with the last vehicles rolling to shore only this morning. The jeep stopped next to the command tent and Hirshson walked inside. A small, dark colonel waved to him from next to a large map table: "Hello, Ephraim. Congratulations on your promotion." The colonel saluted. "As you can see we're setting up. I think we will be ready for a formal inspection tomorrow."

"No hurry," responded Hirshson. "Inspections can wait. The German air force attempts to penetrate our perimeter several times a week. Don't let them closer than fifteen kilometers."

"Yes, sir. If you'll come with me I'll show you what we've done so far."

The two officers walked around AA batteries, anti-aircraft missile clusters with radar and fire control computers. Hirshson stopped by one of the tanks. “Sergeant Frumin, how are you doing?”

The move back in time meant many Israelis had odd family relations. Sergeant Frumin would have been Hirshson’s great-uncle, murdered in the Holocaust. In this time line he was just a younger member of the newly extended family Ephraim had just met and advised a few months ago. He smiled at the memory of Wolf’s crush on Ephraim’s great-aunt Sheina. Luckily they were not blood relations – Wolf was Ephraim’s maternal great uncle and Sheina was his paternal great aunt. Neither had survived in the original history.

Wolf Frumin and the three soldiers next to him jumped to attention and saluted. “I’m fine, sir. Thank you for the inquiry.” He tried to brush some hair from his eyes but only succeeding in smearing black grease on his forehead. He had been in the process of cleaning and lubricating the main cannon – a job for the whole crew.

The Colonel nodded. “Carry on, guys.” The two officers continued on their walk.

“Colonel, one reason I came to take a look at how things are going is that the rest of your brigade will be here day after tomorrow. The same ships are carrying the twenty-seventh armored, as well as most of Golani. As the senior officer of this encampment it will be up to you to decide who goes where. I’m glad to see that you have the positions for the others marked, but we will have to make some changes.

“You will have to spend more time here than anticipated. I was notified that the operation will likely start only in July. I requested mobile homes to replace your tents – the weather here may become rainy and cold and I don’t want the men living in tents unless it’s absolutely necessary. We will house at least half your soldiers in the refugee quarters and feed all of them at the cafeteria there. I expect you to visit my office soon to coordinate with my chief of operations.

“Another issue we have to discuss soon is how to handle the British forces that will start arriving in a month or so. We don’t want them too close to ours but we need to do it without creating antagonism. Your advice would be welcome.”

✡✡✡

Jacob Hirshson, the 20 year old grandfather of General Ephraim Hirshson, finished packing his bag. He was as ready as he expected to be for tomorrow’s trip to the local recruitment office. He was a refugee from Lithuania, one of a group who volunteered to go back to Nazi-controlled Europe to persuade his fellow Jews to leave. Jacob had come to Israel a year ago with his mother Sara and sister Sheina, both of whom were murdered in the Holocaust in the old time line.

Jacob sat on his bed for a moment, then went into the living room. It was a bit crowded with family members who had come to send him off. Jacob's son from the other timeline, sixty-two year-old industrialist Ze'ev Hirshson, was there with his American wife Linda and youngest son Benjamin. The conversation stopped when Jacob entered.

"So how do you feel now about becoming a soldier?" Benjamin asked.

"A bit conflicted. It's not easy to abandon a new business and leave for six months or maybe longer."

"Don't worry," Jacob's uncle Chaim said. "The business will be fine. Just take care of yourself." Chaim and his family also hadn't survived the Holocaust in the old timeline.

Jacob smiled. "I know that you will take good care of it. I'm conflicted about the long-term. Having a business and obligations makes joining the professional army more difficult. After all, Chaim, you're not a surveyor and a surveying business needs a licensed professional at the helm."

"I'm glad you see that," Ze'ev said. "Hopefully you will weigh your options carefully and decide to join the reserves and not the professionals. It may be selfish of me but it's enough that I have a son and Wolf in the army; both are likely to see action soon."

"Enough serious talk," Jacob's mother Sara said. "Let's eat something. Jacob has six months to make up his mind and things can change."

✡✡✡

Nitzan Liebler, Israeli Defense Minister and retired general, looked at the executives around his conference table. It seemed to him that most of them didn't feel in their guts that the country was at war; the urgency was lacking.

"Gentlemen, I will repeat again: we have to go from making one Merkava tank a week to making one a day. Please don't give me excuses; I know it's going to be difficult. So let's take it from the top.

"Itamar what's your situation?"

Itamar Herz, Managing Director of Israel Aircraft Industries, checked the file in front of him: "I don't know all the details of our subsidiaries' operations but we will not have a significant problem quadrupling our output. Going to seven times the current output will take us several months.

"I'm sure that Elbit has about the same capabilities."

The president of Elbit nodded. "We can do it, although for some parts and for the Trophy system we rely on RAFAEL. If they are good, we are good."

The Chairman of the Armaments Development Authority (RAFAEL) just nodded his agreement.

The Minister looked at the Engineering Corps' Commander. "Well, it looks like it's up to you."

"Not entirely." The general looked at the Israeli Military Industries Chairman. "IMI seems to be the one having problems. But it may be best for their Chairman to explain. The other potential problem may be at Consolidated."

Ze'ev Hirshson, President of Consolidated Industries, responded, "The only problem we are having just now is a slight delay in steel-making capacity. If we use all of our large casting capacity we will be able to make four hull and turret sets a week. To go up to seven or eight we will need our new facility in Refidim to go online. That will take another two to three months. The four sets a week now will be possible only if we do nothing else, so I'll need you to coordinate with the Infrastructure Minister."

"That will not be a problem," Nitzan Liebler responded. "What about engines, transmissions, and guns?" he asked the IMI Chairman.

"Guns are a separate issue," replied the Chairman. "If we retool the 60mm line that is making guns for the Brits, we will be able to supply about ten additional 120mm tubes each week. That should cover both assembly and replacement requirements. It will take us about a month to retool.

"Engines should not be a problem either, as we are assembling them mostly from parts supplied by turbine manufacturers and they have spare capacity. Transmissions are a different story. Our current plant is running at capacity. I think that we can make two transmissions a week if we run it in three shifts. Beyond that we need a new plant."

"How long to set up a new plant?" asked the Minister.

"Probably six to eight months, maybe a year."

"Unacceptable," Nitzan Liebler almost shouted.

Ze'ev raised his hand in a calming motion. "We can probably start making parts within a month or so. Our machining shops have spare capacity due to lack of exports. We can also immediately start supplying precision castings. Hopefully this will let IMI assemble three or four transmissions a week starting in, say two months. We can gear up to make complete transmissions in about four months."

Nitzan smiled for the first time in the meeting. "Good. I will have an order for you by the end of the week. And," he turned to the IMI Chairman, "you will do your best to assist Consolidated. It is a good idea to have two sources for transmissions anyway."

Chapter 2
March 1942

"Dr. Epstein, you've been testing our tetracycline for a month now. What's your opinion?" The representative of Lancaster Pharmaceuticals was sitting on the edge of his chair – a picture of eager expectation.

The Medical Director of the Montefiore Hospital in New York City looked at the file in front of him. "I have to admit that the results were spectacularly good. I've never seen any medicine that could cure pneumonia and other infections so quickly. I did see another drug, penicillin, mentioned in research papers as having potentially similar abilities. We don't have access to it. Merck told us they're working on it and may be able to give us samples in five or six months. Does your drug have any connection to penicillin?"

The rep nodded. "It belongs to the same general family of drugs as penicillin but is far more advanced."

Dr. Epstein leaned back in his chair. "Who is Lancaster Pharmaceuticals and how did you get so far ahead of everyone else in the business?"

"We are a British company and a fully owned subsidiary of 'Teva' – a pharmaceutical company in Palestine. As you can see, the packaging says the drug is made in Israel. You know, Eretz Yisrael.

"Would you like to order some for your hospital?"

"Yes, and I will certainly recommend to every physician that is accredited with us," Dr. Epstein responded. "Do you have any other drugs to offer?"

"We have a large variety, but I would recommend that you start with three classes: antibiotics, analgesics and anti-acids. For stomach ulcer sufferers we have a special medication that cures ulcers completely in 85% of patients."

The Teva/Lancaster rep, an Israeli employee of Teva, decided to hire more representatives and ask headquarters to set up a training program in the U.S. He envisioned explosive sales growth.

✡✡✡

General Henry Maitland Wilson was the first, and so far only, British military officer to visit Israel. When Israel arrived in 1941 the British forces were fighting French Vichy in Syria. The Israelis gave Wilson valuable assistance. Churchill deemed him smart, and since he was the only other Brit to know the secret of Israel's time displacement the general was appointed liaison to the Israeli ambassador, meeting with him regularly.

"How do you do, Ambassador?"

"How do you do, general?" responded Mizrahi. He sat in front of Wilson's desk. Wilson occupied a suite at the War Office, which offered privacy.

"General, my government would appreciate the help of His Majesty's government in leasing a piece of land in Canada. It will, of course, be done discreetly through a private corporation."

Wilson nodded. "We are always willing to help, but you will need to give me more information: what do you intend it for, where do you want it, and what size should it be?"

"We intend to set up a landing strip. The idea is to make it easy for American Jews to go to Israel. We could fly them from a Canadian strip in the southwest corner of New Brunswick. To make it safe, we would need about a mile long runway and some support buildings. Probably two square miles would be satisfactory."

"You don't want to build it in the U.S.? It seems to me that building it closer to your target population would make it more useful."

Mizrahi smiled. "The U.S. is fighting a war in the Pacific. We're not their ally and have only the most tenuous contacts with them, so we can't expect easy cooperation. Of course, this may change in the near future. We might accelerate the process if you find it difficult to assist us with the Canadians."

Wilson extended a hand in a pacifying movement. "Please don't misunderstand me. I was just curious. We probably can do something about Canada."

Chapter 3
April 1942

It was a beautiful day. Michella would have preferred to be walking on the nearby Tel Aviv beach, instead of reporting to her boss, the Manager of the South European Desk of the Mossad.

"I finished reading the file and did some research of my own. The only thing I'm missing is the purpose of this exercise. What am I to do with the information?"

The Manager leaned forward in his chair. "It's quite simple and I'm sure you've guessed what we want: If the government decides to go ahead we will need Mussolini to die quickly of an incurable disease. Any ideas?"

Michella smiled: "Sure. How long will I have to prepare?"

"The decision won't be made until August, so you have three, maybe four, months."

Michella's face assumed a cold, clinical, expression. "The subject has syphilis. It seems to be well-controlled by his doctor, Ambrogio Binda. There's not much information on the medication the doctor is using, but since he's visiting Mussolini regularly and il Duce usually rests for a couple of hours after these visits, I assume it's a version of Salvarsan or Neosalvarsan, you know, one of those nasty Arsenic based compounds they used to use to control syphilis symptoms. It really doesn't matter as long as it's an injection.

"I will befriend the doctor, probably get him to hire me as his nurse or pharmacologist and, when the order comes, add some polonium to the injection. Radiation symptoms will appear to be a worsening of his condition and he'll die. Since polonium is fatal only if injected or swallowed no one else will be in danger."

"Good. Sounds like a plan. You will have some time to study your identity and fly to Brindisi. Good luck."

✡✡✡

Jacob Hirshson was dead tired. Only two weeks remained until the end of basic training and he wasn't sure he'd survive. His day started at six in the morning. A light breakfast was followed, on most days, by marching drills. After that came weapons training, different modes of infantry assault - some with live ammunition, hand-to-hand, more weapons training and more live ammo. The only rest came at about noon in the form of lunch.

By the time they were done with military stuff for the day the newcomers were in for an hour or so of Hebrew training, especially military jargon and acronyms.

Now he was preparing to go to sleep. At least today nobody called. Most days his mother called on his cell phone to remind him to eat and making sure he was healthy. His uncle called to update him on the business. Jacob really appreciated the rest and relaxation of the Sabbath. He also learned that five minutes were a very long time in which he could catch a nap, do his bed or even shower.

It seemed like the training achieved its main objective: turn a civilian into a soldier that obeyed orders first and asked questions, if necessary, later.

Someone stopped by his bed. Jacob opened one eye and jumped up to attention. His sergeant stood next to him.

"As you were," the sergeant said. Jacob sat on the bed and the Sergeant sat next to him.

"I made some inquiries as you asked. There was a change in policy last month. If you want to go on to advanced infantry training and even to a commando unit it is possible. Your performance up to now is acceptable, so it's up to you. Let me know by the end of next week. I need to submit the paperwork before you are done with basic."

"What was that about?" Jacob's friend and neighbor on the next bed inquired after the sergeant had left.

"You didn't hear?"

"No, he spoke too quietly for that. Are you in trouble?"

"That depends," Jacob smiled. "It seems that we are eligible for advanced infantry training and even commando units. I really don't know what to do."

"Well, I'm not going for infantry training. I'll train as an auto mechanic. At least it has some use in civilian life and besides I'm dead tired of running around all day long."

"I'm tired too but it's temporary. This is what basic training is all about. I already have a profession so there may be some utility in obtaining training in something different, but I'm not that excited about it. After my experience at the hands of the Germans and Lithuanians I wanted to become a commando but I guess I'll have to think some more."

✡✡✡

Amos Nir, the Prime Minister of Israel, stretched and took another sip of his lukewarm coffee. It had been a long day and he still had one visitor to deal with.

Dr. Ahmad Mazen, Chairman of the Palestinian Authority, entered and, at an inviting gesture from Amos, sat in the proffered armchair. Mazen had lost some weight since they met last time. He also looked tired and worried.

"Well, Mr. Chairman, you asked for a meeting. The floor is yours."

"I appreciate you meeting me so soon." Mazen smiled. "I know how busy you are.

"Last time we met I promised to give you an answer: will we or will we not agree to leave to another time. We have come to a decision. It will be abided by all factions, including Hamas."

"Please enlighten me," said Amos.

"We've decided to stay. There's no reason we can't negotiate an autonomy agreement and continue to have our own limited government within the framework of the Palestinian Authority. If the principle is acceptable we can go into details."

Amos was silent for a long while. Mazen became visibly uncomfortable. Finally Amos said, "I remember no such option being mentioned at our last meeting. The Palestinian Authority will cease to exist. The choice your leadership needs to make is simple: you can either leave to another time or you can stay. If you stay, you will all become citizens of Israel. No more separate autonomous government, especially as you have broken every agreement with Israel and there's no reason for us to believe that you won't break this one at the first opportunity. We've had enough.

"Just in case you misunderstand me: if you stay, you and your colleagues on the PLO council will become private citizens. The PLO, Fatah, Hamas, and all your other organizations will become illegal and disbanded. The PA armed forces will be disbanded, all sixty thousand of them, and disarmed. We also did some thinking and decided that we really don't want Arab political or terrorist prisoners in our jails. All these will be released no matter what you decide. They will be sent into the far past to fend for themselves. The same will be done with all future murderous fanatics. So do you still want to stay?"

Mazen was visibly shaken. “But this is unfair. We have a right to this land. Generations of our forefathers from times immemorial lived here. It is our land as much as it is yours. More in fact. We deserve some autonomy and our own elected leadership.”

Amos was annoyed and close to losing his temper. “Dr. Mazen, you also pronounced a while ago that Jesus was a Palestinian. Shall I treat all your statements as seriously as the Jesus one? You said just now that generations of your forefathers lived here. Can you tell me how many generations of your own family lived here? I can tell you: exactly two. Your grandparents came to Palestine in the 1890s from Algiers via Damascus. You would still be living in Safed, if it wasn’t for your parents’ idea that the Jews would seek retribution for the massacre of 1929. You yourself said that was the reason they left for Jordan and then Damascus in 1948 and took you with them. You’re not an exception either. You know why so many of your people bear the name al-Masri? It means ‘from Egypt’ and this is exactly where they came from not so long ago. So much for having lived here from times immemorial. But this is all in the past.

“Why do you think you deserve anything from us? You broke every agreement you made with us. We offered you not just autonomy: we offered you an independent state. What was your response? You wanted your state to be completely free of Jews and you wanted to settle millions of hostile Arabs in Israel. You refused to accept the largest possible state we could offer you and still survive ourselves. Your response to that offer was riots and terror that cost us thousands of lives. Clearly your existence as a people is predicated on only one desire: the destruction of Israel and the Jewish people.

“Your response to the latest events – the time travel incident – confirms this. You sent emissaries to the Nazis and to your revered Hajj Amin al Husseini, Hitler’s best friend, with an offer of the knowledge to build a nuclear bomb. You deserve the same treatment as the Nazis.

“As to elected leadership: You, Mr. Chairman, are now in the tenth year of your four year term. Do you actually represent anybody?” Amos relaxed and smiled, a bit incongruous in light of his short speech.

Mazen sat up straight and asked, “Is any of this negotiable?”

Amos responded, “I thought it was clear that you have choices but these are not negotiable. We are done negotiating. We’ve tried that. More than a century of talk is enough, especially since the Arabs have never negotiated in good faith.”

Dr. Ahmed Mazen nodded. “The Hamas leader predicted this. What exactly will happen if we decide to leave?”

"We can work out the details later. The rough picture is simple: All Arab settlements in Judea and Samaria outside the security barrier will be transported to the past. You will have a say in what time you're sent to. All those living in the affected areas will have no choice – they will go. Arabs living in Jerusalem and all Arabs holding Israeli citizenship will have the option to join you, though I don't imagine many will take it, even though we would compensate them for their loss of property. We will do our best to give you as a group enough supplies to survive until you can support yourselves.

"I expect a final response from you by the end of April."

✡✡✡

Gad Yaari, the Chief of General Staff, looked at the assembled generals. "We have a number of assignments and need to prepare plans."

The room quieted down as Yaari continued. "We need to make it easier for the Brits to bomb Germany. This means removal of the German long-range Freya radars along the Atlantic coast to enable the bombers to come in undetected. It also means seriously thinning out the Wurzburg radars that control the anti-air defenses around cities. This mission can start as soon as we're ready.

"In about a month, sometime in May, we will start receiving British forces at our Brindisi base. These will eventually amount to two full armies, approximately 300,000 troops. The British High Command expects to have at least two million men in Europe, but that will happen gradually over the next year. Our forces will move through Italy sometime in July or August. We don't expect fighting in Italy and will deploy in northern Italy. As you know, we're still working on detailed plans.

"Any questions?"

As expected the Commander of the Air Force had a question. "I'm assuming the first mission is mine?"

"That depends on what we decide. For the moment let's assume so. What do you propose?"

"We will obviously need detailed planning, but it looks like a classic mission for the Heron 3 drone," the Air Force commander said. "We can equip the Herons with one ton bombs with radar sensors. It means about one bomb per drone but we have enough of them to finish off 80 Freya radars in a single run. The Freya is different from the British 'Chain Home' in that the individual stations have a longer detection range and are more accurate. They also are more compact, and easier to destroy."

The Chief of Military Intelligence stirred in his seat. "The Germans have only sixty-three operational Freyas so your plan is good. You would have to launch the drones from the Brindisi base. Going from here will take too long, assuming you want to hit the Wurzburg radars the same way."

The assembled generals looked at the Chief of General Staff. Yaari nodded. "Seems like a plan. Let me know the details."

✡✡✡

Michella followed the middle-aged woman and made sure she had a key to the door of a doctor's office facing a quiet alley near the Roman Coliseum. It was a fairly expensive district and an appropriate location for the office of Il Duce's doctor. The plaque next to the heavy door said just: "Dottore Ambrogio Binda". The woman was the doctor's nurse, receptionist, and secretary. Apparently the doctor was concerned about privacy and having just one employee made sense.

The next step was studying the woman's routine, habits and friends, if any. Three days later Michella decided she knew enough to formulate a plan of action. The Mossad archivist told her that the nurse was a spinster and had some family, including several nieces and nephews, who lived in the Milan area. Michella didn't see any signs of friends.

The courtyard of the house where the nurse rented a small apartment was empty in the middle of the day. Michella was certain that she wasn't seen as she entered the stairs leading to the third floor. The lock was simple and in a couple of minutes she was inside the apartment. It was spotlessly clean. The kitchen was well-stocked; it looked like the nurse liked to cook and did so frequently. Michella decided that she needed to make sure that the nurse would call in sick the next day and stay away from work for at least a week. The simplest way would be food poisoning, which in the absence of antibiotics could be very serious indeed. Some powdered E-coli, Salmonella and mild hallucinogen mixture judiciously applied to the bread should do the trick.

The next morning Michella observed a neighbor's boy run to the doctor's office. The nurse didn't leave the apartment. A couple of hours later Michella entered the apartment. The woman was in bed. She looked sick and was somewhat delirious. She accepted Michella as her niece, come to take care of her. When Dr. Binda arrived to check on his nurse he found her being taken care of by her niece, a qualified nurse herself.

"You say your name is Maria? She never told me about you," the doctor said.

"My aunt is a very private person and we're not that close. As it happens I came to Rome looking for a temporary job and found her very sick."

The doctor thought for a moment. “It looks like your aunt has food poisoning, but I’ll take some samples just to make sure.” He opened his bag. “In the meantime, please give her these every couple of hours and apply cold compresses to her forehead until the fever drops. She should be OK in a couple of days.

“Now I need to find a replacement,” the doctor muttered as he prepared to leave.

“Doctor, if the medication works my aunt should be out of danger by tomorrow. I could save you some trouble and help while she’s recovering. One of the neighbors can look in on her while I’m at work.”

Doctor Binda thought for a moment. “Good. Come to the office tomorrow at eight in the morning. Just to be clear, I don’t have a permanent position. After your aunt recovers I might be able to give you a recommendation.”

The next day Michella knocked on the door at eight sharp. The doctor let her in. It took him close to an hour to show her all he wanted her to do, explain the routines and carefully instruct her on how to answer the phone. After that he disappeared into the inner office and didn’t emerge until one in the afternoon. At that time he locked the door to the inner office, politely said goodbye and informed her that he was going to see a patient and would not be back until the next day. He also left her a key to the outside door and told her to come at nine the next morning.

As soon as he was gone Michella locked the outside door and picked the lock of the inner office. It took her almost an hour to find what she was looking for. During that time the telephone rang once. It was il Duce’s office and they wanted to know whether the doctor had already left. When she confirmed, the secretary on the other end of the line simply hung up.

Michella took a number of photographs of an object at different angles, plus a number of macro close-ups. She transmitted the images to the drone that was circling Rome at forty thousand feet waiting for her signal. The drone re-transmitted the images to the Brindisi base and from there they went to the Mossad.

Three days later a special courier arrived from Brindisi and met Michella outside her “aunt’s” apartment. He handed her a small package. By then the aunt was recovering and Michella kept feeding her small doses of a mild hallucinogen to keep her from recovering completely and recognizing the “niece” for the stranger she was.

The next day, when the doctor again left at noon, this time with the promise to return by about two in the afternoon, Michella again unlocked the inner office. She found the tin with a cardboard insert of fifteen spaces, of which ten were filled with glass ampoules. She took out the ampoule to be used next and replaced it with what looked like an identical copy. It also had the Bayer company logo and the drug name: Neosalvarsan.

Just as she was leaving the room the outer door handle began jiggling. She closed and quickly locked the door. As she approached the front door it opened.

Doctor Ambrogio Binda stood in front of Michella. "Why do you lock the front door? Where are you during working hours? What if it was an emergency?" He was angry and somewhat agitated.

Michella assumed a supplicant position: head down, hands clasped in front of her.

"I am so very sorry. I had to attend to a call of nature and thought it best to lock the door. It was locked for less than five minutes. I apologize."

The doctor made a non-committal sound: "How's your aunt doing?"

"I think she's fine," responded Michella. "She wanted to return to work tomorrow."

"Good. Please tell her to do so. What you did is inexcusable. Do not return."

Michella sighed with relief. Her mission was over and she was sure it would be a success. From the office she went to her "aunt's" apartment to tell her that she was expected at work the next day. Her next stop was the railway station. The trains ran somewhat better under Mussolini and she caught the seven p.m. to Naples and from there a connection to Bari. There was a slow local train from Bari to Brindisi.

✡✡✡

Ephraim Hirshson's General Staff phone was ringing. It was a conference call with the Chief of General Staff and the Commander of the Logistics Branch.

"Ephraim, we need you to be prepared to accept the British Eight Army and another force of similar size, probably the first Army, sometime in June or July. What do you need to receive them?"

Hirshson pulled up his notes. "That would depend on what they're bringing with them and what supplies they will continue to stream after the main force arrives. We would be able to feed the whole force for about a week."

The Logistics Commander responded. “That would leave you empty. We will get more food to you but be judicious with its use. It’s only for an emergency if the Brits screw up with their supply line.”

General Hirshson had a question. “I’m assuming that everyone is aware that the Italian navy is just around the corner from us in Taranto. What if they become hostile?”

“If they do we’ll have to deal with them, although our intelligence people assure me that this is unlikely,” the Chief of General Staff responded. “They also assure me that the situation will be resolved soon. Do you have enough space in the current confines of the base to accommodate everybody?”

“I think we’re fine with that. Of course, the Brits will have to live mostly in field conditions – tents and so on.”

“Okay. If you have any specific requests, contact the Logistics Branch Commander directly.”

After the call was over Hirshson called in his deputy. “We need a final survey of the base. In another two months we have to accommodate two British armies. I want the terrain properly graded and prepared for them. The Engineers should be particularly careful about the positioning and depth of the latrines they dig.”

Next Hirshson contacted both the armored brigades and Golani commanders. The conversation with them was short: “Gentlemen, the Brits will be arriving in a couple of months. Assuming that you want to keep up your normal training schedules please consider this. There will be only simulator training after they arrive.

“As you know we promised the Brits access to our intelligence. A decision was made at a higher level that all the information we give them will be in the form of radio transmissions. They don’t get access to our data networks. Be sure your troops know that these are classified assets not to be revealed to the Brits.”

✡✡✡

The Prime Minister raised his hand. The cabinet ministers quieted down. “We have a number of items on the agenda. Number one is the management of our war against Germany. The Chief of General Staff will make a quick presentation and we’ll go from there. Gad, the floor is yours.”

Gad Yaari turned on the projector and a map of Europe appeared on the far wall. “As you can see, the Germans have a line of Freya radars along the Atlantic coast. The idea is to detect British bombers early and be able to jump fighters up to intercept them before they can reach the large industrial centers and cities. These radars are quite advanced, much more advanced in fact than the British Chain Home system. They are more accurate in estimating both distance and direction. Since some of their night fighters also have radars, albeit only short-range, the Freya chain points the fighters close enough to make the bombers very vulnerable.

"In a week or so we start destroying the Freya radars. There are about sixty of them. We will use drones to drop bombs directly on the antenna arrays. Since the electronics shacks are next to the antennas one-ton bombs will destroy both. Now, the Germans have some spares that they will undoubtedly install with all due speed. We will destroy them as well. This will leave a couple of mobile systems on trains or trucks. We discussed this with the Brits and they think that we should leave them alone for the time being. Their reasoning is that if we destroy all their radars they will sense that something is wrong and try developing new and better systems. The Brits don't want that and our intelligence people agree – always leave the enemy hoping.

"Our next operation will be to destroy some of the Wurzburg radars. These are short-range and used to direct anti-aircraft fire around large cities. We will destroy some of them and leave the rest for the RAF to deal with. Any questions up to this point?"

The Minister for Infrastructure had one: "Why use drones? Isn't the danger of losing one higher than losing a manned aircraft?"

Yaari nodded. "Indeed it is higher, but there are other considerations. We normally lose small drones at a rate of one every fifteen hundred flight hours. We've never lost a Heron, except the prototype that crashed several years ago. If we do lose a drone the Germans will be able to learn very little from it, at least very little information useful in the short term. The electronics are solid state and the engine is a turboprop. The engine is actually the one useful item they might learn from. On the other hand a manned jet is a different proposition, starting with the pilot. I don't think I need to go into details.

"There is one aspect of this operation that also has to be mentioned: If we lose a craft, be it a drone or manned, the Germans will likely become aware of our participation in the war against them."

"What about the bombs? Won't they be able to determine our complicity from analyzing those?"

"Not easily. With the agreement of the Brits we are using bombs actually made by Royal Ordnance with all the appropriate markings. We only install the primary and secondary detonators and, of course, the radar detector and servo guidance system. In our test everything but one of the detonators is reduced to mush and what remains of the detonator doesn't look unusual."

Amos Nir continued with the agenda. "Our next item is still the war, but from a different aspect. We have several goals. Achieving all of them will not be easy or simple. Just to remind you: we want Germany defeated and defeated in a way that will deter them, as much as possible, from starting another world war. We also want the Soviets to stop at their old international border. And we want to achieve all this without U.S. participation."

"Why are you so opposed to the U.S. joining the European war?"

Amos smiled. "It's not just me. I think that almost all present agree on this. But let me remind you that Hitler didn't declare war on the U.S. and there is no will in the U.S. to fight a two front war. Charles Lindbergh and Henry Ford are popular and both argue, loudly, for either support of Nazi Germany or, at least, non-intervention in Europe.

"But suppose that somehow the U.S. gets involved. What's the guarantee that Roosevelt will not do what he did before and give Stalin all of Eastern Europe with Churchill reduced to futile objecting? With our presence the objections could have more weight but it will mean a confrontation with the Americans that we don't want.

Another point already discussed is that if the U.S. joins the war in Europe it will build up both its industry and armed forces, making the country into a superpower. Do we really want that? As of now, we know that the Manhattan project has been slowed down to almost nothing and they lost some of their first-tier scientists, including Klaus Fuchs the mathematician, who were Soviet spies. This also insures that Stalin won't get the bomb any time soon. If the States join the European war, research will get more funding from Congress and we don't know where that will lead.

"Now, we need to discuss how to do all the things we want to do. I think that the Head of the Mossad has some ideas."

"Well, it's more of an observation and analysis," the spymaster said carefully. "The simple observation is that Nazi Germany is a balanced structure that can be destabilized with some effort. Political and police powers are held by the Nazi party while military power is in the hands of the armed forces. In time of war this may be exploited to cause difficulties.

"The Nazi party also has some military power in the form of the SS and their own military intelligence apparatus in the SD. The military has, theoretically, to follow the Fuehrer's orders. But what happens if the military is suspected by the party of an attempt to grab control of the country? Remember Stalin's purge of the military in 1937? I am quite certain that the German military, if handled properly, will not be as passive as the Soviets were."

The cabinet meeting went on for several more hours and eventually a plan of action was approved.

Chapter 4
May 1942

The duty officer in the radar control center just south of the port city of Bremen relaxed a little. The time was close to two in the morning and a stiff breeze was blowing from the North Sea. It was a clear night and since none of the Freya radars under his supervision detected British bombers it was unlikely that any were coming this night. All the lights on his board were green – all radar stations nominal.

As he was about to get himself another cup of the ersatz coffee one of the lights went red. The major picked up his field phone and spun the handle. “Give me station FSZ 3.”

After a short delay a voice answered, “Sir, the station doesn’t respond. It looks like the line is cut. We are sending someone to repair it.”

This was strange. The major heard of sabotage but not in Germany. Station 3 was just west of him. While he was waiting for the line to be repaired the rest of the board turned red in fast succession. He called the Luftwaffe control center in Hamburg – They were the next higher coordinating authority.

“Yes, Kurt. What’s the problem?” the duty officer responded.

“My board is completely red. You know what’s up?”

“No idea, but you are not alone. We’re taking care of this so sit tight.” The line went dead.

The board didn’t go back to normal. At dawn Kurt finally heard from the line repair people: the four radar stations reporting to him were gone, completely destroyed by direct bomb hits.

Several days later an investigative team of military and civilian experts was sifting through the ruins of station FSZ 3. They found, as usual in such cases, remnants of the bomb’s casing and its tail fin. The fin was in fairly good condition. It was painted pale yellow, somewhat charred but still clearly an RAF color. It also was clear to the team that the bomb was steerable since one of the motors moving the fins partly survived the explosion. This wasn’t a big surprise since the Luftwaffe also used bombs that could be steered by radio. The team’s conclusion was that the Freya chain was destroyed by the RAF using bombs equipped with radar sensors. The conclusion was confirmed several nights later when a number of Wurzburg anti-aircraft artillery control radars were destroyed by bombs with similar tail assemblies.

The specialist from Lorentz argued with the one from Telefunken about the best method of disabling these sensors. Finally they agreed that the only thing to do was to shut down the surviving radars when an attack wasn't in progress. This was the team's final recommendation to the Luftwaffe.

When two days later a similar attack destroyed half of the Wurzburg radars the recommendation was the same: keep the radar off until there's evidence of enemy bombers in the vicinity.

Several days after that the Luftwaffe placed an order for a hundred modified Freya radars and a hundred and fifty Wurzburg units. This was a serious expenditure of resources but Germany could not be left without a bomber warning system.

✡✡✡

"Your Excellency," Albert Conforti bowed his head slightly, "I appreciate you meeting with me." Conforti was a veteran of the Israeli Foreign Service and a past Israeli ambassador to Italy.

The Italian Foreign Minister, Count Gian Galeazzo Ciano, rose from his seat in the opulent office and extended his hand. "Frankly I was curious to meet a representative of the secretive people from Brindisi.

"Il Duce agreed to Herr Hitler's request and never heard from the people on whose behalf the request was made. I was beginning to suspect that we made a mistake."

Conforti smiled. "Minister, you may regret it yet but I do hope to assuage any suspicions you may have.

"I am the ambassador to Italy, assuming you will agree to accept my credentials when the time comes, from a state located in what you know as Palestine. We have developed a very strong entity and, as you may have concluded on your own, have the cooperation of both the British Empire and Germany."

Ciano nodded. "Yes, we know about that, although it's beyond my understanding how you got those bitter enemies to agree on anything.

"But excuse my rudeness. Please be seated. Would you like something to drink? We have excellent coffee, tea, and of course, wine."

Conforti sat in the closest armchair. "Thank you. I'll take a cup of tea, please."

Ciano also sat and after ringing for a server said, “So how did you persuade the two enemies to cooperate with you?”

“It’s usually simple if you are strong enough to enforce your will and smart enough not to cross some boundaries,” Conforti responded.

“So you are, apparently, strong enough to discourage both powers from interfering with whatever you are doing,” Ciano stated.

Conforti smiled again. “Apparently we are, but we are also careful not to step on toes if it’s not absolutely necessary.

“I was dispatched here because my government has a proposition for you, Minister.”

“Ah, I like the direct approach.” Ciano paused while their drinks were served.

“So, what is your proposition?” he asked when the server had left.

Conforti stirred his tea. “First, your Excellency, let me clarify something: are you aware of the seriousness of the Duce’s condition?”

Ciano was a little startled. “How do you know about that?”

“Oh, we have excellent sources. Since your father-in-law has been ill for some time now we took the liberty to investigate.” Conforti paused, looked at Ciano and decided not to add anything.

“How does il Duce’s condition matter to you?”

“We are interested in who the next Prime Minister is going to be,” Conforti responded.

“And what is your interest in that? The only thing of mutual interest between us is your base in Brindisi. Are you afraid that the next Prime Minister will cancel your privileges and expel you?”

“No, Minister, we are not concerned about that.

“From your response I take it that you are aware of il Duce’s serious condition?”

Ciano nodded. “Yes, I am aware of it. His doctor gives him mere weeks to live, unless a miracle happens, of course.”

“Your Excellency, purely hypothetically, if Il Duce dies do you have a good chance of becoming Prime Minister? That is, do you think the king is likely to appoint you and is the Fascist High Council likely to accept you?”

“Purely hypothetically, of course,” Ciano responded, “the council will accept the king’s decision as long as the appointee is not someone outrageously unfit. They would accept me.

"There is some chance that the king will appoint me, but I will have to persuade him. I had no plans of doing so as I have no desire to become Prime Minister. Not under current conditions."

"Yes, I see," Conforti said. "I am assuming, and please correct me if I am wrong, that you do not particularly approve of Italy's partnership with Germany?"

"That and some other things," responded the Foreign Minister.

Conforti put aside his almost full cup of tea. "With your permission I would like to describe a hypothetical scenario.

"What if you were offered the opportunity to join us and the British in a coalition against Germany? This is, of course, purely hypothetical."

Ciano put his cup, very carefully, on the table between them. "What would Italy gain from such an alliance? I have my doubts about Britain's ability to effectively fight Germany, and I know nothing about your abilities."

"Minister, we are not offering that you join an alliance against Germany. A coalition is a less demanding and violent arrangement. But to answer your question: If Italy agrees to join such a coalition, all Italian prisoners of war now held by Britain will be immediately repatriated. From them you will learn how much stronger than Germany we really are. Please recall that the Africa Corps and your own armed forces were thoroughly defeated within six months by the British Eighth Army, which was numerically much smaller than your combined forces. If this doesn't convince you, we will welcome your visit to Brindisi."

Ciano thought for a moment. "What do you expect from Italy if, hypothetically, we agree to become members of your coalition?"

"It is fairly simple," Conforti responded. "We want Italy's permission and assistance to move our combined forces to Northern Italy in order to attack the Germans. We realize that this will anger Herr Hitler, who will, likely, order the extermination of Italian troops anywhere he can catch them.

"We will therefore not announce the agreement immediately giving Italy some time to extract troops from Greece, Albania and, most importantly, Russia."

Ciano shrugged. "I'm sure this is not all you want."

"After we start our operations against the Germans, Italy may decide to join us and become a full-fledged member of the winning alliance." Conforti paused. "We think that Germany has already lost the war. They failed to conquer Britain and are now stuck in a war they can't win in Russia. It's only a matter of time before everyone sees it."

Ciano got up, signaling the end of the interview. "If I were, purely hypothetically, to become Prime Minister, I would support this policy."

✡✡✡

"You idiots. You call yourselves generals? My dog could plan these operations better!" Hitler was furious and expressed himself forcefully and loudly.

Members of the OKW (Oberkommando der Wehrmacht, the German High Command) stood in front of the map table looking down at it, not daring to look at their furious Fuehrer.

The operational maps showed the current positions of German and Soviet troops. In the south, along the Don River, they were approximately where they had been a month ago before the German push towards Stalingrad. In the north, opposite Moscow, the Soviet salient in the Demyansk/Rzhev area wasn't a salient anymore. The Soviets were approaching Voronezh, had taken Demyansk, and were close to Novgorod.

After a long pause General Wilhelm Keitel finally said, "Mein Fuehrer, I'm not saying that the OKW are geniuses but something strange happened. The Russians seemed to anticipate our moves and every attempt to cross the Don was blocked. They are disorganized but given the amount of artillery and tanks they managed to concentrate, not to mention infantry, the Wehrmacht had a serious problem. We estimate that the Russians lost close to one hundred thousand troops and hundreds of tanks in this battle. Our losses were much smaller, but we will need time to reorganize for a repeat attack.

"On the Moscow front we planned a two-pronged attack from Rzhev. Two SS divisions were to attack in the direction of Demyansk while the rest - an armored corps and a mechanized division - were to attack in the direction of Mozhaisk and Moscow. The SS were supposed to meet up with our forces in Demyansk, thus liquidating the pocket. We expected to take Mozhaisk in forty-eight hours and be on our way to Moscow.

"The Russians brought up an army-sized force to Rzhev and attacked our forces a full day before we were ready to move. They also apparently reinforced their forces in the salient. The attack on Rzhev was repulsed but we suffered losses and will need time to replenish and reorganize. Their reinforcements attacked Demyansk, which, as you know, was held by a small infantry force. The Russians took Demyansk and kept advancing."

Keitel pointed at the map: "This is the result."

Hitler returned to his seat and said in a quiet, menacing voice, "These are my orders: Army Group South will attack immediately in two directions, east in the direction of Stalingrad and south towards Maikop and the oil fields.

"Army Group Center will attack in the direction of Moscow and Army Group North will stop the Russian advance on Novgorod."

The Fuehrer got up and marched out of the conference room.

General Jodl, the Chief of Operations of the OKW, looked at Keitel and shrugged. "I'm going to prepare the orders. Will you get them to the Fuhrer for approval and signature or shall I do it?"

"I will have them signed," Keitel responded.

✡✡✡

Ze'ev Hirshson arrived home early Friday. Consolidated Industries always closed early on the afternoon before Sabbath so he and his employees had time to prepare. Usually these days Friday dinner was limited to himself and his wife Linda. Their kids were married and had families of their own, except for the youngest that was spending more and more time with his girlfriend. Ze'ev hoped they'd be married soon.

Today there were a number of cars parked in front of the house. They were expecting their daughter Shoshanna, with her husband, and their son Chaim, with his family. The names were a little confusing. According to Ashkenazi Jewish custom children were named after deceased relatives. Ze'ev's son Chaim had been named after Ze'ev's great uncle, murdered in the Holocaust. In this timeline the great uncle was well and alive and coming to dinner, as were Ze'ev's maternal grandparents, Nachman and Tzila Frumin. Both perished in the Holocaust but were now alive and well here and younger than Ze'ev.

"Hi, everyone," Ze'ev announced from the door.

A chorus of greetings responded. A bit later he was seated at the head of the table. Linda, his wife, lit the Sabbath candles, joined by three women, each with her own set of two candles. The meal was served when they were done.

"So what's new with you guys?" Ze'ev asked his son-in-law.

Noam was an architect and partner in a firm that had received a government order to design a new city. It was doing well and growing fast.

"Nothing much," Noam responded. "As usual, I'm going to abandon Shosh for my six weeks of reserve service, which is annoying with the new baby and all."

"Don't worry, I'll manage just fine," his wife responded. "Sara is going to move in with me for the duration." Sara was Ze'ev's paternal grandmother, rescued from Europe with her son - Ze'ev's father - and daughter.

"Ah, that's good," Ze'ev smiled. "Jacob will not be back from his service for several months yet."

He turned to Nachman Frumin. "I hear that your business is doing well. I also get news from time to time from Wolf."

"Yes, we really appreciate the ability to communicate with him daily by phone." Nachman smiled. "Who could have imagined that we'd use all this modern stuff."

"How is Wolf doing? I get only secondhand news and even that not frequently. Ephraim is a bit busy these days." Ze'ev was referring to his second son: General Ephraim Hirshson, commander of the Brindisi base.

"Wolf is happy, although he sounds a little frustrated." Nachman looked at his wife, who nodded. "He seems to be eager to go into action, which to tell you the truth we're not so eager to see.

"He's also completely taken by Sheina. They exchange several emails every day, including pictures. I doubt that he has enough time to do his military duties."

"Don't worry," Noam smiled. "He's in the Seventh Armored and they don't have slackers."

"Speaking of slackers, where are you going to do your reserve service this year?" Ze'ev wanted to know.

"Hey, I'm not a slacker. You think they would promote a slacker to Captain and Company Commander in the 927th?" Noam responded. "To answer your question, we're going to be deployed in the area between the Sea of Galilee and the Dead Sea. Apparently there are Bedouin tribes moving around the area who are either not aware or don't believe that we're here. It will be my job to make them believe."

"I didn't know. Congratulations on your promotion." Linda said.

"Thank you."

Everybody else joined in the congratulations and Ze'ev called for a toast.

"Oh, I completely forgot," Ze'ev turned to Nachman. "I was making inquiries about Esther." Esther was Nachman's and Tzila's daughter, and Ze'ev's mother in the other timeline.

"There are indications that she's indeed in Samarkand, at a nursing or medical school. The more important thing is that Israel has established relations with the Soviets and very soon we will have emissaries going there to repatriate as many Jews as possible.

"I'm doing my best to have her at the top of the list. You know how it is, personal connections count for something and people owe me. I hope that we will have her back here soon."

✡✡✡

The two ambassadors were drinking tea, a beverage preferred by both. Soviet Ambassador Maisky was curiously looking around the cozy room of the Israeli embassy in London he was visiting for the first time, but there was nothing unusual about it.

Mizrahi said, "I understand that congratulations are in order. The Red Army gave the Germans a nice flogging."

"Yes, yes indeed," Maisky agreed. "We owe you some thanks for the intelligence. It was very helpful, although to tell the truth we have our own sources that gave us the same information."

Mizrahi smiled. "Yes, the Red Orchestra is very good at what it does. But it can't provide you with the details we gave you."

Maisky looked slightly surprised. "Red Orchestra? What's that?"

"If you really don't know, any inquiries may not be very healthy."

Mizrahi nodded at the papers he was spreading on the table. "I will give you these photographs as well as the relevant German operational orders. The rest is up to the Red Army. But perhaps this is the time to discuss the quid pro quo?"

"Yes, I suspected that the information was not going to be free."

"The cliché is that nothing in life is. On the other hand, some things are more expensive than others. Unlike the Americans and the British, we're not asking for gold. Our request is much more modest and I'm sure that you personally will support it.

"Let me start from the beginning. We are well aware that you are a scion of a Polish-Jewish family, an assimilated one, but Jewish none the less."

Maisky sat upright, making pushing motions with his hands. "This is untrue. I have heard it many times but I'm not Jewish."

"Mr. Maisky, or shall I call you Mr. Lachowiecki? I could, if you wish, provide you with the full genealogy of your family but I'm sure you will agree that it's not important to the way the world sees you. Mr. Chamberlain referred to you in private as 'the little Jew' and Mr. Stalin and the others are saying similar things. A Jew is always a Jew.

"I'm saying all this just to establish a common ground. We are thankful for what you did, at the request of the chief rabbi of Palestine, for the Jewish students from Poland that were trapped in Lithuania. Getting them Soviet travel permits was a life saver and delivered them to safety in Palestine. We also appreciate your communications with Professor Weizmann and the encouragement and help you gave him."

Maisky leaned forward. "I was just showing a human interest in those poor students. My communications with Professor Weitzman were in the interests of the Soviet Union. If they seem friendly and supportive that's because they were."

Mizrahi smiled. "I was just saying that one can be our friend and a loyal Soviet citizen. We appreciate our friends and help them when they're in need.

"Let's go to the other issue," Mizrahi continued. "What we want for the information we're giving you is cheap: We want the Soviet Union to give its Jews the freedom to emigrate to Palestine. This will entail the release of those in concentration camps, the repatriation of Western Jews who escaped from the Germans, and the release of Soviet Jews that choose to move. This is somewhat similar to the agreement you signed with Sikorski for the release of Polish citizens in July of 1941."

Maisky nodded, "This may be doable, but I will need agreement of the British government and also some kind of assurance that we are dealing with a legitimate sovereign entity.

"I have a question though. It will be asked by my government, so I may as well be open and get an answer from you instead of guessing: What will happen if my government refuses?"

"If your government refuses to cooperate on such a small and insignificant issue, our stance will change from allies to neutrals, at best. Obviously all cooperation will cease."

The Soviet ambassador looked skeptical. "You will help the Nazis if we refuse your request?"

Mizrahi looked at him for a moment. "No, we will not help you, which is not the same."

"What if the Nazis win?"

"We've already come to an arrangement with them to let all the Jews under their control leave. More importantly, the Soviet Union losing doesn't necessarily mean the Nazis winning.

"On the other hand, I see no real need to discuss this possibility unless you think there is a real danger of your government refusing our request."

Maisky nodded, "I agree."

✡✡✡

Amos Nir gestured for quiet. He was presiding over yet another cabinet meeting. "First, several updates: British forces are trickling into Brindisi. They will probably be at full count by the end of June. Our joint operations should start soon thereafter, subject to the events in Italy going as planned. The British troop numbers will be larger than what they initially told us but we can deal with that. Foreign Minister?"

"After his conversation with our representative in Italy, who hopefully soon will become a fully accredited ambassador, Count Ciano met twice with King Victor Emanuel. Ciano called for a meeting of the Supreme Fascist Council next week. We foresee no difficulties. Apparently he's so sure of his position that he already instructed the Italian Ministry of Defense to recall their troops. Of course, the recall from Germany will need his personal touch. My estimate is that the Italians will be ready to move by the end of July."

"Good." Amos looked around the table. "Questions?"

"What if the Germans refuse to let the Italian troops go?"

The Foreign Minister responded, "This is unlikely since their opinion of the Italian's fighting ability is low. Whether it's justified is another question. The Italians pose a logistical burden on the German army with, as far as they're concerned, little to show for it. The only reason they didn't dismiss them already is that Hitler was reluctant to offend Mussolini. If the Italian Prime Minister asks…" The Minister shrugged. "There may be a problem if the Germans dawdle, not letting them go immediately but not refusing straight out. We, and the Italians, will cross this bridge if we get to it."

Amos Nir waited for a moment to allow for more questions. "The next update is from the Brits. They will have five commando teams in Germany by mid-July. As you know, we will have three of our own there at about the same time. This, in addition to our drones and air force, should be enough to execute Operation Earthquake."

No one had any questions about that.

Amos continued, "The next item is the Palestinian Authority. Mazen informed me that they decided to leave and have picked a target time. We transported a sensor package there and its recordings show conditions that are slightly cooler and rainier than here and now. Generally a good place for crops and for building a civilization. It will take us several months to set up the transport system and to gather supplies for them.

The Justice Minister stirred. She was a proponent of continuing "peace" talks with the Palestinians and derived not insignificant political benefits from supporting the Palestinians.

"I'm still not certain that transporting them into the past is legal, but my question is simple: would there be a possibility of them returning?"

The Prime Minister looked pained and a bit angry. "If you think it's illegal to transport them into the past please cite the law. Otherwise, I'm sure this gathering doesn't want to hear about it.

"To answer your question: they will have no equipment to affect a return. If they succeed in building it, they will be able to move around in time but are not likely to return since they won't have the exact coordinates they're leaving from. We could bring them back at any time if we want but I don't anticipate doing so."

"If they are in trouble and likely to perish, it is our responsibility to rescue them," said the Justice Minister.

The Defense Minister looked surprised. "Why are we responsible for them?"

"If we exile them we are responsible," the Justice Minister responded.

Amos Nir looked amused: "Minister, please feel free to bring it up for discussion before the full government and even the Knesset. As far as I'm concerned we have no responsibilities towards people who want to murder us and tried for more than a century. Besides, this is their choice. Would you suggest that if we exile some of the Nazis instead of executing them we would also be responsible for their well-being?"

"Well, not the Nazis."

"And what exactly is the difference?" asked the Finance Minister. "The same ideology and the same goal, just a difference in name.

"This discussion gives me an idea. Do we really have to remain here? I mean, after we collect all the Jews that want to come to us, why don't we leave into the past as well? That would solve a number of problems. For us it would be a world without anti-Semitism, except the self-haters, who I hope will choose to stay here. For the rest of the world, it will be a fulfillment of a dream: a world without Israel or Jews."

Nitzan Liebler, the Defense Minister, responded, "A world without Jews would give the final victory to Hitler, but I see no real need to keep suffering if we have a solution that will allow us to live in peace."

The Prime Minister said, "This is an interesting idea. I suggest that we devote a full meeting to it. There are many factors to consider. We also need time to collect the rest of our people.

"In any case, we need to discuss it in more detail."

✡✡✡

The leadership of the PLO and the other terrorist organizations were meeting, at the Chairman's request, in the basement of his presidential palace in Ramallah. There were no windows and all electronics were carefully removed. They could be reasonably certain that there would be no eavesdropping.

Ahmed Mazen called the meeting to order. "I notified the Israelis that we are ready to go into the past just as they wanted."

"A brilliant move," Mohammad al-Husseini, the head of Hamas in Jenin and a nephew of the Jerusalem Mufti, pronounced. "Now we can strike a death blow to the Zionist entity."

"This is our last chance to destroy them," Mazen agreed. "We need to breach the border with Jordan and send enough people across to be able to give the Mufti, and his friends the Germans, information on how to make an atom bomb. We failed in our previous attempt because the few agents we sent were caught crossing the Israeli border. This time we will not fail.

"If enough of our fighters manage to get through we have a good chance to take control of Jordan."

"Wouldn't the Arab Legion and the British defend King Abdullah?" asked the representative of the Islamic Jihad.

Mazen smiled. "It's a good thing I'm a historian. In 1942 the Arab Legion only had about 1600 soldiers and those are dispersed between Syria, Jordan and Palestine. Of course those in Palestine were lost. This leaves only several hundred actually defending the Hashemite emir.

"The British have only service and headquarters troops in Amman. The rest of their forces are fighting in Africa and suppressing uprisings in Iraq and elsewhere." He looked triumphantly at his colleagues. "We have a real chance to have our own state and defeat Israel when the Germans win and help us."

The head of the Islamic Jihad had another question: "What will happen to the population we leave behind? Won't the Israelis send them to the past?"

"No, they won't," the head of Hamas said. "As soon as fighting starts, and especially after our people cross the border, the Israelis will do what they normally do: try to negotiate some more."

Mazen nodded his agreement. "We need to make plans for a military assault. Our Security Force will lead. We have tens of thousands of

American-trained soldiers. We always called them 'Police' but we all know what they are – soldiers of jihad."

The commander of the Presidential Security Force pointed to a map hanging on the wall. "We will attack along the whole front from the northern edge of the Dead Sea to the Bardala area at the intersection of the old Israeli and Jordanian border. That's about 10 miles south of Bet Shean. This will not bring our forces into contact with the Israelis until the last moment and will afford us the greatest surprise.

"I also recommend that we attack at night. The best timing would be the night before they want to transport us. We will surprise them completely.

"We will use about twenty thousand troops for the initial assault and five thousand to exploit any breaches."

"What kind of defenses do the Israelis have along the Jordan river?" asked the head of the Palestinian Liberation front.

The commander pointed to the map. "When coming from Jordan there are minefields close to the border, but there are large openings in them where the terrain is rugged. Then there is a sensor fence and beyond that observation towers and bunkers. The area is normally patrolled by less than a regiment of second-tier infantry. It should be easy to cross in many places."

"What if they discover our forces moving into assault positions?"

"We will concentrate in the large Arab villages along the highway in the Jordan valley. This should not be noticeable. From these villages it's less than a mile in some places to the border proper. There won't be enough time for the Israelis to call up reinforcements even if they figure out what's going on."

"Why not attack across the road from the Dead Sea to Eilat?" asked another participant. "The terrain there is basically flat and we won't have to cross the river."

"The terrain is indeed much better there but we would have to cross areas inhabited by Jews and they would be alerted well ahead of the time of the attack," responded the commander.

The leadership agreed on the plan and dispersed.

Chapter 5
June 1942

Normally the Israeli weather in June was mild and pleasant but today was one of the hot, dusty, dry days when winds from the Sahara blow across the Mediterranean and reach the shores.

Captain Noam Shaviv finished inspecting his company's proposed deployment area. His company would be responsible for about half a mile of the Jordanian border near the Arab village of Zubaydat, between the Dead Sea and the Sea of Galilee. The infantry company was reinforced with two armored platoons - tanks and their supporting infantry - attached for this mission.

A combat engineer major drove up. "We're here to construct a defensive line. So tell me what you want and where."

Noam shrugged. "I see that headquarters takes the rumors of a Palestinian attack seriously."

The two officers explored the terrain and hashed out a plan.

Noam brought up his misgiving at the battalion staff meeting. The battalion commander smiled. "Let me first address the 'rumor' issue. We have firm intelligence that the PA Security Forces are setting up supply points and scouting out the terrain. The current intelligence estimate is that they will attack soon.

"The terrain in this area will make it difficult for an attacking force to maneuver - too many ridges. To get to the river the attackers will have to either get through wadis that lead directly to the river or climb steep ridges. This will be made difficult by the artillery support you all have available. There are a couple of helicopter gunships and an air force wing to support you.

"I have to warn everybody here. This is a serious threat – The attack may include up to forty thousand Arab troops, all American trained and armed.

"The main problem is that we have no idea when they will attack. All we have are rumors. My bet is it will happen at night, probably close to the departure date."

✡✡✡

"I would like to know how our energy project is going," Ze'ev Hirshson asked.

He was in his old college roommate's office at the Technion. The owner of said office, now a full Professor, was present as well as his former doctoral student, Dr. Arye Kidron, the man who invented the quantum shield that deposited them all in the past. Dr. Lisa Meisner, a Nobel Prize candidate in physics who had been rescued from Nazi Germany only months before, was with them as well. Lisa was an employee of Ze'ev's company. Consolidated Industries was footing the bill for their research.

Arye fidgeted in his seat. "We have an excellent design for an impenetrable security fence."

Ze'ev visibly calmed himself before speaking. "I know that none of you are stupid, so why are you researching security fences when you were supposed to spend my money on 'Zero Point' energy?" He pointed at Arye. "That was your idea."

The Professor smiled calmly, "Ze'ev, you were always a hothead. Please let Arye finish."

Arye Kidron nodded at Lisa: "While we were trying to figure out the Casimir effect and how to draw energy from it, we came to a better understanding of how our quantum boxes work. We developed a fairly simple algorithm to predict how far into the past you can go for a particular expenditure of energy."

"Wait," Ze'ev interrupted. "I thought you were dubious about this event having been time travel. Yitzhak," he pointed at Professor Wisotzky, "was missing an aunt that he distinctly remembered from his youth. I can't see how I exist since my father is not likely to meet my mother or have a child with her. How can this be time travel?"

Professor Wisotzky responded, "The quantum boxes don't make the volume between them travel in time. They do something more basic: they change the probabilities of quantum events. When the probability of us being in 1941 became high enough we found ourselves here.

"If you look at everything as a collection of probabilities it becomes clear that events that we see as not happening, like your parents surviving the Holocaust, were low probability to begin with. Such events happen, but are less likely than high probability events, like the Moon still being around."

"So how come I'm here even if I won't be born?" Ze'ev looked puzzled.

"Simple," replied Arye. "You were born already and so the probability of that is 100% - adjusted for the chance of travelling back in time. This didn't change in your reality so you're still here, as are we all.

"Lisa asked a really interesting question: 'What will happen if we feed our algorithm negative values of probability.' The answer was that it would open a gateway into a different universe. The properties of that universe depend on the magnitude of the negative numbers and a couple of other parameters."

Lisa intervened. "It wasn't as simple as that. We had also to redesign the quantum boxes. The new ones can move us in time but they can also move between universes.

"In fact, we explored two possibilities. The first was a relatively high probability universe, similar to ours but where humans never developed. The other one was a more improbable combination: an earth with an atmosphere where nitrogen was replaced by argon. Since it has oxygen it apparently has some sort of life but the existence of such an earth is highly improbable. We didn't explore what we call 'near universes' – ones that are almost like ours with a few small differences."

Ze'ev looked from Lisa to Arye. "But no infinite compact energy source? We need to discuss this. I see how a fence where the space between two layers would be in a different universe would be one application. Sending intruders into a different universe is a bit drastic but will work.

"Under our contract all patentable inventions belong to Consolidated, with each of you receiving a share. Physics discoveries can't be patented but the algorithm and the boxes probably can. My lawyers, both the contract and patent guys, will be here tomorrow to figure out the details.

"Arye, if Yitzhak will let you go, I have an employment proposition for you. You can run our new physics lab together with Lisa. Think about it. The budget will be much more than you have here and you will be compensated better. Besides, you will always be able to keep talking to Yitzhak Wisotzky."

Hans Frank, the Governor General of the German-occupied Polish Territories, SS-Obergruppenführer, Reich Minister, leader of the National Socialist Lawyers Bund, and a close collaborator of Hitler's, exited his mansion in Krakow. The sky was overcast with low, leaden clouds, threatening rain. He looked at the wide courtyard and was about to walk down the steps to his waiting Mercedes when a rocket slammed into him. The impact carried him back into the foyer, where the warhead exploded.

The rocket was a modification of a 21cm Wurfgranate for the Nebelwerfer 42. The modification was being worked on by the Luftwaffe under the code name Bordrakete 21 and carried 40kg of explosives. That was enough to partially collapse the building. The Governor General's body was eventually identified by his wife. She recognized a mole on his left foot – the only part that was left intact.

The drone carrying the 150kg rocket had waited in the general area for several hours and after identifying the Governor it fired the rocket. Its on-board computer had to compensate for a strong side wind and for the rocket's high ballistic fall but it was definitely up to its task.

✡✡✡

Moshe Cohen, a veteran Mossad agent with experience operating in Nazi Germany, and two associates boarded a train in Venice. A couple of switches and several stops landed them in Potsdam, southwest of Berlin.

In Potsdam the three were met by another Mossad agent who provided them with a Mercedes and fake plates. The car had been stolen from the mansion of a Deutsche Bank executive in Berlin. It was his personal car, only used on weekends, so the theft wasn't likely to be discovered before their mission was completed.

The three, now dressed in Wehrmacht uniforms, continued to Schwanenwerder Island, a residential enclave favored by the rich and high ranking Nazis. It was close to the Wannsee district and convenient to both the city and the surrounding forests. They arrived in the early hours of the morning, when the light was uncertain and deceptive.

A post with three SS guarded the bridge to the island.

Moshe, dressed as a Wehrmacht colonel, presented his orders, apparently signed by OKW Chief of Operations General Alfred Jodl.

The sergeant of the guard carefully read the orders: "Why are you coming to see the Reichsminister?"

"As my orders say, I have to hand him a package with secret documents."

"Really?" The SS man smirked. "I have to call the OKW to verify that you are who you say you are and that the orders are genuine. Wait here."

His call was intercepted by a little box spliced into the phone line. The Mossad agent who had provided the stolen Mercedes answered the call.

"Everything seems to be in order," the guard said, coming back from the booth. "Do you know where the entrance to the house is?"

"Yes," said Moshe. "I have been here before."

The agents stopped on the driveway of 10 Inselstraße some distance from the house. First they unfurled a blanket-like object carried in a suitcase. It covered the width of the narrow driveway and extended ten feet along it. The blanket was made of a thin layer of RDX high explosive with a pre-fragmented metal mesh on top. It was less than one quarter of an inch thick and, after some gravel was brushed on top of it, blended perfectly with the rest of the driveway.

After this was done they drove to the double swing gates in front of the house. The driver flashed the lights summoning the guard from a booth not far from the gate.

"What do you want?" The SS guard was borderline rude.

"I have a letter from the OKW for Reichsminister Goebbels," the colonel said. "You will hand it to him personally. Unopened."

The guard saluted and departed.

Several hours later Goebbels' chief of security handed him the manila envelope. "Reichsminister, for your eyes only, from General Jodl."

Goebbels turned the envelope in his hands, read the 'Top Secret' stamps. "Put it on my desk. We are going out now. I'll read it when we come back."

The family had plans for the day - shopping and lunch in Berlin.

When Goebbels' car drove over the hidden "blanket" an explosion lifted the car several feet into the air, piercing it with thousands of steel fragments from the blanket's cover.

The drone operator in Brindisi had spent hours watching the images sent by the circling drone. He waited for one of two events: either an explosion inside the house, in which case the drone would return to base, or a car driving out the house gate, in which case he had to activate the radio detonator embedded in the explosive blanket. The car he saw was now broken into several pieces and burning on the driveway.

✡✡✡

The Jerusalem Mufti, Hajj Amin al-Husseini, enjoyed his breakfast in Berlin. Life was good. He lived in a mansion taken from a Jew on the quiet and elegant Klopstock Street. And Hitler obviously liked him.

The Mufti was anticipating his weekly broadcast today to the Arab world on Berlin radio: another fiery call to kill the Jews and cleanse the land.

One of his guards entered the room. "Your Excellency a courier with an envelope from the Fuehrer has just arrived."

The courier was a Wehrmacht sergeant, obviously not young and limping slightly. "Your Excellency, I have a packet for your eyes only from the Fuehrer."

The sergeant handed him the envelope, saluted and left. When he was outside mounting his motorcycle he heard an explosion. He returned the motorcycle to the general transport depot of the Army, where a colleague of his put it back on the available list. They both belonged to a group supporting Carl Goerdeler, the former mayor of Leipzig who was opposed to the Nazis and cooperated with the British. The sergeant himself was, in fact, a member of British intelligence and now on his way back home.

Al-Husseini's right hand was gone, along with several fingers on his left. His face was severely burned and he lost both eyes. The explosive in the envelope had been laced with aeromonas hydrophila – a flesh eating bacterium. In the absence of immediate antibiotic treatment it killed the Mufti, slowly.

✡✡✡

At six in the afternoon Martin Bormann carefully knocked on the Fuehrer's office door.

"Mein Fuehrer, Himmler and Goering are here for the meeting you called."

"Good. You come in as well. We need loyal people here."

After everyone was seated Hitler got up and started pacing – a sure sign of agitation. "Himmler, what are the results of your investigation into these attacks?"

"We now know that Reichsminister Goebbels and his family were killed by a bomb under their car. It seems to have been pre-positioned. We also discovered that the Wehrmacht colonel who went through the bridge checkpoint this morning left an envelope for Joseph. It contains a large explosive charge. He would have died if he opened it.

"Hans Frank was killed early this morning by a Nebelwerfer 42 rocket. We think that it was shot from an aircraft, probably a light one since no engine noise was heard at the time."

Goering stirred in his seat. "I'm investigating this as well. The Luftwaffe is working on adapting those rockets to be carried under a plane's wing. They might be very useful in disrupting bomber formations, especially at night. It is possible that someone stole the modification plans and used them to make some of these rockets."

Hitler stopped in his pacing. "Himmler, set 'Gestapo' Mueller on this as well. We need to know where the evidence leads."

Himmler continued. "The next attack was on the Jerusalem Mufti. An explosive envelope was delivered to him this morning by a Wehrmacht sergeant. The envelope had, as far as we can tell, stamps of the Chancellery and was marked for his eyes only. It exploded when he opened it. The Mufti is in serious condition at the Queen Elizabeth hospital.

"There were also attacks on the staff of three Waffen SS divisions: the 'Leibstandarte Adolf Hitler', 'Totenkopf' and 'Wiking'.

"The attack on the 'Leibstandarte' killed the commander, General Otto Kumm, his battalion commanders, chief of staff, and injured the rest of the division staff.

"The attack on the 'Totenkopf' killed the commander, General Helmut Becker, his deputy and a battalion commander. It also injured most of the junior staff.

"The attack on the 'Wiking' killed the commander, Oberfuhrer Karl Ulrich, and most of his staff.

"At first we thought that the attacks on the 'Leibstandarte Adolf Hitler' and the 'Totenkopf' were done by the Russians. Both divisions are now at the Eastern Front, though not on the front lines. Regrettably, a cursory investigation turned up that both were bombed using the same type of rocket that killed Hans Frank. We are still working on the incident with the 'Wiking'. They are positioned in northern France and the explosion looks like a pre-positioned bomb. It was an inside job aimed at removing the leadership of the three best Waffen-SS divisions."

Hitler went back to his chair. "This looks like an organized assault on the soul of the Fatherland. I have an idea where it came from but we need more accurate information to pinpoint the guilty. It shouldn't be too hard to find. Such a huge conspiracy will be difficult to hide. Take into account that there is only one element in the Reich that would benefit from weakening the Waffen-SS. I'm sure that the Wehrmacht is involved.

"Martin," Hitler turned to Bormann, "I want you to put the party apparatus on full alert. We need to be vigilant and not allow any future attempts to succeed.

"Goebbels' death will be declared an accident. A grand state funeral will be arranged. We won't mention the others."

✡✡✡

Soviet Ambassador Ivan Maisky shook hands with his Israeli counterpart and settled in the proffered seat. They were again in the cozy sitting room at the Israeli embassy. Tea was served.

Maisky began. "Ambassador, I have good news: my government agreed to your terms. You may send emissaries to try and persuade the Jews living in the Soviet Union to leave for Palestine. Jews held in detention will be released. They will be allowed to travel only after your emissaries formally 'take possession' of them.

"May I ask how you intend to transport the few that will agree to go?"

Avigdor Mizrahi smiled, "We would appreciate your assistance in moving them to one of the Black Sea ports. Batumi or Sochi will do nicely. From there we will load them on ships and they'll be out of your hair."

✡✡✡

Jacob Hirshson was busy. He had been working very hard on a computer literacy course. In another week he would be transferred to the Combat Engineers for advanced training.

The Combat Engineers course was not going to be easy. Besides learning modern techniques he will also have to master doing accurate work under pressures of time and combat conditions. They also promised to train him in the use of heavy equipment. Jacob was confident that his training was making him more useful to Israel than if he'd joined a commando unit.

Chapter 6

July 1942

Ephraim Hirshson, newly promoted Major General and Commanding General of the IDF European Command, looked at the officers assembled in the auditorium of the Brindisi base. Next to him sat his Chief of Staff, Brigadier General Uri Sadot, with IDF division commanders and their staff in front of them.

"Gentlemen, I want everyone to know what forces and at what strength we have available." Hirshson looked at his Chief of Staff. "Uri, will you do the honors, please?"

Uri Sadot turned on the overhead projector. "We have close to fifty thousand troops at the base now. I'm referring to our troops only. The Brits are under a separate command and operating independently except for a couple of matters I will mention later.

"This diagram shows the distribution of forces. We have 480 tanks, mostly Merkava 5. Our support includes six artillery battalions, all of them self-propelled 155mm. Our air support includes 12 Cobra and 10 Apache helicopter gunships and a squadron of Kfir jets. Besides mechanized infantry in Namer Infantry Fighting Vehicles – IFV - we also have several infantry brigades with their support: Golani, Givati, Nahal and the Maglan Special Forces. Just to remind those of you who haven't deal with infantry lately, all infantry brigades are equipped with Namer IFVs that carry 25mm automatic cannon instead of the usual .50 caliber machine gun.

"We also have the normal compliment of intelligence drones and anti-aircraft equipment. The only special addition is the short wave radio listening and decrypting unit. This unit will also provide strategic intelligence to the British-French armies."

Hirshson got up and switched the display on the screen to a map of Northern Italy. "The general plan for this operation was developed taking into account two parameters: Our forces are much smaller than the troops Germany has available to oppose us, and we are much more sensitive to casualties than they are. This in conjunction with the fact that losses are always higher for the attacker dictated the strategy. Of course, we are also much more technologically advanced, which should give us a decisive advantage.

"If you look at the map of northeastern Italy, the part that borders on Slovenia and Austria, you will see that the terrain is rugged with only a few access roads…."

General Hirshson went on to explain the topology and then continued, "The Intelligence Command estimates that the Germans will advance on three roads in the Montefalcone area and will likely use the coastal road through Trieste. Another part of the German force, coming through Austria, is expected to take the Brenner Pass. I agree with that estimate. The German High Command will not expect much resistance from the Italians and so isn't likely to consolidate their forces until they need them against the British and French.

"We will wait for them in the town of Vipiteno near the Brenner Pass and at Palmanova down by the sea. Questions?"

The commander of the 7th Armored Brigade had one. "General, why not wait for them on the border or even across it if the terrain is favorable?"

Hirshson smiled a predatory smile. "Our objective is not just to stop and destroy the German forces. We want to break their spirit. To do that we need to give them the impression that they're advancing and winning before they are destroyed. We could destroy most of them from the air but this is not effective as far as future combat with the same troops or breaking the morale of any others that might follow. We have seen it in North Africa – the Afrika Corps suffered terrible losses from our air attack but the units that survived kept fighting. This was much less apparent in our timeline when they were beaten up by the Russians. We want to destroy their fighting spirit and make the Germans expect defeat when they meet us the next time."

✡✡✡

Noam Shaviv's reserve duty was close to its end. He had been in the Jordan valley for four weeks and expected to be released in another two.

At about six in the afternoon the tactical terminal in his dugout sounded an alarm. Several drones reported a number of columns approaching from the West. They were using barely visible trails and canyons.

From the drone images Noam estimated that his company was facing at least two, maybe three thousand fighters. They were going to come out of the hills in about an hour, unless they chose to slow down and rest before attacking after dark.

Another drone image showed a lot of activity in the Arab village of Zubaydat, just west of the main north-south road of the Jordan valley.

Noam used the network to alert the platoon commanders to what was happening and order the second platoon to move a machine gun crew forward.

The communications terminal blinked with a text message from battalion: “To all line units: Do not try to stop every single fighter. If they cross the river we will deal with them later.”

Noam’s second in command looked a bit puzzled. “Won’t they try to disperse and find a German agent to contact in Jordan?”

“I have no doubt that’s their plan,” Noam responded. “Their problem is that there are none within a hundred kilometers from our borders. They were eliminated early on. We couldn’t take the risk of a visual report getting back to the Nazis. The stupid Arabs will have to go deep into Syria to find one and even those will likely not have a radio. So for them it will be all the way to Turkey.”

Noam turned to the company sergeant major. “Remind everyone to put on their night vision goggles as soon as it gets dark.”

They didn’t need to wait for full darkness. Apparently the Palestinian Security Force was eager to roll over a few Jews and victoriously cross into Jordan. In fact, their commander figured that it would be a good idea to show the Jews how many Arab warriors were coming and so intimidate them into running away. Somehow he neglected to remember the training he underwent and the American instructor’s advice: Never expect the enemy to run away; do your best to attack in the dark and always assume that the enemy can see you even at night. He also consistently underestimated the Jews.

The terrain in front of him was rugged. The valley was divided in the north-south direction by a two lane paved road, Route 90. The Palestinian forces were approaching from the Judean hills, to the west of the road, where the foothills flattened out for about a thousand feet. On the same west side of the road was the Arab village of Zubaydat, a small village where some of the fighters were already setting up a command post and preparing defensive positions. They knew that the Jews avoided firing at civilians and so encouraged the inhabitants to stay put.

On the other side of the road, to the east, the terrain was flat for about fifteen hundred feet, becoming more rugged in the direction of the Jordan River and the border. According to the commander’s map the terrain looked like a comb with teeth ridges running to the river and meeting a backbone ridge running north to south. Just south of the village was a break in the difficult terrain. On the map it looked like a funnel: the wide part facing the road and the narrow part leading directly to the river and border. This was the only clear area where his forces could pass quickly.

The commander decided that his original plan was good: attack with most of his force into the opening of the funnel and send two small forces on top of the ridges to flank the defenders inside the funnel on both sides. The flat funnel area was about twelve hundred feet wide. The map showed that it narrowed down to about three hundred at the river.

His soldiers left the cover of the Judean hills and were approaching Route 90. There was no response to his advance and the commander decided, to his credit, that this might be an ambush. He ordered six of his 80mm mortars and a machine gun section to dig in on the west side of the road - the roadside ditch was handy for that - and suppress any fire that might descend on the troops.

Two of Noam's platoons were dug in between the two ridge lines about two thousand feet back from the entrance to the funnel. The flanks were protected by a platoon on either side and machine guns on the ridge slopes. Six tanks were positioned in line with the infantry, dug in to make them less visible from the road. A mortar platoon behind the infantry line completed the defense position. It all looked somewhat appropriate for a First World War setup.

Noam's plan was for the forward machine gun team to start shooting and then fall back to the rest of the company when the enemy started advancing on them. This would put the attackers in a prepared field of crossfire.

When he saw the mortar teams taking up positions in front of him beyond the road he considered calling his artillery support to attack them. He hesitated – the Palestinian position was only a couple hundred feet from the outskirts of the village and artillery could easily drop a shell off the mark. He didn't want to harm civilians. Noam decided on an alternative: he ordered his tanks to target the mortar positions with high explosive rounds, to be fired on his command.

Now he needed to wait, the hardest part of any battle. After fifteen more minutes, in the darkening dusk, he gave his order: "Machine gun crew start firing for effect."

Theirs was the only position in front of the company. A trench led back, with a couple of Claymore mines installed in its walls to be primed by the retreating crew – in case some of the Arab fighters decided to use the trench.

The PA Security Force soldiers in front threw themselves to the ground but continued to advance in small groups. They were well-trained and disciplined.

Noam gave the order to retreat and waited for the machine gun crew to run in front of him. He followed, setting the Claymores as he passed them. When he was less than ten feet from their main position his world went black.

His deputy took over and ordered, “Tanks, fire on the marked point. Keep firing as long as mortar fire persists.”

Six 120mm air burst shells exploded above the mortars and machine gun crews across the road; 80mm proximity fused mortar shells followed close behind them. Now it became clear that just digging a roadside ditch deeper was not a wise decision. Without a zigzag in the ditch one round could send shock waves and deadly fragments great distances. The first salvo wiped out the machine gun and all but one mortar. The last mortar crew wisely chose not to fire again.

Next the lieutenant called on the artillery to attack the advancing infantry. Shells were falling as close as 300 feet from the company’s position. The reaction of the attackers surprised him: most of the crawling soldiers got up and tried to close the short distance at a run. They might have succeeded since the company’s fire power was not enough to kill two thousand fighters but the Palestinian troops were taking heavy losses and seriously slowed down by barbed wire starting at 200 feet from their position. They still would have had a chance against the vastly smaller defending force.

Noam’s plan worked: the tanks positioned in between the infantry opened up with antipersonnel rounds. Thousands of flechettes were shot out of each 120mm main tank gun at over four thousand feet per second. The effect of the tiny steel arrows was devastating. After several salvos there were a couple of hundred stragglers still alive and trying to get out of the area. Very few of them survived the artillery that kept laying a blocking curtain of fire parallel to the road in back of the attackers.

The attack on the ridges followed a similar pattern, except that those attackers didn’t have mortar support and had to climb a steep ridge under fire from its defenders and from the forces below. When it looked like some of them might get over the top and into an area where the defendant’s fire couldn’t reach, a helicopter gunship rose above the ridge and opened up with its mini-gun. The firestorm swept the attackers from the ridge.

In this sector the whole affair was over in less than an hour. It didn’t end bloodlessly for the Israeli forces. The cost of the battle was thirty-seven wounded and sixteen dead. Sixty percent of the casualties were officers and noncoms. That was the price of leading by example.

After the battle the PA Security Force ceased to exist as a coherent unit. Most of the surviving soldiers threw away their weapons, returned to their homes and got out of uniform in the hope that they could disappear among the general population.

✡✡✡

The next morning Ze'ev was awakened by his phone. It was six in the morning. He was groggy and responded in an angry voice, "What's so urgent?"

His daughter Shoshanna was on the line. "Dad, Noam was in a battle on the Jordan river. He's at the Shaare Zedek Medical Center. I'm on my way there now."

"Wait a second. What's his condition? Where was he injured?"

"Dad, I don't know. They just notified me. He's alive, that's all I know. I've got to go." She hung up.

Linda woke up and looked askance at her husband. Ze'ev gave her Shoshanna's message. He was up and preparing to go.

"Ze'ev, I'm coming with you. Before we go you will eat something so don't rush. You won't be able to do anything and Shosh is strong and will manage without us for an hour. So stay calm and slow down."

Ze'ev did his best to follow his wife's orders. "I have an appointment with the Prime Minister later in the day. You want to take two cars?"

"No. We will go to Jerusalem together. If the situation isn't grave, you will leave me at the hospital, go to your appointment and pick me up afterwards. If it's bad, I'm sure the PM will understand."

✡✡✡

Hitler was foaming at the mouth. "What do you mean you don't have sufficient proof of who was responsible for all the assassinations?"

Mueller cringed in his seat but didn't back down. "Mein Fuehrer, we definitely have a connection to the Army. Army personnel were present at the assassination of Reichsminister Goebbels and at the attack on the Mufti. The other attacks used Wehrmacht rockets. We had difficulty determining who exactly in the Army was responsible."

The head of the Inland-SD (Sicherheitsdienst), SS Gruppenführer Otto Ohlendorf, moved in his chair and nodded in agreement. "We have a lead that points to the staff of Field Marshall von Rundstedt but we have no names." Ohlendorf fidgeted a lot. He felt unbalanced without his left arm and half the right leg. Both were lost when the "Caliph" attacked and destroyed Einsatzgruppe E, which he commanded.

Hitler looked at Himmler: "Suggestions?"

Himmler straightened in his chair. “I would like to arrest some of the members of Rundstedt’s staff, at the rank of colonel, and start interrogating them. I need your approval. This may cause some disaffection in the Wehrmacht and we need to prepare for that.”

“I assume that your subordinates here agree?” Hitler nodded at ‘Gestapo’ Mueller and Ohlendorf.

Both nodded agreement.

“You have my permission to start the operation, but move cautiously. The generals are a bit touchy. On the other hand, some of them are traitors, so don’t dawdle.”

✡✡✡

The major was arrested in Paris and brought to the local Gestapo. He was held in a relatively comfortable cell but never told why he was arrested. After a couple of days he was brought to an interrogation room. It was dark and a bright light was set to shine in his eyes. He thought that in addition to the interrogator on the other side of the heavy table to which the major was handcuffed there was another person in the room, but that person never said a word or even made a noise.

“Your name is Hans Gruber?

“Yes.”

“You are the adjutant to Colonel Bombach?”

“Yes.”

“Did you ever hear the colonel say anything disrespectful of the Party?”

“No.”

“Never? Even when you were all drunk at that bash at the bistro around the corner of the headquarters two weeks ago?”

“No. He never said anything disrespectful of the Party or the Fuehrer.”

“You are lying, Hans. May I call you Hans?” The interrogator was smiling now, an unpleasant expression.

“No. I’m telling the truth.”

“Are you telling me that in your drunken condition you remember everything said by the colonel and the others? Every word?”

“No… I don’t really remember.”

“So you did lie to me!”

After two days without sleep the major signed a confession. It implicated his commanding officer in un-patriotic activities and named several other potential enemies of the state. The major was released and returned to his duties.

Colonel Bombach was next. He was a tougher nut but eventually cracked and signed his confession. Everybody confessed to the Gestapo; it was only a question of time.

The colonel had some real anti-Nazi contacts, not where the Paris Gestapo were looking but in the command of Army Group South on the Eastern front. Most were people who voiced vague dissatisfaction with the way the country, or the war, was run and one even quoted his general as saying that 'Hitler is just a stupid corporal playing with toy soldiers.' The colonel didn't single out any of them but what he said was enough for Himmler's hounds to start on their trail.

✡✡✡

General Henry Maitland Wilson was putting the final touches on a plan he was revising.

"General," the Israeli ambassador greeted him.

"Ambassador, a pleasure seeing you. Tea as usual?"

"Please." Mizrahi settled in a chair opposite Wilson's desk. "I think that it's time to discuss the second phase of our German plan."

"I agree," Wilson said. "Our forces in Brindisi are almost ready. By the time we need to move they'll all be in place. Our people tell me that your forces are ready as well."

Mizrahi smiled. "Not just our forces but also the Italians. They have as many of their soldiers back in Italy as they expect to return. Prime Minister Count Ciano let us know that they're ready to transport our combined task force to Northern Italy as soon as we say so."

Wilson nodded. "Yes, our people in Italy confirm this, though I doubt the Italian railroad's efficiency and ability."

Mizrahi shrugged. "We doubt that as well. We have observers with secure communications equipment at all the major junctions and will do our best to alleviate any problems.

"But this is not the reason for my visit today. We have clear indications from Germany that there is growing unrest among the generals, especially in the east. It seems to us that the time is ripe for a second push."

Wilson extended the papers he was reviewing when Mizrahi came in. “This is what we propose to do. It’s based on our discussions and hopefully reflects both our countries abilities in this field.”

Mizrahi placed the bundle in his briefcase. “I will give you my government’s opinion as soon as possible.”

✡✡✡

Consciousness was slowly returning; Noam Shaviv tried to remember what had happened. It took him several seconds to remember the battle and his sudden blackout. He took inventory of his body: a headache, left arm slightly numb, can’t feel his legs. He opened his eyes.

At first he saw only whiteness but a moment later his eyes refocused and a ceiling came into focus, then a familiar voice. “Noam, how are you feeling?” His wife Shoshanna, sitting next to his bed looking worried.

He tried to speak but nothing came out. Shosh gave him a drinking cup with a bent straw.

He sipped and cleared his throat. “Much better. My throat was bone dry. Where are we?”

“At the Share Zedek Medical Center in Jerusalem, because my stupid husband got himself injured. So how are you feeling?”

“I don’t know.” Noam turned his head and saw the IV stuck in his left arm. “Do I have legs or are they gone? I can’t feel them.”

“You have legs.” The speaker was Ze’ev Hirshson, Noam’s father-in-law. “I just spoke to the doctors. You were very lucky. A mortar bomb exploded behind you. A large fragment hit you in the left leg and went through the knee. The other knee got a smaller fragment through it. You also have a concussion and a bunch of bruises.”

Shoshanna nodded. “Like dad said, you have legs. What you decide to do with them is another matter. You don’t feel them because of an anesthetic nerve block. After all, two torn and broken knees would be very painful.”

Noam tried nodding and winced. His head was very painful.

“Try not to move and get some sleep. You are suffering from a serious concussion,” Shoshanna said.

Noam closed his eyes. “I wish I could sleep but the thought of not ever being able to walk normally is a bit bothersome.”

A new voice entered the conversation. “I’m the surgeon. Who said anything about not being able to walk? I fully expect you to walk normally within a couple of months. We just need to replace your knees: a simple operation."

"When?" Noam croaked.

"As soon as you recover from the concussion, young man. That will take at least a week. We'll see how it goes.

"In the meantime I need you to relax." The doctor faced the visitors. "You guys have to be absolutely quiet. Noam needs to rest."

"Actually, please keep talking," said Noam. "It makes me feel better, like we're all together at home."

Linda asked Shoshanna, "Who's taking care of the children?"

"Sara has been staying with me since Noam was called up for his reserve duty, so she took over. That reminds me, I need to call her. She is worried sick about Noam and apprehensive about Jacob as well."

Noam said, "Call her from here. I'll say hello as well."

Ze'ev got up. "I have a meeting in about forty minutes. With this traffic I better get going. See you later."

A new voice joined the conversation. "Baby, what happened to you?" Noam's mother and father came into the room.

Noam tried to wave to them but gave up in the middle of the motion, "Nothing big. I just stumbled on a walk by the river."

✡✡✡

"Prime Minister, Dr. Ze'ev Hirshson is waiting."

Amos got up to greet Ze'ev. "Dr. Hirshson, what brings you here?"

"Just Ze'ev, please. I need to share some information with you, Prime Minister, which may be important to your future considerations of policy. You are familiar with the work of Arye Kidron at the Technion." It was a statement, not a question.

Amos nodded, "The Shield inventor, yes."

"I have been funding his work for some time now in the hopes of finding a new compact source of energy. That doesn't seem to be working out, but while working on an energy source he, and a physicist in my employ, discovered a way to open a portal to parallel universes. The theory will take too long to explain. In a nutshell, the effect is similar to what the Shield does but the affected area is transported to a universe different from ours."

Amos scratched his head. "A different universe? How do they know it's a different universe?"

"Well, one of those universes is apparently, as far as they could ascertain, free of human life. There is another where the atmosphere is a mix of oxygen and argon with life really different from ours.

"I also have to mention," Ze'ev continued, "that my company owns the patents on the transport equipment and algorithms. I believe that we can arrive at an agreement if the government wants to make use of it."

"A different universe? You mean that whatever happens there has no chance of changing anything here?"

"That's what I understood from the physicists."

Amos smiled. "I really appreciate you bringing this to my attention. Assuming this is indeed true it solves a problem that's been bothering me for a long while.

"How soon would your equipment be available? I would like a demonstration to ascertain that there's no misunderstanding or mistake."

"We have prototypes that will send an area of about ten by ten meters. If you need more, we will have to see how many of the boxes are necessary. It takes several hours to make one box by hand - we call them U-nodes. If you need more than a hundred we will have to manufacture them at our new facility in Refidim. The facility will be ready in a month or so."

Amos looked Ze'ev in the eyes. "What I'm going to say is confidential. Can I rely on you to keep the secret, at least for a while?"

"Certainly," Ze'ev responded.

"In that case, we will need enough of your U-nodes to send all of Judea and Samaria, excluding Jewish settlements. We will also, probably, want to send some of the Israeli Arab villages and maybe parts of Jerusalem. Can you figure out how many we will need?"

"The definition of Israeli Arab villages is a bit vague. How about defining the whole project as Judea, Samaria and 50% extra?"

Amos nodded. "Good. After a satisfactory demonstration and approval by independent observers your company will receive a formal request for a quote from the Ministry of Defense. Assuming, of course, that we can come to an understanding on who owns the rights to what."

✡✡✡

Wolf's tank was equipped with a data terminal and keyboard, usually used for tactical information and control. Since they arrived in Brindisi it was connected to the base's intranet and through it to the Israeli internet.

Now he was busy composing an email in Yiddish to Sheina who was, like him, one of those who hadn't survived the Holocaust in the other timeline. They were both, separately, related to Ze'ev Hirshson and met at a family reunion. Wolf was courting the beautiful girl, and she seemed receptive.

> Dear Sheina,
>
> I've been busy today. We are training on our tanks - cleaning and maintaining them - and have little time for anything else.
>
> In recent weeks large numbers of English soldiers started arriving here. They brought with them tanks, artillery and lots of infantry. Their tanks look quite good but nowhere as advanced as ours. Same is true for the artillery.
>
> I have no idea how their people are – we have a completely separate camp and never meet. Our company commander told us in the last briefing several days ago that we will start studying English so we can communicate with them. He also said that we can say nothing to them about our weapons and other equipment. So I suppose soon I'll get to meet and talk with them.
>
> How are you doing? I heard on the news today that there was a large battle with the Arabs with many casualties. Is the family safe?
>
> Yours, Wolf

He was a bit surprised when his terminal beeped an hour later. There was a new email for him.

> Dear Wolf,
>
> Shoshanna's husband Noam was in that battle. You should remember them. We all met at Ze'ev's house. He's a captain and was injured. Mother is taking care of their kids and told me that Shoshanna is going to spend a lot of time with him at the hospital. He's at Shaare Zedek.
>
> I called Shoshanna earlier. He is in serious condition with both knees gone but she's upbeat and expects

him to walk in a couple of months. She spoke from his room so I didn't want to prolong the conversation. I will ask her next time how he can be expected to make such a recovery.

Please be very careful and don't get injured.

The last picture you sent me was nice. Who is the girl in the background?

Yours with love, Sheina

✡✡✡

Two British agents arrived at the Tegernsee Lake in Bavaria in a light truck. They wore uniforms of the Todt organization and had appropriate documents. They parked the truck on Buchberweg, close to the intersection of the main road running around the lake. Even though the road seemed to be in good shape, the two started a standard pothole repair procedure, with some modifications. They dug out a hole, buried a German anti-tank mine, and then filled it in with gravel, laying asphalt on top. The asphalt was thumped down to be precisely at the same level as the old road. They admired their work for a moment – it was done to the best German standard as befitted a road leading to Reichsführer SS Heinrich Himmler's house.

The mine was connected to a miniature radio receiver. Two days later a drone arrived over the area. It parked at a high altitude and stayed until it was replaced by a fresh one two days later. After the second drone exchange the operator finally had his target: a convoy of four cars approaching the intersection. Either the second or the third car carried Himmler – the procedure was changed frequently. The drone operator exploded the mine in the gap between the second and third cars. The explosion of more than twenty pounds of TNT caused both cars to burst into flames.

The drone operator was puzzled. "Why didn't we dig two holes and have one mine in each so we kill the guy for sure?" he asked his supervisor.

The supervisor smiled, "I'm sure that if we wanted him dead we would have done exactly what you suggested."

Himmler survived. He was slightly burned and had several shrapnel wounds – mostly from the car's windshield but nothing life threatening. His rival and colleague Herman Goering wasn't so lucky.

The same British team that worked on Himmler's mine had prepared the road to Goering's palatial residence, Carinhall in Brandenburg, with two mines at a placed distance with separate receivers. Everything, including the receiver on one of the mines, was of German manufacture. Only one mine was necessary to kill Goering, the other was a backup and piece of evidence for the investigators to find.

Chapter 7
August 1942

"Gentlemen, I have grave news." Admiral Wilhelm Canaris, the head of the German Abwehr intelligence service, looked into the eyes of each of the attendees.

"After that last attempt on Himmler's life and the death of Goering, the Fuehrer approved a large scale operation against high-ranking Wehrmacht officers. Arrests are scheduled to begin in about two weeks. We are assumed guilty and will have to prove our innocence or be executed. You all know our chances of survival. I will also give you a longer list of those to be arrested in a second wave of, as the Fuehrer called it, 'cleansing'. I suppose you have questions and I will do my best to answer them."

"How many people on the first list and what ranks?" asked General Ludwig Beck.

Canaris' deputy, General Hans Oster answered, "Eighty-three generals and six civilians. Everyone present is on the list."

"That leaves us with few options," said the newly promoted General Henning von Tresckow. "We either fight or die."

"True," agreed one of the two civilians in the group, the former mayor of Leipzig, Carl Goerdeler. "We will have to fight and we have only two weeks to organize. Can we succeed?"

Canaris nodded. "We have a chance but have to quickly persuade some of the most senior commanders to join us. Since Generals Rommel, Paulus, von Mackensen and von Kleist are on the first list I believe it will not be too difficult to convince them, and their troops, to join us.

"The second list includes von Rundstedt. He might join if confronted with the information. He also knows that many officers at his headquarters have been arrested and interrogated by the Gestapo and SD, but he is an old-fashioned loyalist and will not break his oath of allegiance to the Fuehrer lightly. I think it's safe to talk to him – He will not betray us."

"We may also have some help from the outside. I believe that under certain conditions the British might assist us," said Ulrich von Hassell, a senior official at the foreign Ministry.

The discussion and planning went on for most of the night. Close to dawn the participants left General Franz Halder's Berlin apartment one by one. Halder was the commanding general of the OKH (High Command of the Army) and had frequent disagreements with Hitler on strategy. After recent setbacks on the Eastern Front he decided that it might be advisable for him to prepare a fallback position and free the army of Hitler's constant meddling.

✡✡✡

Albert Conforti, now the fully accredited Israeli ambassador to Italy, bowed slightly as he entered the official reception room of the Italian Prime Minister, Count Galeazzo Ciano. "Your Excellency, I appreciate the prompt meeting."

Ciano gestured for the ambassador to take a seat on an ornate sofa opposite him. "What was so urgent, Ambassador?"

"Prime Minister, now that most of your troops are out of reach of the Germans we would like to proceed with our plans. As I pointed out to you in our previous meetings, we need your assistance.

"There are two British armies and one of ours waiting at the base in Brindisi. They need your permission to move to the north of your country and the use of your railroads to facilitate the move."

Ciano thought for a moment. "Yes, if I remember correctly I promised you that my agreement and assistance would be forthcoming when all our troops were safe. There is a hitch though: we are still waiting for the Germans to release the last several work battalions. They claim they need them for fortification work in Russia."

"Yes, we know about that. I have a transcript of a communication exchange between the German High Command and Army Group South." He handed several pages to Ciano.

"As you can see they have no intention of ever releasing your people. The German offensive in the east has been stalled for months and all their attempts to break through the Russian lines have failed. The Italian work battalions will not do the Germans any good and they know it. In my government's opinion the Germans are holding on to them mostly as hostages."

"I agree," said Ciano, "but I'm also reluctant to provoke the Germans. Besides harming the hostages, they might also invade Italy."

"Oh, I have no doubt they will and quite soon. The only thing that will stop them is our deployment on your northern border. We don't have to announce anything. If you prefer, Italy can play the role of an occupied country. But this will also make it difficult for us, and especially the British, who just finished fighting you, to fully trust our arrangements."

"You are right. It's high time for us to choose sides. We are definitely not choosing Hitler.

"I will make all the arrangements with the Ministry of Defense and the railroads. I want you to inform your British allies that we want to immediately establish full diplomatic relations with them. After your forces are deployed and ours are deployed to back you up we will, together, announce our new alliance."

"There may be another partner to the alliance," said Conforti. "The French navy is going to move from Algiers and land several divisions of French troops from North Africa and the Free French from Britain in Marseille. This will be coordinated with the British move from Brindisi."

Ciano smiled. "I hope you don't rely too much on the French. In any case, we will have to iron out the disputed territories we took from them in the north. But this is for later."

✡✡✡

Peter Gershman had come to Israel from the former Soviet Union as a teenager. He retained his Moscow area Russian accent and now used it to good advantage.

The NKVD (Soviet Secret Police) operative in the Black Sea port of Sochi was a bit confused as a ship came into the port under a flag he had never seen before. The port captain had orders to allow it to dock. Now this individual from the ship demanded to see General Vereshchagin, the regional commander of the NKVD.

"What is your business with the general?"

Peter looked at the official. "That is between me and the general. I do advise you to call his office now. Any delay will have serious consequences."

The official shrugged and picked up his phone. It took more than half an hour to connect, although the general's office was just a couple of miles away on the other side of town. Finally the phone rang and the call went through. "A man off that newly arrived ship wants to talk to the Comrade General. What shall I do?"

The official listened for a minute and then hung up the phone. "They are sending a car for you." He sounded respectful.

A lieutenant accompanying Peter on the ride led him to the general's office, knocked on the door, opened it and closed it from the outside.

General Vereshchagin got up from behind his desk to shake hands. He was a compact, burly man in his fifties with a powerful handshake. Peter, who was six feet tall, looked lanky next to him.

"Please sit," General Vereshchagin pointed to a chair across from his desk. "Would you like some tea?"

"I'd appreciate some."

"According to my records you are Peter Gershman?" the general asked.

Peter offered his ID for inspection. It was printed in Russian and had his picture affixed to it. It also stated that he was a citizen of Palestine.

The general examined the document and returned it to Peter. "I have instructions from Moscow to issue you an NKVD ID as a colonel in the service. How many others came with you?"

Peter smiled. "Only fourteen on this ship. More may follow, depending on how the job goes."

"Good. In that case we will start with you. Bring the others here in pairs, or maybe three at a time, to get their papers. We don't want to attract too much attention.

"I also have instructions to assist you in obtaining transportation and securing cooperation from other regional commands. I'm not going to ask what your mission is – I don't want to know anything about it.

"Comrade Beria will come here day after tomorrow for an inspection. You will be free to leave after that."

Peter was surprised. Beria's visit wasn't part of his instructions. The People's Commissar of the NKVD asked him several questions about Palestine, which Peter evaded as best he could. Beria seemed to have expected evasive responses and just smiled a very unpleasant smile that did nothing to improve Peter's already low opinion of the man. After their short conversation Beria asked for a tour of the ship. He was given a tour that excluded the bridge and engine room. Since the ship was sovereign Palestinian territory Beria didn't complain.

With his papers Peter had no problem obtaining a place on a train that, after many stops and a week later, deposited him in the capital of Uzbekistan, Tashkent. He started a systematic search for Jews that had escaped from the advancing Germans. He had lists that were based on family records and memories. That helped but it was a tedious and time-consuming job.

He met with the refugees. The procedure was always the same: He introduced himself, explained that he was on a mission from Palestine and assured them that his mission has been approved by the authorities. This was the trickiest part – Everybody was aware of the constant presence of informers and was afraid to end up in the GULAG. The fact that the Soviet press started a series of positive articles about Zionism helped: At least being a Zionist wasn't a crime anymore.

He explained to the refugees that their families had survived and were waiting for them in Palestine. For some of them he had pictures and letters – a full suitcase in fact. A minority had no family in Palestine and were more difficult to persuade, but not too hard. The conditions were bad. They weren't any better where he travelled next, to Samarkand and Bukhara. People were starving. A promise of work and food backed up by an immediate distribution of ration coupons was all he needed in most cases for people to agree to move.

Peter didn't neglect the local Jewish communities. There was less information about them. On the other hand, they were largely observant. A combination of the pull of the Holy Land with the promise of a better life and the push of difficult conditions under the oppressive Soviet regime caused many to abandon their established lives.

When someone agreed to move Peter gave them travel papers, which were essential to leaving the area they were assigned to, and a travel assignment to get a place on a train.

It took him close to a month to finish his job in Uzbekistan. Then he went to the Chuvash Republic on the Volga River and located a Jewish labor battalion in the tiny town of Pervomayskiy, in the midst of dense forests on the north bank of the Volga River, across from the town of Cheboksary. These individuals had escaped western Poland when the Germans invaded in 1939 and were lucky enough to cross into the Soviet controlled part of Poland. Most of them continued to Lvov in the Ukraine. The Soviets, who occupied Lvov in 1939, gave them a choice: accept Soviet citizenship and be released into the Soviet Union or reject it and serve in labor battalions. Many Jews accepted citizenship but some were reluctant – they didn't want to become subjects of the Soviets, hoping to return to a free West after the war. As Soviet Citizens they would be prohibited from travel outside of the Soviet Union and have only limited travel rights within its borders. The Jews in Pervomayskiy were the individuals that hadn't accepted the offer of Soviet citizenship. Instead they felled trees to be shipped down river. It was hard work with minimal food. By the time Peter arrived in the area only the young and healthy were alive. Most people older than forty had died.

Peter asked to meet with the leaders of the labor battalion and was invited to a largish tent that served as headquarters. The commander was seated behind a makeshift desk. "Welcome to our battalion. How can we be of assistance?" His second in command, a big burly man, smiled. "You need trees cut down?"

"No trees for me. Let me introduce myself." Peter sat down on the chair offered by the commander. "Despite what my papers say I'm not a colonel or even a member of the NKVD. I am an emissary from Palestine. We are an independent state allied with Britain and the Soviet Union in the war against Germany. According to our agreement with the Soviet Union, we are empowered to offer all Jews the opportunity to leave for Palestine. To make it easier all our emissaries were issued NKVD papers."

The commander shrugged. "You have any proof of this?"

"Yes. We have already rescued the Jews that were trapped in Europe under the Nazis and moved them to Palestine. Your families are among them. I have letters from them to you." He opened his suitcase, now almost empty. "You are Jacob Solomon. You have a brother Simha that got stuck in Bialystok. Here is a letter from him. It was written a couple of months ago – I've been visiting other Jewish communities.

"Mr. Reich," he addressed the deputy commander, "your sister from Bochnia also sends you a letter."

The two men said nothing until they were done reading.

"This is proof that they were alive and, if you're not lying, in Palestine," the commander said.

"I have more letters. Hopefully they will convince you we are for real."

Reich, the deputy commander said, "My wife had a sister. Do you have a letter from her?"

Peter nodded. "Yes, I do. Please give it to her."

"I would like to finish our business here. I have limited time and want to find more Jews. Will your people be willing to leave now?"

The deputy smiled. "Leave the pleasant, easy life here? What do you think? Sure, we will move. Do you have more letters?"

Peter took out a bundle of letters tied with a string. "These are all I have for your group. Not everyone gets one but we had only a limited time to prepare."

Solomon and Reich looked at each other. Reich nodded. "I think that we can be ready as soon as you are."

It took another week for the Soviets to arrange a train to Sochi.

✡✡✡

Sergeant Wolf Frumin looked at the city as they passed through. The train, made up of flatbed cars carrying armored personnel carriers and tanks and passenger cars for troops, was slowly rolling through Vipiteno in northern Italy. The flatbeds were piled with equipment and supplies that barely fit in between the armored vehicles.

The next several trains carried self-propelled artillery, more tanks, plus anti-aircraft batteries and missiles. Everything was covered with tarps to make it as inconspicuous as possible. Wolf wasn't sure this was working, since they passed crowds of people at several stations waving to the troops.

Just north of Vipiteno the train stopped and orders came to unload. It took them two days to unload the armored vehicles. They brought special ramps, also used to drive the tanks onto the train cars, but the Italians were very slow in installing them despite their government having insisted on doing it. After several hours with no real progress the regiment commander ordered his own mobile maintenance depot to unload their cranes and do the job. The Italians protested but not too much.

The IDF 7th Armored Regiment spent the next three days taking up positions near the only road crossing the mountains into Austria. Trains kept arriving with supplies, mostly ammunition and fuel. A small combat engineers unit prepared a landing pad for their Cobra attack helicopters, with fuel dumps and ammunition storage nearby. The intelligence company found a good spot to launch their drones. Then everyone went into waiting mode.

Wolf's tank was with a company assigned to the south flank, positioned about a mile south from the main road to Austria. An infantry company served as their screen. Wolf and his comrades were busy monitoring their tactical displays, rotating guard duties and performing maintenance. Their company commander took his jeep on a tour of the area and decided to set up several static cameras about four miles away on a secondary road leading into Austria. You could never know which way the Germans might choose to attack. Drones might fail to alert them if the weather was exceptionally foul. He wasn't going to take any chances.

The plan was to stop any German forces that might try invading Italy from the direction of Innsbruck. A different force guarded the South-Eastern sector bordering on Slovenia.

Italian troops took up positions close to the Austrian border and would be the first line of defense. The Israelis expected them to fall back after only token resistance, but one could never tell. Some Italian units in North Africa fought valiantly and they might do so again, especially when fighting for their country and if properly supported from the air.

The Israelis and Brits agreed to operate separately on two different fronts. Israel was responsible for the border between Italy, Austria and

Slovenia. Britain was responsible for the border with Vichy France. Now that everybody was in place, the allies waited for the French Algerian fleet to land Free French forces at Marseilles. Their landing would be the signal for the British army to invade Vichy France from Italy and create a united front with the Free French. Israel, with much smaller forces, was supposed to protect the flank and rear.

✡✡✡

General Ludwig von Kleist carefully listened to his guest. Admiral Canaris put a typed list of names on the general's desk. "General, your name is the second on this list. They will arrest you as soon as you step off the plane in Berlin."

Kleist waved his left hand chasing away an invisible fly. "What are you proposing? I was summoned to see the Fuehrer and I have to go. Are you saying I should disobey a direct order by the leader to whom I swore personal allegiance?"

Canaris nodded. "Just a wild guess, I bet that your chief of staff was also summoned."

Kleist shook his head. "No, he wasn't. If he was, I would know about it."

"Ask him."

Kleist hesitated, than picked up his phone. "Zeitzler, did you get a summons to Berlin?

"Why didn't you notify me?" He listened to the response than hung up.

"You are correct, Admiral. My chief of staff didn't notify me because those were his orders. He wasn't ordered not to answer my question though. Very strange. I also find it strange that we are ordered to go see the Fuehrer one day apart. On the other hand, as strange as it is it doesn't warrant disobeying an order."

Canaris had an idea. "General, how about asking for a short delay? After all, you command a panzer group and we are at war. There are unforeseen circumstances. If you ask for a delay of, say, a week and the Fuehrer agrees, then I grant you I might be wrong. I predict that they will insist on you coming exactly when summoned and not a day later, even if the Russians start a big offensive."

Kleist drummed his fingers on the polished surface of his desk. "I agree that calling both of us to Berlin at this time and making us come separately looks suspicious.

"It makes sense to ask for a short delay. I'll think about it."

Canaris presented the same arguments to Rommel and to Eberhard von Mackensen. Both had the same general attitude: a German general couldn't refuse an order. Being a master spy Canaris was both patient and resourceful. He decided to wait.

When four days later von Kleist's plane landed in Berlin, the general was met by a Gestapo agent and three SS guards. They relieved him of his side arm and pushed him, somewhat roughly, into a waiting car.

An Abwehr agent carefully photographed the proceedings using a telephoto lens. He also followed the Gestapo car to their headquarters at 8 Prinz Albrecht Strasse and photographed the handcuffed general being taken inside. The photographs were delivered by airplane to Admiral Canaris, waiting at the headquarters of the first Panzer group in Donetsk, southeast of Kiev. Canaris showed them to General Zeitzler, von Kleist's Chief of Staff, who was scheduled to go to Berlin the next day. After that Canaris met with General Eberhard von Mackensen, positioned nearby commanding the third Army Corps of Army Group South. From there he flew to meet with Erwin Rommel in France.

The photographs seemed to be much more persuasive than anything the head of the Abwehr could have said.

✡✡✡

Lavrentiy Beria, the People's Commissar for Internal Affairs, nodded to his deputy, Ivan Serov, and pointed to a chair in front of his desk. "Ivan Aleksandrovich, you know of our arrangement with the Palestinians. They are, as we speak, transporting large numbers of Jews to their homeland. We know nothing about them and this is an unacceptable situation. Any idea what we can do?"

Serov thought for a moment. "The simplest would be to find a couple of Jews that are members of our security apparatus and have them go to Palestine with the rest. They'll let us know what's up."

"My friend, you're a genius." His voice was dripping with sarcasm. "You think that I can't come up with such a clever idea by myself? What will you do when your agents are recognized by other Jews and reported to the Palestinians?"

Serov, who had served under Beria for a number of years and was used to his boss' style, smiled. "Comrade Commissar, you are the smartest man I know. It never crossed my mind that my idea was clever. It does have the advantage of being simple. We can find someone that is unknown as our agent. I know one such person. He's from Latvia and did a great job for us there in 1939. Now he's a translator with Military Intelligence, using his excellent knowledge of German.

"Very few people outside our command structure know about him, so he should be safe. I might find another one with a similar background."

Beria shrugged. "I never said you were stupid, comrade. Does this Jew have a family?

"He has a wife and a child, a daughter I think," Serov responded. "He also has a couple of cousins that he helped escape Latvia. I think that we will have to let his immediate family go with him – too many people know about them and it will look suspicious if they stay. His cousins are a different story. They'll make excellent hostages."

Beria smiled. "Very good. Make sure that a Palestinian emissary finds him soon."

✡✡✡

The management meeting at Consolidated's headquarters in Herzliya finally got to the part Ze'ev enjoyed most: an update by his VP for Research and Development.

The VP turned on a projector and started his presentation. "We have been busy developing a modern car that will sell and can be manufactured now. Our main concern was the power train. We tried to make it as simple and reliable as we could. This, and drivability, caused us to abandon a turbine engine.

"A turbine looks attractive at first glance, especially as we're tooling up to make Merkava transmissions, but on closer examination it's not practical for a car that needs much less power than a tank and must have absolutely no delay in power delivery – even a second might lead to an accident. Another problem was cost. A turbine is much less complicated than an internal combustion engine of comparable power but due to its high speed it requires an expensive transmission and some exotic materials if we want it to be reliable and efficient.

"After looking at several options we zeroed in on an external combustion engine – a Stirling Cycle reciprocating engine. It has many advantages which are enumerated in the handout. It has two major disadvantages for automotive applications: it needs a warm up time before the car can move and it's not easy to change the power output to quickly accelerate. We overcame both problems. We managed to shorten the warm up time. It varies from two to four seconds – depending on ambient temperature. To enable the car to move immediately and to eliminate a transmission we utilized a simple hybrid design with lead-acid batteries. We also utilized variable output burners and the ability to disconnect cylinder pairs. This gave us enough control of the power output to make the car drivable.

"This is what it looks like." He showed a slide of a car with an open hood and a clear view of the engine.

Ze'ev asked: "This car looks kind of antique. What body did you use?"

"We purchased a number of Fiat 2800 Berlina models, all newly manufactured by Fiat in Italy. We also purchased several Lancia Ardea cars. They're smaller than the Fiat and probably better suited to our local market."

Chaim, Ze'ev's son and the manager of one of Consolidated's plants, asked, "Can we make them here or do we need to keep buying them from Fiat? And do they comply with our modern safety standards?"

The VP smiled. "They comply with no modern standard, safety or otherwise, and we can't make them here. We discovered, with the help of a number of automotive engineers who were rescued from Europe, that this body can quite easily be adapted to comply with most of the standards. Since the power train is compliant, we will have no problems.

"To be able to make these cars in Israel we need a source of automotive sheet metal, presses to form it and, of course, all the little things liked gauges, upholstery, etc.

"The real problem now is obtaining sheet metal. I'm afraid we will have to roll our own."

Ze'ev intervened. "I suggest that we distribute the three prototypes to everyone here so that each of us drives one for a couple of days. If the general assessment is positive, we can specify to Fiat and Lancia what we want them to do to make the body safety-compliant and maybe modernize the styling. We can buy from them while we tool up to make our own. Assuming we find it necessary."

✡✡✡

The Supreme Court in Jerusalem finally rendered its decision: The judges agreed with the prosecution that the Palestinian leadership and its armed forces acted in bad faith and committed treason against its own people as well as against the State of Israel. The sentence was exile.

A representative of the court read the sentence to the assembled Palestinian Arab leaders and three thousand members of their "security" force. That was the formal part of the proceedings.

"The sentence will be carried out immediately. There are containers behind you with supplies that should last you six months. There are also weapons and tools. Do you have questions?"

Ahmed Mazen approached the microphone. “I just want to say that this is an unjust sentence and we will do all in our power to return and take our revenge.”

The crowd cheered but quickly quieted down when the court representative spoke. “You will do what you always do and frankly we don’t care. Good luck to you all.”

With that he retreated behind a fence surrounding the crowd and nodded to the technician waiting by a switch. A quiet hum started and the crowd disappeared. The surface of the ground inside the fence was a couple of feet lower than it had been seconds before. Grass was growing where only dust and stones used to be. The traitors had been exiled to a different universe.

✡✡✡

The Theodor Herzl passenger ship arrived at the port of Ashdod at dawn. The passengers disembarked in groups of twenty and walked over to a temporary building on the quay. The area was heavily guarded. From that building the passengers emerged directly into the port’s terminal.

Alfred Goldberg with his wife and five year old daughter were in the third group to be released. They expected to be delayed for no more that fifteen minutes – like the groups before them. Whatever happened in the small building didn’t take very long.

As they entered, each individual was directed to a separate room. Alfred went in first, leaving his wife and daughter behind.

“Please take a seat,” a polite young woman told him. She was seated behind a desk with a keyboard and a monitor. Alfred took the seat.

“Your name and date of birth, please.”

Three questions later the process slowed down. She looked at the monitor with a slightly puzzled expression.

Alfred didn’t know what the monitor was but he was smart enough to figure that something was wrong. “Is there a problem?” he asked.

The interviewer shook her head. “No problem. Are your wife and daughter with you?”

“They’re waiting outside.”

“Good, this will only take a minute.” She picked up a phone and said in Hebrew, “I think we have one.”

The door behind her opened a moment later and a middle-aged man came in. He gestured to Alfred. “Please come with me.”

"What about my family?"

"Your family will be fine where they are," the man responded.

He took Alfred through a number of corridors to a room guarded by an armed soldier. The door clicked behind them with a sound that indicated it was heavy. The room was very quiet.

"Sit, please." The man indicated a chair in front of a simple desk.

Alfred recognized the setup: an interrogation room. He was worried. The man sat opposite him, took out what looked like a flat box from the desk's drawer, and started the interrogation.

"You are Alfred Goldberg from Riga. Correct?"

"Yes."

The man examined the box carefully. "Your NKVD employee number is 7295176. Correct?"

"What? What NKVD number? I'm Jewish and barely escaped from the Nazis."

"Alfred, I never said you were not Jewish or didn't escape from the Nazis. I need to know whether the number I just read to you is your NKVD employee number? Don't try lying to me, it will land you in a heap of trouble."

Alfred was thinking as fast as he knew how. What would happen if he admitted that this was his number? What if he tried to deny everything?

The man seemed to read his thoughts. "Your direct supervisor at the GRU was one captain Oleg Vyshinski. Your NKVD supervisor in Riga was Nicolai Drugulin and in Moscow it was one Boris Nikodimov."

Alfred gave up. "Yes, the number is my serial number in the NKVD."

The man smiled. "See, it's much easier this way. Now you will tell me what your orders are and after that you will join your family. We'll have to give you an injection first. Nothing serious, but it will enable us to know where you are, geographically speaking. When the time comes, you will be contacted and instructed regarding reports to send to your former bosses."

"They will kill me for sure," Alfred Goldberg whispered, "but I had no choice. If I refused they would have killed me and my family anyway."

The man smiled and this time it was a genuine smile. "We will protect you. You, and most important, your family will be safe here." The smile disappeared. "You are lucky that you may be of use to us and that we're not as blood-thirsty as your Communist friends, otherwise your crimes against your fellow Jews deported to Siberia would warrant at least a lengthy prison term."

✡✡✡

Nachman and Tzila Frumin finally arrived at the port of Ashdod. It had taken them a while. Public transportation was much better than it had been when they arrived in Israel nine months ago, but it was still time-consuming. Ze'ev had promised to meet them at the gates of the port. They waited for only a couple of minutes before he arrived. Together they went into the new passenger terminal.

The large, open area was cool. People were milling around, obviously families waiting for new arrivals. Two lines of poles extended the width of the space. Each had a letter of the alphabet displayed on a plaque at the top. The letters were Hebrew, Latin and Cyrillic. The Frumins and Ze'ev congregated under the F. There were several other groups waiting there, obviously everyone with last names starting with F, פ and Ф.

They waited for almost an hour before the first immigrants started leaving the customs area. Finally a girl approached them. Ze'ev recognized his mother, Esther, from the photographs he had of her when she was seventeen. At eighteen she looked not much different, except for being sickly thin.

Nachman and Tzila hugged their daughter. It took a little while before everyone calmed down enough to introduce Ze'ev.

Esther was completely confused. She was surprised that she had family in Palestine and confused by the unbelievable time travel story. Finally Ze'ev said, "Let's go to my house. We can talk on the way there. In any case, the rest of the family is waiting there."

On the way Ze'ev tried to explain, again, the strange incident of Israel traveling back in time. He wasn't sure whether he was explaining everything persuasively or whether it was the car they were riding in and the obviously advanced country they were rolling through that made her accept the story.

After a while Esther asked, "Where is Wolf and the uncles and their families?"

Her father answered. "Wolf is serving in the Israel Defense Forces. He's a tank commander and a sergeant. Right now he's in Italy and maybe soon will fight the Nazis. The uncles will meet us at Ze'ev's house."

Ze'ev added, "You will also meet the rest of the family there. It's a big family."

When they arrived at the house in Hertzlia Pituach the family was waiting to meet the new arrival.

Esther was overwhelmed. For a year she had been living with only a female friend from her town and no news. Only rumors of what was happening in occupied Europe penetrated the Soviet propaganda barrier. She thought that they were all under German occupation and in grave danger. The Hirshson part of the family was new and difficult to accept. The rescue of all the Jews from Nazi Europe was a surprise, even though the Palestinian emissary had brought her a letter from her parents.

Ze'ev's wife Linda invited everyone to the table. Jacob, sitting across the table, assumed that the general introductions were too overwhelming for Esther to absorb and so introduced himself again: "I'm Jacob Hirshson. He smiled. Supposedly I'm Ze'ev's father but we just call each other by first names."

Esther looked at him closely for the first time. She liked the slim young man with a dark complexion. He looked good in uniform. "I find this whole thing very confusing. How did you manage to accept having a son forty years your senior?"

"Who said I accepted it? It is what it is and I'm just glad to be out of Europe and the clutches of the Nazis. That Ze'ev is my son is a claim I can live with but I'll always have difficulty accepting emotionally, though I don't doubt that in some other history it was true. He's not really my son - or yours. He's the son we might have had if things had been different."

Esther considered his words. "I think I will suspend my disbelief and emotional judgment for a while.

"So, what are you doing in uniform? And what is your rank?"

Jacob explained about his compulsory service and how he had been promoted to corporal only a short time ago. He liked this girl. She seemed serious and mature beyond her years, probably because of living in the Soviet Union by herself.

"I'm keeping you from enjoying the food. You look like you need feeding," Jacob said.

"They fed us well on the ship from Russia, but you're right. I was hungry most of the time since I left home in June of '41."

After dinner Jacob invited Esther for a walk on the beach. She refused. Jacob didn't press but had to comment. "I can see that you're uncomfortable with me. Forget about that other reality. Just enjoy this life."

Esther nodded. "I agree. How about tomorrow? Are you still going to be here?"

✡✡✡

Three men entered Emir Abdullah's public office, or throne room, at his palace in Amman. The meeting has been arranged through a sheikh of one of the Bedouin tribes in the Jordan River valley. The visitor was Ambassador Yaron Weizmann. The other two were his body-guards.

"Please be seated," Emir Abdullah invited them politely. "I understand that you are the Ambassador from Israel. I wasn't aware that the Jews of Palestine declared independence, though rumors fly around."

The Ambassador introduced himself: "Your highness, my name is Yaron Weizmann - no connection to Professor Weizmann, and I do indeed represent the State of Israel. We are not only independent but also allied with Britain and the Soviet Union against Nazi Germany. We are also allies with the United States."

"This implies a strong state, unless you are just a symbolical ally not really doing much. Like Syria is now a Free French ally."

"I assure you that we are indeed a very strong state. If we establish diplomatic relations you will have an opportunity to see for yourself. We offer you friendship and support and, if need be, protection against your enemies."

"And what will you want in return?" asked the Emir.

"Reciprocity. We want the neighborhood we live in to be friendly to us."

The Emir nodded. "A noble desire. Good relations would be beneficial to both parties. But to be clear, if we establish diplomatic relations it doesn't mean an alliance. This is probably a good issue for the future."

The Israeli Ambassador nodded agreement. "My government completely agrees with this sentiment. May I suggest that our two states exchange ambassadors within the week?"

"That fast? As you know, Transjordan is a British protectorate and I can't exchange ambassadors without their agreement."

"My government knows about this potential obstacle. We requested the British Foreign Office issue a letter of agreement. It will be presented to you by Sir Alec Kirkbride, who is on his way as we speak."

"I am not sure whether to be offended or gratified," Abdullah said. "Your government seems to know a lot about my affairs and isn't shy about interfering."

“Your highness, it is our intention to set up relations as fast as possible. I can explain as soon as I have presented my credentials, which I have with me.”

There was a knock on the door. “Come in,” Abdullah said.

The door opened and the majordomo announced, “Sir Alec Kirkbride.”

“Let him in,” Abdullah said.

When the British Ambassador appeared Abdullah greeted him. “Come in, old friend. Join us and explain to me what is going on.”

Sir Alec shook hands with Ambassador Weizmann and settled on a comfortably overstuffed chair next to him.

“I see you know each other,” Emir Abdullah said. “How did that happen?”

“We haven’t known each other for very long,” Sir Alec responded. “I was ordered to meet the Ambassador at the RAF Marka base and make sure he got a proper reception there. I was also asked to inform your highness that Israel is a very powerful and valued ally of Great Britain.”

“The Ambassador told me that you would have a letter for me from your Foreign Office.”

The British representative opened his slim briefcase and handed an envelope to the emir. “Yes, your Highness. This is a letter signed by Secretary Eden. It removes British authority over your ability to establish diplomatic relations with Israel.”

✡✡✡

The Prime Minister asked the Foreign Minister to present a general update to the Israeli cabinet.

The minister shuffled the papers in front of him and said, “A number of things have happened in the last week. Our ambassador to Britain met with John Winant, the U.S. ambassador. They discussed establishing mutual relations and trade. We expect to send a representative to Washington within a couple of weeks. Regarding trade: We expect to start trading directly with the U.S. instead of through British companies. This will take a couple of months, although I must admit that as it is we are making tons of money selling medicines. Teva is complaining about excessive taxation but in truth they’re prospering and happy.

“On a related issue, in cooperation with the Absorption and Immigration Ministry and the Jewish Agency, we have dispatched a group of emissaries to the U.S. There are more than four million Jews living there now and we are trying to bring as many of them home as we can. We have sent individual emissaries to prominent people. Albert Einstein, Chaim Weitzman, who at the invitation of FDR is working in the U.S. on synthetic rubber, Jonas Salk, and others.

"Two weeks ago we signed a mutual defense pact with Italy. Britain joined it the next day. We also have a trading agreement with Italy and have already started limited imports.

"The most interesting news comes from our new representative in Moscow. Since we didn't want to have a Soviet ambassador in Israel we only asked for a representative to take care of our nationals and to transfer military intelligence to them directly. By the way, the people we sent to collect the Jews of Russia are doing well. We are receiving two ships a week from Sochi. Very soon we will need to lease more passenger ships. The old Theodore Herzl can make only two trips every week and that won't be enough. The head of the Security Service may update you on the spies the Soviets tried to slip in with the legitimate immigrants.

"The Germans haven't missed all this immigration traffic. Our base in Brindisi got a call from Alois Brunner, Eichmann's replacement, asking what our ships are doing in Sochi. The Germans have a good spy network in Turkey and were informed about our ships going through the Bosporus. The new base commander told them the truth: that we are collecting Jews from there. I think that they are getting suspicious and will soon realize that they have been the victims of a gigantic hoax. They will probably decide to attack then but the Defense Minister tells me we're ready for them.

"Last week we established diplomatic relations with the Emirate of Transjordan. As we agreed, in a couple of days our ambassador will present the Palestinian question to Abdullah.

"I also need the Defense Minister to elaborate on his activities in Moscow, of which I'm somewhat wary.

"This is all the news for now. Questions?"

The Finance Minister had a question: "How many people do you expect to get out of Russia?"

"The Jewish population of the Soviet Union is more than four million. We expect that at first under a million will move. Another million, or maybe two, can be expected to arrive in a couple of years, after establishment of full relations."

Amos asked the Defense minister, "Nitzan, what are you up to in Moscow that the Foreign Minister doesn't like?"

Nitzan Liebler smiled a crooked smile. "Nothing out of the ordinary, except I'm not as trusting in diplomatic relations and promises as my colleague. It seemed reasonable to be ready for some underhanded action by the Soviets, so I directed the Air Force to have a long-range drone over Moscow at all times and a jet on call if necessary. Just in case."

The Minister for Internal Security was next. "Last week we expelled the Arab leadership and their thugs who survived the fight on the Jordanian border. Since then the Arabs of Judea and Samaria plus some of the Israeli Arabs are rioting. We had stones and firebombs thrown at traffic in Jerusalem, riots and tire burning in the Galilee, and attacks and shootings in Judea and Samaria. I invited their local leadership for a conversation and got an earful of threats.

"My recommendation is to send them all to some place where they won't be able to harm us."

The Justice Minister said, "Surely not all the Arabs participate. We can't punish everyone for the crimes of a few."

"I don't know how many don't participate," the Internal Security Minister responded. "We had about thirty thousand Arabs from several villages trying to force the Qalandia checkpoint into Jerusalem. They came from villages with a total population of about thirty-five thousand. Draw your own conclusions how many, including women and children, are peaceful."

The Prime Minister said, "I agree that we need to send them away. We agreed the population of Judea and Samaria would be transported to a different universe, now that we have the means to do so. I think that we should notify the others that they will also be sent away if calm isn't restored immediately. We need a couple of months to finish the system anyway. So let's give them one last chance."

✡✡✡

"Himmler, what's going on with your investigation?" Hitler was pacing again, sharply turning when he reached a wall.

"Mein Fuehrer, von Kleist admitted to some dissatisfaction among the generals but refused to admit any knowledge of the assassinations. Personally, I don't believe him. We have a demonstration of his lies: His chief of staff, General Kurt Zeitzler, was also summoned and was supposed to present himself here two days ago. He didn't arrive and hasn't contacted us.

"I dispatched a contingent of SS and a senior Gestapo agent to detain him. He had his troops waiting and arrested my people. We have an open rebellion on our hands. It has to be suppressed."

Hitler stopped pacing. "We need to act swiftly and decisively. I want you to dispatch the Waffen SS to take care of this traitor. Use the most loyal and experienced troops: Wiking, Prinz Eugen, Hohenstaufen and Totenkopf divisions. Appoint Paul Hausser as group commander.

"You will exterminate the rebel generals and any troops that support them. I also want you to put all Waffen SS units on high alert. They have to be ready for action at any moment. Report to me by the end of today. I will be at the OKW – The stupid generals there need guidance about France."

When Hitler arrived at the High Command of the Wehrmacht he found a bunch of agitated generals.

Jodl, the chief of staff, explained. "The French fleet left Algiers and arrived in Marseille yesterday. They unloaded an army - French forces withdrawn from North Africa as well as De Gaul's Free French. In all they now have 12 divisions, including three to four hundred tanks. The French are moving northwest. In addition, more than twenty British divisions with at least five hundred tanks are moving from northern Italy and are forming a front with the French based on Grenoble-Lyon and west.

"We have enough forces in France to stop and defeat them, but it will take time. Most of our forces are on the Atlantic coast."

"Why didn't you know about their movements before now?" Hitler asked.

"We lost a number of reconnaissance aircraft patrolling the Mediterranean. When we received reports of the fleet within visual range of the coast the Luftwaffe tried attacking. We lost a whole wing of Stuka dive bombers and several Messerschmitt fighters. We're still investigating what happened."

Hitler started pacing, but stopped immediately. "I assume you have recommendations?"

"We recommend defense on a line in central France. Since the British obviously have an agreement with Italy we recommend an attack on Italy through Austria. This will allow us to cut off the British and take control of Italy, denying the British and French supplies through that route. It will also allow us a two-pronged attack on the combined British-French front."

"What forces do you recommend we send into Italy?"

"We have two SS Panzer divisions in southern Austria. Two Wehrmacht mechanized divisions are in Slovenia and Croatia. There's also a Wehrmacht division stationed in Serbia on the Croatian border. These can be ready to go within five days.

"We recommend utilizing the major roads from Austria and Slovenia. This will allow faster advance in the mountains. I hope that the Luftwaffe can help. We will need close support and forward observation."

Hitler nodded. "Good. Go ahead."

✡✡✡

Jacob Hirshson was ready to go. He called his mother and sister and told them not to worry. The Combat Engineers unit was in the port of Haifa waiting for their heavy equipment to be loaded for transport to Italy. Jacob's compulsory service was supposed to end in a couple of weeks. If the IDF still needed him after that, they would call him up for special reserve duty and extend his service.

The IDF General Staff had decided to beef up the Engineers in northern Italy. Since Jacob's unit was composed mostly of new soldiers, they were being sent on what was considered a safe mission to gain some experience.

"Hi, Jacob," said a familiar voice.

Jacob looked up. Benjamin Hirshson, Ze'ev's youngest son and, theoretically, Jacob's grandson, stood in front of him. "Hi to yourself. What are you doing here? I thought you were a menswear designer."

Benjamin laughed. "And I thought you were a surveyor. We all wear several hats in this country. I'm also a navy Staff Sergeant." He pointed to the chevrons on his sleeve. "We will be escorting your transport to Italy. You will be landing in Venice. We'll stay in the neighborhood to keep an eye on the sea and air."

Jacob nodded. "True, we all have at least two jobs. But I see that I'm the lowest ranking military person in this family." He smiled. "How depressing."

Benjamin became serious. "If this war goes on long enough, they will likely try to persuade you to go to officer school. The way you run your business shows you have leadership skills and you are a surveyor, which puts you on a fast track with the Combat Engineers. But I have to run, we're preparing to sail."

The heavy engineering equipment was secured on the ship and Jacob's unit started boarding. Mechanized infantry and artillery joined them, filling the ship to capacity. They had to wait for another two hours before the vessel was ready to leave port.

The journey lasted four days and, as far as Jacob could tell, went without a hitch. He did see a few missiles launched by their escorts but never saw their targets.

Venice was pleasant at the end of August, much cooler than Haifa. The transport unloaded at a military pier. All the troops were headed for their various destinations by early afternoon. Jacob's Combat Engineers regiment was on its way to the Brenner Pass, or rather to a village just south of it on the Italian side of the border. They travelled in trucks with their heavy armored D9 bulldozers. The roads were narrow and started climbing soon after Venice, which made for slow-going. The unit got to its destination three days later.

As soon as they arrived the quartermaster company started erecting tents, setting up space heaters, kitchens and dining tents. The rest of the regiment helped enthusiastically. While the soldiers were working, the officers went with the regiment commander to explore the terrain and get their assignments. They drove from their encampment just south of the village of Vipiteno to north of the village, where the valley was wider.

"B Company, liaison with the armor units and determine where they want positions prepared for their tanks and IFVs. C Company, prepare mine fields where the armor commander tells you. Don't forget to make detailed maps of the mines you lay."

They kept driving the few miles to just south of the pass and the Austrian border.

"D and E Companies, you see the steep cliffs on both sides of the valley? I want you to prepare them to be dropped to close the valley about a thousand feet south of the Brenner Pass. We also have a requirement from the local commander that a narrow path in the middle remain passable to vehicles. Use radio-controlled detonators and be careful to leave no evidence of your work here."

The commander of D Company had a question: "Should we set the explosives off as soon as the Germans attack?"

The regiment commander smiled. "That would be way too simple. The idea is to let them in and start a battle in front of the village. When they decide they don't like our welcome and start retreating, we drop the cliffs to slow them down. We do want some troops to escape and spread the word."

✡✡✡

"Your highness, my government instructed me to present to you an idea that," the Israeli Ambassador to Transjordan smiled, "may be beneficial to both of us."

Emir Abdullah nodded. "Go ahead, Ambassador."

Ambassador Weizmann continued. "As you know, we have a fairly large Arab population. About nine hundred thousand of them live in an autonomous area. Their leadership is exceptionally corrupt and is following the Jerusalem Mufti's hateful teachings. One of their important leaders, Yasser Arafat, now deceased, was a nephew of Haj Amin al-Husseini. A short time ago their armed forces, which numbered in the tens of thousands, tried to break through our border with you and invade Transjordan."

Emir Abdullah slightly rose from his seat. "What? You have armed followers of Haj Amin al-Husseini running around free? Is your government suicidal?" Abdullah visibly calmed himself. "I hope that none crossed the border. That would be a catastrophe."

"No, your highness. None did. We destroyed those who attacked our border forces and deported the leadership and all their remaining armed men. We tried to negotiate with them for a peaceful agreement but to no avail – They break the agreements we reach and incessantly engage in violence."

Emir Abdullah nodded. "You couldn't expect anything else from disciples of al-Husseini."

"My government is going to deport the whole population. We don't want to harm them but we also can't live with them. Here's the opportunity I mentioned earlier: we know that not everyone in this group is an active murderer. We are willing to let those villagers who are peaceful immigrate to Transjordan. They will boost your population, which really needs it, and will bring with them some advances they learned from us."

The Emir raised an eyebrow. "This is not a gift I would necessarily want. If they've been infected by al-Husseini's madness they will be as dangerous to me as they are to you."

"My government agrees, your highness, and proposes that you send your own officials to evaluate the people to determine who might be dangerous and who might bring some benefits. If you decide to take some of them we will let them decide if they want to go to Transjordan or join their brethren in exile. Those who choose emigration and who comply with our criteria will be granted emigration permits and enough funds to buy a farmstead and some livestock. They will also be permitted to take their possessions and livestock with them."

Emir Abdullah looked slightly disgusted. "I've told some people in the Yishuv that they have no idea how to deal with the Palestinian Arabs. You are soft and that doesn't go down well with Arabs." He thought for a moment, then shrugged. "I will send several of my Bedouin to interview potential immigrants."

Chapter 8

September 1942

"General, according to intelligence a Waffen SS group is advancing towards us from the west. I have a message from their commander, General Paul Hausser." The adjutant handed General Zeitzler a radio message slip.

> To: General Zeitzler
>
> From: General SS Paul Hausser
>
> By command of the Fuehrer you are to immediately surrender to me. If you do not obey this order I will have no choice but to use force to take you into custody.

Zeitzler looked grim. "Captain, I need to speak to General von Manstein."

The field telephone line was crackling but clear enough. "General," Zeitzler said, "a Waffen SS group is advancing on us. Their commander, Paul Hausser, wants me to surrender to him."

Manstein was quiet for a long while. "As we have agreed, you will let him know that he has to stop his advance and contact me directly. I will do my best to resolve this matter peacefully. If this fails, are you prepared to fight and will your troops support you?"

"Sir, we are being betrayed by our own Fuehrer. Yes, we are ready to fight, though there may be Nazi loyalists among us that will become a problem."

Fifteen minutes later General Paul Hausser received a message:

> To: General Hausser
>
> From: General Zeitzler

> We will not surrender. Please contact General von Manstein.

After speaking to Manstein on the radio Hausser sent a message to Himmler:

> To: Reichsführer SS Himmler
>
> From: General Paul Hausser
>
> I spoke to General Manstein. He refuses to give up Zeitzler or any of the others. He threatened me that if we try to use force the whole Army Group South will attack us.
>
> Awaiting your orders.

✡✡✡

Lior Lapid waited for almost twenty minutes and was becoming impatient when the door opened and a Navy Commander entered.

Lior was a respected historian. His latest book, "The History of the U.S. Involvement in Iran," had been published less than two years earlier. He was a close friend and supporter of Amos Nir, the current Prime Minister of Israel. Amos appointed him Ambassador to the United States to "make sure that things get done the way we want them." His immediate task was to establish trade relations with the U.S. Not being a professional diplomat he was going about his job with a directness that would have been rejected by the seasoned employees of the diplomatic corps. Being a historian helped him see Israel's historical significance in this world without false caution or modesty.

"Ambassador, the President will see you now."

Roosevelt was seated behind his desk and got up when Lior entered. "Ambassador, welcome to the U.S."

"Mr. President, it is my pleasure to be here. Allow me to present my credentials." He extended his letter of credence. Roosevelt accepted it and gave it to Secretary of State Cordell Hull who was seated in front of the President's desk. The third person in the room was Jesse Jones, the Secretary of Commerce.

"Ambassador, please be seated. We agreed to accept your accreditation on the request of Prime Minister Churchill. He assured us that 'Israel' is indeed a free and independent state and a British ally against the Nazis. We're looking forward to hearing more about Israel."

"Mr. President, Israel is a democratic state with a President as the titular head of state and a Prime Minister as the executive. We are quite advanced technologically and have abilities that are not common. I trust you remember the doctor who treated you last year. I see that the treatment was successful and you don't need a wheelchair anymore."

Roosevelt nodded. "Yes, I can walk, although I still need a cane and can't walk very far. It's an immense improvement. I remember Dr. Brown explaining to me that you had a large number of experts from all over Europe. But how did you become independent and such an important ally of the British?"

Lior Lapid had a prepared response; the answer had to be truthful and obtuse at the same time. The Americans knew nothing of the time travel incident and Israel preferred to keep it that way for a while longer. He said, "As you know, advanced science and engineering lead to, among other things, advanced weapons. Also, don't underestimate our fighting ability and spirit, especially since you had an opportunity to benefit from them last year." Seeing FDR's eyebrows lift in a question he continued, "You surely remember the warning the British ambassador gave you at the beginning of November 1941 regarding the planned Japanese attack on Pearl Harbor."

Cordell Hull shrugged. "Whatever your fighting spirit I can't see a handful of Jews making a difference."

Lior asked, "What do you mean by 'a handful'?"

Hull responded, "Your total population is what, six hundred thousand?"

"No, you're forgetting the six million we rescued from the Nazis and almost a million from the Arab countries. We are also now absorbing a couple of million Russian Jews. So we are smaller than the U.S. But science and technology are an immense force multiplier.

"Oh, before I forget, Dr. Brown gave me a package for you. He figured that you would be running out of your pills soon." Lior put a box the size of a book on the President's desk. "There should be enough here for another six months.

"Now, since my mission here is to promote trade, can we can discuss that?"

"Please give my best regards and thanks to Dr. Brown. I also appreciate the warning about the Japanese attack. I wasn't aware that it came from you.

"Mr. Ambassador, please give us a general understanding of what your government expects." Roosevelt leaned back in his chair prepared to listen.

"Our expectations are quite modest. We would like to purchase some equipment, including earth-moving rigs and machining tools. Also rolled steel stock and plate."

The three Americans looked at each other. Jones nodded, "Those are materials and equipment essential for our war effort. We would not be able to supply you with much, if at all. How do you propose to pay for your purchases?"

Lior smiled, "We hope you'll accept good old U.S. dollars."

"You sure you have enough funds? When I prepared for this meeting I found out that the Palestinian community is poor."

"The State of Israel is not poor. As you know, we supply close to forty percent of all the antibiotics used in the U.S. The market is still growing and we expect to be the largest supplier of analgesics, antibiotics and many other lifesaving drugs for the foreseeable future. Your own Department of Defense is our largest customer.

"This brings me to the next issue: we would like to establish a tariff exemption for our exports, so that we would be able to sell directly to U.S. customers and bypass the British. Your consumers and the government would see a reduction in the price of our drugs."

Roosevelt asked, "What can you sell that might be of interest to us?"

"You mean besides the drugs we're already selling? After we settle the principles, a meeting can be set up between experts on both sides. We would like to reach an agreement as soon as possible. It would be to both our countries' advantage."

✡✡✡

The internet was connected. The IDF communications people set up a series of digital transceivers on balloons along the Adriatic coast of Italy and into the Alps while they were working on setting up antenna towers.

Wolf Frumin received an email from Sheina:

> Dear Wolf,
>
> I spoke with Jacob last week and he told me he was on his way to Italy. Maybe you will meet.
>
> We have good news from Noam. He has recovered from the concussion and undergone surgery to replace both knees. I have no idea how that's possible but the doctors promise that he will be able to walk soon.

> Best regards and love from your sister Esther. She arrived here a couple of weeks ago but I had no way of informing you. She is now studying at the Ben Gurion University. We share an apartment with my cousin Tzipora. Esther is attending Hebrew courses and also learning about computers and modern technology. She plans on going to medical school.
>
> Please be careful.
>
> Love, Sheina

Wolf thought for a moment. Jacob was with the Combat Engineers and a regiment had just arrived. It made sense that Jacob might be right here, in the valley. Since he had some time before his next guard shift Wolf walked over to the company commander's tent. "Sir, it's possible that my relative with the Combat Engineers just arrived. How can I check where he's posted?"

"You can contact their headquarters directly. Look up their cell number in the network directory. If they give you grief, tell them I asked to know."

They didn't give him grief. Jacob was in a tent next to the headquarters, probably asleep – it was past eleven. The next day he was supposed to do some work northwest of the village of Vipiteno, which was exactly where Wolf's company was deployed.

In the morning Wolf sat on top of his tank and examined the terrain through binoculars. It didn't take him long to spot Jacob.

"Welcome to our Alpine resort."

"Wolf, good to see you. I didn't know you were deployed here. How are you?"

"I'm fine. I'm sure you haven't had an opportunity to contact home since you left. I have an internet connection in the tank. Would you like to send email?"

"Sure," Jacob hesitated, "but I have to finish my job first. I'll find you in the early afternoon. Thanks."

As it happened Jacob couldn't make the meeting. A general alert was announced at about noon. German forces had been spotted by a drone fifty miles east of Innsbruck, which put them about 70 miles from the Brenner Pass. The work the Engineers were required to do became urgent. They worked through the night and the next day.

Jacob came to visit Wolf two days after the alert.

"Wolf, I would appreciate sending a message or two. I think that the most efficient way would be to send an email to Sheina and let her notify the rest of the family. What do you think?"

Wolf nodded. "Make it as short as you can. The connection is very slow. I'm sure that our command is using the link for their communications and they have priority."

Jacob sent his message:

> Dear Sheina,
>
> Please let the family know that both Wolf and I are in the same area in Italy. We are fine, sitting here and waiting for the Germans to arrive.
>
> Best regards and love to everybody.
>
> Jacob

✡✡✡

Israel's PM Amos Nir couldn't decide what to do about the Palestinians so he sought advice from experts: the head of the Mossad, the head of the Security Service, and a psychologist.

"As you know, the cabinet decided a while ago to send the Arabs from Judea and Samaria into the past. We anticipated a simple operation that would give the Arabs the independence they claim they want and give us peace. It didn't turn out that way. Mazen and their leadership ordered an attack by their armed forces to breach the Jordanian border. We stopped the incursion but with a high number of casualties. After a somewhat strange legal procedure the Supreme Court allowed us to deport the leadership and fighters. A recent technological breakthrough allowed us to send them into a parallel universe so hopefully we will never hear from them again.

"I have no doubts about transporting the rest of the population but we have an old problem: the Israeli Arabs. After the recent fighting they demonstrated and attacked Jews on roads that pass by their villages. We know that some of them are armed and ready to attack us. I need opinions."

The head of the Mossad responded, "We need to be careful. There are several Arab villages that are generally hostile and others that are not."

"There are a number of very hostile villages where a great majority of the population is ready to riot at a drop of a hat," the head of the

Security Service added. “There are places like Nazareth, where some are always angry but some want to live in peace. We generally don’t need to worry about the Druze and Christian Arabs.”

Amos nodded and the Security Service man continued, “I would suggest conducting polls in every Arab and Bedouin settlement with more than, say, a couple of hundred people. First, explain to them what may happen and then ask what they want. We should also present the option of emigrating to Jordan to those that have been approved by the Emir and passed by us.”

The psychologist added, “That’s not a bad idea, but we have to be careful how we word the question, or questions, and what we tell them by way of explanations. If I understand correctly we are proposing a move to an uninhabited Earth. I would present this as an opportunity for them, which it is. They get to move to a new, unpolluted, fertile and empty land where they can establish any form of government they want and claim as much land as they want. No Jews or Israeli government to oppress them. They take their houses, fields and all their possessions with them – What could be better? I don’t believe we’ll have many volunteers moving to Jordan – Why exchange one government for another, less enlightened, if they can have full independence? Some of them still remember their brutal treatment at the hands of King Hussein, Abdullah’s grandson, and will not be willing to live under the Emir.”

The head of the Security Service said, “I agree the presentation is important, especially if we are selling them the truth. Are we going to send them to join their leadership?”

Amos Nir shook his head. “We can’t do that. When we send an area to an alternate universe an equal area from that universe replaces it. Since we don’t know where on their alternate Earth the leadership moved we might bring them back. We don’t want to. Also, I see no reason to burden the whole population with the same corrupt band of gangsters that ruled them for years. Let them choose a new leadership. At least they’ll have a chance for improvement.”

✡✡✡

Jeffrey Rosen entered the office of Abraham Cahan, owner and editor-in-chief of the Jewish Daily Forward.

Cahan took off his glasses and looked at Jeffrey. “Mr. Rosen, I was expecting someone to come and explain to me what happened to our correspondent in Palestine and why we are not allowed to send anyone there. I hope you have an explanation.” Cahan put his glasses back on and looked expectantly.

"Please call me Jeff - all my friends do. The question of Palestine is a bit complicated. First let me show you something. It will take only a couple of minutes and will make all I say afterwards much easier to accept."

"May I close the door? This is confidential. You'll see why as soon as I start the presentation." Jeff opened his bag and took out a large laptop computer.

Finally Jeff started a video. The short movie was entitled "Welcome to Israel." It presented modern Israel to a potential immigrant.

Cahan said nothing during the twenty minutes it took to watch the film. When it was done he said, "Very impressive. Not believable, but an impressive cinematic achievement."

Jeff smiled. "Would you care to closely examine the equipment?"

Cahan got up, took a magnifying glass from a drawer and examined the laptop. Jeff opened the tray and showed him the disk.

"Where do you think I acquired this equipment?"

Cahan examined it again. "I have no idea. This looks completely unfamiliar to me."

Jeff nodded. "I came from the future. Please don't think this is a trick or hoax. Israel was transported, replacing 1941 Palestine. That is why you lost contact with your people. We didn't contact you before now because we were quite busy for a while rescuing the European Jews from the Nazis and needed secrecy."

"What about the British? They let you do things in Europe? I don't remember them being very friendly to Jews. They never responded to our inquiries and were, in fact, quite rude about it."

Jeff smiled. "Indeed they were never friendly to us but when a state with advanced weapons and strong military offers assistance even John Bull is smart enough to accept."

Cahan fidgeted in his chair. "And why are you telling me this story now?"

"Simple. We want to encourage the Jews of the United States to join us in Israel. To advance this idea I would like to extend an invitation for you to come visit, all expenses paid, to see for yourself."

"I think there's something fishy about your story. But there's no harm in checking it out. That's what journalists do. I'll send one of my correspondents."

“Good, but maybe you should send several, just to make sure we don’t pull the wool over anyone’s eyes. If they want to bring their spouses it would be even better,” Jeff said.

“We have women writing for us but it will take at least two, maybe three, weeks to get to Palestine and as long to get back, plus a week there. I will lose whoever goes for a month and a half. I don’t know that I can send more than one,” Cahan said.

“Your calculation is wrong. You need to send your people to the Port of New York where they’ll be picked up by a boat and deposited in New Brunswick. From there we will fly them to Israel. They will return the same way. Travel time is two days each way. You can have your people back in ten days. Do we have a deal?”

Cahan looked at Jeff for almost a minute. “For some reason I trust you, outrageous story and all. You have a deal. When and where should they report?”

“I will let you know a week before departure. Probably by the end of this month. Let me know the travelers’ names as soon as possible.”

Jeff had three more appointments that day. Rabbi Stephen Wise, like Cahan, offered to send a replacement.

His last appointment was with Hillel Kook, also known as Peter Bergson, the head of the Bergson Group, who had come to the U.S. in 1940 from Palestine by way of Poland with Ze’ev Jabotinsky. Kook, the brother of the future Chief Rabbi of mandatory Palestine, used the name Bergson so as not to embarrass his family. In the original history he very actively tried to save European Jewry.

“Finally someone from Palestine! A little while ago we were asked by a Palestinian representative to make our protests louder, which I couldn’t as we were as loud as I knew how to be. What’s going on there? Are you from the Irgun?”

“The situation is much more complicated than you can imagine. Let me show you a short film and we will talk after that,” Jeff said with a smile.

After watching the film, Kook carefully examined the laptop and finally asked, “What happened to my family?”

Jeff took out two envelopes and several printed pages from his bag. “Here are letters from your daughters and a copy of several pages from a history book. I’ll wait.”

It took Kook close to an hour to finish reading. Finally he asked: “So what do you want from me?”

"We want to bring as many Jews as we can to Israel. You are a public figure with lots of followers. If you're convinced that our story is true, I'm sure you can convince others. We would like you to come for a week-long visit and then do whatever you want with the information."

"What about my mission here?" Kook asked.

"The reason we asked you a little while ago to intensify your activities was because we were in the process of moving the European Jews to Israel. The noise you were making helped us deceive the Nazis. Now there are no Jews left in Europe, so your mission is over. We hope you will accept a new one. You don't have to decide right now. Come and see for yourself. You can act with conviction only if you believe this incredible story. And bring more people with you.

"How long will the trip take?"

"About ten days round-trip. You will have about a week in Israel."

Kook smiled. "Future Israel. Sounds too good to be true and I'm very curious. Count me in."

✡✡✡

Himmler jumped from his seat when the Fuehrer entered. "Mein Fuehrer, they told me to wait in your office."

"Yes, yes, those were my orders. Sit. What's so urgent?"

"We have a serious problem. I just received a message from General Hausser. He was warned by Manstein that if he tried to execute the orders we gave him his group would be attacked and disarmed by the Army Group South. Obviously Manstein has vastly superior forces so Hausser stopped and asked for instructions. Besides, if the Soviets realize that two German forces are fighting each other…"

Hitler leaned back, the fingers of his left hand drumming on the desktop. "That's unexpected. I didn't think that Manstein was a traitor. I suppose that if I order him to give up his command there is no assurance he will. What do you suggest?"

Himmler rubbed his chin, a nervous gesture he had recently acquired. "We can't arrest Manstein and the other generals and we can't let it go. Maybe we should just kill them all? That will prevent further investigation but is better than nothing."

"That's a good idea. Send Otto Skorzeny to liquidate von Rundstedt. This will confuse the traitors. They don't expect us to know the members of this conspiracy. Rundstedt is in France and will be easier to get to. After he's taken care of we will take care of Manstein." Hitler thought for a moment and added, “Maybe Manstein and Zeitzler can be treated at the same time. Keep me up to date.”

✡✡✡

All fourteen ministers - constituting the full Government of Israel - sat in session. The debate over the Arab issue was loud, threatening to become violent. Since the time travel event Israel enjoyed a national unity government. It looked like this unity might not last much longer.

The divisions were clear: the right and center parties wanted to present the Israeli Arabs with the option to resettle on an alternate Earth; the left objected to resettling even the Arabs of Judea and Samaria.

After two hours of arguing and shouting the Prime Minister used his gavel and best command voice. “Ladies and Gentlemen, the arguments on both sides have been repeated at least ten times. I will summarize:

“The pro-resettlement group wants to hold to the resolution of resettling the Arabs from Judea and Samaria and add an open and public resettlement proposal for Israeli Arabs, who would be free to accept or reject it. Those who were invited by Jordan and whom we approve will be free to move there.

“The anti-resettlement group wants to rescind the original resolution and do nothing.

“I suggest that we vote now.”

The vote showed a sharp difference in opinion: ten ministers were for resettlement and four were against. Amos Nir concluded: “The resolution for resettlement passed.” He was about to adjourn the meeting when a minister from the Labor party stopped him. “The resolution passed in the government but we insist on bringing it before the full Knesset. If this is not done we will leave the government.” The other three opposed nodded in agreement.

Amos was a bit surprised. “You would leave the government at a time when the country is at war with Nazi Germany in order to force us to rescind a resolution you voted for only six months ago? Would you have done that if the security cabinet approved the decision without your involvement?”

“It’s the deportation of Israeli citizens,” responded the minister from Labor.

“But we’re not deporting citizens; we only propose giving them the option to leave.”

The Labor minister got up. “Either the government brings this to the full Knesset or we walk out.”

Amos smiled. "And what will happen when the Knesset majority decides the same thing?"

"They will side with us," said the Labor minister.

Amos thought for a moment and then surprised everyone. "I agree. Let's bring this decision before the Knesset and ask it to pass a law that will put this issue to rest."

After the meeting the Minister of Defense stayed behind. "Amos, why did you agree to this foolishness?"

"We are nearing elections and I think this kind of thinking needs to be clearly presented to the public. There's nobody better than the left to bury itself. I believe that a great majority of our population, especially those who were rescued from the Nazis, will have little tolerance for the leftist fools who are playing with our security and existence while we're fighting a war."

✡✡✡

Noam Shaviv was reading in his hospital bed when his father-in-law came to visit.

"Hi, Noam. How are you doing?" Ze'ev inquired.

Noam smiled. "As good as can be expected. They torture me with physical therapy twice a day, but at least the food is good."

Shoshanna entered the private room.

Ze'ev waved to her. "So what's new with you? We haven't heard from you for two days now," he joked.

"Actually I needed to ask you something. You know that Esther, Sheina and Tzipora share an apartment in Beer Sheva. Since your grandmother is helping me I get all the news and gossip. She told me that Esther wants to go to medical school. I mean she really wants to. She finished a year of medical training in Samarkand and liked it."

Ze'ev nodded. "Your grandmother was a good doctor. The best diagnostician I ever met. She loved the profession and had great instincts."

Shoshanna smiled. "Yes, I remember. The question is how to help this Esther? Grandma graduated from medical school in Russia. To get into a medical program here is very difficult. Even the one at Ben Gurion is very picky."

Noam interrupted, "Ze'ev, don't you know someone or somebody who knows someone?"

Ze'ev nodded. "I'll have to think but I'm sure you're correct. I have doubts about using this kind of connection though. I did a favor once, a long time ago, for a friend who wanted her son to have a safe job in the army. Years later I married Linda and told her about this 'good deed'. She convinced me that it wasn't a favor to the son, although the mother was happy enough. I'll ask Esther and see what she wants."

A nurse came into the room. "Noam, it's time for your exercises."

Noam groaned miserably. "You see, guys. They're going to torture me again." He threw off the blanket and almost nimbly lowered his feet to the floor. Apparently he could walk using a cane and supervised by the nurse on one side and his wife on the other.

Ze'ev asked jokingly, "How soon will he be able to run?"

"Probably in a month or so if he continues to exercise after he goes home," the nurse responded seriously.

"Interesting," Noam smiled. "You ask the same questions as my dad."

✡✡✡

The armor company commander looked at his troops. They were at parade rest with a beautiful Alpine landscape in the background. The morning air was crisp, almost freezing.

"You all know why we're here so I will not make you stand in the cold and listen to one more explanation. The Nazis are close and we expect to see them in this valley within the next several hours. I would like to remind you of an absolute truth of war: you have to fight in order to live. The enemy will kill you if you let him, especially this enemy. It's kill or be killed, so show no weakness or hesitation.

"We are facing two SS armored divisions. According to our intelligence they have 417 tanks, plus artillery and mechanized infantry, about forty thousand soldiers in all. These are seasoned troops that have seen action. We will defeat them. You know what your tanks can do and what the artillery behind you can do.

"They outnumber us three to one, which means that they're doomed. But don't be too cocky. These are excellent troops and they have an Alpine infantry element with them, so be careful.

"As to our tactics: we don't go into our normal maneuver and attack mode until after the enemy starts retreating. Our job is to stand and let them smash themselves against us. We don't want them to escape after defeat, so we've made provisions to close the exit of the valley by the Brenner Pass before they can leave. We do want some to escape and carry the word so that others will be afraid even before they encounter us. We all carry oversize unit and country flags for exactly that reason – We want these Nazis to know who is killing them.

"Good luck to us all."

The intelligence people slightly underestimated the speed at which the Germans could move. Their lead scouts arrived at the pass just before ten in the morning and were engaged by Italian units. The firefight went on for close to an hour until several German tanks arrived and an artillery battery opened up on the Italians. At this point the Italian commander decided, prudently, to withdraw. It was an orderly retreat with the Germans following cautiously.

One of the Italian units equipped and trained for mountain warfare positioned on a slope a mile from the pass opened up on the German tanks. The tanks didn't have enough elevation to return fire and had to retreat. Even though the Italians used antiquated light artillery a direct hit into the thin top armor could kill a Panzer IV. The victory was short-lived as German artillery quickly got the range and very soon their infantry began firing from below. The Italians had to abandon two of their five artillery pieces and withdraw behind the peak of the ridge.

Since the Israeli positions were only about eight miles from the pass, the Germans arrived within firing range of the tanks before noon.

At first the SS scouts didn't notice the Merkava tanks –waiting in a hull down position with only the flat turrets sticking out. The scouts did take notice of artillery coming down on them. Of the five German armored half-tracks and three armored cars, only one armored car managed to escape.

The valley was quiet for a short while with the only noise coming from ammunition cooking off in the burning vehicles a mile and a half from the Israeli line. Then the lead Panzer IV tanks appeared. Israeli drones transmitted images of German artillery taking up positions about twelve miles away – their longest range. Israeli artillery with a range of twenty-five miles opened up before the Germans had time to set up. The 155mm shells directed by an artillery observer using drone images were deadly. The SS group commander withdrew his artillery. It did him little good since they had to travel more than ten miles to get out of range of the Israeli guns. By the time the maneuver was completed only two artillery batteries were still in a semblance of working order. Those six surviving cannon didn't get to fire in this battle.

The German tanks were careful. After the Italians abandoned their position a panzer platoon advanced slowly to locate the opposition. The accompanying infantry was slightly behind the tanks, also spread over the width of the valley.

A coordinated volley from three Merkava tanks killed the panzers at a range of half a mile, causing the infantry to stop and dig in.

The Germans would have followed up with their standard tactic - an encirclement movement - but the valley was too narrow for that. The alternative was to bring up more tanks and try an assault on the offending position. The width of the valley at this point was about 2000 ft. and the ten panzers filled it. Ten more panzers were in a second line. Both lines were steadily moving forward.

The four Merkava tanks in position in front of the hamlet of Colle Isarco started slowly retreating to the main Israeli position 2.8 miles to the south. They shot as they moved, and soon there were 12 burning panzers, replaced by new ones and still advancing.

The German infantry also advanced, although some elements dug in to hold the terrain taken.

As a tank commander Wolf was expected to keep an eye on what was going on and didn't really have much to do. The German tanks fired on his platoon a couple of times but the shots went wide; they couldn't aim very well while moving and half a mile was far enough to be relatively safe.

Every so often a marker popped up on the tank's display marking an enemy tank. The gunner saw the marker as well so the only thing Wolf had to do is tell him to fire. At this point in the battle the platoon commander was calling the shots. There was time for Wolf to take care of some of the infantry advancing with the SS tanks. He used the machinegun slaved to one of his sights, taking down a German soldier or two. The other three tanks did the same, so the Germans became very cautious. From time to time Wolf also sighted and shot his 60mm mortar. This took a bit of time since he used only proximity fuses set to burst fifteen feet above ground. Those seemed more effective than the machinegun.

The slow retreat seemed to work - a display on one of the monitors slaved to a drone above the valley showed German forces pouring through the Brenner Pass, massing behind their forward attacking formation. About half an hour later Wolf's platoon commander ordered them to destroy the German tanks attacking them and retreat into the waiting defensive line.

By the time Wolf's tank joined the rest of the company it was close to four in the afternoon and parts of the valley were in shadow from the surrounding mountains. The platoon was resupplied with ammunition and topped off its fuel tanks. They had time to rest and eat. An hour later the Germans attacked in force. A mass of tanks raced toward the Israeli positions, infantry running between and behind them. German infantry units peeled off the main force and started climbing the ridges on both sides of the valley. They were doing their best to get into a commanding position over the valley and their opponent's forces.

It seemed that the German commander had figured out that he was dealing with an enemy with superior equipment, which wasn't a first for him. After all, the Soviet T34 tanks had been a nasty surprise. Those had been overcome with superior tactics and discipline. Since the German didn't know that his tanks' guns couldn't harm the enemy, he was trying to close the distance and use numbers and infantry to overwhelm them. This was someone experienced in combined arms fighting. At this point in the battle Wolf had no more time to contemplate the action – the order came to destroy the enemy.

His orders were to start with the farthest targets and not to worry about the enemy infantry. He found a panzer two miles away, designated it to the gunner and issued the order to fire. While he was deciding on the next target his tank fired and the Panzer IV was hit by a sub-caliber 120mm tungsten penetrator. The result was spectacular: the tank exploded with the turret lifting off and landing ten feet away. The next one did the same, killing and injuring scores of their accompanying infantry. Wolf knew he could kill a much heavier tank than the Panzer IV at 3 miles but targets farther than 2 miles disappeared behind a curve of the valley.

He kept shooting at panzers coming out from behind the bend until they stopped emerging. At closer ranges there were not many panzers moving. The valley floor was littered with burning tanks, dead soldiers, and burning German half-tracks. Wolf carefully examined the slopes leading down to the valley floor. With moderate magnification he could see infantry in Waffen SS uniforms digging in on his right where the lightly forested slope wasn't too steep.

Wolf decided they were not worth wasting an explosive shell on and settled in to wait for new developments. He didn't have to wait very long. German infantry was cautiously infiltrating the valley. They were weaving in between the burning tanks and skillfully using the terrain for concealment. In the meantime the sun was completely down behind the mountains and the valley was getting dark.

✡✡✡

Esther Frumin's story was interesting but unusual only in one aspect. When Germany attacked the Soviet Union on June 22, 1941, Esther and ten other girls from her high school class were on a field trip with their history teacher who, unbeknownst to them, was a NKVD officer. As it turned out, the teacher was a decent man – this was the unusual aspect of the story. He told his charges that by the time they'd make it back to town the Germans would likely already be there. He also told them that the Nazis treated Jews badly and they were not likely to survive if they went back. The teacher offered to put the girls on a train going east into Russia, as far away from the Germans as possible. Of the eleven girls only two decided to return to the village; the others took the offer and ended up in the Soviet Union. Esther and a friend got as far as Samarkand in Uzbekistan. In the old history she was the only member of her family to survive the Holocaust. In the altered history, she spent a year far away from her family, fending for herself in a country under siege, with little food and no knowledge of what was happening to her parents and brother.

After a month sharing an apartment in Beer Sheva with Sheina Hirshson, Esther went to a Ben Gurion University Career Councilor. She wanted to know what options would be open to her after she became fluent in Hebrew.

They were sitting in the councilor's tiny office in the administration building.

"Your options depend on your interests and on how hard you want to work," the councilor said.

Esther didn't need to think about what she wanted. "I want to study medicine. I finished one year of medical study in Samarkand and I really liked it."

The councilor looked skeptical. "Medical schools of this era are not considered adequate. So having finished a year at one of those is no asset."

"What do I need to do to be accepted into a medical school in Israel?"

"You would have to take an exam. It's not easy. They test your knowledge of physics, chemistry, math and life sciences. Only the top scorers are accepted.

"Our medical schools grant a degree after six years. If you have a bachelor's degree in biology or other life science you may be accepted into a medical school and your degree might be counted as an equivalent of up to two years of med school.

"Your best bet is enrolling in biology or biochemistry classes and trying to switch in a year or two. Since our population grew so much so fast all the universities are expanding their medical schools and building new ones, so in a couple of years the competition may be not as fierce."

✡✡✡

SS Colonel Otto Skorzeny and two assistants came to Paris on a morning train from Berlin. They had a complicated assignment: to assassinate Field Marshal Gerd von Rundstedt, the commander of Army

Group D, currently occupying France and the Low Countries, in a way that would not look like a French Resistance attack and make clear what awaits anyone opposing Hitler.

Skorzeny got all the help he needed from the local Gestapo. He changed his uniform to that of a Wehrmacht colonel and went to explore the scene. He determined very quickly that the military headquarters at Hotel George V, where Rundstedt spent most of his time, would be difficult to access. An assassination there would be difficult due to the presence of so many armed guards and officers on duty.

Skorzeny decided that Rundstedt's living suite was a much easier target. It was in a different wing of the hotel, well-protected against resistance or commando action but vulnerable to an inside job. In addition, to Skorzeny's delight, several senior SS officers had their lodgings two floors below the Field Marshal's rooms. Skorzeny decided on the most direct approach. He had the local Gestapo chief secure rooms at the hotel for himself and his two assistants. He used a false name and wore some makeup to conceal the easily recognizable scar on his face.

The actual operation proved to be very simple. The three SS officers went up to the fifth floor at two in the morning. The two guards outside Von Rundstedt's suite were stabbed by Skorzeny's assistants. The slight commotion caused one of the guards inside to open the door. He was beckoned by Skorzeny and stabbed as soon as he was outside the room.

The three assassins entered the suite and shot the last guard, using a silenced pistol. They knew that an orderly and a secretary were in the suit, but didn't try to find them. The door to the main bedroom was unlocked. Skorzeny entered and shot the sleeping von Rundstedt in the head. The three left the suite and the hotel. A Gestapo car waited for them around the corner.

✡✡✡

Admiral Canaris was somewhat surprised to hear that von Rundstedt has been assassinated. The Field Marshal had not been on the first list of suspects. He was killed in a manner that left no doubt that it was a sanctioned assassination to intimidate other potential conspirators. The admiral notified his co-conspirators of the new danger and advised everyone to take special precautions.

Canaris' warning saved von Manstein's life and cost the life of Otto Skorzeny.

When the assassin entered von Manstein's unguarded bedroom in a building next to the Army Group South headquarters in Donetsk and shot at the figure in the wide bed he was seized by several guards waiting in an ambush inside the room. In the ensuing scuffle Skorzeny managed to stab two of them and was shot in the shoulder by the third. He was given medical attention and then interrogated none too gently. Skorzeny was loyal to the Fuehrer but he learned that the Gestapo was not the only entity in the Reich that knew something about torture. His injured shoulder was used to the torturer's best advantage. He was not allowed to pass out and when the shoulder was numb Skorzeny was brought into a cell equipped by the Soviet NKVD. It included hooks on the walls with piano wire and other implements. He was promised either a quick death if he confessed or days of torture, including loss of limbs.

After one of his eyes was squeezed out of its socket Skorzeny wrote down the orders he received from Himmler and the fact that Himmler told him the orders came from the Fuehrer. After signing the document he was dispatched, as promised, by a shot to the back of his head.

✡✡✡

As darkness descended on the valley the sounds of battle died down. The German troops tried shooting flares in an attempt to illuminate the scene. They stopped after artillery responded to the source of every flare.

The Israeli sharpshooter sections moved forward. They were not snipers trained to conceal themselves and wait long periods for a target. These troops were equipped with .50cal sniper rifles with day/night scopes. Their objective was twofold: to dispose of as many enemy officers and noncoms as possible and to make the rest afraid to move. They discovered a lot of movement among the Germans. Crews with horses were trying to move burned out tanks to clear a passage for tomorrow's attack, infantry units were moving up on the slopes of the valley, and new units were arriving from the direction of the Brenner Pass. The sharpshooters didn't interfere with the operation to open the road.

With night vision and their heavy rifles the Israelis could hit targets at a mile and a half. They started by killing the team leaders of the groups climbing the ridges. Most of the climbers were stopped but some decided to crawl and there was enough ground cover to allow them to do so.

Wolf was extremely tired, especially after the hard work of replenishing the tank's ammo, but he couldn't sleep and so took the first watch. The tank's auxiliary engine was murmuring quietly in the background, keeping the tank warm and the batteries charged. Wolf set the motion detectors to warn him of any movement and concentrated his attention on his main display, which showed a combined infrared and enhanced light picture of the area in front of his tank.

After close to an hour of nothing happening and almost falling asleep, a bright spot moving on the display caught his attention. It disappeared almost as soon as it appeared. Wolf increased the magnification and concentrated on the area where he had seen the light. There was movement at the top of the ridge defining the southern edge of the valley. His ranging laser told him that this was almost three miles away. The movement stopped but by now Wolf had the coordinates and doubled the magnification. There was a blind built into the slope with the opening facing Wolf. He decided to alert his platoon commander.

"Blue, this is Blue Three."

A voice responded, "Blue Three this is Blue. What's the problem?"

"I see what looks like a concealed observation post with two people inside." Wolf transmitted the coordinates directly to his commander's computer.

"Blue Three information received. I'll deal with it. Out."

Ten minutes later the company commander's tank fired a high explosive shell into the observation post. The hit was spectacular in the dark.

A couple of seconds later Wolf's radio came on. "Blue Three this is Blue. The commander removed the threat and asked me to express his thanks. Blue out."

The rest of the night was uneventful for the tank crew, except for one strange incident. A short time after the observation post was taken out, a salvo of six rockets was shot by the Germans. The launcher was behind the bend of the valley and invisible to Wolf, although it was clearly visible on the drone's images. The rockets fell to the side of the Israeli position but without an observer to correct the aim no more were fired. A couple of minutes later artillery opened up on the German position and a big explosion lit up the sky – a Nebelwerfer ammunition truck was hit.

Wolf went to sleep as soon as his watch was over. He lay down in the empty infantry compartment and, after what seemed only minutes, was shaken awake by the driver who had the last watch.

The light outside was gray and uncertain, full of shadows offering concealment, except when viewed through the tanks sensors. These showed clearly that the Germans were on the move.

Israeli artillery opened up again at targets too far away for Wolf to see. The floor of the valley in front of him was almost clear of debris: the Germans did an excellent job of moving the dead tanks and half-tracks off the main road. They arranged the burned out hulls to make a barricade for infantry to hide behind.

A fresh batch of panzers rolled into the last two miles of the valley. As far as Wolf could tell from the overhead drone's images there were about sixty of the tanks, with only a fraction within his sight and no more panzers behind this batch.

The company commander came on the radio. “Prepare to repeat yesterday’s protocol.”

They waited. The Germans didn’t move. They were also waiting for something. Ten minutes later Wolf’s tactical display blinked a red alert symbol and a message: “Incoming hostile aircraft at 80 miles and closing.” They waited for almost half an hour. The display showed a group of planes over the Brenner Pass, then almost on top of Wolf’s tank. Almost but not quite. The anti-aircraft defense went into action.

Wolf wondered what happened: Why would they let the German planes get so close? In fact it was a calculated move by the regimental command – to reveal a minimum of their true capabilities and strike a maximum blow to the enemy’s morale.

The Luftwaffe group was clearly visible. It consisted mostly of Junkers Ju-87 “Stuka” dive bombers and a few Messerschmitt Bf 109 fighters. Just as the bombers were about to go into a dive to attack the Israeli positions they started exploding. The simplest and least expensive radar directed missiles in the Israeli arsenal dispatched all 36 bombers. The fighters tried to run for it but none of them escaped.

The German armor was immobile for close to forty minutes while their command tried to decide on a new tactical solution. Finally some of the tanks turned around and started moving back. Soldiers began digging positions for the remaining tanks.

After a short consultation at the regiment command post the order came to move forward and finish the Nazis off.

Wolf’s orders were simple: move forward and destroy tanks or anything else that was armored and not dead yet. The Israelis moved several tanks abreast covering the floor of the valley. Namer armored Infantry Fighting Vehicles (IFVs) were intermixed with the tanks. About half the force stayed in position to serve as a reserve and take care of any surprises.

Wolf was surprised within the first ten minutes. The Germans had concealed an intact Panzer IV behind several burned out hulls. Now the panzer opened up at the closest Merkava tank from a distance of barely four hundred feet. The 75mm armor piercing round hit the Merkava in the front left side of the turret. A modern 120mm round would have done some damage; the 75mm round bounced off, leaving an inch deep gash on the surface. The noise inside the Merkava was very loud and the crew, none of whom had experienced a hit before, was startled.

Wolf reacted quickly despite the surprise and started slewing the turret for a shot but didn’t fire – the panzer’s crew was abandoning the tank. They realized that their puny gun only attracted the monsters’ attention and knew what was bound to happen next. They were somewhat mistaken. The Namer IFV rolling behind Wolf's tank opened up at the panzer with its 25mm high velocity gun. In a couple of seconds the panzer was burning merrily.

Later, when thinking about the battle and discussing it with friends, Wolf was always amazed at the Germans' fighting spirit. Their infantry did its best to stop the assault. They threw grenades, tried to throw anti-tank mines under the tracks and even tried to swarm the tanks and the IFVs. None of this had any chance of success since the Trophy defense systems of the tanks and the Iron Fist installed on the Namer killed the attackers and destroyed anything they could throw at the vehicles, while the tanks' and IFVs' machine guns contributed their deadly fire.

This fighting spirit lasted only as long as the troops thought they might have a chance to survive and inflict damage. Some of the ferocity was brought out by the large Israeli flags that all the vehicles carried. The sight of the Star of David seemed to make the SS crazy.

After Wolf's tank advanced about three miles the picture changed abruptly. The German infantry stopped attacking and ran; the surviving panzers also tried to escape. This was difficult in a narrow valley with steep inclines on both sides. Some of the infantry did get away but not many. The regimental commander estimated that close to thirty thousand Germans died in the eight mile stretch between the Brenner Pass and the town of Vipiteno. No panzers or any other mechanized equipment survived.

The command post of the SS group positioned close to the Brenner Pass retreated as soon as they figured out that defeat was imminent. They didn't survive: Cobra helicopter gunships went after them. The combination of rockets and fast-firing Gatling Mini-Guns brought on their speedy demise.

Two SS Panzer divisions ceased to exist. The survivors were on the run, mostly into Austria and Germany carrying the news of a terrible Jewish army moving on Germany.

After the battle Israeli combat engineers removed the explosives they had installed to close the valley as well as the mine fields. None of this turned out to be necessary but, like Jacob's platoon commander said, "You never know what a crazy Nazi is capable of."

Two days later, at a company level debriefing discussion, Wolf questioned the company commander. "We have seen the Germans fight and later run but I have seen none trying to surrender. Why?"

"The infantry did see the SS surrender, when our soldiers were out of their armored vehicles. Maybe the Nazis were too intimidated by the armor, though that's unlikely. I think that they were afraid of the Star of David flags on our vehicles and figured that we would kill them all anyway. We captured about three thousand prisoners of war. Not a large number compared to the number of dead."

"What will we do with them?" Wolf asked.

"That's not my decision and command doesn't ask my opinion, which is lucky for the SS. I heard that they'll be transferred to the Italians who, by the way, don't like them much either."

Chapter 9
October 1942

The head of the Mossad gestured for his guest to sit. "I have an assignment for you. It's going to be somewhat dangerous but one you might enjoy."

The man sitting in front of the Mossad chief was in his early forties, close to six feet tall and built like a bear.

"You know I enjoy peace and quiet."

"It's going to be peaceful and quiet indeed. I want to you to join our legation in Moscow. Your new name is Avram Zaretzky and you are a member of the Palestine Communist Party. Zaretzky was born in 1900 so you are aged appropriately.

"You met Leopold Trepper, one of the founders of the party, before he was expelled by the British in 1929. He may or may not remember your name but you need to remember him. Right now he is the head of the Soviet Red Orchestra spy ring in Germany, though he spends most of his time in Paris. Read his file from when he was in Palestine, it may be important.

"Since Zaretzky's name was on the Comintern lists of Communist party members we expect the security branch of the NKVD to approach you. Your mission is to serve as bait to discourage them from picking on someone else and to feed them information, or disinformation, we want them to have about us."

"Lovely," Zaretzky responded. "Now I'm bait. Who am I expecting to devour me?"

The head of the Mossad smiled. "No devouring. We expect them to be curious about us. Their normal modus operandi would be to either kidnap one of our people or subvert one. They don't normally kidnap foreign diplomats but who knows whether they will consider us poor Palestinians proper diplomats. So we are offering them bait in the form of a known Communist who has already communicated with them and given them information on the British Mandate in Palestine.

"The head of the legation is expecting you and actually has a job for you but knows nothing about this mission. Your official position will be

First Secretary of the Palestinian Legation. We already have a security guy there. You will help him and collect as much intelligence as you can, but bear in mind that your primary mission is to keep Beria and friends happy. We have in mind a secondary purpose: If possible, we want to undermine Beria's standing with Stalin."

"Yes," responded Zaretzky, "the guy is an animal, torturer and pedophile."

"All true, but that's not the main reason we want to undermine him," said the head of the Mossad. "He's very effective at what he does and one of the things he does is consolidate intelligence and organize special projects. Stealing the atomic bomb secrets was his initiative as well as organizing and guiding the team that developed the Soviet bomb. With him either gone or losing his standing with Stalin those special projects will be significantly slowed down or not developed at all."

"They will have a couple of questions regarding our spying abilities for you that may be tricky. Here's what you tell them…"

✡✡✡

The Prime Minister waited for the Speaker of the Knesset to bang her gravel and silence to fall. "My fellow members of the Knesset, before we start debating I have some news to share. Our forces in Northern Italy fought their first battle against the Nazis. The victory in this battle was complete. We destroyed two SS divisions near the Brenner Pass and three Wehrmacht divisions on the Italian-Slovenian border. Our losses were less than a hundred casualties with eight dead. The news is being disseminated to the public at this time so you will find more details and pictures in the papers."

A member of the Knesset, from one of the Arab parties got up and yelled, "The Prime Minister should be ashamed. The government initiated a war of aggression and we will all pay the price." A general hubbub erupted after this interruption. It took the speaker some time to quiet the room.

Amos Nir waited patiently before responding, "The Knesset member seems to think that we started this war. May I remind you that the Nazis started it. We are just acting to protect ourselves and to fulfill our obligations to our allies, the British and Soviets. But that's not what we need to discuss.

"I would like to present a law to the Knesset for acceptance.

"This law is quite simple. Any citizen of Israel who wants to join the Arabs from Judea and Samaria in their trip to an alternative universe or to Jordan will be free to do so. The State will do everything in its power to insure that these citizens travel with all their possessions. The move to the alternate universe will include their homes, fields, cars and anything else they choose to take with them. If this proves impossible, the state will compensate such citizens with items of equal or greater value of their choice. If for example a majority of a village decides to move, the whole village will be moved even if a minority of its inhabitants objects. Those who decide not to move with the village will be free to stay with no special compensation.

"The government and the Knesset Internal Affairs Committee both recommend approval of the law as written."

The debate lasted the rest of the day and into the next. It ended in the afternoon when the speaker called for a vote. Of the 120 members 23 voted against the law – members of the Arab parties, the Communist Party, and two other leftist groups. The rest, including the left of center ones like Labor who had demanded the vote, voted for the law. Since every law had to survive three such votes it took another day to pass.

✡✡✡

Hitler was pacing in front of the map table at the OKW headquarters as General Alfred Jodl explained the operation against the British forces. He started with France. "Our forces successfully executed a pivoting maneuver and are now converging on Lyon. We estimate that about sixteen enemy divisions are concentrated in that area. We think that nine of them are British and the rest are French. Elements of the Eighth Panzer encountered a British force near Saint Etienne.

"We estimate that the British force was about battalion-sized. Our forces had to retreat after losing a third of our tanks. It seems that the British are using a new tank that our Panzer III can't penetrate at any angle. Panzer IVs with new guns can't penetrate its front or most of the side armor. Their guns are deadly to us at long ranges.

"This incident caused us to slow the armored units and wait for artillery support. We also requested close support from the Luftwaffe."

Hitler stopped his pacing. "Are you all crazy? We need to attack them as soon as possible. Put Rommel in command of Army Group D. We have to crush them." He looked around. The generals lowered their eyes. Jodl clicked his heels. "As you command, my Fuehrer."

Hitler nodded. "What's going on in Italy? Have our forces positioned themselves to attack the British rear?"

Jodl shook his head. "My Fuehrer, we are still collecting information on what happened in Italy. Preliminary reports are coming in but everything is confused. We can't establish contact with the two Waffen

SS divisions that attacked across the Brenner Pass. Contact was also lost with the sixth Panzer division. We have reports from the 13th Panzer division and the 25th Panzer regiment. Neither one has any tanks left. They lost close to 80% of their personnel. The Luftwaffe reports the loss of 82 Stukas and 12 Messerschmitt fighters - all the planes they sent into action at both locations, the Brenner Pass and the Slovenian border."

Jodl paused indecisively and continued after a moment. "We have several unconfirmed reports that the opposing forces displayed flags with Jewish stars."

Hitler stopped, leaning heavily on the map table. "Jodl, are you telling me that we lost five divisions, including some of our best, and a hundred aircraft to some pig-dog Jews?"

Jodl hesitated. "My Fuehrer, I am not sure what happened. Our losses were heavy and our forces didn't achieve their objective. We still don't know how it happened."

Hitler considered the statement. "Then find out. That's what you're here for."

Jodl clicked his heels again.

Hitler asked, "What's new on the Eastern Front?"

Jodl gestured to a colonel standing nearby, who changed the maps on the table. "We seem to be unable to dislodge the Russians on the Don line. They are attacking on the Northern Front and slowly moving northwest from the direction of Moscow. If we don't stop them they will break our ring around Leningrad."

Hitler pointed at the assembled generals. "Devise a plan to stop their advance and break through to the other side of the Don. Present it to me in two days." He turned around and left.

At his office in the Chancellery Hitler told his secretary to summon Albert Speer and General Robert Ritter von Greim, the new commander of the Luftwaffe replacing the assassinated Goering. In the meantime he met with Himmler.

"We need to stop our actions against the generals. Only temporarily, you understand. We have problems on all fronts. I had to appoint Rommel to lead the defense of France. The Russians are getting frisky and we can't afford an open insurrection. I have decided to postpone our actions."

Himmler nodded. "I understand. I can start moving the Waffen and other SS troops to be in position to act when the time comes. Slowly concentrate them in the Army Group South territory ready to strike."

Hitler shrugged. "Good, do that. In the meantime I need you to investigate a strange claim. According to the High Command, our troops invading Italy were repulsed by forces under a flag with a Jewish star. Did you hear anything about that?"

Himmler fidgeted in his chair. "Just before coming here I received a disturbing report. The two SS divisions that were supposed to go through the Brenner Pass indeed claim to have fought against a force under a Jewish star flag. The survivors are ready to go back into the fight but the debriefing officer said they didn't believe they could win."

Hitler got up and immediately sat down. "Well, investigate this and tell me when you have definite information. I also want you to call the Caliph's base in Brindisi. Maybe there is a connection." Hitler thought for a moment. "Actually don't call the base personally. Tell Alois Brunner to call." Brunner replaced Adolf Eichmann after Eichmann's execution by the Israelis in Lithuania.

As Himmler left the office, Albert Speer and General von Greim entered. Hitler gestured for them to sit. "Albert, what is the status of the modified Panzer IV?"

"My Fuehrer, the Variant F2 is now in production. That's the one with a 75mm high performance gun. As you know, it is successful against the Russian T34. We should be able to replace all the Panzer IIIs by the middle of next year."

Hitler got up and started pacing. "What about a larger gun?"

"That would take a while. I'm not certain what's available in the way of guns, but a larger caliber with a higher muzzle velocity will also require a new, larger turret and a new hull. It means a new tank design. I will check with Krupp and with Daimler-Benz."

Hitler addressed the commander of the Luftwaffe. "I want you to closely support our forces in France. At the moment, this is the most dangerous front and Rommel must have the support he needs."

General von Greim thought for a moment. "We have two Air Armies available. Luftflotte 2 with 177 aircraft and Luftflotte 3 with 752 aircraft. Luftflotte 2 is now located in Greece and already lost some aircraft in Northern Italy. We need them in that area against the Yugoslav partisans and other threats. Luftflotte 3 is positioned in France, Holland and Belgium. It would mostly be their assignment to act against the Franco-British invasion of France. We can, possibly, take some bombers from the Luftwaffe Command Center in Germany, but they have only 46 Do217 and 18 Ju-88. Any other reinforcements would have to come from the Eastern Front."

Hitler made an impatient gesture. "Take all the bombers from the Command Center. We'll see how it goes and decide on more later, if needed. We need to be extremely responsive to the requirements of the French front."

✡✡✡

Wolf settled in the tent he shared with his crew. It wasn't bad, insulated and with a propane heater. It even had internet access, although he had to use a battery operated-tablet to send an email to Sheina.

> Dear Sheina,
>
> We have just been through a major battle. Thank G-d my group came through with no injuries. There were some casualties in some of the other companies and some people were treated in our field hospital. It doesn't seem to be too bad.
>
> I was promoted. I am now First Sergeant and as soon as things settle down will become Platoon Sergeant. My company commander promoted me because of my "resourcefulness and initiative in combat."
>
> The weather here is cold. During the night the temperature falls close to freezing and it's not that hot during the day either. We have warm clothing and warm tents with heaters. I'm lucky to be in an armored unit. Our tanks have heaters and we're all very comfortable.
>
> Right now I'm in an encampment several kilometers away from the Brenner Pass, on the Italian side. There's talk about us crossing into Austria but no orders yet.
>
> Jacob sends his best regards. He's doing very well and was promoted to sergeant. He told me that his unit is reorganizing and that they are going to release him from service into the reserves within a couple of weeks. He should be home soon.
>
> Give my best regards to Esther. How is she doing and does she have an email address? I would like to write to her directly.
>
> They promised that our cell phones would have a connection within a couple of weeks. I will call my parents as soon as I can. In the meantime please inform them that everything is good here. I can't write to them since they don't have email.
>
> With love, Wolf

A response arrived within an hour:

Dear Brother,

Sheina gave me your email address and as you see I have my own now.

I called our parents and told them that you're doing well. They were having second thoughts about having signed your request to serve in a combat unit but seem to be reassured now. Father is very proud of you and Mother thinks you're a hero. They want to know whether you need anything they could send to you.

Having had some little experience with war I have only one piece of advice for you: don't be tempted to become an officer. The wounded in the hospital in Samarkand where we trained all agreed that new second lieutenants have a very short life expectancy.

I'm doing as well as can be expected. I'm studying Hebrew and as you can see this email is part Yiddish and part Hebrew. My basic computer literacy is improving but I may have difficulty getting into medical school. There is still some time before I need to decide and will update you later.

In the meantime Sheina wants her computer back to write an email to you. By the way, she's a very nice girl and we have become really good friends. I also like her cousin Tzipora, though I can see why you were attracted to Sheina.

Wish you the best.

With love, your sister Esther.

✡✡✡

Major General Ephraim Hirshson, the commanding general of the Israeli Expeditionary Forces in Europe looked over his staff, assembled in the command tent and waiting for him to start the meeting.

"Good morning, everyone. First an update on what the General Staff requires us to do: We stay where we are and let the Germans come to us. If they don't take the bait, we advance until they do. It's up to us to decide where and how.

"I want to consolidate our position. We need a good logistics base close to the port of Venice. We also need a subsidiary base by the Brenner Pass."

Ephraim turned to his Chief of Operations. "Please take care of the planning.

"What's the status of our anti-air capabilities?"

The Colonel responsible responded, "We have local and regional capabilities. The regional is the 107th squadron of Kfir fighters. They're mostly obsolete where we came from but are extremely capable, especially when armed with Derby air-to-air missiles. In this configuration they are capable of dealing with aircraft up to twenty miles away.

"Local capabilities are the Machbet/Racquet system mounted on Centurion tank chassis. It has a 20mm Vulcan cannon plus missile launchers with a maximum range of about four miles. We used them in the last battle and they're deadly, especially as we're dealing with slow flying aircraft. We also have several SPIDER batteries, which are basically Derby missiles modified for ground-to-air use."

Ephraim nodded. "That confirms my assumption that we don't really need a Kfir squadron for air defense. We may use it for ground attack but, judging by their performance in the last battle, our air defenses are more than good enough.

"I am bothered by the distance the Kfirs have to fly to get where they might be needed. Brindisi is 450 miles from us and even farther to where the Brits are. I would like to have the Kfirs close. Maybe the logistics base can also serve as an air force base. Get a combined air force and engineers proposal on my desk in a day or two. If need be we can get construction assistance from the Italians.

"If any of you are wondering why I mentioned the Brits, it's because they asked for assistance. I'll let our chef of intelligence explain."

The Brigadier General responsible for the Expeditionary Force's Military Intelligence stood in front of a large scale map of Southern France. "The combined French/British forces are slowly advancing in the face of German opposition. They are holding the line at Lyon and advanced and took Clermont-Ferrand. This makes for a reasonably narrow front, only 150 miles from the Swiss border to Clermont-Ferrand. From there the front goes to Toulouse. The Allies are holding about 400 miles in all.

"We are providing them with intercepts and transcripts of German communications. We also have several drones flying constantly over the area, including at least one equipped with long range radar. That combined with satellite images gives us excellent information on what the Germans are planning and doing.

We know from our intercepts that the Luftwaffe is moving its Third Air Army very close to the front. This caused the British to move significant numbers of Hurricane and Spitfire fighters into the area. Their Centurion tanks are performing extremely well. There are three confirmed reports of Centurions knocking out Tiger I tanks. The Panzer IV and IIIs are defenseless against them.

"Now to the request for assistance: Montgomery is a capable commander but not as good as Rommel, especially in open terrain like France. He suffered several small setbacks and is now overly cautious. I think that his natural overly aggressive personality will soon be back. I have no doubt that he will eventually push the Germans out of France but it might take him a year and, what's more important, not convince the German command soon enough that the war in the West is lost. Especially if he makes a major mistake, which, as we know from history, he's liable to do. He requested our assistance in the air until his reinforcements arrive. I recommended that we use our jets not only against the Luftwaffe but also against ground troops. That should quickly convince Rommel and the rest of their command that they are losing."

Ephraim summarized. "I want plans for a logistics base, air-force base and air force deployment by end of day tomorrow. We need to start urgent work on winter quarters for our troops, especially those at high elevations.

"One last item. We are going to be deployed here for a while. Some Italian businessmen offered us their services. I'm all for purchasing local produce and other foodstuffs. Just remind the procurement officers that all food they buy has to be certified kosher by our rabbis and not to neglect the resources of the local observant Jewish community.

"We had several proposals to set up brothels – which is apparently common practice for armies here. I refused and warned the businessmen who proposed this not to try setting up illicitly. Speaking of this issue, we will start rotating troops on home leave in about a month, after we have winter shelters and a landing strip close by that can accept C130 transports."

✡✡✡

The Israeli Colonel commanding the Brindisi base was ready to call it a day when his telephone rang.

"Colonel, I have Alois Brunner on the line."

"Put him through."

There were clicks and noise on the line and then Brunner's distant voice. "I need to speak to Colonel Rakhman, commander of the base."

"My dear friend Rakhman has been promoted. He's now General Rakhman. I am the new commander of the base."

"How shall I address you?" asked Brunner.

"My name is Hussein bin Abdul Hamid. You may call me Colonel Hussein. What can I do for you?"

"We have a little problem and hope you can help us. Our forces had fighting incidents with some unknown forces near the Brenner Pass and near Udine. We have reports of the opposing forces flying a flag very similar to the one you used when transporting Jews to Palestine. Would you know who they might be?"

The Colonel answered without hesitation. "I can say only that they were not forces of the Caliph. If they would have been, the Caliph would have destroyed a major German city for an attack on his soldiers."

Brunner wasn't done. "British forces attacked our forces in France. They came through Italy. The Fuehrer asked the Italian ambassador for clarifications before ordering the takeover of Italy by our army. Were you aware of any such goings on?"

The Colonel did his best to sound angry. "Colonel Brunner, are you trying to interrogate an officer of the Caliph? Do you know what might happen to you and to Germany if I chose to take offense? I'll let it go this time, but if I hear any such questions again you and your Fuehrer will be very sorry." He hung up.

✡✡✡

Lior Lapid, the Israeli Ambassador to the U.S., waited on a comfortable settee in a conference room at the Department of Commerce. He had a meeting with the Secretary.

The door opened and Jones came in, accompanied by several assistants. "Don't get up, please." He shook hands with the ambassador and sat next to him.

"How is our request for purchase of equipment and steel progressing?"

Jones shrugged. "The materials and equipment you requested are governed by the export control act of 1940 as amended in 1942. You need export licenses and it's up to the President to grant them. Whether the President will sign an export license depends on the quantities and specific machinery you need.

"Submit a specific request and, if it's not going to burden our industry unreasonably or impinge on the needs of the Department of War, it will be granted."

"Mr. Secretary, I have the application right here. We want to purchase about two hundred Caterpillar D8 bulldozers, up to five thousand tons of steel every year, and assorted machining equipment – lathes, milling machines and such."

Jones carefully read the application. "There might be a problem with so many bulldozers. I'm not sure how many Caterpillar is making right now and how many are bought by the Department of War. My staff will check and I'll get back to you."

Jones visibly shifted gears. "Mr. Ambassador, my staff checked the information you gave us and it seems that you underestimated your share of the U.S. patent medicine market. It's in our best interests to grant you the direct import privileges you requested. It will save us money. But we have one condition: you have to grant American companies licenses for the most popular drugs."

Lior smiled. "We were planning to stop marketing through Britain and let our manufacturers start direct sales next month. I guess they will just have to pay the tariffs."

"What do you mean? Your manufacturers will have to pay a lot. Won't it harm sales?"

"Not really," Lior responded. "If the Department of War wants the drugs it will either pay what it has to or apply for an exemption. I would assume that the public will not be happy to see higher prices. If our manufacturers decide to negotiate licensing agreements with American companies they will do so. The Government of Israel tries not to interfere with free markets and trade."

✡✡✡

Admiral Canaris was worried. Germany's military position was deteriorating faster than he had expected. British bombers were exploiting holes in the coastal radar defense and hitting Luftwaffe landing strips in France and the Low Countries. Large numbers of planes were destroyed on the ground, and the new British bombs created fire storms destroying fuel tanks and repair facilities. Cities weren't doing much better; large swaths of German urban areas were in ruins, including most of Hamburg, burned down in a firestorm.

The presence of a combined British and French army in Southern France would have been inconceivable a couple of months ago yet there they were, defeating all German efforts to dislodge them. Canaris decided that the information warranted a face to face meeting with Rommel. He took his car from the Abwehr headquarters at 76/78 Tirpitzufer in Berlin to the airport and from there boarded a flight to Paris. Rommel's chauffer met him at the airport, taking him to the Hotel George V where Army Group D had its headquarters. Lunch was served in Rommel's office.

"General," Canaris started after coffee was served, "I hear that things aren't going so well on the new French front."

Rommel leaned back in his comfortable chair. "This is not a secret. You don't need the glorious Abwehr to know that we're having problems."

"True, but the nature of these problems isn't exactly public knowledge. I know that the British suddenly deployed a new type of tank that's beating the stuffing out of our Panzer IV and defeats even the Tiger. I also know that their infantry is armed with new automatic rifles and anti-tank rockets that kill our armor and infantry. Neither of these new weapons nor a combination of them could cause the Desert Fox to lose several battles in a row. So what's going on?"

Rommel's right hand fingers started drumming on the table. He got up and closed the door, sat back in his chair and started drumming again. "Admiral Canaris, what I'm going to tell you should not leave this room. You agree?"

Canaris nodded.

Rommel continued, "From the very first days of the Allied landing and invasion through Italy I noticed a strange phenomenon. They had no planes in the air. Moments before our aircraft would have appeared the Brits had their fighters in just the right area to intercept them. I interviewed several Luftwaffe commanders who fought over Britain last year and concluded that their aircraft must be guided by radar that can see ours coming from afar. The problem is that the Allies had no radar in the area. They're building some now, but several weeks ago they had none."

Canaris nodded. "But this isn't what stopped you from defeating them in battle?"

Rommel looked pained. "No. We have another problem that is more serious and for which we haven't found a solution yet. The Allies are deployed in what is essentially a defensive line. As you know, in order to prevent a static line from being breached by a mobile enemy one needs enormous forces, enormous fortifications, or favorable terrain because the defenders can't predict with any certainty from where an attack will come. The attacker, if he's mobile enough, can gather superior forces at one point and breach the defensive line, especially in this flat terrain.

"This theory doesn't work anymore with the Allies. They have only about sixteen divisions on the ground yet they manage to have a concentration of their forces exactly where we attack. The results are disastrous in two respects. Our attacks fail, sometimes at a very high price, and the Allies immediately counterattack at the point I removed units for the original attack.

"Army Group D has 23 divisions, including some holding down the Low Countries and Northern France. The enemy now has at least eleven of their sixteen divisions facing us. When they get more reinforcements and attack we will be in serious trouble."

Canaris took a sip of his, by now cold, coffee. "Do you suspect a spy in your organization?"

"I did in the beginning. The Sicherheitsdienst found no leaks. We conducted a simple test: my orders were encoded with an Enigma machine and radioed to the front under my personal supervision and that of two SD agents. It didn't help. We then did the same over the telephone lines. That didn't change the outcome either. I finally decided to send a runner with written orders. This did improve the situation but not much, certainly not enough to make a difference. The Allies still seemed to know what we were about to do.

"Now you know my problems. I need a solution soon. It's my estimate that if we let this to go on for another month, the Allies will have enough forces to attack and we will have even more serious problems."

Canaris crossed his legs. "Now let me share something with you, on the condition it doesn't leave this room."

Rommel nodded agreement.

"Last month the Fuehrer ordered two Waffen SS divisions and three Wehrmacht armor divisions to enter northern Italy through the Brenner Pass and through Venice. The plan was to cut off the British supply lines, invade and subdue the Italians and, after reinforcing this group with several more divisions, mainly SS, attack the Allies from Italy and take Marseille. That would leave them with no supplies and they would have to surrender."

Rommel leaned forward. "Not a bad plan. I wasn't consulted but I was informed about it. Was it successful?"

"It was a catastrophe." Canaris rubbed his forehead and suddenly felt very tired. "The combined SS-Wehrmacht group met something in the north of Italy that gave it battle. At the end of two days of slaughter only about 20% of our troops survived. All the tanks and artillery were destroyed, as were close to 100 Luftwaffe Stuka bombers and Messerschmitt fighters."

"What do you mean 'met something'?" Rommel asked.

Canaris leaned forward. "I mean that we don't really know what we were fighting. Some of the survivors claim that the opposing forces used huge tanks and carried flags with a Star of David on them.

"Now, think about your experience in North Africa. Didn't the British also start anticipating your moves at some point?"

"Yes, but with only one road and a narrow coastal strip to fight on, it wasn't so strange. Though now that you mention it, I did wonder what they were using."

Canaris got up. "Don't feel bad about this. There is a Luftwaffe force in Greece with almost 180 aircraft that doesn't dare fly anywhere close to the Italian coast. and the Luftwaffe doesn't dare fly over the Adriatic either. Something makes their aircraft explode in midair.

"Well, I have to return to Berlin. Please give some thought to what the future holds if we are fighting an enemy we can't see."

✡✡✡

Jeff Rosen greeted the last of the Jewish leaders to arrive at the brand-new New Brunswick passenger facility. The hall was full and noisy. Jeff used the PA system to announce, "Ladies and Gentlemen, we will be boarding our flight to Israel within the hour. I would just like to remind you that the flight will be nonstop, approximately twelve hours long. You will be fed and served drinks and will be able to rest and sleep during the flight. For those of you observing dietary laws: the food is certified kosher by the Chief Rabbinate of Israel."

Boarding started ten minutes later. It was a slow process. Every single passenger had to be identified, photographed, and led to their seat. The procedure was designed to prevent unauthorized personnel boarding the 747 and to provide photo IDs to every passenger on arrival to Israel.

When the passengers saw the plane they were about to board, a Boeing 747-400, they were amazed. A well-dressed man said to his wife, "Frankly, I thought they were selling us a bunch of goods – time travel and all. I believe it now."

The flight was uneventful and indeed lasted about twelve hours, not the customary eleven. They couldn't fly by the northern route over Ireland and France. With the Germans still controlling France the decision was made to fly over Northern Africa.

They landed at Ben Gurion airport in the early afternoon. The passengers were taken by a convoy of buses to the Crown Plaza Hotel at the Azrieli Towers in Tel Aviv. Their first three days were spent touring the country. Three more days were spent in small groups: doctors went to visit medical facilities, lawyers visited court houses, etc.

A few people went to meet family and re-acquaint themselves with a country that looked both familiar and alien.

Most of the delegates spent Saturday with people from the organizations they supported in 1942.

Morris and Emma Schaver spent the day at Kibbutz Kfar Blum, a community founded in 1943 by the Labor Zionists; Morris was a founding member and leader of the Detroit chapter. Another Detroit couple, Rabbi Morris and Golda Adler, spent Saturday as honored guests of the Schechter Institute in Jerusalem, where his writings were part of the curriculum.

On the last day before departure back to the U.S. the crowd was seated in the Arison Auditorium at Habima square in Tel Aviv. The auditorium could hold about four hundred people and was just the right size for the crowd. The Absorption Minister gave a short speech and then called for questions.

"Minister, you said you want us to convince as many of our coreligionists as possible to come to Israel. How can we do that without telling them about the time travel incident? And how do we persuade them that it's true short of schlepping all of them here for a visit?"

"If you have to tell them about the time travel, then go ahead and tell them, just keep the information within the community. How to persuade them it's true is a different issue. I have no formula but I assume that you are all trusted leaders and if people have doubts you can show them some of the items you collected here. Our emissaries might help with movies.

"The most persuasive argument is making aliyah personally. People follow you."

Another question came from a distinguished looking man. "I am a doctor. If I make aliyah I will have to pass a licensing exam. They told me that it will take me at least two years to qualify. Why should I bother? I have a nice comfortable life in the U.S."

"How comfortable is your life? Can you be accredited at any hospital you want or are you admitted to practice only in a few, mostly Jewish ones? Can you buy a house anywhere you want or are communities free to exclude you because you are Jewish? Were you comfortable listening to Father Coughlin? You know that he was forced off the air in 1939 because of his opposition to the President not because of his rabid anti-Semitism. Do you feel comfortable listening to Henry Ford and Charles Lindbergh rant in support of Hitler and against Jews?

"If any of that makes you uncomfortable, you belong here. You will gain a life without anti-Semitism and a future of freedom for your children. I'm not mentioning the fact that you will have access to vastly superior medicine, transportation and conveniences. And your children will have access to a superior education.

"The most important thing though is that in this country when somebody tells you that you are a dirty Jew, you better take a shower. We are all Jews here."

✡✡✡

Prime Minister Amos Nir had a busy schedule. His first visitors were three members of the Knesset from far left parties. Amos felt that he needed to persuade them and an informal conversation seemed like a good idea.

After the customary polite small talk and cup of tea Amos started the discussion. "You wanted to talk about our decision to transport the Arab inhabitants of Judea and Samaria to another universe?"

"Yes, but this also concerns Israeli citizens who are now subject to deportation," replied the senior Knesset member.

"What are your concerns?"

"We see no reason to deport anyone. There was a violent attempt to breach our border, but the people responsible have already been deported. All of us are united in our opposition to the deportation of innocent people and to collective punishment. It is a violation of their basic human rights."

Amos nodded. "I understand your opposition, but I think that you may be missing something.

"Your position regarding the defense of basic human rights is admirable but we're not infringing on anyone's rights. They will be moved to exactly the same location. All their possessions – including fields and houses – will be transported with them. The climate of the new place is a bit cooler and a bit moister than here so it's better. The only thing that will not move with them is the State of Israel, which they hate. Those who choose to emigrate to Jordan will definitely exercise their human rights. Their leadership and most of the population accepted the move. Please explain to me what the violation is?"

"You're moving them away from their centers of culture and religion."

Amos smiled. "Ah, you hit the nail on the head. Let's see. This world has no Islamists. The last outbreak of Muslim fanaticism was, if I'm not mistaken, during the Mahdi uprising in Sudan in about 1870. Do you want to introduce Islamism with all its associated horrors of beheadings, crucifixion and terrorism within the next year?"

The Knesset members looked at each other. "I don't understand," said the senior one, "what the deportation has to do with Islamism?"

"Everything. The ideology that permeates the modern Muslim population in Israel is Islamism. Not all of them are the same flavor and not all Muslims are fanatics. But it doesn't matter. In the time we came from only a small minority were fanatics. The majority just wanted to be left in peace to live their lives. They, and a large chunk of the West, discovered too late that if you don't act against evil it owns you. This is a lesson that is being taught in this timeline as well. How many Germans are devout Nazis? Probably less than 10% of their population. The other 90% are now owned by them because they just went about their business and didn't do anything to oppose them.

"So I ask again: Do you want to introduce Islamism to this time? It will spread as soon as we open our borders, which will happen soon."

The members of the Knesset exchanged glances and then the senior one said, "This is an aspect of the problem we didn't consider, but does it warrant expulsion? Maybe we can re-educate them, provide them with better conditions?"

Amos shrugged. "None of the Islamists are poor. They're mostly from well-to-do families. So that argument is a dead end. Did you have in mind a re-education program like the Cultural Revolution in China?"

One of the visitors nodded. "If necessary that would do."

Amos smiled. "You would put people in camps, torture and brainwash them just to avoid expulsion? I wouldn't do it to them and, more importantly, wouldn't do it to us. Feel free, though, to raise it in the full Knesset for debate."

The senior member of the delegation got up. "We appreciate your time. This conversation has been very enlightening." They left.

The Prime Minister took a sip of his cold tea and called for the next visitors. The Defense and Internal Security Ministers came in, followed by the head of the Security Service.

"Gentlemen, how are the preparations going?" asked the Prime Minister.

"We're almost ready," responded the Internal Security Minister. "We need to install more transport nodes to assure that important historic structures, like the Church of the Nativity, do not go away. There are also some adjustments to account for possible archeological sites and for the few Christian Arabs left in the Palestinian Authority."

"What's the mood in the Israeli Arab villages that decided to leave?"

The head of the Security Service responded. "Most of them are celebrating the upcoming move but are apprehensive as to how they'll survive without government support. We were surprised that a large number of Bedouin tribes decided to leave."

"Not so surprising," interjected the Defense Minister. "Being nomads they like the idea of going to a place where they will be able to move all over the world with no civilization stopping them."

"We'll need a lot of troops to make sure that travel day goes smoothly. We don't want people going who don't want to go and vice versa. When will we be ready?" asked Amos.

"We'll need to call up some reserves for a week or so. We can do the transport two weeks from today," said the Defense Minister.

"What about emigrants to Jordan?" asked the Prime Minister.

"Personally I was somewhat surprised that Emir Abdullah invited less than fifty thousand Palestinians to come to Jordan. Not so surprising is the fact that less than ten thousand decided to move. Most of them, or maybe all of them, have family there," responded the head of the Security Service.

✡✡✡

Ze'ev and Linda Hirshson hosted their first large Saturday night family dinner since Noam had been wounded. Most of the family was together again, including Noam, who was slowly moving around with some help from a set of crutches.

Ze'ev's eldest son, Chaim, drove from Beer Sheva, where he ran one of the company's plants. He also brought his wife and kids, plus the three girls studying at the university: Sheina, Tzipora and Esther. Esther's parents, Nachman and Tzila Frumin, were present, as was Jacob, who was done with his active army service and back from Italy. Ze'ev's youngest son, Benjamin, was also there, having finished his four week reserve service with the navy.

Linda managed to seat Jacob between his sister Sheina and Esther Frumin, hoping to develop the budding romance.

To Jacob's surprise Esther, who had done her best to discourage his attention the last time they met, started a conversation. "I heard from Wolf that you were promoted to sergeant. He told me that you're a hero."

Jacob smiled. "A hero I'm not, but I tend to give my all to the job at hand. I worked hard and they promoted me. I really didn't do anything exceptional."

"Men are weird. Wolf says the same about his promotion."

"No, no! Wolf was promoted for initiative and courage in battle. That's a real hero. I just worked."

Esther smiled. "Yes, so you said before. Combat Engineers are just a work outfit, right? So why is 'Combat' in the name?"

Benjamin, who sat across the table from the couple, said, "Don't let him convince you otherwise. Combat Engineers is a unit of volunteers that do all kinds of dangerous work, often under fire. Just thinking of all the explosives they handle makes me shiver."

"Don't listen to him," Jacob responded. "This immature grandson of ours has no clue what he's talking about. Besides, he's in the navy. What would he know about Engineers?"

Esther laughed. "You guys are strange but nice," she conceded. "Are you in the reserves?" she asked Benjamin.

"Yes, this is the second time I've been called up. Normally the Navy doesn't keep its reservists; they transfer us to land-based units. But we're in a war and they need to rotate troops. The reserves relieve the regular guys so they can go home for a couple of weeks."

Esther looked at Jacob and asked quietly, "How soon do you expect to be called up and for how long?"

Jacob smiled. "I'm a bit wet behind the ears and have no experience in this. I can only tell you what they told us: As a sergeant I can expect to be called up for five weeks every year. I should have about a year before my first call up, unless there's an emergency."

Noam Shaviv said, "From what I hear they might leave you alone for the full year. The Generals don't expect to need many more forces in Europe, at least for a while." He looked directly at Esther. "You know it's all a question of luck. He may serve out his term, until they kick him out because of advanced age, without a scratch. I got unlucky and all my planning was for nothing."

His wife Shoshanna elbowed him none too gently. "Don't tempt luck. You're here, alive, and will walk well soon. There were lots of people who died in that battle."

Noam smiled and raised both hands in surrender. "Yes, boss."

Esther asked him, "From what I heard you got brand new knees. Is that true?"

Noam nodded. "Yes, it's true. It's not a big deal. Medicine has advanced a lot and Israel is always on the cutting edge. Now I have two knees made mostly from titanium. I'm still learning to walk and the implants are still healing but I expect everything will be as good as it was before I was injured."

“That’s why I started studying medicine – to help people,” Esther said. “That, and the fact that they fed medical students enough to only starve slowly.”

After dinner Ze’ev invited Esther to his study. “How are your studies going?” he asked.

“Not too bad,” she replied. “My Hebrew is decent, although it needs some work, and I can use a computer now. In a month or so I’ll be ready to start regular studies.”

“Even now your Hebrew is less accented than mine is. I still have remnants of the Russian and Yiddish my parents spoke at home.

“Did you explore the possibility of being accepted to medical school?”

“I did. The information I got is not encouraging. The advisor at Ben Gurion University told me that the only way for me to get into any medical school would be to start a biology or similar program and try transferring after the first year.”

“And your year of medical school in Russia doesn’t count?”

“That’s what she told me.”

Ze’ev hesitated for a moment then decided that he may as well come out with his proposal. “Would you want me to inquire and see if I can help with that?”

Esther thought for a moment. “I don’t want anything irregular. If it’s only a question of overcoming stupid bureaucracy, I guess it’s acceptable.”

“Good. I’ll contact a couple of friends and see what can be done.”

After Esther left, Ze’ev’s eldest son Chaim came into the study. “What was that all about?” he inquired.

“Esther wants to go to medical school but the councilor at Ben Gurion told her that her year of medical training in Russia doesn’t count and her chances of acceptance are very low. I offered to help. Do you know anyone?”

“I’ll have to think about it but I know for sure that the councilor was wrong. One of the criteria they’re looking at is how much an applicant wants to be a doctor. Finishing a year of med school and still wanting to continue is a good first step.

“On a different subject, I’ve been driving the new car for several days and wanted to share impressions. What do you think of it?”

Ze’ev shrugged. “I drove it for three days. It’s a car, what else can I say?”

Chaim smiled. "Yeah, that's what happens when an old man tests a car. I'll tell you what I think. It has pluses and minuses. On the plus side: It is quiet – quieter than my wife's Lexus. The acceleration is decent and it's drivable. On the minus side: The body is 1942 style and looks old to me. I would like more refinement and a faster start time."

Ze'ev made a stern face. "Who you calling an 'old man'? So the trick worked. I didn't want to influence your opinion.

"I mostly agree with you but in my opinion the car isn't drivable enough. It doesn't behave like a good internal combustion powered vehicle. I think that it needs more power when cold, which may be solved by reducing the engine's thermal inertia or better cooling. We'll see what R&D comes up with.

"The body will have to go. I hope we can get together with Fiat designers and come up with something a bit more modern-looking with a modern suspension. The Fiat Berlina was considered a good car in its day but we know better. I would also like to reduce the whine from the electric motors."

"You think it's worth investing in? This is going to be an expensive project."

"Definitely worth investing in. Don't' forget the size of the market. If we build a good car we can sell it worldwide. We'll beat the competition hands down. Our car will be unique in its performance, quiet and ability to use different fuels."

✡✡✡

Lavrentiy Beria, the head of the Soviet People's Commissariat for Internal Affairs (NKVD), waved for Boris Merkulov to sit. Merkulov was Beria's deputy responsible for internal security.

"Boris, what can you tell me about the 'Palestinians' we have here?"

Merkulov looked glum. "Not much, comrade Commissar. Each of their 'emissaries' is accompanied by an 'assistant' or 'interpreter'. The problem is that they say nothing we don't already know.

"Their legation in Moscow is completely opaque to us. The bugs we planted before they took possession of the building are working but all we hear through them are trivial conversations, in Hebrew."

Beria rubbed his chin. "There must be something we can do. What about the cleaning crew that we offered them?"

"Comrade Commissar, they surprised us by accepting our offer and now the crew goes in twice a week. They haven't found anything out of the ordinary."

Beria nodded. “I want to know more about them. The official line is that they’re independent of the British and have very advanced knowledge. There must be something to this because, as you know, they provide us with excellent intelligence on the Fascists. On the other hand, I smell a rat. That can’t be the whole story.”

“We could grab one of their people and interrogate him. It would be a while before they miss an emissary,” offered Merkulov.

“I’m quite sure they know nothing useful, otherwise they would not be so exposed. You have any other ideas?” Beria said.

“There were five of them in the permanent mission. It’s housed on Olkhovskaya Street in a little building we found for them – easy to keep an eye on and easy to bug. A sixth guy arrived last week. He’s the First Secretary of their legation. I had my department check his name and crosscheck with our records of useful people. Apparently he’s a member of the Palestine Communist Party and probably knows Trepper. We can try recruiting him. This would provide us with the most reliable information.”

“This First Secretary hasn’t contacted us yet? Very strange. Maybe he didn’t have enough time to settle in. Do these people spend all their time at the legation building?”

“Some come out infrequently. Our guy likes the Writer’s Club. In the week he’s been here he’s visited three times already.” Merkulov hesitated. “That may be the best place to approach him.”

“I think you’re correct, comrade Merkulov. He’s probably looking for a contact. Just be careful; we don’t want to try recruiting the wrong guy.”

Chapter 10
November 1942

General Ephraim Hirshson, the commander of the Israeli Expeditionary Force in Europe, examined the map in front of him with his Chief of Staff, General Uri Sadot.

"Uri, I was considering our next move. We can't sit here and do nothing for an extended period. The Germans seem reluctant to attack. From the intelligence we're getting they will leave us alone as long as we don't bother them. I want to prod them a bit. It would also be useful if we could cut off their access to the Adriatic and the Balkans."

Sadot looked at the large monitor displaying the map of the Adriatic coast, Slovenia and Croatia. "There's not much point in going into Slovenia. Since Italy joined us and pulled out their troops they have been replaced by Germans extending their garrisons from Lower Styria and Upper Carniola. The Germans are very thinly spread and I doubt that we can find a good meaty target there. Besides, the Slovenians are doing a fair job of harassing the Nazis.

"I suggest that we go down the Adriatic coast to Croatia. Not many Germans there right now but the Croatians have their own, quite numerous, army. We could go down the coast as far as the Albanian border, or we could go to the capital, Zagreb, and make a detour from there, liberating the concentration camp of Jasenovac."

General Hirshson considered for a moment. "I generally agree with your reasoning but now that I'm looking at the map it seems like an awfully long trip for our forces with no clearly defined objective. Maybe we can repeat our passive plan: send a relatively small force in the direction of Lubliana and park it in a good defensible position. Let the Germans attack us and exhaust themselves. After we're done with them we can move to Lubliana and formally liberate it. I'm sure we can scrounge up enough obsolete weapons from the Italians and British to arm the resistance there to hold the city and county for a while.

"In the meantime we send some of our air force to destroy the Luftwaffe and Croatian air force in the Balkans. Shouldn't take long even if we use just a handful of planes – it's a short flight from Brindisi."

"You're the boss. Would 10% of our total force be too big, too small or just right?"

Ephraim Hirshson smiled. "You're the chief of operations, figure it out. Just to be clear, from Lubliana I would like to move on Croatia, unless, of course, the Germans wake up."

✡✡✡

Ben Mosowitz was a fairly good-looking man, 6 feet tall with wide shoulders and strong, muscular arms. Tonight, he looked tired and his thick black hair was disheveled. Ben came home late, as usual. He was delayed at the synagogue and by the time he, the three kids and his wife Evelyn sat down to dinner it was late. November wasn't a pleasant time of year in Wilmington, Delaware. The cold, damp, weather didn't agree with Ben. He was one of the 'relatively well-to-do' members of the Jewish community. Not rich but not poor either. His furniture business was doing reasonably well, but he felt guilty. After Pearl Harbor he tried enlisting in the U.S. Army and was disqualified – He was 29 years old with three kids and flat feet. It bothered him, especially since his Jewish neighbor's 23 year old son, who worked for Ben, enlisted and left his widower father to fend for himself. Ben's wife visited the old man frequently. In fact the old man wasn't that old, he was in his mid-fifties, but that looked old to both Ben and his wife.

"How was your day?" Evelyn asked.

"Nothing special. Not many customers today, so I closed a bit early and went to the synagogue. Just made it to evening services. The rabbi gave an interesting talk and promised to repeat it Saturday."

"What was the topic that he's going to repeat himself? Do I have to pull it out of you with pliers or will you tell me willingly?" Evelyn smiled.

"Evie, I'll tell you but promise not to laugh."

"I promise. So go ahead already."

"You know that our rabbi went to Palestine last month. Now he has a story. He told us that there is a Jewish state there called Israel. It supposedly was transported from the future. He was very enthusiastic about it and the advanced stuff they have. He's going to give a presentation Sunday night. Including a movie."

"That's it or did he say anything else?"

"He's going to make aliyah and wants everyone to come with hm. He says it's the Promised Land of milk, honey and miracles."

Evelyn ate quietly for a while. "Do you want to go?"

Ben nodded. “I would like to see his presentation and also talk to the representative from Palestine, or Israel, who will be there Sunday night. If everything the rabbi told us today is true, I would seriously consider moving.”

“But why? The business is doing well, Bea will start school next year, and we live in a reasonably comfortable house. Why move into the unknown?”

Ben waved a hand in negation. “You always see the glass half full. Look at the other half: I tried getting a contract to supply office furniture to the DuPont Company. You remember what they told me? ‘We prefer not to do business with Jews.’ I have people come in from the street, look at the merchandise and when they discover that I’m Jewish, walk out. Not many, but enough to make me feel unwelcome.

“You’re also right about Bea. What school will she go to? At the public school she’ll be harassed. I don’t make enough money to send her to the Jewish school without help and I don’t want a handout. You want our kids to go through life as second rate citizens like we did. In a Jewish country they will be part of the majority. Wouldn’t that be nice?”

✡✡✡

“The Germans have accelerated their tank production and are making many more Tiger I, or rather Panzer VI, tanks than in the old timeline,” Zvi Kaplan, the Chief of Military Intelligence, told the assembled General Staff.

“Since they stopped investing in submarine production after we started helping the Brits, a lot of industrial capacity was released. All that rolled steel is now going into tanks.”

“What are the implications for us?” asked Gad Yaari, the Chief of General Staff.

“In the very short term, on the order of a couple of months, there will be no measurable change. The Germans are still training crews and maintenance teams. Eventually it could get tough for the Russians. Their main battle tank is the T-34 and it’s vulnerable to the Panzer VI’s gun. The Germans are using the 88mm KwK36 gun. We hear some discussions about replacing it with the longer KwK43 but it will not happen soon – They need a new turret design for that.

“In any case, the T-34 can’t kill a Panzer VI from the front, except with an extremely lucky shot. It *can* kill it from the side. Taking into account the training levels of the Russian armor units, they will suffer serious losses when they encounter large numbers of the new German tanks.

“There won’t be much impact on the British. The Centurion will be able to kill the new panzers with the 20 pounder gun the Brits are phasing in now and has enough armor to survive a hit by the German gun. The most important factor though is training. The Brits are becoming quite good in combined arms warfare and the RPGs they’re making are deadly to all German tanks.

“Our forces will have no problems with the new German tanks.”

Gad Yaari nodded. “Maybe we should tell the Russians about the upcoming German surprise. They can install a better gun in their T-34 before the Germans give them conniptions.”

The generals present agreed. “Good, then I will notify the Prime Minister of our recommendation.

“Another issue we need to discuss is the German air force. The Luftwaffe is making a nuisance of itself both in France and on the Eastern Front. They’re also active in suppressing the partisans in the Balkans. What should we recommend to the government?”

The Commander of the air force smiled. “It may sound simplistic, but I would send another squadron of our jets to destroy as many Luftwaffe assets as possible. We can damage their airstrips, destroy fuel dumps and aircraft.

“I looked up their manufacturing numbers and they’re impressive. In the five years from 1940 to 1945 they made more than 15,000 fighters. In my opinion destroying their aircraft will help everyone but destroying fuel dumps would probably prove more effective.”

The Chief of General Staff nodded. “I agree. Let’s do it with one caveat: I don’t want extremely long-range missions. Our air activities should be limited to ranges accessible for rescue in case we lose a plane.”

✡✡✡

‘Departure Day’ for the Palestinians was cold and bright like it sometimes is in Israel in November. Thousands of IDF reservists were checking, for the last time, the positioning of the transport boxes. The job was seriously tedious in places like Jerusalem where the Muslim, Jewish and various Christian communities were intertwined. Only Muslims were leaving and the troops were making sure that boxes were present where they were supposed to be. Those emigrating to Jordan were already gone. Their houses would be transported with the rest.

At two in the afternoon air raid sirens sounded in areas that were about to be transported. After the sirens a pleasant female voice, the same one that used to announce ‘Red Alert’ when rockets were fired from Gaza or Lebanon, announced: "Ten minutes to activation. Please leave transport areas now if don't want to be transported."

Ten minutes later another siren sounded and areas in Judea, Samaria and Israeli Arab villages blinked out of existence and were replaced, mostly, with grassy terrain.

The transport was done. Israel hoped that the appearance of Islamists in this world would be delayed many years or prevented altogether.

✡✡✡

Noam Shaviv got out of the car. He had come to this hill northeast of Jerusalem with a crew from his company. He could stand and walk short distances but had difficulty driving. They finally had accurate elevation maps of the new terrain and were preparing to start work on the design of a new city in the Samarian hills.

"So, Jacob, what do you think of this land?" Noam asked Jacob Hirshson, whose company he had hired as his surveyors.

"Looks like good agricultural land," Jacob responded. "Why would anybody want to build a city here?"

Noam shrugged. "There's indeed good soil here but it's also hilly and not easy to cultivate. I guess the government wants a place for people to live that's not a desert. I hope that people from the Tel Aviv area move here. I'm considering it myself."

"You're a city boy," Jacob smiled. "I got used to my own separate house. I wouldn't move to a high rise no matter where it was. You know that a desert is a desert only as long as it's dry. Give it some water and it blooms. Just look at Refidim. We're in the middle of the Sinai desert and it's a city of gardens and parks."

Noam nodded. "Yes, I'm a city boy. There are lots of people like me and lots like you, so we build communities for both."

"I'll have a crew here by the end of the week and submit the results to you two weeks after that. Is this satisfactory?" Jacob asked.

"Perfect," Noam responded. "Are you going to work on this personally or will someone else lead the crew?"

"Do you want me to work on this?"

"It's up to you. I was just curious. This place is not close to where your base is. It's a long drive from central Sinai."

"A long drive indeed, except I take the train to Jerusalem through Tel Aviv and rent a car in Jerusalem. So I got here rested and do some useful work on the train.

"By the way, I'm moving to Beer Sheva. It's temporary, for the duration of my studies."

"Studies? You never told anyone. What are you going to study?"

"We haven't had any big family dinners for a while so I haven't had the opportunity to broadcast the news. I'm enrolled at Ben Gurion University in their civil engineering department.

"I figured that adding a civil engineering degree would help my business and enable me to expand. I promise not to compete with you," he added with a smile.

"Are you moving completely to Beer Sheva or is everything staying in Refidim?"

"I rented a small apartment near the university and will use it during the week. I'll go back home on weekends. My mother will stay at the house and the business is, of course, based in Refidim. It's a fairly short and comfortable train ride to Beer Sheva. I would have preferred to study in Refidim but we'll get a university branch there only sometime next year, if the gods smile on us."

"Well, good luck." Noam shook Jacob's hand. "I'm sure you will make an excellent engineer."

✡✡✡

"Herr General, the attacks on our airfields in the Balkans still continue." The adjutant clicked his heels and put a typed list in front of General Robert Ritter von Greim, commander of the Luftwaffe.

The list enumerated all the airfields that had been destroyed in the last three days. It was a long list. "Captain, please ask General Kreipe to come in."

The Luftwaffe Chief of Staff, General Werner Kreipe, came into his commander's office a couple of minutes later.

"Have you seen this list?" von Greim asked.

"Yes, I have. I also carefully read the other reports."

"Good, and what's your conclusion?"

"The reports sound strange. Arrow-shaped aircraft flying very fast and making thunder-like noise. I'd say someone had too much Schnapps, but they couldn't all have been drunk at the same time."

"I noticed that before they bomb the runways they always destroy our aircraft parked in revetments, from a great altitude, since the witnesses didn't see or really hear anything until the bombs hit, always inside the revetments and only those that were occupied," von Greim said. "So who might it be attacking us there?"

"I know that Messerschmitt is experimenting with rocket- and jet-driven aircraft but they're nothing like what the reports describe. Maybe the British developed something new?" Kreipe said.

Von Greim shook his head. "I don't think so. Two of the reports mention the markings on these aircraft."

"Yes," Kreipe said unhappily, "white Jewish stars on a blue background. I wonder who it is we're fighting."

"I don't care who it is. We must find a solution before they destroy us. The Luftwaffe must not be helpless against an enemy. Not on my watch," von Greim almost shouted. "Do we have any information that may be useful?"

"They always come in pairs. You remember that yesterday we thought we might be able to swarm them with as many 109s as we could muster?"

"Yes, I remember. What happened to that idea?"

"First, it's extremely difficult to swarm something you can't see. We know they're there only after bombs start exploding amongst our planes. We tried this morning. They attacked an airfield in Macedonia we use to bomb partisans in southern Serbia. There is another airfield in Bulgaria only 140 kilometers away that had a flight of Bf-109s. They were scrambled as soon as the attack in Macedonia started and got there within minutes."

"And what happened?" Von Greim rose up from his chair a bit.

"The two aircraft somehow shot down the eight Messerschmitts without even stopping their bombing of the airfield. I have no idea how they did it."

Von Greim sagged in his chair. "I'm expected at the OKW in an hour. The Fuehrer will be there expecting a report. He knows about the Balkan attacks. I'm not sure what to tell him."

There was a knock on the door and the adjutant entered. "Herr General, we just received a message from Dijon." He handed the typed sheet to von Greim.

Von Greim read it and with a sour face handed it to Kreipe.

The message read:

From Commander Dijon airfield

> To: General von Greim, Commander of the Luftwaffe
>
> Copy to: Field Marshall Ervin Rommel, Commander Army Group D
>
> As ordered I report an unusual attack on the airfield.
>
> At 1100 the field was bombed and all aircraft parked inside revetments were destroyed. Several minutes later two aircraft of unknown origin bombed the landing strip and left it in an unusable condition. The two aircraft also strafed the aircraft parked by the runway and destroyed them, as well as our three aviation fuel tanks.
>
> As of now the airfield is nonoperational.

Kreipe looked up at von Greim. "So they're destroying us in the Balkans and now also in France. I hope you have a brilliant idea of what to do about this mess."

"Not really," responded von Greim. "They are destroying aircraft at a slower rate than we can build them, at least for now. The immediate problem is the loss of aviation fuel. We have difficulty replenishing so much. I will try to acquire more construction capacity and bury fuel dumps deep enough so they'll be safe."

"How deep might that be?" Kreipe asked with a smirk.

"How should I know." von Greim was annoyed. "As deep as practicable."

✡✡✡

The room was noisy with everybody talking, at the same time. The Prime Minister looked at his watch; it was time to start the weekly meeting. "The Cabinet meeting is formally open. Let's start with the first item on the agenda. The Absorption Minister, please."

"I have two items. First is the final report on immigration of Jews from Arab and Muslim countries. Most of them have moved here. As you know, in our previous history the well-to-do Jews from North Africa went mostly to France and well-to-do Syrian Jews went to the U.S. This time around they all came here. I think that all who want to leave are here now. We are organizing the exodus from Yemen. The overall numbers are relatively small, approximately 900,000 all together.

"Next is immigration from the Soviet Union: It started recently and is still growing. Our experts expect approximately a million, maybe a bit more. We may be underestimating the numbers but as long as we don't announce ourselves as the 'State of Israel' people think they're invited to come to Palestine, a land of desert and camels. As bad as it is in the Soviet Union, people who have been living there for many years are reluctant to move.

"We are carefully screening all new arrivals from the Soviet Union. You may remember that in our original timeline there were a number of Soviet spies among them. Since Stalin is still in power we expected even more this time around, but the actual numbers are small. Possibly because most of the Jews arriving now are 'Western' refugees. When long-time Soviet residents start arriving we will likely find more spies.

"We just started working on repatriating North American Jews. The numbers are still small but we're not in a great hurry. They're in no imminent danger and we need to smoothly absorb the millions of other immigrants who came here in the last year."

The Minister for Internal Security was next. "As you're all aware 'Departure Day' was last week. In all it went smoothly. We had several attempts to move transport boxes but nothing serious. The Ministry of Infrastructure may have a report."

"Nothing really urgent. We are in the process of laying out several cities as was agreed at previous meetings.

"We have a problem with electric power supply. Our generating capacity is at its limit. Last year we started construction of a natural gas power station on the Sinai coast. It will be partly operational in a couple of weeks and fully operational by the middle of next year.

"As an intermediate measure we re-activated the old Reading power station in Tel Aviv. It was modified to use our own natural gas so the pollution is minimal. We're also running several 100 Mw gas turbine generators.

"We now have enough heavy earth-moving equipment, specifically bulldozers and excavators, to accelerate the hydroelectric plant and Mediterranean-to-Dead Sea canal. It will become operational in a year or so. The earth-moving equipment is new but antiquated. It should suffice."

The Foreign Minister picked up. "There is one more matter of importance I need to mention: It seems that the time has come for a meeting between the three leaders of the anti-Nazi alliance. I suggest that we initiate negotiations with Britain and the Soviets for Amos, Churchill and Stalin to meet. We need to organize further coordinated action against Germany and prepare for peace negotiations."

Amos Nir, the Prime Minister, nodded agreement. "We are close to a point where at least parts of the German army will figure out that the war is lost and will try to negotiate a peace agreement. We need to be ready.

"The disadvantage of this inevitable step is that the Soviets will know with some certainty what we are. I see no alternative, and we will need to deal with consequences of this disclosure sooner or later anyway. We'll keep you apprised of our progress."

He looked at the Defense Minister. "Nitzan it's your show."

Nitzan Liebler smiled. "First we need to increase the military budget." The statement caused a general fidgeting and murmuring among the Ministers.

"Just joking," Liebler said. "Actually we're doing unexpectedly well. As you know, we've had few casualties in the action so far. Financially, our main expense was in ammunition. Also maintenance for vehicle engine and cannon barrel wear and flying hours for the air force. We're well within the budget. I can't assure you that it will stay that way for long.

"Ephraim Hirshson, the General Commanding our European Expeditionary Forces, wants to become more aggressive. I agree with him. We need to push the Germans more both to ease the pressure on the Brits and accelerate the Nazi collapse.

"Our Soviet allies are doing moderately well. They successfully opened a corridor into besieged Leningrad and are holding the Germans off on all fronts. Right now the Wehrmacht is training several more army-sized formations. You've received the IDF's intelligence reports and analyses regarding German tank production so I'll not repeat that information.

"The Soviets are also working hard. They brought lots of tanks, artillery and Katyusha rockets to the front. They also have several new models of aircraft that are finally proving a match for the Germans. With no huge losses in previous battles and no battle of Stalingrad they're in good shape as far as personnel goes. Their command is something else. Our estimate is that if we stopped streaming intelligence to them we might have a German breakthrough. The Soviet command seems to be slowly improving in defense but is still incompetent in offense. Our estimate is that the Eastern Front is likely to stay static for a while.

"The General Staff asked for permission to warn the Soviets about the accelerated deployment of more powerful German tanks so they can prepare. Taking into account our political objectives and the balance of power between Germany and the Soviet Union, the Prime Minister and I decided to refuse the request. This fits with our vison of post-war Europe. To prevent Stalin from taking over all of Eastern Europe we need to prevent a sudden German collapse and insure that when Germany surrenders, the Soviets will not be tempted to pursue their objectives on their own. In other words: Germany should not be perceived by the Soviet Union as a pushover.

"There's one more issue that is connected to infrastructure and budget. I discussed it already with both ministers: the possibility of establishing a Global Positioning System (GPS) satellite network. The military needs it for precise navigation and weapons deployment. I don't have to tell you how convenient GPS is for civilian use.

"We will need a dedicated budget to launch the satellites and to maintain them. For system maintenance we will need ground stations around the world but this is not an immediate need. We can manage with a station in Israel and one in Northern Italy. To insure proper flight navigation to the U.S. we will need one in North America as well.

"If the Cabinet approves we will present a budget next month and discuss it in detail."

"Aren't we stretched financially as is?" asked the Foreign Minister.

"Not really," the Finance Minister responded. "Our economy grew 300% in the last eight months and keeps growing at a nice clip. All the new immigrants are adding to our tax base and increasing the gross national product. Sales of medicine to our allies give us a nice tax income. If you add the income from arms sales to the Brits and the Commonwealth we have very respectable exports. Due to the enormous increase in our tax base we have a budget surplus, war and all."

✡✡✡

"Gentlemen, we're here because there are problems to be discussed and decisions to be made." General Franz Halder paused and looked at each of the leaders present at his Berlin apartment. "I'll let Admiral Canaris give you the details."

Wilhelm Canaris got up, unrolled a map and pinned it to a wall panel. "As you see, this map shows our positions in August of 1942 and our positions now. In the past three months there has been little change on the Eastern Front, except that the Bolsheviks managed to open a corridor to Leningrad. The city is not blockaded anymore. The situation doesn't bode well for us. We seem not to be able to dislodge the Russians and they're slowly gaining. If this turns into a war of attrition they will win.

"In the West the situation is worse. In August we controlled all of the northern part of France, with the Vichy government having nominal control over the southern part of the country. Now the combined French-British forces control everything south of the Lyon-Nantes line. There is worse news. They are advancing, albeit slowly, and pushing us steadily north and east. General Rommel might give you more details later.

"There are two more pieces of information that are important. You have all probably heard by now about the failed attempt by a four division group to invade Italy and strike at the British from behind. That was not just a defeat but a catastrophe. The four divisions were wiped out. We lost hundreds of panzers, artillery pieces, and more than a hundred aircraft. We're still not sure who did the damage. You have all heard the strange reports after that fiasco.

"The second piece of information is new and still ongoing: the Luftwaffe and allied air forces in the Balkans have been completely wiped out. The attackers used very advanced aircraft and suffered no losses as far as we can tell. Simultaneously similar aircraft attacked our air strips in France. General Rommel will tell you that there is no air support to speak of for his Army Group D."

"Any comments?" asked Halder.

"I have a question," said General von Tresckow. "What is happening now on the Italian-Austrian border? Did the force that defeated us move at all?"

"Yes, but not much. They pushed our forces from the southern part of Slovenia and then moved into Austria – the Klagenfurt area. Another group is occupying Innsbruck. Both cities surrendered after receiving a radio communication from the attackers and a threat of destruction. That was after any defenders we had in the area were decimated from the air. The local commanders deemed it wise to evacuate the cities."

Canaris continued, "I delivered all this information to Generals von Bock and von Manstein. I believe that General von Tresckow represents them here."

Halder nodded at the map. "My assessment is quite dark. I believe we've lost this war. It will just take some time and a long butcher's bill to make it clear to everyone. Make no mistake: The butcher's bill is growing and it's not just our military that is paying it. We have very little left of our radar warning net along the Atlantic and it is destroyed as soon as we attempt rebuilding it. You have seen the results on the way here. Block upon block of ruined and burned buildings as well as flattened industrial areas. I can't say I'm surprised. My predecessor, General Beck, who regrettably couldn't attend today, warned the Fuehrer not to attack British cities for fear of retaliation."

Rommel, who had been listening quietly from the back of the room, spoke up. "I was summoned to Berlin by the Fuehrer to report on the situation in France, which is lousy." Rommel repeated the report he had given to Canaris at their private meeting in Paris several weeks earlier.

"Last week I asked for reinforcements," he continued, "mostly more new panzers, and was promised five new divisions soon."

General Paulus nodded. "We also asked for reinforcements. The Eastern Front will have to consolidate if the Russians organize a coordinated attack. We were also promised reinforcements with no timetable and told to hold fast. I was also summoned to the same OKW meeting as General Rommel."

"When are you scheduled to be at the OKW?" asked Canaris.

"Three days from today," Rommel answered.

"Maybe it's an opportunity to present to the Fuehrer and OKW the true situation and propose a peace initiative or at least opening negotiations with the British, French and whoever it is that's sitting now in southern Austria," Halder said.

Canaris raised a hand. "I don't know. All present here are on Hitler's liquidation list. He doesn't trust us and might arrest on the spot those who make such a proposal. I would not like losing General Rommel or General Paulus. Such a proposal is sure to trigger repressions against all of us. I would suggest saying nothing for now. We have some time; after all, we're not in danger of imminent collapse. Without a plan for action, proposing peace would be suicide."

✡✡✡

Zaretzky finished his second glass of tea. The Writer's Union was a place where those entrusted with manufacturing and distributing Soviet propaganda could come to enjoy their privileges. In addition to tea there was some food available without the need to present ration cards. Here he could meet interesting and, sometimes, famous writers.

One couldn't just walk in the door. A pass was necessary. Zaretzky asked for one from the People's Commissariat for Foreign Affairs. It was granted with very little delay and none of the usual bureaucratic dance. He knew that the NKVD must have been involved but they hadn't approached him yet, even though this was his fourth visit to the place.

"Excuse me, comrade, may I join you?" a bookish looking man asked Zaretzky, interrupting his reverie.

"Sure, sure. Please, sit."

The man extended his hand. "I'm Boris Ivanovich Andreyev, correspondent for the 'Red Star' Army newspaper."

Zaretzky responded, "Avram Moiseevich Zaretzky, a diplomat with the Palestinian legation."

"Yes, I know who you are. How long have you been a member of the Communist party?"

"I joined the Palestine Communist party almost immediately after it was founded. In 1923 we united with the Communist Party of Palestine. Why are you asking?"

Andreyev shrugged, "Just curious. Do you know Leopold Trepper?"

"Sure. He was the one who persuaded me to join. Do you know what became of him after he was expelled from Palestine by the British?"

"When did that happen?" Andreyev asked.

"Around 1929 just before the big crash and failure of capitalism. After that I lost contact with him."

Andreyev sipped his tea in silence, than nodded to himself and said, "You think Leopold will remember you?"

Zaretzky smiled. "Sure he will. We argued like crazy but worked well together. He was a great leader and organizer."

Andreyev was silent for a while longer then seemed to come to a decision. "Leopold Trepper is working for the Soviet Union in a secret capacity. Would you be willing to follow in his steps and help us our current struggle?"

Zaretzky fidgeted in his seat, clearly broadcasting discomfort. "The days I knew him were long ago. I am working for a state that's on its way to Socialism and, to paraphrase comrade Stalin, will become a force for the Revolution in the Middle East. I don't want to do anything to harm it. On the other hand, I am willing to help our common cause."

Andreyev smiled a wide, sincere smile. "In that case, I welcome you. We are allies with the British and Palestine in the fight against the Fascists. By helping us you will help both Palestine and the Communist cause." He extended his hand.

"I would like to meet you in a day or two in a more private environment. Can you come here day after tomorrow? A guard will meet you."

"Sure, comrade Andreyev. I'll be here."

✡✡✡

The OKW meeting was stormy. The Fuehrer paced in front of the map table then screamed, "Greim, do you have an explanation for the lack of Luftwaffe support for Army Group D?"

General von Greim clicked his heels. "My Fuehrer, we are being attacked by very advanced aircraft. We have no effective defense. We're still receiving more aircraft from the manufacturers than the enemy destroys but our fuel situation is getting critical. We also lost a number of airfields close to the front. This combination of factors severely limits our ability to support General Rommel."

Hitler stopped in front of Rommel. "You will receive all the support the Luftwaffe can give you. Will this solve the problems you're having?"

Rommel hesitated. "My Fuehrer, we have several kinds of problems. The enemy has air superiority. I haven't seen any advanced planes but the British and French have increasing numbers of Spitfires and Dewoitines. They're strafing, bombing, and generally making a nuisance of themselves.

"Our other problem is the enemy's ground forces. Their tanks are better than anything we can deploy and they have a new anti-tank infantry weapon. I believe it's some kind of rocket. It is devastating to our armor and fortifications. Their infantry is armed mostly with automatic weapons and has much more firepower than we have encountered in the past.

"All this wouldn't have been so deadly if we could figure out how they know about our movements in advance. It's very difficult to fight an enemy that seems to have a clear view of the battlefield whereas we suffer from the usual fog of war."

Hitler turned to the third general, not a member of the OKW. "Paulus, what is your report?"

"Mein Fuehrer, we suffer from a problem similar to the one General Rommel has: the Soviet enemy seem to have a clear view of the battlefield. This allows them to effectively defend against our attacks. We have some advantage with the new tanks but it's not enough to break through their defenses."

Hitler paced for a while, and then turned to the OKW Chief of Staff. "Jodl, what is going on in Austria?"

"We have a peculiar situation there," General Jodl responded. "The enemy took Innsbruck and Klagenfurt with what seemed like minimal effort and is now sitting in place. We do have some intelligence coming out of Klagenfurt, or rather that came out of Klagenfurt before the enemy sealed it." Jodl stopped with a questioning expression.

Hitler nodded, and Jodl continued. "The occupying force is definitely Jewish. They speak several languages and communicate with the population quite well. According to at least one knowledgeable Gestapo agent they speak Hebrew among themselves.

"The force occupying the Innsbruck area is probably a division or a division and a half. The one in Klagenfurt is larger, probably three divisions. There is also a third, smaller force approaching Lubliana. We have very little in the area to oppose them."

Hitler stopped pacing, took his usual seat at the conference table and motioned for the others to sit as well. He spoke with an artificially calm voice. "I don't believe one word of this report. We are being manipulated by someone and should ignore this dangerous propaganda.

"Here's what I want you to do: send immediate reinforcements to Rommel. Of the twenty-two reserve divisions we have, send eleven to Rommel, including most of the new Tiger tanks. The other ten divisions plus an armored corps will attack the enemy in Innsbruck. Attach to this force the 6th SS Alpine Division North."

He turned to von Greim. "The Luftwaffe will concentrate on supporting the attack on Innsbruck and softening the enemy. I will personally coordinate the attack on Innsbruck.

"Jodl, when will the forces be ready?"

"We will have to move them into position. That will take a week or two, depending on which direction we attack from. This area has few roads and is very rugged."

Hitler smiled a predatory smile. "I want to surprise them and the only way to do it is an attack from where they don't expect it. We will have a small force, about a division, move in from the east. This will create a diversion while the main force attacks from the direction of Lichtenstein.

"Prepare detailed plans for my review. I want to start the attack not later than next week."

✡✡✡

Ze'ev Hirshson looked at the view from his office window. It wasn't much, just the old industrial buildings where his company, Consolidated Industries, began. They were still active. Consolidated's original steel foundry, heat treating facilities, and machining shops were located here.

The company had expanded through the years and now owned plants in the Haifa area, as well as in the Upper Galilee and Beer Sheva. The new, much larger foundry in Refidim was operational and still expanding. The Refidim location also had new plants making the interdimensional transport boxes and precision parts for the Merkava tank project.

Ze'ev wasn't happy with the expansion and intended to discuss it at the management meeting about to start. He thought that the plants were too spread out for effective control and too small to warrant a separate management structure. He had a solution.

When Ze'ev entered the conference room next to his office he nodded to the senior managers and took his seat. "We have only a couple of items on the agenda. I would like to start with an idea I had.

"Some of you had a long drive or train ride to get here today." He looked at the manager of the Hatzor facility. "How long did it take you to get to this meeting?"

"Almost two hours."

Ze'ev looked at his son Chaim who managed the plant in Beer Sheva and oversaw the one in Refidim. "You came today from Refidim. How long did it take you?"

"Three hours to Tel Aviv and another thirty five minutes to get here."

Ze'ev nodded. "We are wasting an enormous amount of time. Theoretically we could communicate by phone or video conference, but there may be a better solution that will have additional advantages.

"What do you," he made a wide gesture to include everyone at the table, "think of consolidating most of our operations right here close to our headquarters?"

Chaim smiled. "That would be nice. Some of us would have to move but it would be worth it. Did you find an empty piece of land no one knows about?"

Ze'ev nodded. "As a matter of fact I did. There's unlimited land we can use if we move some of our operations to a different universe."

The room was silent for a minute and then everyone started talking at once. Ze'ev slapped his hand on the table. "We will now hear objections, remarks and ideas, but one by one." He pointed at Chaim. "You begin."

"I really have no objections, assuming the technology is stable and reliable. I do have two questions: first, *is* the technology reliable; second, do we have the resources to start from scratch? We will have to supply everything for this new location - power, water, even sewers."

The VP for research and development responded. "The technology is stable. We tried and tested it in different configurations for several months and never had a failure. As to power and water, we probably would be able to connect to our facility here. We only tested this once, but it seems that a cable thrown through a portal will carry power. Keeping a portal open consumes 500 watts per every square meter of its area, so the energy expenditure for a portal to carry utilities will be minimal."

After everyone had their say, Ze'ev declared, "Since the only serious objection we heard was money, I propose a plan. We don't need to move any of our operations just now. We can prepare a site in a suitable universe. From this site we could fly exploratory flights in a light plane to make sure this universe is what we think it is. Personally I would prefer a place that has no animals like a Tyrannosaurus Rex or a competing civilization. After that we can start development. In the meantime we can make other preparations.

"One of the things I would do, after we are done exploring, is sell the rights to use some of the natural resources. This will generate the income and capital we need for development."

Chaim cut in. "You did talk to our lawyers about declaring this hypothetical universe 'our property'?"

Ze'ev smiled. "You know me well, my son. Yes, I did speak to our legal department. The consensus is that we can declare the property ours and proceed to do what we want with it as long as it contains no self-aware creatures. If it does, they are the owners and we would be better off finding another place.

"There is, of course, the question why anyone would buy rights from us if they can open up their own private universe? The answer is twofold: we own the technology to open a portal and also it makes more sense to pool resources than to go it alone."

"Just to remind you, the government used our technology twice to open portals. This was done under a special agreement. They paid for the hardware but we retained the rights to the technology itself. At the time, we had a legal argument with the government: they claimed that our development is based on research done at the Technion on a government grant, resulting in the creation of the Shield. This is true, but the grant was unconditional and didn't reserve any rights for the government. Basic research grants are often like that. Since the portal-opening hardware and computer algorithms were developed by us, we own them, the same way the government owns the shield technology."

After the meeting was over Ze'ev called Esther. "I promised to check the options you might have to enter medical school. There are some that your advisor didn't mention to you, although they're not necessarily good."

"Apparently Tel Aviv University still has their program for foreign students. You know that to become an MD in Israel you have to study for six years, much like in Europe. Tel Aviv's program was designed for Americans. Getting in is difficult; you have to demonstrate college-level knowledge of biology and chemistry.

"You could continue at Beer Sheva University, graduate with a degree in life sciences and continue to medical school. Since we really need more doctors there are plans to expand the existing medical schools and there is a good possibility that after two years at Beer Sheva you'll be able to switch to medical school.

"Another possibility would be to train as a pharmacist. It's much easier to get into those programs and they would likely take you in next year.

"A third possibility that my daughter Shoshanna mentioned is to go to nursing school. If your goal is to practice medicine and treat people, this may be a good option. You can always continue your education and in four years become a nurse practitioner or physician's assistant.

"I'll have to think about it and discuss my options with the girls and Jacob. We'll see you next week for Shabbat and can talk about it more then. Thanks."

✡✡✡

Ben Mosowitz was impatient. He brought his family to synagogue early on Sunday evening to hear the rabbi's full story about Israel.

The rabbi introduced a youngish man. "This is the Jewish Agency representative from Philadelphia here to give us information about Israel and to answer questions."

The representative surprised everyone by asking for the light to be dimmed. Only then did Ben notice that a large screen had been erected at the front of the sanctuary. With the lights dimmed the Israeli produced a little box-like device and pressed a button. A projector positioned on a tripod in the back of the room came to life and a documentary about the creation of the state of Israel and life in modern Israel appeared on the screen. Since the film had been produced after the time travel incident that, and the rescue of European Jews, were featured.

The questions came quickly.

"We have seen well-made movies before," one of the congregants said. "What assurance do we have that it's not just a fantasy? We all know what Hollywood can do."

"Ask your rabbi if what the movie shows about current life in Israel is true."

Soon the questions shifted to the practical. People wanted to know how they would manage: would they be able to find a job, was their training or profession in demand, where would they live, what were the schools like.

On their way home Ben and Evelyn were quiet for a while, digesting the information and the answers Ben got to his questions. Finally Evelyn said, "So, are you still considering moving to Palestine?"

"Moving to Israel," Ben corrected. "And yes, I think I want to move. There are still a number of questions I need answered but I see no reason to stay here."

Evelyn shook her head. "The only Hebrew you know is from the prayer book. How do you expect to run a business in a place you know nothing about? When Bea goes to school she will need to learn a new language. I will most likely not be able to help even with simple homework and the things I do here, like running the household, may be beyond me there. We'll have to live just on your income, which will likely be lower in Israel. All this trouble, for what?"

"Evie, you're pointing out temporary difficulties. I'm quite sure that we will settle in like millions of others. We will learn Hebrew, as will Bea. If my furniture and business abilities aren't enough to make a living I will try something new."

"You may be right and all the difficulties are temporary, but so is life. Why abandon our comfortable home here for an iffy future in a faraway, socialist, land?"

Ben shook his head. "First, Israel is not a socialist country. This has been clarified by the film as well as the rabbi. It's not the Palestine we knew about.

"There is one great advantage to living in Israel: We will be among our own people, part of the majority. We will also benefit from advanced science, like much better medical care when we need it. Wouldn't you rather go to a Jewish doctor that has knowledge your doctor here never dreamt of? What about hospitals? You realize that if we need serious medical care here it will eat all our savings. In Israel they have insurance. Besides, from what I understand some conditions considered incurable here are trivial in Israel.

"You make it sound easy," Evelyn responded.

"It will definitely not be easy. We'll have plenty of aggravation and will probably be angry and disappointed more than once, but we will acclimate and within a year or two we will be happy we moved. At least I hope so.

Evelyn shrugged. "I'm uneasy about this. We'll be throwing away bread and going someplace to look for crumbs."

Ben was quiet for a moment, concentrating on driving. "Look, I really want to go. The rabbi is going; Joe and Shelly with their two kids are going. Even your friend Rosa is going with her husband, six children and elderly mother. Must have been a tough decision for them.

"What will you do when your whole maj group leaves? And how can we have a good Jewish life here if the rabbi and most of the community emigrates?

"Maybe you should talk to your friends and see what people are thinking."

"Okay." Evelyn shrugged. "We did talk about this at a sisterhood meeting but that was just after the rabbi came back. There wasn't much information available. I might feel different after discussing it with my friends.

"I'm somewhat surprised how you feel. I thought that you were used to dealing with gentiles and anti-Semites."

✡✡✡

Avigdor Mizrahi, the Israeli ambassador to Britain, greeted General Wilson and got right to business. "General, my government is of the opinion that the time is ripe for a tripartite conference with our Soviet allies. What do you think of both of us meeting with the Soviet ambassador, Maisky, to discuss such a conference?"

Wilson looked slightly uncomfortable. "Ambassador, I have already contacted Mr. Maisky. We're supposed to meet next week to discuss a summit."

"You didn't consider it necessary to consult with us before doing this?"

"Well, like you told me once, we're allies but we're independent," Wilson responded.

"I have an impression, and I sincerely hope I'm wrong, that His Majesty's Government is reverting to treating the Jews the way it always has." Mizrahi let anger show in his voice. "Shall we reciprocate and negotiate with the Soviets separately? Is that what the Prime Minister wants?"

"Absolutely not. Mr. Ambassador, it was my mistake. The Prime Minister told me to arrange a summit and I assumed, mistakenly, that he meant himself and Mr. Stalin. A stupid oversight for which I apologize."

Mizrahi sat back in his chair. "General, if I didn't have some experience with you I could interpret this episode the wrong way. As it is, I trust your integrity and will recommend to my government to accept your apology.

"But to prevent any further misunderstandings, cancel your meeting with Mr. Maisky now. I will make an appointment for both of us.

"We need to coordinate our positions before we speak to Maisky. Stalin won't want to meet in Britain; he may have no safe way of getting here. I suggest that we meet in Israel. Mr. Churchill, I'm sure, will enjoy the visit and Stalin can get there easily, although he'll refuse and propose a location in the Soviet Union."

Wilson looked surprised, "You are ready to disclose to the Soviets who you really are?"

"Not really," Mizrahi responded. "We will just let them see but offer no explanations. They can think whatever they choose to."

"If you don't offer an explanation Stalin may be seriously offended."

"Yes, he may be, but I doubt it." Mizrahi smiled. "He will likely never ask directly – that would be admitting ignorance and not in his character. He also understands secrecy."

"But why would you want to disclose anything to him?" Wilson sounded very curious.

"General, I'm thinking about the future and we, I mean Israel and Britain, will have serious disagreements with the Soviets. Please ask yourself whether your position would be improved or worsened by having an ally on your side that Stalin at least respects or is somewhat apprehensive of?"

"Yes, I see what you are trying to achieve. Britain alone would have difficulty dictating conditions to the Soviets. Together we might be able to pull it off.

"This brings me to the next point: what is the endgame you propose? To finish off the Germans and not let the Soviets take control of half of Europe?"

Mizrahi pulled out a sheaf of papers from his briefcase. "Please give this to the Prime Minister. This is my government's desired outcome of this war. I suggest that we meet again to discuss this in detail.

"One remark though: My government asked that you stop the advance in France. We will not advance any further in Austria. The Soviets will become aware of this lack of progress soon enough and Stalin will have an incentive to meet and negotiate."

Chapter 11
November 1942

November weather in the Alps can be unpleasant. This morning low clouds were racing over Innsbruck, releasing snow. It was cold. The Israelis prepared to receive a German force outnumbering them several times over.

Brigadier General Oded Almog, commanding the Israeli force in Innsbruck, knew that although German communications spoke of more than ten divisions closing on his position, the actual force was only about five or six times larger than his. German divisions became smaller as the war progressed and losses mounted. Still, more than sixty thousand troops, with tanks and artillery, were nothing to sneeze at.

After several long discussions the staff recommended attacking from the air the smaller German force coming from the east. The combined infantry and armor division moving on a single road would be decimated before ever reaching the Israeli positions west of Innsbruck. The tactic was to be repeated on the main force approaching from the west. Since that force was much larger – almost 50,000 thousand strong – it was assumed that more planes and more sorties would be necessary to destroy it. The planners expected that the remnants of this force would retreat or, if they decide to continue with their mission, be mostly harmless.

It was a good plan that very quickly became obsolete. The larger German force was moving in from the west. A cold front moving from the northwest brought a low cloud ceiling and close to zero visibility. The air force could still do some damage but not close to what was called for by the plan. The situation in the east was much better. Just fifteen miles in that direction the sky was clear. The German division was advancing fast enough to come into the proposed killing zone within the next couple of hours.

General Almog made his decision. Close to twenty jets, mostly obsolete Kfirs and some even older Phantoms, took off from the new air strip near Venice. With the airstrip only 130 miles from their objective they could keep up a nonstop attack even with some planes going back to refuel and rearm.

The first to see the attacking planes was an officer on the last truck in the German convoy. The truck carried a quad 20mm antiaircraft mount. "Fritz, point your gun there. Open fire when they're in range." Next he pounded on the cabin roof of the truck and yelled at the radio operator inside. "Notify command that we're coming under air attack from the east." The truck exploded before the radio operator could obey the order. The attacking jets used rockets to destroy almost a mile of the column before they ran out of rockets. The next wave took over seamlessly.

Minutes later the column stopped and troops jumped off the trucks. Tanks driving on the road in-between the trucks tried going into the fields. Everyone was shooting into the sky, including several antiaircraft batteries of 88mm guns and 20mm quad mounts. It's very difficult to hit a fast, low flying jet with a manually controlled 88mm mount. It's slightly more practical with a mechanized 20mm mount but not if the attackers use long range rockets to attack from a distance. None of the German projectiles did any damage.

Two hours later the German 27th division and its attached mechanized regiment ceased to exist as a coherent unit. Israeli jets chased individual tanks and artillery, strafing vehicles still parked on and by the road. Of the jets participating in the attack three returned with bullet holes but no serious damage.

General Almog had ongoing reports from both the air force and his observers just east of Innsbruck. When the last jet left for its base Almog gave his orders: "Tell the two tank companies in the east to transfer to the west and park just east of the Inn River Bridge west of Innsbruck University. Keep the two infantry companies in place north of the Friedberg Castle. They're to block the road and dispose of any stragglers."

Several minutes later his adjutant came into the office, "Sir, we intercepted a transmission from the commander of the western force. He asks for permission to stop where he is and regroup. Our drones can see in infrared that their vehicles have stopped. It seems that he didn't wait permission."

General Almog looked out the window of his office on the western outskirts of town. He had a good view of the mountains and valley but there wasn't much to see now. Low clouds obscured not just the mountains but also much of the valley floor. He got up and gestured the adjutant to follow. In the room next door, the hotel's dining room, a map table was set up with a large scale map of Innsbruck and surrounds.

"Where are their forward units?" Almog asked his chief of staff.

"About 10 miles west of our positions, on both banks of the Inn River."

Almog looked at his watch. "We have three, maybe four, hours of daylight left. If the Germans delay much longer and decide to advance anyway they will be much easier to deal with. The dark is our friend. What's the weather forecast?"

The meteorologist sitting in the far corner spoke up. "There are clouds extending several hundred miles to our west and about 200 miles to the north. The wind shifted and is now North-Northeast at 15 miles per hour. If it continues blowing from the same direction and speed for the next eight hours, the Germans will be out from under the clouds."

Almog thought for a moment. "I want artillery observers high on the sides of the valley in front of us. Make sure everyone has their infrared equipment ready and functioning. Use a helicopter to position the observers. The less accessible their positions, the safer they'll be."

"Sir," the Chief of Staff said, "I'm not sure about the helicopter. The clouds are touching the bottom of the valley. They might not be able to fly in this soup."

"Ask their commander," Almog responded. "If they can't, they can't, but I think that if our observers can see using their shortwave infrared binoculars in this soup the helicopter pilots can as well."

The General returned to his office to review, for the umpteenth time, his force disposition and ammunition reserves. The most worrisome issues were his tanks and artillery not having enough ammunition to break the German force without the assistance of the air force. He repeated his calculations and compared them to the work done by his quartermaster. The numbers looked good so General Almog went back to the command center. He wanted one more look at the map.

He was greeted by his Chief of Staff. "Oded, you came in just as I was going to report. The Germans got their orders. They are supposed to dig in, establish anti-air defenses, and shut the valley so that we can't move down the road to Garmish and Munich. This will require them to advance another couple of miles.

"According to the same communication from the OKH, they are moving another force of at least four full Waffen SS divisions to cut us off from the east. Our intelligence guys are sure that these were taken off the Eastern Front and are full strength, about 80,000 men with several hundred tanks and artillery. They should be in place in another week."

"Incredible," Almog responded. "They expect us to sit here and wait to be almost surrounded."

"Or retreat to the Brenner Pass," responded the Chief of Staff.

"We will do neither. I want our lead units to advance west beyond the Garmisch-Partenkirchen intersection. We'll see if the Germans want to fight for it. In the meantime prepare a detailed plan to defeat the force to our west."

"How far do you want to advance to defeat them?"

"As far as necessary. We need to destroy them before the eastern forces arrive."

✡✡✡

Zaretzky arrived at the Writer's Union just as the streets of Moscow were getting dark. Lights were out because of the German air raids and blackout. It would be difficult to get back to the legation unless his new friend Ivan Andreyev provided transportation. Zaretzky went directly to the room indicated in their previous meeting. Andreyev was waiting. "Good evening, comrade Zaretzky."

"Good evening," Zaretzky responded.

"Would you like cookies with your tea?" Andreyev inquired.

Zaretzky looked pleased. After all, cookies were a luxury in wartime Moscow and cookies without the need to present a ration card were a privilege of the powerful. "Yes, comrade Andreyev. I'd appreciate some."

"Comrade Zaretzky," Andreyev began, "there are many things we don't know or understand about your country. Would you mind if I asked you some questions? Just to satisfy my personal curiosity, you understand."

"Go ahead. I will answer your questions to the best of my ability. Just as long as you remember that I'm a simple diplomat."

Andreyev smiled. "Come comrade, you're the first secretary of the Palestinian legation. That's not so simple. But first, can you tell me why we didn't hear from you for so long?"

Zaretzky shrugged. "It wasn't that long. If I remember correctly the last time I sent a letter to my dear aunt was in 1938. Since then there were all kinds of difficulties. I was under British surveillance as a suspected Communist. Then the war started and sending mail to the Soviet Union became very complicated. I have to say that I would have managed but I got no requests or questions so I kept quiet.

"We figured something like that. Now that you're here we have questions. Can you tell me how you became a First Secretary? This is quite a senior position. Don't they know you're a Communist?"

"I don't advertise it but I'm sure they know and don't care. Being a Communist isn't a crime in independent Palestine.

"I worked in the Foreign Section of the Jewish Agency for a long time and when we gained independence I became a senior functionary in the Foreign Ministry. I volunteered to come to Moscow. It's considered a dangerous assignment because of the war."

"What's the population of Palestine?" asked Andreyev.

Zaretzky pretended to think. "It's more than seven million now."

"More than seven million? How did that happen?"

"I hope you won't hold me to the exact number," Zaretzky responded. "The government rescued about six million from Nazi-occupied Europe and the Arab countries. There are Jews coming in now from the Soviet Union and the rest of the world, in addition to those who lived in Palestine before."

Andreyev made notes. "Ok, comrade, it's getting late. I suggest that we break now and continue next time. Would you like a ride to your legation?"

✡✡✡

Amos Nir, the Prime Minister of Israel, was in a good mood. Things were going according to plan, as much as could be expected in a war. Time for the weekly cabinet meeting.

"Good morning, everyone. First, the Foreign Minister's report."

"I have some good and some puzzling news. Our ambassador to London was surprised by General Wilson. He met with Wilson to arrange a conference with the Soviet ambassador in order to set up an allied leaders' meeting. Wilson told him that he had already made an appointment with the Soviets. Mizrahi, our ambassador, threatened consequences and Wilson apologized, cancelled the appointment and let Mizrahi set up a meeting."

"What was Wilson explanation?" asked the Defense Minister.

"He claimed it was his mistake and misinterpretation of Churchill's instructions. Sounds like a bit of a stretch to me. More likely they tried to create a situation where we would play a secondary role as a junior partner."

"I doubt it," interjected Amos. "Churchill is devious but not stupid. He knows he needs a strong ally at his side when bargaining with Stalin. I tend to believe Wilson. He probably just screwed up. Old habits die hard and even Wilson sometimes thinks of us as 'poor Palestinians'. To be sure, we need to be watchful and respond forcefully to any clear manifestation of antisemitism.

"We proposed to the Soviets a summit meeting in Tel Aviv. We have discussed this before so just let me sum up the reason why: the location will impress Stalin and his aides plus convincing them that we're not to be slighted. We are doing a job on their intelligence service right now to confuse them about our origins. I doubt that they'll ask direct questions while they're here. The chances of a leak will be minimal – Both the Soviets and the Brits will be surrounded by our security people at all times. This includes everyone: waiters, drivers, house cleaners - anyone they may come in contact with. We can't prevent them from arriving at conclusions from what they see.

"Any opinions on what to do if they refuse our proposal?"

The Foreign Minister responded. "I see no reason why Stalin won't propose a summit in Teheran, like in our old timeline. It's occupied by the Soviets and the Brits, it's close to his border. He can bring a sizeable security detail. I would accept meeting in Teheran. We will have to make it clear to Stalin and his generals that we're a serious power."

There were nods of agreement from other members of the cabinet.

"Very well," Amos agreed. "We will find a way to impress them or scare them, whichever we find more useful."

✡✡✡

An anticipatory mood prevailed at the Supreme Command of the Armed Forces as Hitler examined the map one more time.

"It looks like we may be able to encircle those pesky Jews or whoever they are. Paul Hausser with his group of four Waffen SS divisions is on the way to Innsbruck. He will be joined by four Hungarian divisions that our ally Admiral Horty is sending. Rommel's contributing four divisions to the forces west of Innsbruck since the British/French offensive is stopped and the front in France is stable."

"My Fuehrer, the staff and I recommend that we hold the line east of Innsbruck and consolidate all the forces in the west before attacking," Jodl suggested in a somewhat timid voice.

Hitler nodded. "That is my intent. I also want to concentrate at least three hundred fighter planes and two dozen bombers on airstrips within fifty kilometers of Innsbruck. When we attack it has to be devastating.

"Jodl, how long will it take to set up all the forces east of Innsbruck?"

Jodl looked at his notes. "The Hungarians will arrive first; they are already moving. General Hausser should be there within seven days, and the forces sent by General Rommel will arrive at about the same time.

Taking into account the need to organize the forces, we need eight to nine days. It also depends on who is going to be in command."

"Let Field Marshall Günter von Kluge know that he's in command. He will present himself to me tomorrow."

Hitler got up signaling the end of the meeting.

✡✡✡

Wolf's unit advanced, although not very far. They were supposed to take up positions just west of an intersection three miles away. The armor company was positioned in a relatively wide valley. From the top of his tank Wolf could see two roads. The northern one, he knew, was the road to Garmisch-Partenkirchen, a town on the way to Munich. The southern road lead east to where a large German force was positioned. Since the valley was almost a mile and a half wide, the company spread out. Two infantry battalions with their Namer IFVs were spreading behind and in between the tanks, with anti-aircraft batteries just behind them.

Night was descending on the valley and the temperature was dropping. Next to Wolf's position an infantry company of the 927th was hard at work erecting tents, installing heaters and otherwise preparing to be comfortable. Wolf's immediate concern was food; he didn't like the ready-to-eat meals. Several times before, most recently during the fighting by the Brenner Pass, he had had the 927th as a neighbor and knew they had decent cooks. It was only natural to walk over to their company sergeant and try to arrange a hot meal for his crew.

The sergeant looked him over and nodded. "Sure. As soon as we're ready. It will take a while. I'll send someone to invite you guys."

Back in Wolf's tank a message waited on his terminal. His gunner, who assumed the commander's duties while the commander was away, pointed it out to Wolf. "The platoon commander saw you walk over to the infantry and didn't like it. We're supposed to be on full combat alert."

Wolf smiled. "I'll explain it to him." He sent a message to the platoon commander about the hot food.

The response came immediately. "Wolf, I don't care about hot food. The orders are clear and I don't want you leaving your tank for anything, except, maybe, to empty your bladder. Even then don't go farther than the tank's track."

When a soldier came running from the infantry position inviting them to eat, Wolf waved at him from the turret. "Give my thanks to your sergeant but we can't come. Our orders are not to leave the tank. Aren't you guys on combat alert?"

The soldier nodded, which was barely visible in the uncertain light. “Sure we are. We have a crew of five, including myself, that deliver hot food to the positions. I can bring some for you guys if you want.”

“Thanks,” Wolf replied, “we’d like that.”

Nothing happened for the next forty minutes. Wolf checked his displays and tried to pick up images from a drone he knew was circling the valley overhead. They were still in dense fog. His infrared showed nothing unusual. The drone broadcast showed some movement to the north but that was likely to be either an animal or a civilian from the village they were straddling.

Just as Wolf and his crew gave up on the hot food and were considering opening their ready meals the infantry food carrier arrived. He had a medium-sized sealed pot which he placed on top of the tank’s track cover. He climbed on top of the tank and prepared to dispense the hot stew. Wolf got down inside the tank, collected the mess kits from his crew and popped up through the hatch. He handed the kits to the soldier, who ladled stew into them, handing them back one by one. Just as Wolf picked up his mess kit and was about to dive inside, the attack began.

A series of explosions walked across the Israeli position. One of them was next to Wolf’s tank. The flash and bang of the explosion stunned him. He saw the food bearer fall off the tank and almost jumped out after him, but his training took over. He dived into the tank and closed the hatch. There was still nothing on the monitors.

Seconds later the radio came alive on the company command frequency. “All units: We have a large armored force approaching from the west. Prepare for action.”

Wolf acknowledged receipt of the message and looked at the drone monitor. It was indeed showing a column of warm objects approaching from the west. He also noticed a dark drip on the monitor. It looked like blood. “I seem to have been hit.”

Wolf woke up in a brightly lit white room. He tried to get up but couldn’t. His head was on fire and he had no feeling in his left arm.

“Relax,” a voice said. “You were injured. This is a hospital. I’ll call a nurse.”

Wolf turned his head, slowly and carefully. There was a bed next to his with a young man in it. “Who are you?” Wolf inquired quietly.

“Sergeant Yitzhak Kaufmann, Company B the 927th”

Wolf tried to focus his eyes, which wasn’t easy. “Are you the guy that sent us the food?”

“That’s me.”

"What's wrong with you?"

Kaufmann smiled. "Nothing much. A couple of pieces of shrapnel in my arm."

"You guys are supposed to be resting. Stop babbling and rest."

The newcomer was dressed in a white coat over his uniform and introduced himself as The Doctor. He addressed Wolf, "Look at me. Try to follow my finger with your eyes.

"Good, now close your eyes and tell me if you feel anything."

Wolf almost jumped when he felt a needle stab his left arm.

The Doctor exhaled audibly. "Very good. It seems that feeling is returning to your arm."

"What's wrong with me?" Wolf wanted to know.

The Doctor examined the monitor above Wolf's bed. "You will live. You were extremely lucky. A piece of a mortar bomb hit you in the head just above the rim of your helmet. You had a bleeding cut and a concussion. Two other fragments hit your left shoulder and upper arm.

"You seem to be recovering from the concussion. The arm is regaining some feeling but you will not be able to use it for a while. It's broken in two places and you need to recover from surgery."

"Surgery? How long ago was I injured? How did the battle end? What happened to my crew?"

The Doctor looked at his watch, "They brought you here almost exactly six hours ago. According to the medics who brought you in your crew is fine, in fact they fought very well and saved your life. The battle is not really over yet."

Wolf felt his concentration wavering but he had one more question. "Where are we?"

"We're in the University of Innsbruck Hospital. Not a bad facility. Combined with our equipment it makes a much better operating environment than a field hospital."

Wolf fell asleep.

✡✡✡

General Ephraim Hirshson was angry. Uri Sadot, his Chief of Staff, had never seen him so angry.

Hirshson was looking at the map in front of him. "What in hell compelled this idiot Almog to go on the offensive? We have a strategy and he acts like he doesn't comprehend it." He waved at the communications officer on the other side of the large room. "Get him on the radio." Hirshson looked at Uri Sadot. "We'll see how it goes. Are you ready to take over from him?"

"Of course, but are you sure it's necessary?"

"As commander of the Expeditionary Force it's my responsibility to do what the General Staff wants us to do. If one of my subordinates either doesn't understand the strategy or deliberately disrupts the operation..."

The communications officer waved. General Almog was on the line.

"Oded, what's going on in Innsbruck?" Hirshson asked.

"I moved some forces slightly west beyond the Garmisch-Partenkirchen intersection to prevent the Germans taking and fortifying it. We came under a sudden and unexpected mortar and armor attack. We stopped them and keep destroying their attacking forces. They seem to be running out of steam. I'm considering pressing an attack soon."

Hirshson shook his head, though he knew Almog couldn't see him. "What are your losses?"

"We have 52 dead and 73 wounded. The medics tell me about 20 will return to service within a day or two."

Hirshson looked at Sadot and shook his head. "Oded, do you remember the strategy we're following? You were not supposed to attack at all, just sit there and let them come to you. No matter how well they dig in they will, eventually, have to come to you.

"You should have consulted with me before doing anything that is contrary to your standing orders. Had you contacted me, I would have told you to sit tight and save the lives of your soldiers. I'm sending reinforcements, a division and several battalions. Fifteen thousand people in all. Uri Sadot will lead them. When he arrives, which will be in three days, he will become the commanding officer of the Innsbruck enclave. Is that clear? In the meantime you will not counterattack. Just sit where you are."

"That makes sense. I see no need to retreat to my original positions."

"You are correct. Stay in your current position and let them come to you."

✡✡✡

Jacob was preparing a light lunch at his apartment in Beer Sheva before leaving for a couple of evening lectures at the University. The TV was on and he was listening with one ear to a soap opera – good training in colloquial Hebrew. He was startled when the broadcast was interrupted by a news flash. "Our reporter with the IDF in Austria just informed us that a big battle was fought by our Expeditionary Force against a much larger German army. Our forces were victorious but we had significant losses. We will have more details in the regular news broadcast."

Jacob picked up the phone and called Sheina. She didn't answer. He concluded that she must be at class. Next he called Esther. She picked up on the first ring, "Hi, Esther, it's Jacob. Did you hear from Wolf?"

"No, should I have?"

"There was a battle where he's stationed and I was wondering whether he emailed you."

"He didn't. I'll call my parents. Maybe they know something. I'll call you as soon as I have news."

Jacob was finishing his lunch when the phone rang.

Esther was on the line. "I just finished talking to my parents. They were visited by an IDF officer and a nurse.

"Wolf was injured in the battle. They operated on him and the prognosis is good. This is all I know."

"I'll be at your place in five minutes. Just have to make a call. Maybe I can find out more details."

Next Jacob called Ze'ev, who didn't answer his phone, so he called Ze'ev's wife Linda. "Do you have any details on Wolf's condition?"

Linda chuckled. "You seem to be telepathic. I was just about to call you since for some reason I don't have Esther's phone number. We got an email from Ephraim. You know that he's the commander of the Expeditionary Force? He doesn't have much time but he also doesn't have a relative injured in battle all that often.

"Anyway, he says that Wolf was hit by shrapnel. One hit his helmet and gave him a concussion. Two pieces struck his left shoulder. His left arm was also broken in two places. They had to operate to take out the shrapnel and, more importantly, repair damage to his shoulder. They expect him to recover but don't yet have any idea whether he will have full use of his left arm.

"Wolf will be on his way home in three or four days. You call Esther and I will call her parents."

Jacob called Esther and then ran over to her dorm. He wasn't sure how she might take the news, though she seemed like a tough young woman and the news was not all bad.

✡✡✡

Ze'ev Hirshson hadn't answered Jacob's call because he was just entering a conference room at the Foreign Ministry. The Minister and several other people were waiting for him.

"Dr. Hirshson, as my secretary told you we would like to discuss an automobile issue."

"Yes, that's what she said, with no elaboration, so I'm still in the dark."

The Foreign Minister smiled. "Apparently she's a diplomat as well. Let me shed light on this and hopefully you can help us.

"As you know, we now have diplomatic missions in several countries. All these embassies need transportation and, in some countries, we think it's vital for our image to use our own home-grown cars.

"We have heard about your company's efforts to develop a domestic car and I signed off on your import requests from Italy. So, is there anything we could use?"

"Why not use one of the cars you're using here? No one will recognize a car from the future if new and different badges are fabricated."

"In some countries - like the U.S., Russia and Italy - we don't want the time travel incident to become an issue. A car that looks correct for this time would be preferable. Is there anything you can offer us?"

"As a matter of fact I can, but there may be a small problem." He pulled out several photographs from his briefcase. "These are the two cars we're setting up to manufacture. The bodies will be, at first, imported. We settled on the Fiat 2800 Berlina and Lancia Ardea. The Fiat is a large luxury model and the Lancia is a smaller family sedan. These cars look almost like the originals, except for some changes to the bumpers that are required by our safety laws. We're calling the Fiat Alpha 290 or Aleph 290 in Hebrew and the Lancia is the Beta 180 or Bet 180. The number designation is simply the horsepower of the motor. Both cars will carry the line name 'Sabra' and Consolidated's logo."

The Minister and his two assistants looked through the photos. One of the assistants said, "I'm a bit of a car enthusiast. I know that the Fiat 2800 had an engine of about 85 horsepower. What will happen to the transmission and differential with a 290hp engine?"

Ze'ev smiled. "You laid your finger on the problem. Not the mechanical one but the one of time travel. We gutted the bodies and are using a Stirling cycle motor spinning an electric generator. There's no transmission and no differential. The car is propelled by four electric motors in the wheel hubs. The result is a very quiet and powerful car. Look at the photos of the interior: we have seat belts, the instrument panel looks 'normal' but in fact it's a flat panel display. It will be obvious to anyone taking a close look that this in no regular instrument array. Anybody lifting the hood of this car will see that it's a bit unusual. They might also notice the radial tires.

"Would you guys like to see one and maybe drive it?"

The Minister looked at his watch. "I really don't have the time to go to your plant. Sorry."

"The car is in the parking lot downstairs - I drove it here."

The others looked at each other and as one got up to follow Ze'ev downstairs. After a short drive around the parking lot the Minister looked carefully at the logo. "Sabra, and it actually has a little fruit growing on the front of the hood. Interesting design."

"Our chief designer studied in Italy, many years in the future and is very proud of the design. He and his team are working on new car bodies. He is going to be famous yet. I'm sure you'll hear about Hassan Amjad in years to come."

The Foreign Minister looked at his assistants, who nodded. "Dr. Hirshson, I think that the Foreign Ministry will be your first government customer. We will buy both models for our overseas missions. We will also probably buy some for the ministry here. Our older cars are wearing out and need to be replaced soon."

You'll have to change the shape of both models, at least the cars that will go to our embassies, to make them look less like Fiat and Lancias."

"That will not be a problem. Starting next month both Fiat and Lancia will start supplying us with bodies made to our specification. They look slightly more modern but not too futuristic. We have several prototypes at our plant if you want to see them."

✡✡✡

Zaretzky met with Boris Andreyev again, this time in an office building not far from the Palestinian legation. The building was cold but the first floor room they were using had a puffing and steaming samovar promising hot tea. The room was drab, with peeling greenish paint and squeaky wood floors. The windows were dirty and, as usual in Russia in winter, painted shut. At least the windows were double framed, which offered some hope of warmth if the samovar was left going for a while.

When Zaretzky came into the interrogation room, as this is what it was, Andreyev was already there sipping from a steaming glass of tea in an elaborate metal holder.

"Comrade Zaretzky, please sit. Help yourself to a glass of tea. We also have sugar."

Zaretzky poured himself tea and settled at the small table opposite Andreyev.

"How can I help you today?" Zaretzky asked.

Andreyev smiled. "There are a number of issues we need to clarify. You know, just to understand what's going on in the big, wide world.

"Can you tell me when and how the British agreed to grant you independence?"

"That's an easy question." Zaretzky smiled. "You should have had the answers as soon as it happened, but I'll tell you the story.

"In June of 1941 the British were in very bad shape. The Germans were helping the Italians in North Africa and both were beating the living daylights out of the British. We made the British an offer they couldn't refuse: grant us independence and we'll help defeat Rommel or refuse and we'll rise up against you. What can I say, they chose wisely." Zaretzky smiled and sipped from his glass of tea.

"I'm still not clear on how you could help the British beat Rommel? After all, if they couldn't stop him how could a bunch of Jews in Palestine do that?" Andreyev was now looking intently at Zaretzky.

"Comrade Andreyev, you must have figured out by now that the 'bunch of Jews' had something to offer. I really can't tell you what it was except, as you know, we are a smart people and when necessary we are also very inventive and industrious. I don't think that Mr. Churchill ever regretted the deal."

"You can't or you won't tell me?" Andreyev's tone was slightly threatening.

Zaretzky made calming gestures with both hands. "I'm not an engineer, so I don't know anything that makes sense, at least not so I could tell a coherent tale. I could tell you about teleportation and remote viewing and such but this is just babbling without understanding."

Andreyev made notes in a small notebook. "So this is how you are able to give us such accurate information about the Germans?"

"I didn't say that. It's your conclusion. The only thing I know for sure is that every evening a little machine that sits on my boss's desk spits out some pictures and printed sheets that he delivers to your High Command. I have no clue how it's done."

Andreyev made more notes. "So let's assume that you have some kind of magic that lets you look at the front lines and the German forces for hundreds of kilometers in depth and lets you know what they're planning. Can you use the same magic to know what we and everyone else in the world is doing or planning?"

"This is an excellent question, comrade Andreyev. I don't know for sure but my assumption is that the Germans are not different in this respect from anyone else."

Andreyev wrote some more in his notebook. "I understand that you also can do damage to your enemies at a distance. Is that true?"

Zaretzky visibly hesitated then seemed to make a decision. "I really shouldn't say anything but you probably know at least part of the story already. We got the Nazis to turn over all the Jews in Europe to us. It was done in part by diplomacy, but you know Hitler. Diplomacy not supported by a show of force wouldn't have worked. I will only say that he had his demonstration. It was fierce enough to make our diplomatic offer attractive. I also understand that we did serious damage to Rommel's Afrika Corps, so serious that he lost the North African war quite quickly."

"Can you tell me how this was done?" Andreyev was leaning forward, a hungry expression on his face.

"Sorry to disappoint you, comrade." Zaretzky smiled apologetically. "As I said before I have no idea how the mechanics of these things work or what exactly was done to the Germans."

"What if your leadership decided to, say, destroy a city, like Moscow?" Andreyev was waiting with his pencil poised over the notebook.

Zaretzky looked surprised. "Why would they do that? You're our friends and we don't attack friends."

Andreyev nodded. "Sorry for the bad choice of targets. How about destroying Berlin?"

Zaretzky shook his head in indignation. "Just because something is possible doesn't mean that it's going to be done or should be done, Boris Ivanovich. We are not barbarians. Destroying a city means murdering thousands upon thousands of innocent people. We would never commit a crime like that."

Andreyev made a couple more hasty notes. "I appreciate your openness, comrade Zaretzky. Maybe we should meet here again soon. Someone will call you to set up a meeting."

"Certainly," Zaretzky smiled. "I serve the Communist Party."

✡✡✡

Wolf could sit up in bed. His platoon commander came to visit and sat on a chair next to Wolf's bed. "How are you doing?"

"As good as can be expected. The doctor told me that they'll have to take me back home for some rehab. How are the guys doing? Was anybody else injured?"

"The guys are mostly doing fine. The night you were wounded the company had several more casualties, none in our platoon. The medics notified me that you will be transported back home. I brought some of your stuff, including your tablet. The guys send their best."

"Do you know what happened? I mean, how did the Germans surprise us? I looked at all the monitors just before the attack and there was nothing there."

"That's one mystery we solved. Apparently some of their mountain troops climbed the slopes of the valley just north of us and stayed hidden beyond the summit. None of the drones were observing that area so they surprised us," the lieutenant responded.

A nearby artillery battery opened up and the building shook slightly.

"I better go," the lieutenant said. "It looks like the Nazis are getting frisky again. Be well and keep in touch." They shook hands and he was gone.

Wolf took his tablet out of its case and started an email to his sister just as a medic came in. "Wolf Frumin?" the medic asked.

"That's me," Wolf responded.

"The doctor told me that you may be able to walk short distances. Want to try?" the medic asked.

Wolf threw off the blanket and started to get out of bed. He slowed down immediately – his head started spinning. The medic noticed and helped him.

"Take it easy. You lost some blood and are not fully recovered from surgery. Four days are enough to make it safe for you to move but only if you don't try running," he joked.

With the medic's help Wolf got up and dressed in loose fitting tanker's overalls. He could walk if he leaned on the medic.

"Let's start slowly moving out of here. There's a helicopter waiting for you and others to take you on the first leg home."

"What about my stuff here?" Wolf asked.

"I'll pick it up as soon as I settle you in. It will take only five minutes and I have to get one more wounded guy from the next room anyway."

Half an hour later the helicopter was on its way to an airstrip near Venice. The weather was much better than it had been the night Wolf was wounded. It was sunny and calm. The air was cold and the helicopter's heater was blasting. The flight took longer than the fifty mile air distance to Venice would suggest. They had to follow directions that kept the heavy helicopter within the range of Israeli air defenses – there was no point in offering the Germans an easy target.

They landed near Venice an hour later. The wounded were transferred to a waiting C130 Hercules, which took off for Israel.

Wolf slept most of the six hours on the plane in a bunk. He kept waking up with a painful reminder of his injuries whenever he tried to turn onto his left side.

Minutes after landing the passengers were loaded onto another helicopter that brought them to the Rambam Medical Center in Haifa.

After he settled in his room, Wolf could finally call his parents.

"I'm at the Rambam Medical Center. I'm doing fine. They examined me after I arrived here. Everything seems to be healing well. They will allow me to walk around later in the day so if you come in the evening we can party."

"We will be there. In the meantime I'll call your sister and let her know. Be well and we shall see you soon."

✡✡✡

General Uri Sadot settled into his Innsbruck headquarters. His first order of business was a review of the tactical situation with his staff and General Oded Almog, who was now the second-in-command.

"I want a Falcon AWACS system in the air at all times," Sadot ordered. "It should let us know of any air activity or major ground advances. The German aircraft assembling in Munich and Vienna airports are here to support a ground attack, which is likely to start when the force to the east arrives. I would like to do two things: reduce the ground forces that are assembling against us in the east and destroy the Luftwaffe forces that are likely to attack us." He looked around the conference table. "Any proposals?"

"We have one easy option: the Hungarian force is just being loaded onto trains. If we move reasonably fast we can attack and destroy them from the air," General Almog proposed.

Others at the table were nodding agreement. "Good, let's make it so," Sadot said. "Any other ideas?"

The air force liaison, a colonel, said, "From the intelligence we have, which is mostly radio intercepts and satellite imagery, it looks like the Luftwaffe really pulled out all the stops. We're looking at hundreds of aircraft, most of them bombers but also a fair number of fighters like the Bf-109, and even heavy fighters like the Me-110. If they attack together, which the Germans did sometimes in the Battle of Britain, we will have to expend a large number of missiles to destroy them. I suggest that we attack both the Munich and Vienna airports tomorrow, or even better, tonight. Ninety percent of their forces are in place and we can easily destroy them on the ground. A second attack will take care of their fuel tanks. By the way, some of the tanks are buried deep and protected by layers of reinforced concrete. We will have to use some of our bunker busters to get to them."

"Why at night? Won't it be easier to hit the targets in daylight?" General Sadot wanted to know.

"A night attack will be less dangerous. The Germans have lots of quad 20mm anti-air mounts at both airports. Not a concern if we are coming in at 8,000 or 10,000 feet but dangerous at the altitude we need to destroy their aircraft. In the dark the danger they pose will be much reduced. Our planes, even the older ones, are equipped with night vision sights and ground reflection radar. They'll do a fine job on the Nazis."

"That makes sense as far as it goes," Sadot said, "but I have a question: why not eliminate the danger to our aircraft altogether? Why not drop some medium-sized thermobaric bombs to eliminate their anti-air defenses from high altitude and then come in for a low level attack on what remains?"

The air force colonel shrugged but before he could say anything General Almog intervened. "Dropping thermobaric bombs is not exactly the most civil thing to do. Fuel-air bombs kill in a large radius and we might kill innocent civilians."

Uri Sadot's eyebrows crawled up his forehead. "You mean that we can't bomb or otherwise attack any facility that has civilians present?"

Almog nodded. "In essence that's the situation. We were attacked by human rights organizations for years and years and they always demanded that we abide by the Geneva conventions, which we always do."

General Sadot nodded. "Do you know what exactly the conventions say regarding civilians and which convention we're talking about?"

"It's the fourth Geneva Convention but I really can't cite from it," Almog responded.

"You are partially correct. The relevant rules are in Protocol 1 of the Fourth Geneva Convention as amended in 1977. Since the Fourth Convention dates to 1949, neither it nor the amended protocol can bind us in 1942. Besides, in the time we came from the USA and several other countries refrained from ratifying the protocol so all this nonsense is not binding on us.

"The specific articles that protect civilians are Articles 51 and 54 which outlaw indiscriminate attacks on civilian populations and destruction of food, water, and other materials needed for survival. Indiscriminate is the key. Are we intending to harm civilians in our attack? The answer is no, therefore any civilians that are close to a military target are not protected. Civilians that are engaged in activities that support the enemy don't fall under the protection of this convention at all. The fact that this was used against us for years doesn't mean it was justified or that we should change our tactics and endanger our lives. Israel was singled out for these kind of attacks and accused of killing 'innocent civilians', but did you notice that no one, not even the Palestinians, wanted to go to the International Court and file formal accusations? The accusers always knew that the accusations were bogus, just a propaganda tool.

"So to summarize: My orders are to bomb both Munich and Vienna airports in the morning. We start with a high altitude attack using five thousand pound thermobaric bombs. After their air defenses are gone we drop bunker busters on the underground fuel tanks." Sadot looked at the air force colonel. "You decide what size you need. If after all this there are aircraft still intact we destroy them. Is this clear?"

"Crystal clear," the colonel responded.

✡✡✡

Friday night was approaching and for the first time in weeks the family was assembling at Ze'ev's house for a Sabbath dinner. The crowd included Ze'ev and Linda's youngest son, Benjamin, plus their daughter Shoshanna with her husband Noam and their kids. Jacob brought his sister Sheina, mother Sara, cousin Tzipora, and Esther Frumin. Esther's brother Wolf and her parents, Nachman and Tzila, were also present. Wolf's left arm was still in a sling. Ze'ev's son Chaim's family was also at the table.

After the women finished lighting the Sabbath candles and the meal was served the conversation began.

"How do you like your new car?" Ze'ev asked Jacob, who had driven his brand new Sabra from Beer Sheva.

"I love it. It drives well and is so quiet," Jacob responded.

"Isn't it a bit small?" Chaim asked.

"I picked up Esther, Sheina, Tzipora and my mother. We all fit, a bit tight but not too bad. I didn't want the larger model; it's much more difficult to park."

Chaim looked at Ze'ev. "You know that Jacob isn't a connoisseur of automobiles. I think that a gasoline powered car would drive somewhat better. Why not drop the Stirling engine and switch to something normal?"

Ze'ev shook his head. "Chaim, you are missing the point. The current model drives worse than the cars we're used to but better than its contemporary competition. And it's our first attempt. The next generations will be even better.

"The more important point is that soon, maybe even before the war is over, we will start exporting our cars. Do you think we could compete with Detroit selling gasoline powered vehicles? Never. This car though, and trucks built on the same power train, will kill them. I'm sure they will want to license the technology, which I'm prepared to do."

Ze'ev turned to Wolf. "How are you feeling?"

Wolf smiled. "Quite well, thank you. I appreciate you not calling me a hero. My sister and parents can't stop. It's embarrassing, especially as so many of my comrades died and the battle is not done yet."

Noam Shaviv nodded. "You are not alone, my friend. Welcome to the brotherhood and please suffer heroically. Do you know whether you're going back to Europe?"

Wolf shrugged and winced; the shrug was painful. "I hope so. The unit liaison officer told me that when my medical profile is at least 75%, they'll take me back. Otherwise I'll probably become an instructor. It's still a ways off. The doctors at Rambam told me that it will be at least a month before I can take off the sling."

"Did they have a prediction for what you can expect?" Ze'ev asked.

"Yes, I asked that question as well. The doctor said that I might regain close to 100% of my arm function after exercises and therapy. I'm optimistic, but it will take months," Wolf responded.

Linda entered the conversation. "I trust our doctors but you need to follow directions and use your own brain. Don't try being a hero; you will be of no use if you return to your unit prematurely. If you served in the American military you would have gotten a medal just for having been wounded. You're a hero already and have nothing more to prove."

"You sound like my mother."

Tzila Frumin, Wolf's mother smiled. "Just because I'm your mother doesn't mean I'm wrong."

Shoshanna, Noam's wife, turned to Esther. "How you are doing? Did you decide what to do about your studies?"

"I decided to enroll in Ben Gurion University and study biology. That way after one year I might be able to transfer to the Tel Aviv University and become an M.D. after four more years."

✡✡✡

Amos Nir, the Prime Minister of Israel, was tired and looking forward to going home. Just one more meeting.

The Foreign Minister, the Defense Minister, and the head of the Mossad came in together. After the greetings were done and everyone had their cup of coffee, Amos began. "We need to discuss our relationship with the U.S. In this timeline, they are not a superpower but still a major player. I think that we need to forge a friendship with the U.S. based on mutual respect and a commonality of interests."

Amos nodded at the Defense Minister, who was shaking his head. "I know that this sounds trite, especially in view of the way things developed in our past. Just hear me out and decide.

"The situation now is that they know very little about us, so we can't really expect respect. We have some limited common interests but we also may develop serious conflicts, like we had in our old timeline. The U.S. is friendly with the Arabs. They have a partnership with the Saudis in ARAMCO, a fact that predates the Roosevelt administration. If the oil companies maintain their influence, we will have tensions, possibly insurmountable, with the Americans. Any ideas on how to solve these problems?"

The Foreign Minister nodded. "I have been thinking about this for a while. We need to show the Americans that we are militarily strong and a valuable ally in their Pacific war. I would prefer to keep the time travel issue in the background. They may already be aware of it but if questions are not asked we shouldn't volunteer this information."

The Defense Minister agreed. "That's what I was thinking as well. Maybe the simplest way to become a useful ally would be to offer them intelligence. They may not be in as bad a situation as the Russians but they are having a tough time with the Japanese navy. But we need to remember that the Americans have a history of rejecting, or just being skeptical, of intelligence.

"In our timeline the Japanese occupied the Philippines shortly after the attack on Pearl Harbor. This time we disrupted that attack and gave General McArthur a chance to hold the Philippines. His air force, which survived due to our intervention, destroyed most of the Japanese air assets on Formosa and sunk most of the Japanese invasion fleet. The problem is that McArthur is arrogant. He managed to ignore a second invasion fleet that invaded the island of Mindoro. Now he's trying to dislodge the Japanese, but with little success.

"The Japanese are building up support for their forces on Mindoro. Also, since there was no battle of Midway, the Japanese aircraft carriers and most of their fleet are still intact. The U.S. had some success in dislodging them from other islands, Papua New Guinea being a good example, but the main problem for the Americans is locating the Japanese fleet. As you know, in the battle of Midway they got lucky and found the Japanese carriers first, but luck is not a reliable thing. We could hugely help them by providing the same kind of timely satellite photos we provide the Russians."

The head of the Mossad shrugged. "We may also be able to help them by breaking Japanese coded messages in real time. The Americans are doing a good job but every time the Japanese change their cipher it takes several days and sometimes weeks to find the new key. It seems that in this timeline the Japanese are changing the ciphers much more often than they did originally. We could provide the Americans, and the Brits, with the ciphers minutes after they are changed. This might help them a lot."

Amos Nir nodded. "Yes, I think we have a base for an approach to the Americans. Since the matters are mostly military, the Ministry of Defense should take the lead. Do we have a military attaché in our Washington embassy?"

"We do, Colonel Oren Shaviv. He is with the air force and participated in the attack in North Africa. He was the only one of our pilots shot down there. A good and smart man," the Defense Minister said.

"Good, then he needs to get all the pertinent information and do his job," Amos Nir concluded.

✡✡✡

When Ben Mosowitz and his wife Evelyn arrived at the Jewish Agency office on Arch and 18th Street in Philadelphia they were greeted by a polite receptionist. She took their names, checked their appointment, and promised they were next on the list. The wait was short and the representative came out to greet them and escort them into his office.

Ben started as soon as they were seated. "We were at your presentation a couple of weeks ago in Wilmington and would like to ask some questions."

"Go ahead," the representative said. "I'll do my best to answer."

"First, we would like to know how much it would cost us to visit Israel? We would like to see what we're getting into before deciding to make aliyah."

"It's not cheap," the shaliach responded. "You have to make your way to New York where we would pick you up and transfer you to New Brunswick, Canada. From there you fly on one of our passenger planes directly to Israel. The total cost for a round trip is about five hundred dollars per person."

"So going on a research trip is expensive." Ben looked at Evelyn, who nodded. "Let's go to our next question: what kind of luggage and household items can we take with us if we decide to move there?"

The shaliach tapped several key on the laptop in front of him. "You have three kids, so you're entitled to two trunks and a large suitcase which the airline will ship with you. You can carry onto the plane a small suitcase per person. In addition you can send about half a boxcar full of possessions. They will have to be packed in what we call a 'container'. It will be delivered to you, you fill it with stuff and we pick it up a day or two before you leave. We can send experienced movers to help you pack it, if you want. The container will arrive in Israel separately, possibly several months after you do, so it shouldn't have anything you expect to need soon after you arrive. American electrical appliances won't work in Israel so don't bring those. You'll get a discount on new ones to replace them."

Ben had his final and most important question. "I'm a business owner with a furniture store and small manufacture in Wilmington. What can I expect to do in Israel?"

"You can open a furniture business. If you manufacture furniture you could be very successful. We're absorbing enormous numbers of immigrants. People have jobs and places to live but furniture is a bit scarce. You will have competition, but you should be used to that. We will help you with information to adjust to local conditions, as well as with any licensing you might need.

"There are many other avenues open to you, everything from working for the government to sales or manufacturing as a salaried employee.

"Your daughter will go to school as soon as you arrive. All four year olds attend a half day kindergarten. If both parents work the kids usually go to a full day establishment for a small payment. Many women do work but it will be up to you."

Ben shifted in his seat. “I almost forgot to ask, the only Hebrew either of us know is a smattering from the prayer books. Is this going to be a problem?”

“Yes and no,” the representative responded. “You can get by with just English, but I doubt you’ll be satisfied. Most new immigrants spend a couple of months in an immersive Hebrew school when they first arrive. It’s free and highly recommended.”

✡✡✡

Hitler finished reviewing the documents Gestapo Muller had given him. The Fuehrer was thoughtful. He turned to Himmler, who also attended the meeting. “Do you agree with Mueller’s recommendations?”

Himmler nodded emphatically. “Yes, my Fuehrer. I have confirmation from several sources and they all agree. We’re facing a serious conspiracy. It involves civilians, civil servants, and the military. Our military difficulties stem from treason.”

Hitler was slightly annoyed. “You didn’t answer my question. Do you agree with Mueller’s recommendations? Arresting most of our top generals and some second level military officers is not a simple affair.”

“Yes, I agree with Mueller. We must act decisively or they will attack us.”

“Who is this ‘us’ they will attack?” Hitler asked quietly.

Himmler looked at the Gestapo chief who answered, “As far as we can ascertain, the attack will be against you personally and, after that, against the Party and its organizations, including the SS, SA and any party official they can get hold of.”

Hitler sat for a short while, his fingers drumming on the desk. Finally he stirred. “Himmler, you think that some of the military problems are due to treason? What about the Luftwaffe?”

Himmler straightened in his seat. “I spoke to the Luftwaffe commander and he seems to agree. By the way, I noticed General von Greim is in the waiting room. Maybe we should invite him in and ask him directly what he thinks.”

Von Greim entered the office, saluted the Fuehrer and took a seat in the chair Hitler indicated.

The Fuehrer looked at the general for a while then said, “General, please give us an update on what’s happening on the different fronts.”

“I can only report with any certainty on issues concerning the Luftwaffe.

"The Eastern Front and the French sector have been quiet for the past week. The only activity of any importance was in Austria." von Greim stopped.

Hitler was impatient. "Go on, man. You're supposed to report not just sit here like a lump."

"Yes, my Fuehrer. Field Marshall von Kluge planned his attack on the Jewish force in Innsbruck for three days from today. We started moving aircraft into the Munich and Vienna airports five days ago. These are relatively large facilities with underground aviation fuel storage tanks. Three days ago, when most of the aircraft were in position, both bases were attacked by the enemy. We lost all but five bombers in Vienna and everything in Munich. Worse than this, the underground tanks, including those in Munich with reinforced concrete protection, were blown up. The attack was carried out in the morning and lasted only fifteen minutes. We think we damaged one enemy plane but we found no debris."

The room was quiet for long minutes. Hitler got up from his seat and started pacing. He stopped in front of von Greim. "How do you think the enemy knew that your force was in position?"

General von Greim hesitated. "I really don't know. We didn't see any planes in the vicinity so it had to be an informant or spy."

Mueller stirred. "Who, besides Luftwaffe personnel, would know the exact location of the fuel tanks?"

Von Greim shrugged. "Many people would have that information. The tanks were built a while ago, before 1939, as part of civilian improvements of the airports."

Mueller nodded. "They were built by the Todd Organization under Wehrmacht supervision. Todd used concentration camp inmates who were later executed. This leaves us with only one set of suspects: Wehrmacht personnel, although some Luftwaffe experts were also involved, especially in designing the bomb protection of the tanks."

Hitler addressed von Greim. "General, please wait outside. I will need to speak with you in private later."

After the Commander of the Luftwaffe was gone, Himmler shook his head. "My Fuehrer, there is another development you need to know about. Yesterday a division of Hungarian troops was destroyed. They were on their way to join our forces east of Innsbruck. One of their trains was attacked from the air. Very few survivors. The following train was also attacked but some of those troops escaped. They observed the attack on the first train and started running away before the second attack began.

"I'm asking myself how did the enemy know when and which trains to attack?"

Hitler returned to his seat. “You convinced me. We will go with your plan, after we deal with the invaders in Innsbruck.”

✡✡✡

“Come in,” Lior Lapid, the Israeli Ambassador to Washington, yelled. The door opened and Colonel Oren Shaviv, the military attaché, entered the room. “Lior, it’s almost time to go. I just wanted to make sure we’re on the same page. You do all the talking; I just answer questions if they ask me directly. Correct?”

“You got it,” Lior said rising from his desk. “The President is likely to ask questions of you as are the military guys. Just remember one thing: any questions about where we came from are for me to answer. If, in the future, I’m not present you can always hide behind your Israeli accent and answer a different question or misinterpret completely what you’re asked. They don’t know that you have an MBA from UCLA.”

They arrived at the White House in their new Sabra-A limousine. It was the first time the limo had been used officially. It provoked some obvious interest at both the White House gate and the North Portico.

An aide took them to the same anteroom where Lior had waited during his first meeting with Roosevelt. Ten minutes later they were invited into the President’s office.

“It’s a pleasure to see you again, Ambassador Lapid,” the President said.

“Thank you, Mr. President,” Lior Lapid responded. “Please allow me to introduce our military attaché, Air Force Colonel Oren Shaviv.”

The President smiled. “Welcome to the U.S.A., Colonel. Allow me to introduce my Secretary of War, Mr. Stimson, Secretary of the Navy, Mr. Knox, Army Chief of Staff, General Marshall, and Navy Chief of Operations, Admiral King.”

“Ambassador Lapid,” the Roosevelt continued, “you requested a meeting to present to the military assistance your country can give us in our war with the Japanese Empire. Prime Minister Churchill assured me that you have been instrumental in winning their war against Germany.”

“Mr. President, we can indeed render significant assistance.

“You have two main difficulties: the first is that in the vast Pacific Ocean it’s not easy to spot an aircraft carrier. It’s even harder to spot a submarine.

“The second difficulty lies in how long it takes you to decode Japanese communications when they change their cipher. If they changed every two weeks you would not be able to decode their messages.”

Secretary Stimson stirred in his seat. "Pardon my blunt question, but how do you know about our decoding operations? These are top secret. Do you have spies in our military?"

"We have no spies in the U.S. We don't need them. We have the ability to know things other people think are secret. Here's an example of what we can give you."

He opened his briefcase and pulled out several satellite images of the Solomon Islands. "These photos of Guadalcanal and vicinity were taken today. As you can see," the Ambassador gave the images to Roosevelt, "there is a train of Japanese vessels running supplies to support their forces on Guadalcanal."

The Americans studied the images for a while before Admiral King said, "You're saying the pictures were taken today?"

"Three hours ago."

"How did you manage to take such high quality pictures and get them here in such a short time?" the President asked.

"Mr. President, we won't share our methods but you can benefit from our information," Lapid responded.

"Can you find the Japanese carriers now and tell us where they are?" the Secretary of the Navy asked.

The Ambassador pulled out another sheet of paper. "As of 12:00 Washington time, today, the carrier Hiryu was 200 miles north of New Guinea. It's on its way to attack Port Moresby. If you examine the image carefully you will note that two of its escorts are submarines, which were submerged when the image was taken."

General Marshall asked, "How do we know that the information in these images is correct?"

Surprisingly, Admiral King answered. "I know the positions of our vessels and the image of the Guadalcanal area is accurate. I don't understand how they determined the names and serial numbers of the vessels, both ours and the Japanese, but the information is accurate.

"Mr. Ambassador, how certain are you that the Hiryu is on its way to Port Moresby, New Guinea?" He looked at the photograph again, "Yes, that's what it says here."

Lapid looked at Colonel Shaviv. "The Colonel can answer that better than I can."

"The images you are looking at are the product of several streams of information. We analyze the images to determine what ship it is and in what direction and at what speed it's travelling. We also consider other available intelligence. In this case, we decoded several messages that mentioned Hiryu. One of these contained orders to bomb Port Moresby."

The room was quiet while Roosevelt fit a cigarette into a holder. Finally the President nodded decisively. "I think that it would benefit both our countries to forge an alliance. Mr. Ambassador, I propose that your government prepare the text of a treaty, we will do the same. Then you and Secretary Hull can meet and come to an agreement."

As the Americans were leaving, Roosevelt signaled for Lapid and Shaviv to remain. "I would like to discuss a couple of issues in private."

"No problem, Mr. President."

"Several Jewish newspapers and some other sources, including officials of Jewish institutions claim that the State of Israel as it now exists in Palestine was transported there from the future. Can you enlighten me on that?"

Lapid smiled. "Sounds like a fascinating story. I suppose that's the only way anti-Semites can account for our knowledge and abilities."

The President also smiled. "I suppose it doesn't really matter. The truth eventually gets out.

"In the meantime what do you think will be your government's response to establishing full bilateral relations, including a U.S. Embassy in Palestine, excuse me, Israel?"

"I'm sure they will be delighted."

Chapter 12
December 1942

Ambassador Mizrahi poured himself another cup of tea. He was tired and impatient. For two hours he had been negotiating with General Wilson and Soviet ambassador Maisky about the location and procedures for the upcoming allied conference.

Wilson was saying, "Mr. Maisky, I appreciate Chairman Stalin's desire to have the conference on Soviet soil. Sochi is a nice place but I have to take into consideration our delegation's safety. As we have discussed already, the city is close to German lines and within reach of German aviation. There is no guarantee of complete protection against their air attacks."

Mizrahi nodded agreement. "Mr. Stalin is reluctant to come to Tel Aviv because it's complicated to get to and is the sovereign territory of another allied power. The same applies to Sochi."

It was Maisky's turn to agree. "I can see your problem gentlemen. I propose a neutral place: Teheran. Would that be acceptable?"

Mizrahi said, "My government will probably accept Teheran. General Wilson?"

Wilson nodded. "I think this is an acceptable compromise."

The meeting broke up. When Wilson left Mizrahi gestured to Maisky to return to his seat. "Mr. Ambassador, my government thinks that this may be a good time to upgrade our relations. We would make our legation a full embassy and you will be able to open an embassy in Jerusalem."

Maisky couldn't hide his surprise. "Just several months ago your government was happy with a legation in Moscow and said nothing about a Soviet embassy in Palestine. Has something changed?"

"Several things, including the fact that we are now actively fighting and destroying Nazi divisions that would otherwise threaten your country," responded Mizrahi. "The most recent change is that we were asked by the United States to establish full bilateral relations with them. It's my government's position that we treat all our allies equally."

"I believe that my government will be happy to establish such relations." Maisky hesitated before adding. "I know of several people that will be very interested in setting up an embassy."

✡✡✡

Rachel Rothstein finished her dinner preparations. Many things had happened since her family came to Israel as tourists in June of last year. A day before they were scheduled to return to Boston, the country was transported into the past. They were stuck but not helpless. Her husband David set up a consulting company in his area of expertise, manufacturing equipment to make microchips. With some initial help from his cousin Ze'ev Hirshson, the company was prospering. The Rothsteins moved from a small rental apartment in Tel Aviv to a new house in Rehovot. Their two sons were prospering as well: Josh graduated from high school in September and was now in the IDF doing basic training. Their younger son, Jake, was starting his last year of high school. Rachel kept herself busy teaching history in one of the local elementary schools – Israel had a severe shortage of teachers from the future.

Dinner was nearly ready. She surveyed her creation for today, smaller than usual. This time she remembered Josh was away and prepared an appropriate amount of food. David was supposed to pick up Jake. They should be home soon.

The phone rang. "May I speak to Rachel Rothstein?" a male voice asked.

"Speaking," Rachel responded.

"Mrs. Rothstein, you may remember the forms you filled out for the Ministry of Absorption several months ago?"

"Yes, I do." Rachel remembered the ads in the Jerusalem Post and on TV asking people with family in 1942 America to submit names. They were promised to be notified if those family members were coming to Israel.

"I just wanted let you know that a Mr. Benjamin Mosowitz from Wilmington, Delaware, signed up to make aliyah with his wife and three children. They are tentatively scheduled to arrive at Ben Gurion airport in two weeks. If you would like to meet them, please go to our website. It will have updated information on their arrival."

Rachel was rarely speechless but this was one of those times, at least for a moment. "Can we take them straight to our home?"

"Certainly," the voice responded, "although not for very long. We recommend that all newcomers go through an immersive Hebrew course.

There is one not too far from where you live so you should have no problem delivering them there within a week of arrival."

David and Jake arrived just as she hung up. "David, Jake, I have wonderful news. My grandparents, mother, and uncles are arriving in Israel!"

✡✡✡

Avigdor Mizrahi shook hands with General Wilson. They had met only several days earlier at the Israeli embassy. "General, it's time to discuss our peace proposal to the Germans."

"Yes, I agree. But first I would like to congratulate your army on the victory in Austria. It was a monumental achievement. Truthfully, neither the Prime Minister nor I thought that your plan was feasible. You offered the Germans an irresistible temptation: a small force vulnerable to being surrounded. We're still not clear about the details but our intelligence indicates that the Germans lost close to twenty divisions, including their tanks and artillery. Incredible. I also heard that Hitler sacked Field Marshall von Kluge. That must have been a sight to behold."

Mizrahi smiled an unpleasant smile. "Maybe the Germans will learn not to mess with the Jews. This victory is exactly the reason my government thinks it's the right time to start talking. With the renewed offensive in France the German High Command must have realized that the war is lost."

Wilson nodded. "Our sources indicate that they're close to making a decision. The French government agrees as well. In fact, their ambassador should be here shortly."

Mizrahi smiled. "I'm glad we finally established relations with them, but please remember that they're in the dark about who exactly we are and where we come from. Let's keep it that way for a while."

The French ambassador entered. "Gentlemen, it's a pleasure to see you again." He turned to Mizrahi, "I hear that congratulations are in order. That was a brilliant victory."

"Yes, we are somewhat pleased. This victory opens the door to finishing the war soon. After a painful defeat the Germans should be open to a negotiated peace. My government gave some thought to what terms we can offer the Germans. It would be as follows…"

After Mizrahi was finished, Wilson asked, "What do we tell the Soviets?"

"I suggest that we keep them informed of all the details," the French ambassador said.

"I don't think that's a good idea," Mizrahi responded. "Our Prime Ministers are going to meet Stalin next month. You don't have an elected government yet, but a representative from the Free French Government will be at the meeting. I think that would be the right time and place to inform the Soviets."

Wilson nodded agreement. "That is also the position of my government. In the meantime, this offer will remain secret. As was agreed earlier, the German representative, a civilian, will be brought to London. All negotiations will be done by me and Ambassador Mizrahi."

The French ambassador bristled. "It was my understanding that we would be represented at those meetings as well."

"I'm sorry for the misunderstanding, Mr. Ambassador. Be assured that your government's positions will be presented by us," Wilson responded. "There's no difference between our positions anyway."

✡✡✡

The group assembled in General Halder's Berlin apartment was subdued. They sat facing the large fireplace, quietly exchanging news and waiting for Halder.

Finally General Halder, the commander of the Army High Command, entered, followed by another man in uniform.

Halder stopped and closed the door. "Gentlemen, please allow me to introduce Field Marshall Günter von Kluge. He decided to join our group and swore, like everyone here, to uphold any decision we make.

"Before we continue I would like the Field Marshall to report on the battle of Innsbruck. It will be a very short report. Field Marshall..." Halder took his customary seat in front of the fireplace.

"Gentlemen, comrades," von Kluge began, "as you know the Fuehrer appointed me to command the special Army Group assembled to liberate Innsbruck. The Fuehrer, despite his promises, interfered and meddled with my orders, but that wasn't the reason we were defeated.

"My group consisted of 19 full-strength German divisions, including five armor divisions, and two Hungarian divisions. We also had at our disposal close to a thousand Luftwaffe aircraft, most of them bombers. The armor divisions were equipped with the latest Panzer VI - some of you know it as the Tiger. Approximately 400,000 personnel participated in this operation. We were supposed to defeat a small force. Our scout reports and intelligence suggested that we faced less than two divisions. Destroying them was supposed to be an easy job, even knowing that a similar force destroyed two Waffen SS divisions several weeks earlier.

"I will make it short, like the battle itself. The Hungarians never reached us – they were destroyed on the way out of Hungary. Not a big loss. Most of the Luftwaffe forces were prepared for jump off at the Munich and Vienna airfields. The airfields, the planes, and the underground fuel tanks were demolished by the enemy in one short morning attack. Our two forces, that were supposed to crush the enemy, could advance not a millimeter. The Tigers were destroyed by both enemy tanks and infantry. Their tanks are absolutely invulnerable to our weapons. Their infantry operates from personnel carriers that are also invulnerable but the soldiers can be destroyed when they leave their vehicles. They don't do it very often and when they do, artillery, tanks and other weapons we didn't recognize, plus some that remained invisible to us, protect them.

"The bottom line is that they trapped our forces in the mountains and destroyed them mostly from the air. We lost all our heavy equipment and at least 90% of our fighting troops. It was a catastrophe. The enemy is still in Innsbruck and if it moves we have nothing to throw against them, which would be futile anyway."

The room was quiet. Finally, Admiral Canaris asked, "Field Marshall, we have heard reports that the enemy is displaying flags with a Star of David and that their soldiers speak Hebrew. Can you confirm this?

"I have seen the flags with my own eyes. According to reports by several Gestapo agents that left Innsbruck after it was occupied, the enemy soldiers do speak Hebrew. Some of them speak Yiddish in addition to Hebrew. I also swear that as I was observing an enemy unit east of Innsbruck I was seen and recognized. A tank gun was trained on my location but then aimed at a position a hundred meters to one side and annihilated it. They never shot at me."

Since there were no other questions Halder said, "In view of what we heard, Mr. Goerdeler has a very interesting report to make."

Carl Goerdeler was the former mayor of Leipzig and a strident opponent of the Nazi regime. He had had several personal run-ins with Hitler over Goerderler's refusal to fly Nazi flags over city hall or remove the statue of Jewish composer Felix Mendelssohn, as well as enforcement of the Nuremberg laws, but somehow Goerdeler survived and even enjoyed some freedom of movement. After his resignation as mayor in 1937 he travelled Europe as the representative of the Bosch Company and met in England with Winston Churchill and with important politicians in France.

Now he got up and moved to the front of the room. "Friends, several days ago I was approached by a British agent. He invited me to come to London to listen to a proposal. I went. I met with two people: General Wilson, who is a representative of Winston Churchill, and Avigdor

Mizrahi, the ambassador to Britain from the State of Israel. I was given no information about this state except that it's a powerful, independent Jewish entity. Britain, Israel, and the Soviet Union are allied against us. The forces Field Marshall von Kluge described are a part of the Israel Defense Force.

"Their proposal is simple: If the Nazis are removed from power and Germany surrenders and goes back to its pre-war borders, the allies will stop fighting.

"They gave me some of the details which are, according to them, nonnegotiable:

> All Nazis above the rank of District Leader and SS ranks above Brigadier General will be tried and, if found guilty of crimes on the attached list, executed.
>
> No former members of the Nazi party will be allowed to hold public office or work for any branch of the government - ever.
>
> Companies that used slave workers will have to reimburse these workers at a rate double what was paid German employees one position senior to them.
>
> All Germans and collaborators who participated in the murder of civilians will be tried for their crimes with the maximum punishment being death. This includes all concentration camp personnel. Detailed lists of such personnel attached.
>
> An elected government will replace the military government of Germany within six months after signing the peace agreement. Germany will be a federal republic.
>
> Allied garrisons will be stationed in Germany for as long as the allies deem necessary.
>
> Germany will have to pay reparations to occupied countries, not punitive reparations like under Versailles but actual damages as agreed upon by a joint committee of allied and German experts.

"Those are the most important points."

"What happens if we continue to fight?" asked Admiral Canaris.

Goerdeler smiled a sad smile. "If we continue to fight, the allies will destroy us. They promised to leave Germany in ruins. I believe them and, according to von Kluge, there's nothing we can do to stop them."

"At least none of us are members of the National Socialist Party. There are few of those among senior Wehrmacht officers.

✡✡✡

“I know we have discussed this issue before but I still don’t agree,” the Defense Minister said while poking his index finger at the Foreign Minister.

“Nitzan,” the Prime Minister responded quietly, “you know better than to yell and lecture. We decided to postpone the decision precisely because of disagreements. Now it’s time to decide. We can’t maintain diplomatic relations and not have full reciprocity of embassies.”

“Why not?” Nitzan Liebler asked. “It allows us to keep technological and scientific secrets safe.”

“And how long do you think we can keep ourselves cut off from the world?” the Foreign Minister wanted to know.

“At least until the end of the war.”

“What exactly will change then? It’s not as if anyone could steal all our secrets at once. Which ones do you consider most important to protect?”

Nitzan Liebler, the Defense Minister, drummed his fingers on the table top. “Nuclear secrets obviously, jet technology, microchips. There might be more but this is what comes to mind.”

The Infrastructure Minister smiled. “How about time and inter-dimensional travel?”

“Yes, that too,” Liebler agreed.

Amos Nir nodded. “Now we’re getting somewhere. Let’s start with nuclear technology. Don’t forget that the Americans, British, and to some extent the Germans know that uranium can be used as a weapon or power source. What exactly do you want to keep secret?”

“How to make a bomb, which as you know is not a simple affair.” the Defense Minister responded.

The Science and Development Minister smiled. “I agree, but this is not exactly information found in public libraries. Even if a spy finds a description of the equipment necessary, the country in question will still have to develop and build it. This is an enormous financial outlay, unless we let everyone look at our classified libraries. Even the U.S. will have a problem marshalling the resources necessary in the absence of war or threat. I can see only the Russians, maybe, trying to develop a bomb, and they will be seriously handicapped by the lack of information. It is true that just knowing that something is possible is a big step, but we already missed that train. The bottom line is that having a foreign embassy here will not endanger our nuclear supremacy in any significant way for a long while.”

Amos Nir nodded. "Good, let's go to the second item: jet technology. As of now the Brits are working on a jet engine and have some designs for a turbofan engine. Messerschmitt has already tested one. So what are we guarding here?"

"I'm not an engineer, but it seems to me that materials and design specifics are very important," the Defense Minister said.

"Are you worried that anyone will soon have jet fighters that would compete with ours?" the Foreign Minister asked.

Nitzan nodded agreement.

"You shouldn't worry," the Science and Development Minister said. "The engine is only one part of a jet. There are other parts, like the fuselage, avionics and weapons. In avionics and weapons we were leaders even in the time we came from. How long do you think it will take the rest of the world to catch up, especially if we continue development? They may be able to learn which alloys work best in a jet turbine, but book learning is also a handicap – it's never as deep as what you learn through research or trial and error.

"I also need to point out that microprocessors are at the heart of almost everything we make. Without them a lot of things are extremely difficult, if not impossible. As an example, a couple of days ago I examined a new car, the Sabra, that is using a Stirling cycle engine. The engine was invented and patented by a Scotsman in 1816. It was never used in automobiles until now. Consolidated developed a smart chip with some nifty programming that made it practical to use this engine in a car. Detroit couldn't duplicate this for all the money in the world.

"Microprocessors are a technology that is virtually impossible to duplicate without developing the underlying infrastructure. Again, in our old timeline Israel manufactured 80% of the equipment used around the world to test microprocessors. In the absence of such equipment, a manufacturer is likely to produce garbage that will fail quickly. We also manufacture, or know how to manufacture, the equipment necessary for a microchip fab. We just need to expand in this area, which is being done already. You think that here and now someone else can do better?"

Nitzan Liebler shook his head. "I'm still against allowing foreign embassies here, but I will not insist. If the majority of the government wants to allow foreigners into our country, I can't stop it."

The Foreign Minister shrugged. "Before we pass the resolution let me add something that's bothering me. The Soviets are not taking us seriously. It's partly because of our attempt to undermine Beria and feed him misleading information but it's also because we're small and Jewish. They treated us the same way in the old timeline until we defeated their surrogates and, in some places, their own troops during the 1967 war.

"We now have an opportunity to change this. An embassy here will make them recognize that we can be a powerful ally but an even more dangerous opponent. It may change the whole fabric of future relations with them. The Americans are not as bad due to FDR's contacts with Churchill, but its second-hand experience. Exposing U.S. State Department employees to our country might enable them to understand viscerally the advantages of being friends with us and the dangers of opposing us. Hopefully they'll change their approach to the Arabs and think twice before interfering with us.

"Of course people see what they want to see so there is a chance we won't be successful with the ingrained anti-Semites. I have to admit that the chances for the optimistic scenario happening are small. Many of the State Department employees are extremely prejudiced, as is a great part of the general U.S. population. On the other hand, I can't see refusing to open a U.S. embassy as a feasible option."

The Defense Minister nodded. "It makes sense. I still think we're making a mistake but I won't vote against it."

The Prime Minister smiled. "This is settled then."

✡✡✡

Ze'ev Hirshson was in a cheerful mood. His plan for a quiet afternoon in the office reviewing company activities was satisfying so far. The first castings for the big Dead Sea hydroelectric project were done and accepted by government inspectors. This was the first product cast at the new foundry in Refidim and clear proof that the company was capable of building its own melting and heat treating equipment – not a small achievement. The first transmission assemblies for the Merkava engines were shipped and the Sabra car was being produced in small quantities. Ze'ev was somewhat surprised that the smaller Sabra-B based on a Lancia model was the more popular. For some reason he thought that the luxury model would sell better. The main customer for the Sabra-A luxury car was, of all things, the government. Almost all of the cars they bought went overseas. The embassies in Britain, U.S., Italy and now Russia were using them.

Ze'ev paused as an idea came to him: why not develop a Stirling engine for the Merkava? It could always be used, with less power, for trucks and other heavy equipment. He made a note to discuss this idea with his V.P. for Research and Development and with the V.P. for marketing. The company was sailing into unknown waters with the automobile and engine business. Hiring a marketing specialist or a consulting company with expertise in cars might be a good idea, especially one with knowledge of marketing in the 1940s.

There was a knock on the door. “Come in,” Ze’ev yelled, somewhat annoyed by the interruption.

His secretary opened the door. “Ze’ev, your cousin David Rothstein is here. He called earlier and you promised to meet with him.”

David looked different from the last time they had met almost six months ago. It took Ze’ev a minute to figure out what it was: David looked Israeli. He was dressed casually and moved with self-assurance. When the Rothstein family got stuck in Israel due to the time travel incident Ze’ev helped his cousin settle in and set up his own consulting business. They used to meet almost every week at Ze’ev house for the family Sabbath dinner but David was too busy these days with his business, a son in the army, and moving to a new house.

“Good to see you, David! It’s been too long. How are things going?”

“Very good. The car you sold me is really great. I appreciate you letting me buy it without waiting in line.”

Ze’ev smiled. “That’s what family’s for. So what brings you here?”

“We were notified that Rachel’s maternal grandparents are immigrating from the U.S. Her mother, who is all of six years old, and two uncles who are toddlers are coming with them. I figured you might have some ideas on how to cope.”

Ze’ev nodded. “Aha, now you’ll understand what confusion is. Having relatives who died coming back to life or a parent who is suddenly a kid is a challenge.”

“True. Rachel is worried already. I’m mentally bracing for my parents moving here. It will happen sooner or later. Rachel was born in 1955, when her mother was nineteen. I clearly remember my mother-in-law when she was in her forties and I remember her maternal grandparents. Nice people but I have no idea how to even address them.”

Ze’ev shrugged. “That depends. I found it easiest to address everyone by their first name.

“What was Rachel’s grandfather doing for a living? Maybe I can help.”

“Ben had a furniture business in Delaware, a store employing five people and a facility where they rebuilt and restored old furniture and made new. That would be a good business here as well. With millions of newcomers, furniture is very difficult to come by. I bought items imported from Italy. He might need some capital to start with but I can lend him that.

“I really stopped by to ask you to have Shabbat dinner with us this week, but, of course, Rachel and Linda will have to formalize it.”

"I accept. Do you have space for the whole family?"

David smiled, "I bought the house with foresight. We have space. I didn't count on resurrected relatives but figured my sons would expand the family sooner or later."

✡✡✡

Stalin lit his pipe and enveloped himself in a cloud of aromatic Georgian tobacco smoke. "Lavrentiy, what can you tell me about these Palestinians? We are going to meet them in Teheran and I need to know as much as possible."

The other members of the State Defense Committee - Voroshilov, Malenkov and Molotov - all waited for Beria, who was seated, as usual, to the side of Stalin's desk so that he could see both the boss and the others without turning his head too much.

"Our information is somewhat limited. As you know, in 1941 we lost most of our intelligence assets in Britain and America; they were arrested within a period of several days. This makes it very difficult to obtain verified information."

Stalin waved his pipe. "Beria, stop with the excuses already. What do you know?"

"I'm not trying to excuse anything. We need to understand that the information we have comes from two sources: the First Secretary of the Palestinian legation and a couple of agents we infiltrated with the Jews going to Palestine.

"The First Secretary, Avram Zaretzky, is an old member of the Party. We verified his identity with Leopold Trepper of the Red Orchestra. The two infiltrators are giving us information that is essentially identical to Zaretzky's."

All present nodded. They all knew the name of Leopold Trepper, the man who ran the "Red Orchestra".

"Zaretzky told us that the Jews in Palestine invented something, or some things, that allow them to obtain images of the front lines and to gather German communications and decrypt them very quickly. They also tricked the Fascists into exiling all European Jews to Palestine, so now they have a substantial population. This is the essence of what we know. Regrettably, Zaretzky isn't an engineer and is not privy to technical secrets. We are now looking into additional sources.

"They were of such serious help to the British that they were granted independence. Of course, they had to threaten the British imperialists with an uprising first.

"Most of the information we're getting from the two agents we infiltrated with the emigrants is contained in letters they send to their 'relatives' here. These agents report a quickly developing country with millions of Jews, mostly recent arrivals. Conditions are tough but they're building housing, roads and factories. Regrettably we only infiltrated two agents since most our Jewish employees are known as such and would have been exposed very quickly."

Stalin smoked in silence for a while. "So what are your recommendations for dealing with the Palestinians?"

Before Beria could respond Molotov stirred in his seat. "Our ambassador in London was approached by the Palestinian ambassador there. They suggest establishment of full diplomatic relations and an embassy in Jerusalem."

"When did that happen?"

"I got the note on my way here."

Stalin smiled. "Good, this is an opportunity. An embassy there will get reliable information useful in Teheran. Molotov, arrange this as fast as you can. Beria, I want your best people to be ready. We will need all the best equipment to eavesdrop on these yokels. Or maybe they're not yokels at all. We'll see."

"Our ambassador to London thinks very highly of them," Molotov added. "He had several meetings with their ambassador - they call the country 'Israel' - and was impressed. I heard from sources at the British Foreign Office that Churchill has a high opinion of them as well. Apparently their help to the British army in North Africa was substantial and contributed in a major way to their defeat of the German army."

"They also consider themselves an equal member of the alliance against the Hitlerites," Beria interjected.

Stalin nodded. "They have some justification for that."

✡✡✡

"You have several choices," the regiment liaison officer said. "The doctors certified your medical profile as temporary 80% and the report says that it should be 97% within another couple of months. You can go to NCO school or join the armor school and help train new soldiers." She looked at a paper in front of her. "Your company commander strongly recommends the NCO school. By the rules you can't be promoted unless you graduate from the Non-Commissioned Officers School."

Wolf Frumin nodded. "I understand that. How long is the NCO course?"

"It's a short course - six weeks for sergeant training." The lieutenant smiled. "After that you'll be fit for a Company First Sergeant or to go on to officer training."

Wolf ignored the bit about officer training. "This means I won't be able to return to my unit for months."

"You may not be able to return to your unit anyway. If you go as an instructor to the armor school you'll need to be trained for four weeks and the instructor stint is at least four months long. If you really want to go back to your unit I would advise you to go to the NCO school. Your company needs a first sergeant; the position has been open for a while and they will probably wait for you. I'll have to notify them as soon as you decide. If you wash out all bets are off."

"What are the chances of me failing to course?"

"Judging by your commanding officer's recommendations and your latest evaluations, you'll graduate."

"I would like to think about this. When do I have to give you an answer?"

"Two weeks would be nice if you want to go to the NCO school. I have to reserve a place for you. Don't ignore the officer school option either. You will likely make a good armor officer and it would be a waste of your abilities not to become an officer. The country needs you."

✡✡✡

"Vladimir, my promise to you and your staff stands. We will shield you from the Soviet government." The Israeli Foreign Minister nodded for emphasis. "You will have to vacate the embassy building. I know that some of your staff are living there."

The former Russian ambassador to Israel smiled. "I'm glad I made that deal with you last year. Can I bother you for one more favor?"

The Foreign Minister nodded. "Sure, go ahead."

"I would like to have permanent residence and work permits for myself and my staff. As soon as Stalin establishes his embassy here we can't be diplomats anymore and I don't want to be caught up in the immigration bureaucracy," the Russian said.

"Vladimir, as long as you are a citizen of the Russian Federation you are a target and vulnerable to the Soviets. You will also be able to leave Israel only as stateless person. Why not take Israeli citizenship?"

"You would give it to us?" Vladimir sounded surprised.

"We will on one condition: you promise never to have any contact with the Soviets. If you do you'll be considered a spy with all the ensuing consequences."

Vladimir extended his hand. "I will shake on this. Thank you.

"Can you tell me where the Soviet embassy will be?"

The Foreign Minister smiled. "Where the rest of them will be: in our capital, Jerusalem."

✡✡✡

Dan McKenzie, the former United States ambassador to Israel, felt uneasy. He was waiting for the Israeli Foreign Minister. It was strange not to be the representative of a superpower or, for that matter, not to be an official diplomat.

The Foreign Minister came into the conference room. "Hi, Dan. How are you doing?"

"Good. I assume that there's something you wanted to discuss with me." Dan McKenzie smiled.

"Yes, we're establishing full bilateral relations with the U.S. This has implications for you and your staff."

"The U.S. is going to establish an embassy here?"

"Yes," the Foreign Minister responded. "They will choose from a selection of sites in Jerusalem."

"But we already have an embassy here, in Tel Aviv," McKenzie said.

"The building in Tel Aviv is owned by the State of Israel and was leased to the U.S. in 1966."

"I don't understand," McKenzie responded.

"It's simple. In this timeline the U.S. is not going to build an embassy compound in Tel Aviv that will open in 1966 on land leased from Israel. All embassies will be located in Jerusalem."

"This is impossible. The United States doesn't recognize Jerusalem as Israel's capital."

The Foreign Minister smiled. "Dan, you mean that the United States that you represented didn't recognize Jerusalem as our capital. I can assure you that the current U.S. will make no such mistake. Neither will any other country. But this is not a matter you need to concern yourself with. I invited you here because you and a significant number of your staff are American citizens holding diplomatic passports. Those passports are null and void unless re-issued by the Roosevelt administration. We accept our responsibility for bringing you to this time, though it wasn't intentional, and issued you work permits. Now you will have to make a choice: either apply for American or Israeli citizenship or become stateless persons. If you or any of your staff choose to remain American citizens you will lose your work permits and have to leave."

Dan McKenzie looked surprised. "Are you saying that we have to decide whether to accept Israeli citizenship or leave? Does this decision apply only to diplomats or to all Americans in Israel?"

"It applies to all the Americans. To have a permanent work permit you have to be a citizen of Israel. As a stateless person you will also be allowed to work here.

"The current U.S. administration doesn't know you from Adam. We can help by certifying to the U.S. authorities that you are a U.S. citizen. We will allow you to stay here until the process is finished, at which point you will have to leave for the U.S. if you're granted citizenship.

"We are offering the same deal to all the foreigners transported during the time travel event, whether diplomats or not. If you need clarifications, contact my office."

✡✡✡

The atmosphere in the room was tense as the Fuehrer stood looking at a map of Austria.

"General Halder, what are you doing to destroy the enemy infesting Innsbruck and Klagenfurt?"

Halder hesitated. He was prepared for this moment. The troops were on high alert and ready to take over the capital, but he still felt uncomfortable saying something that might precipitate the need for action.

There was a knock on the door. It opened a crack and a Wehrmacht captain poked his head in. "A message for the Fuehrer." Hitler nodded, the door opened wider and an SS sergeant entered, saluted and handed an envelope to Hitler. Hitler read the message. His face turned white and then red.

"So, General Halder, speak up," he yelled.

"My Fuehrer, there is nothing we can do against this enemy. I would like to remind you that they destroyed an Army Group within a couple of days and we could do nothing."

Hitler spluttered, "Are you proposing to do nothing? This amounts to surrender and treason! Are you one of the traitors that did this?" He waved the message in Halder's face and threw it on top of the map.

Halder picked it up and read it out loud: "Reichsführer of the SS Heinrich Himmler was assassinated at noon today by a rocket hitting his home. The chief of the Gestapo was assassinated this morning by means of an explosive device under his car."

"My Fuehrer, none of us are traitors and none of us are assassins," Halder said quietly. "We are all German patriots and would lay down our lives for Germany."

Hitler visibly took control of his emotions. "What do you suggest we do about the enemy infesting Austria?"

Halder took a deep breath, "We suggest suing for peace. If they decide to attack, we can't stop them. This is also true for the combined British and French forces. At this point it's not too late to achieve a honorable peace."

"Peace? With the Judeo-Bolsheviks that scared you at Innsbruck? General Halder you are dismissed. The Gestapo and the SA will look into your treasonous activities. Guards!"

The door opened and a detail of Wehrmacht soldiers entered.

Hitler looked at them with surprise. "Where are my SS guards?"

Halder took a step forward and pointed at Hitler. "Captain, arrest this man as a traitor to Germany. Take him to the Spandau Prison. They have a special cell ready for him."

The captain clicked his heels, saluted and put handcuffs on the surprised Hitler. The Fuehrer was escorted, not too gently, downstairs and into a waiting military command car.

Halder turned to the others present. "Gentlemen, I hereby declare Germany to be under martial law. The ruling body, for the time being, will consist of a military committee with a civilian at its head.

"As we have agreed previously, the civilian head of the Emergency Committee for the Welfare of Germany is Carl Goerdeler. The following generals will be members: Franz Halder, Ervin Rommel, Erick von Manstein and Günther von Kluge.

"The first order of the Committee is as follows: All known agents of the Gestapo and SA are to be arrested immediately and imprisoned. The same applies to all senior Nazi party functionaries. A radio transmission announcing the new interim German government will be made within the hour."

The door opened and Field Marshall von Kluge entered. "Gentlemen, apparently word of Hitler's arrest leaked out. Several SS units, about company size, are attempting to take this building. We will see very shortly who is supporting whom in this new arrangement," he said with a predatory smile.

Halder again addressed the assembled officers. "As the Field Marshall said, soon we will know who is loyal to whom. In the meantime those of you who feel uncomfortable supporting the Committee and helping us save Germany from a disaster may stay on the sidelines. You will not be harmed as long as you don't interfere with us." This announcement caused some movement among the assembled. Several generals and a couple of colonels moved to one side of the room.

"Those who have decided not to participate are free to leave."

Before the group left, a young lieutenant burst into the room. "General Halder, sir, there's some fighting at the Spandau Prison, but it's still under Wehrmacht control. The Fuehrer, excuse me, herr Hitler has been delivered there and is being held in a solitary cell."

After that several officers in the small group opposing the coup moved back. The rest of the group left. The others got to work: telephones, radio messages and runners to units from the East Front to France notifying them of the current situation and giving orders of new dispositions.

✡✡✡

The Hirshson family assembled at the Rothstein's house in Rehovot. The living room was large enough to comfortably accommodate more than the twenty people. Most of the youngsters were in what David Rothstein called his 'study' but was in fact the room where he and Rachel enjoyed watching TV.

More than an hour was left before candle lighting and the Sabbath. The men had nothing much to do except talk. Some of the women volunteered to help in the kitchen but were promptly expelled by Rachel and Sarah, Ze'ev's grandmother.

Ze'ev's wife Linda asked Evelyn Mosowitz, "Is the transition to Israel from the U.S. very difficult for you?"

"Yes and no," Evelyn replied. "All the gadgets are bewildering, I know only a couple of words in Hebrew, but everybody is very nice. Most of the people understand English and I also speak some Yiddish so it's not too bad. You sound like a native English speaker. Are you from the U.S.?"

"I was born and raised in Detroit and came here with Ze'ev, whom I met while he was at MIT, many years ago. As to the many English speakers here, don't let it fool you into skipping the ulpan," Linda said, "especially as they're offering you a free immersive one."

"What's an ulpan?" Evelyn inquired. "Is it some kind of school?"

"Exactly. After a month or so you will be able to understand most of what the natives say and to respond in Hebrew. The immersive part is important: you speak nothing but Hebrew for the duration. It's very effective." She was about to add more but was interrupted by one of the Shaviv kids who ran into the room and shouted: "The TV says there is important news from Europe."

The TV was tuned to Channel One, normally broadcasting children's programs in preparation for the Sabbath. The broadcast had been interrupted. "...This is all the news we have for now. Again, approximately two hours ago, German radio interrupted its regularly scheduled broadcasts and announced that Germany is now under full martial law. The government has been replaced by what they call 'The Emergency Committee for the Welfare of Germany'. The new government is removing the Nazi party from power and suing for peace. This is all we know. We will now return to our scheduled programming. More details in the news magazine at nine this evening."

The room was quiet for a minute. Then Tzila Frumin said, "Maybe Wolf will not have to go back to Austria?"

"It's likely that by the time he's ready to go, the fighting will be over. But don't build up your hopes. A lot can go wrong and they might need him elsewhere," Ze'ev responded.

After the meal was mostly finished Jacob addressed Ze'ev. "I had a discussion with Uncle Chaim about a new business. He doesn't agree with me. Let's see what you think: I want to start a computer manufacturing company. Many small mom and pop establishments assemble computers but the market is wide open for mass production. I think this is an opportunity, especially since computers are so hard to come by."

Before Ze'ev could respond Noam Shaviv intervened. "Does that mean that I need to look for a new surveying firm?"

"No, no," Jacob responded. "The idea is that Chaim will continue to run the surveying company just like he does now. I will start a new business but will be available to help with the surveying if necessary. We have several licensed surveyors working for us now, so that shouldn't be a problem."

Ze'ev smiled. "Do you intend to run the company from your college dorm?"

"I have a small apartment next to the university, not a dorm room. Why? Is this important?"

Ze'ev shook his head. "Just an out of time reference. Many years in the future there was a young man who went to college and started such a company from his dorm room. His name was Michael Dell. He became a billionaire.

"It's a great idea, but you'll have to overcome supply problems. Storage media, displays, and other parts are in short supply."

"I guess I'll have to read up on how Dell did it and try to apply his lessons to the current situation. It's hard to argue with success."

Ben Mosowitz joined the conversation. "How difficult is it to start a business here?"

"Net very," Jacob responded, "but it depends on what kind of business. My surveying business or Noam's architectural firm require specific licensing. A computer business does not, except for registration and a general business license. Every company also needs to be registered, but the process is simple."

"I'm hoping to make and sell furniture."

Ze'ev nodded. "I don't see a problem. My advice would be to set up the manufacturing first. It may not be as easy as it seems since you'll likely have to import most of the wood. I can help with that. After you start making furniture you will have no trouble selling it. The market is starved. Our population grew explosively and the existing manufacturers can't cope. You could also import furniture. The problem is from where? Europe is mostly busy with the war and doesn't have sources of high quality mass produced furniture anyway. The U.S. might be a source but transportation would be expensive.

"Did you do your design your furniture in the U.S.?"

Ben shook his head. "Most of the time I just copied popular designs."

"You can do that here too, but you might be more successful if you add original designs to your selection. My youngest son, Benjamin, is a men's clothing designer and knows other designers. When the time comes he might help you find a good one."

✡✡✡

Gad Yaari, Chief of General Staff, Zvi Kaplan, Chief of Military Intelligence, and the head of the Mossad entered Nitzan Liebler's office.

"Gentlemen," the Minister of Defense said, "I need an update on the situation in Germany. I also want to hear what you think we need to do about it."

Zvi Kaplan started. "Events went almost as planned. The Generals arrested Hitler and announced a new regime, as we agreed with the Brits.

The execution of the coup was somewhat inept. Three days after the announcement they're still moving forces and haven't taken control of important objectives."

"If you remember," the head of the Mossad interjected, "I warned against exactly this kind of fiasco. They had to coordinate a military coup in a dictatorship where many of their co-conspirators were loyal to the Nazis. I recommended weakening the Nazis apparatus more before precipitating a coup."

Zvi Kaplan fidgeted in his seat but it was his boss, Gad Yaari, that responded. "It's pointless to assign blame now. At the time the consensus was we couldn't kill more Nazis without provoking Hitler into executing the generals he suspected. In any case, we never had fine control over the situation."

The Defense Minister nodded agreement. "I want to know what the situation is now, as detailed as you can make it without taking all day."

"It's a mess," the Head of the Mossad said. "The Army took control of most of the airfields, so the true believers of the Luftwaffe are neutralized. On the other hand, there is fighting in the streets of almost every major city in Germany. There are large numbers of Nazis and Nazi sympathizers in the Army, and it will take a while to clean those out."

The Chief of Military Intelligence agreed. "Just today the Committee announced that all military personnel supporting them should wear armbands with the old Weimar Republic tricolor flag on it.

"There's also trouble from the expected sources: Gestapo headquarters in almost every city are centers of resistance, as are Nazi party headquarters and SS bases. The generals are planning on dealing with those but they're doing it slowly. We think," he nodded at the head of the Mossad, "that this is due to the relative unreliability of their own troops."

"In other words are you saying that Germany is fighting a civil war?" Liebler asked.

The Chief of the General Staff nodded. "That is partly correct. Our estimate is that the non-Nazi forces are much stronger and will eventually overcome the Nazis. The fighting should be mostly over within a couple of months. It will leave Germany weaker and may open the way for Stalin to get into Western Europe."

"Any recommendations as to how to avoid that?" the Defense Minister wanted to know.

"I'm not sure we need to do anything extraordinary," the head of the Mossad said. "We do need to insure that there are firm agreements with the Soviets about where future borders will be in Europe. I think they will keep their agreements. Stalin always did, as long as he perceived the other parties to any agreement as both strong and resolute."

The Chief of General Staff added, "There's also the consideration that the German High Command is not entirely stupid and will do its best to keep the Eastern Front stable. They know that for now there's nothing to fear from the West."

✡✡✡

The Foreign Minister knew he didn't have the expertise to decide on the issue in front of him and had called for a meeting of experts. There were several people at the conference table.

"I need a clear analysis of what planes to start using to supply our embassies in Europe and Russia," the Minister began. "We have been using the ship that picks up immigrants from the port of Sochi in the Soviet Union to haul supplies to the legation, but from Sochi it's a long way by unreliable trains. We also need a secure delivery line with no interference from their intelligence, who open every shipment that goes by rail. We also need a secure and fast connection to our London embassy."

The man in an air force uniform was the first to respond. "I'm assuming that you want to use period aircraft?"

"I'm not sure, but we don't want to use modern jets. Something with a propeller would be good."

The Aircraft Industries representative said, "The most reliable propeller driven plane we have available is the C130 Hercules. It will get some attention. It's a turboprop and in Russia they will be extremely interested."

"What other alternatives do we have?"

"We have the Arava, but it can't reach Moscow without refueling," the IAI rep said.

The air force officer smiled. "We still have a couple of DC-4s and DC-3s in a museum somewhere. Either one will get to Moscow but whichever you chose it will have to be seriously refurbished, especially the engines."

The historian had said nothing and now fidgeted in his seat. "The Soviets are actually building some licensed DC-3 derivatives as the Lisunov Li-2. It will not draw any attention there."

"Of course the price you pay for anonymity is a very slow and uncomfortable plane," the IAI rep said.

"How long will it take you to get the two planes ready to fly reliably?" the Foreign Minister wanted to know.

"We'll have to examine them to give you a time frame, but I don't think it will take longer then several weeks."

✡✡✡

Admiral King looked worried. "Colonel," he hesitated, "Shaviv, are you telling me that the positions of all the submarines on this map are accurate as of two hour ago? How can that be?"

Colonel Oren Shaviv, the Israeli military attaché to Washington, shrugged. "Admiral, they were accurate two hours ago and are getting less so as we speak. We have the means to track this sort of information quite easily. Locating six Japanese submarines in three locations along the West coast is not such a big deal. If you tell me which ones you wish to attack I can give you updated positions every forty minutes or so."

"It would be a breach of our security to tell a foreign power what we're going to do. We very seldom share operational information even with the British navy."

"Feel free to keep it secret," the Colonel said. "We will know which ones you sink when they disappear from our scans anyway."

"What the heck." Admiral King's expression was both sour and resigned. "We are allies and you probably know more about our operations than I do. I want to attack the three submarines on station outside the port of San Diego. So please keep updating their coordinates," he looked at his watch, "starting two hours from now. They should be destroyed in three hours. If your information is accurate.

"Do you have anything else for me today?"

Colonel Shaviv took out a typed page from his briefcase. "As you know, the Japanese switched to a new cipher yesterday. This is a message we intercepted this morning local Philippines time. The new cipher is at the top of the page." He handed the page and a photograph to King.

The admiral read it. "What the …! They're bringing more forces to Mindoro. Is McArthur asleep at the wheel? His air patrols should have seen them already." King stopped to look at the photograph. "Very good, I really appreciate this. I will let McArthur know where the Japanese transports are, after our naval forces in the area take care of them. That way the arrogant son…cannot interfere."

"Admiral, maybe we can establish a more efficient way of doing this. By the time I come here on my daily visit some of the information is already stale. I'm also taking up an inordinate amount of your time."

King nodded. "I understand that you have, probably, better things to do than waste a couple of hours every day on an old curmudgeon, but I find our sessions interesting. My interest may not last very long, but as long as it does I hope you'll accommodate me. Oh, and please tell General Marshall the same thing. I know he's trying to pump you for information but he'll figure out very soon what I figured out already."

"What's that admiral?"

"That you say only what you want to say and not one word more."

✡✡✡

The Israeli DC-3 was coming in to land at the Bykovo airport in Moscow. The Soviet authorities had refused a landing permit at the much closer Frunze Central Aerodrome. They claimed that the aerodrome was not safe for such a big plane. It was an obvious lie but the new Israeli ambassador said nothing. He suspected that the real reason was a hope on the part of the Soviet security police that if the Israelis had to haul whatever arrived on the plane from Bykovo the police would have a better chance to look at it and, maybe, learn something.

After the plane was on the ground and had taxied to the primitive terminal, it's modified cargo door opened and two cars rolled out: a Sabra-A and a Sabra-B. Both were second generation: no more Fiat and Lancia bodywork. The Sabra-A was copied from a 21st century Lincoln Town car; The Sabra-B was a facsimile of a late model 21st century Subaru. The suspensions were still a work in progress and too soft for serious driving but perfect for the broken streets of Moscow. Both cars carried prominent Israel flags – no mistaking that these were diplomat's vehicles. Diplomatic plates, issued a week earlier by the Soviet Commissariat for Foreign Affairs, were also affixed to both cars.

Several suitcases and large boxes, all with diplomatic seals, were also unloaded and put into the cars. The ambassador, who met the plane, got into the limousine and the two car convoy drove off.

The DC-3 was refueled and left an hour later. Avram Zaretzky, the supposed First Secretary of the old Palestinian legation, left on the outgoing flight. Being a polite man he had told his contact, Boris Andreyev, the day before that he was going to leave and another man would take his place. Andreyev was visibly annoyed. "Who is going to take your place. Can you give me the name of the new First Secretary?"

"I have no idea," Zaretzky responded with a smile. "They didn't tell me."

"I want you to contact me as soon as you get back home. I will need a steady flow of information from you."

"What kind of information, comrade Andreyev? It may be better if you ask me questions and I'll try answering them."

"Maybe. In any case, I need you to contact me first to establish a communications routine. You should know best how to establish communications discretely and safely."

Zaretzky nodded. "I will do my best."

✡✡✡

Merkulov, the head of the NKVD security service, and his underling Andreyev waited patiently. The room was small and drab. Beria's suite at the Kremlin was smaller than that of the other members of the Politburo. He had a much nicer suite and office on the Garden Ring – the loop road around the center of Moscow - and rarely did any business at his Kremlin office.

The receptionist picked up the intercom and, after replacing the handset, told the two to enter the inner office.

Beria was sitting behind his desk and let them stand for a short while. Finally he put aside the paper he had been reading and pointed to a couple of simple wooden chairs. "Sit and tell me what brought you here."

Merkulov nodded to Andreyev. "Comrade Commissar, as you know, yesterday the Israelis brought their first transport with goods for their new embassy. The same plane also took back the old legation's First Secretary, who was our source. He will stay in touch.

"We observed several unusual things about the plane. It was a modified DC-3 with a large cargo door in place of the passenger one and some kind of arrangement that allowed two automobiles to be unloaded with just a couple of people pushing them.

"We never saw such cars before. The shape is…" Andreyev hesitated, "strange or maybe futuristic." He put several photographs in front of Beria. "And they drove in almost absolute silence."

Beria studied the photographs with interest. "What does it say on the back of the trunk?"

Andreyev pulled out a magnifying glass from his briefcase. "On the left it says 'Consolidated', on the right 'Sabra-A'."

"Never heard of such a brand." Beria looked at the photographs again. "The shape does look strange."

Merkulov spoke for the first time in the conversation. "When they asked two days ago for a fuel allotment I instructed the liaison to tell them that we have only five liters of gasoline to give them. They responded that they'll take any liquid fuel for their cars, so I authorized some kerosene and some diesel in addition to the gasoline. They accepted it."

Beria shrugged. "They'll probably sell the kerosene and diesel on the black market to buy gasoline. When they do we will have something on them. Good thinking, Merkulov.

"One thing puzzles me. Do they make their own automobiles? If so, we may have seriously underestimated them. Keep investigating. I want to know what's going on with this State of Israel, Palestine, whatever."

The red telephone on his desk started ringing. Beria waved to Merkulov and Andreyev to get out.

Alexander Nikolaevich Poskrebyshev, Stalin's personal secretary, was on the line. "The leader wants you here in an hour with the two files you were supposed to prepare." The line went dead.

Beria both despised and feared Poskrebyshev. The man was smart, didn't mind taking action and had been close to Stalin for many years. Beria opened a drawer in his desk, pulled out two bound files, stuffed them into his briefcase, and left.

Forty minutes later he entered the anteroom of the leader's suite of offices. Soon Vyacheslav Mikhailovich Molotov, the People's Commissar for Foreign Affairs, joined Beria in the waiting room. They nodded to each other. Molotov took a seat at the farthest end of the room from Beria.

It was Beria's job to spy on everyone, especially people close to the top. He enjoyed the fear he provoked in people but was somewhat apprehensive, if not outright afraid, of those who were personally close to Stalin and under the leader's protection. Beria didn't like fear and hated those who evoked it. One could always hope that a protégé would slip up but the chances of this happening with Molotov were too small for Beria's taste. Beria was hopeful that the upcoming meeting might create an opportunity for him to undermine Molotov and maybe, in the future, topple him.

Twenty minutes later the inner door opened and a guard beckoned for the two to come in. Poskrebyshev got up from his desk, knocked on the door to the inner office and stuck his head in. He opened the door wider, beckoned for the other two to follow him, and entered.

Stalin was seated behind his desk with a benign expression, stuffing his pipe, usually a sign that the leader was in a congenial mood. He gestured to the chairs arranged in front of the desk. The three took their seats and waited.

"Molotov, you asked for this meeting. What is it?" Stalin lit his pipe and puffed a couple of times.

"I wanted your approval of my choice for our ambassador to Israel. I think it's an important post and we need just the right man for it." He paused, waiting for Stalin's response.

Stalin's left eyebrow climbed up in a somewhat mocking expression. "According to Beria it's not all that important. How important can an ambassadorship to a small country of sand and camels be?"

Molotov shrugged at Beria. "Shall I tell the leader or will you?"

Beria didn't look amused. "Yesterday the first direct transport flight arrived with cargo for their embassy. A DC-3 brought two cars. They rolled them out directly from the plane. My engineers tell me that this required a significant and very advanced modification of the frame." He looked at Molotov, who smiled beatifically, or as beatifically as his normally stern expression would allow.

"Here are pictures of the modified plane. The cars were also very interesting," Beria said as he put several more photographs on Stalin's desk. "As you can see, they look different from anything else we have ever seen. We couldn't identify the make or model. They must be manufactured locally. My people also tell me that they are absolutely silent."

Stalin carefully examined the photographs then pushed them over to Poskrebyshev. Molotov said, "I suspected that Beria's estimate of their abilities was somewhat simplistic. Whatever these Palestinians are, they are not living in a country of sand and camels."

"Yes, I think that Beria underestimated them. So who do you propose sending there?"

"I have two candidates. I gave the names to Beria so as not to waste time.

"The two are Boris Yefimovich Shtein and Semyon Ivanovich Aralov. Shtein is an excellent analyst, especially in economics, and has experience in our foreign service. He served as an ambassador to several small countries. He is currently serving in Moscow.

"Aralov is different. He has military experience and used to be the chief of the GRU, the military intelligence service. He also served as an ambassador, so has diplomatic experience. There is one difficulty with him: In 1937 he was relieved of all his duties and appointed to manage the Cultural Museum in Moscow."

Stalin looked at Beria, who pulled out two files. "I carefully studied both of them and have no idea what Yezhov had against Aralov. I don't mind appointing Shtein, but there are two things against him: we urgently need intelligence from Israel and this isn't his forte. Also he is Jewish and I don't know if we can trust him to do his job properly in a Jewish state."

"So you would prefer Aralov. What is your preference?" Stalin asked Molotov.

Molotov shrugged, "Either one is fine with me."

Stalin nodded, "Aralov it is."

Chapter 13
January 1943

"Gentlemen, I want a status report." General Halder, the head of the OKH and a senior member of the Committee for the Welfare of Germany, nodded at Admiral Canaris. "Admiral, will you do the honors, please?"

"The Abwehr is now primarily concerned with collecting intelligence on the Nazis. Our secondary target is the general population.

"I will start with the general population. Two weeks ago the mood of the country was very dark. The damage from the nightly bombing raids on our cities couldn't be denied. Hamburg is a burned out shell and a large part of Berlin is in ruins, as are most of the other major cities. Even Hitler's propaganda machine couldn't conceal the fact that our forces were being pushed back in France and that Austria was successfully invaded.

"The popular mood is much better now, mostly due the pause in bombing raids. There is also some optimism that we can negotiate an acceptable peace.

"We expected that with the popular support we're enjoying the Nazi resistance would dissipate. Regrettably it is not so. Our main difficulty is that our own Wehrmacht troops are not completely reliable. Some of our soldiers and officers are members of the Nazi party and there are even more sympathizers. In every fight with the Nazis we have to always look behind us – is the guy at our back friend or foe?

"Identification armbands help, but the Nazis are devious and sometimes use our colors.

"On the plus side, honest soldiers vastly outnumber Nazis and when we confront them face to face we always win. The maniacs fight to the bitter end, partly because our own soldiers sometimes kill Nazi prisoners.

"This is the general situation. Details are in the reports you have."

General Halder nodded at Field Marshal von Kluge. "Can you give us a summary of what's going on at the fronts?"

"Certainly. The situation is very simple. There is no activity on the French or Austrian fronts. The Eastern Front is relatively quiet. Our intelligence indicates a Russian buildup in the north – around Leningrad.

"Since the French front is so quiet and the British stopped bombing, we need to move at least ten divisions from France, half of them to reinforce the Eastern Front and half to finish off the Nazi resistance. We have negligible forces in Austria. If the Jewish force there decides to move, our chances of stopping them are small, so we left only observers in place."

Halder looked at the others in the conference room. The OKH was much calmer these days with Hitler gone. The assembled generals seemed to agree with von Kluge.

"Rommel, you will have to take charge of the Home Front. We need to finish this civil war nonsense as quickly as possible. Berlin is already clean of this garbage. As agreed, we need to pacify the large cities first. You will implement the strategy we devised."

Rommel rose from his seat. "I accept this appointment and will do my best. I will need at least a month to six weeks to pacify the country. My only doubt is whether the de facto ceasefire with the Western allies will last that long."

Carl Goerdeler spoke for the first time. "As the civilian head of this government I took it upon myself to contact the British. They assured me that both they and the Israelis will wait as long as necessary. They also warned me that they will know of any breach of good faith by us and will immediately resume hostilities. I was given to understand that in such a case only unconditional surrender would be acceptable."

"What about the Soviets?" asked von Kluge.

"No one will guarantee quiet on the Eastern Front," Goerdeler responded, "until after their summit. I don't know where and when this is going to happen."

✡✡✡

The President carefully got up from his chair and carefully made several steps holding on to the edge of his desk. He didn't do this very often; it was difficult. His doctor urged him to exercise his legs as often as he could without overdoing it and he tried to abide by the instructions, including swimming when he could. The whole thing was still amazingly new to him – after so many years of being confined to a wheel chair it was exhilarating to be able to walk even a few steps.

Harry Hopkins entered the room and the President returned to his chair.

The Foreign Secretary and the Secretary of War entered, took their seats, and waited for the President to start.

"Gentlemen, I think that it's time we send an ambassador to Israel," the President began. "We didn't bother when they setup their embassy here. If you remember," he looked at Cordell Hull, "you were against an embassy in a third-rate country, especially as this might offend our friends in Saudi Arabia and elsewhere. The situation has changed. Israel is providing us with vital intelligence. Or am I wrong?" FDR looked at the Secretary of War.

"I don't know about vital but it definitely helps us against Japan. Just a week ago they gave us the coordinates of three submarines that were lurking close to the West coast. We destroyed them. They also warned us of a reinforcement transport bound for the Philippine island of Mindoro. The navy took care of it. It seems that McArthur's command missed them completely. If they had landed, re-taking Mindoro would have become that much more difficult."

The Secretary of State carefully inspected his manicured fingernails. "I still don't know whether it's wise to appoint an ambassador. We really don't want to upset the Saudis and endanger our oil holdings there. Their production isn't significant right now but sources in ARAMCO tell me that they have oil reserves that might be useful in the future. I see no significant advantage to having an embassy in Israel."

FDR deliberately inserted a fresh cigarette in his holder and lit it before responding. "Cordell, did you hear all the rumors about Israel having travelled here from the distant future?"

"Sure. The yellow press was awash for a while with those stupid rumors. What does it matter?"

"If it's true we need to collect information and learn about future science and technology. Just being able to go to a public library there may be enormously beneficial. Having an embassy makes all that easier."

Secretary Stimson shrugged. "Mr. President, if you've already made a decision, why discuss it with us?"

"Always blunt and to the point, Stimson. In fact I wanted to hear objections. Cordell presented the standard State position, which is a bit out of date. We are going to have an ambassador in Israel. How about appointing Hermann Baruch?"

Stimson nodded. Cordell Hull shook his head and said, "Mr. President, I appreciate that Mr. Baruch is a great supporter of the Democratic Party and of you personally. On the other hand, he is Jewish and I would have some doubts about having him represent the interests of the United States in a Jewish country. It is only natural to think so. As you know my wife is Jewish and I'm not prejudiced against Jews."

"I know you're not prejudiced, Cordell. Do you have anybody else in mind?"

The Secretary of State nodded. "We have a very gifted man in Egypt. He's our Ambassador in Cairo and is accredited to Saudi Arabia. He has been in the service of the Department of State since 1915 and served, among other places, as Embassy Counselor and Consul General in Moscow and as Chargé d'affaires in Berlin beginning in May of 1939. He became the senior officer in Germany after we recalled our ambassador because of Kristallnacht. From Berlin he was appointed Embassy Counselor in Rome and from there to his current post in Cairo."

Harry Hopkins, who was silent up to this point, stirred in his seat. "I remember Kirk from his stint in Moscow. He was our senior man there for nine months in between Ambassadors Davies and Steinhardt. I agree, he's a good man."

The President nodded. "Okay, so Kirk will be our man in Israel. Please inform him and make it clear that he needs to take up his post without delay."

✡✡✡

The old Arava turboprop, refurbished and freshly painted, landed at the airstrip in Mehrabad near Teheran without incident. The aerodrome was primitive, with a small control tower and short runways. The place had belonged to an aviation club established in 1938. Since the British-Soviet takeover of Iran it was mostly abandoned. Recently the landing strip had been improved by the British to accommodate the B24 Liberator used by Winston Churchill.

The Arava unloaded a platoon of Israeli soldiers and several engineers. Their job was to examine the landing strip and make it safe for larger aircraft.

The three engineers spent the rest of the day inspecting the tarmac landing strip. It was a bit short and wouldn't withstand many jet landings. The leader of the team connected to headquarters through a geostationary satellite and transferred images, measurements and a recommendation to make the landing strip longer and wider.

The next morning two Israeli Air Force C130s landed. They managed to stop at the very end of the short strip, where one of them disgorged a bulldozer, a grader, and a roller - equipment to lengthen and widen the strip. The work was finished by the evening of the second day with three crews working non-stop.

The whole length of the strip was also sprayed with a stabilizer to make landing a jet safe, at least for a while. The C130 Hercules took off with the crews and their equipment, leaving the Arava and a platoon of Israeli soldiers behind. Also left behind were several Sabra cars and a small group of security personnel.

The second C130 Hercules carrying a paratrooper company, a couple of observation drones with their communication truck, as well as a truck for the troops and some other equipment, stayed parked close by.

The security people left the strip in one of the cars and drove to Teheran. They were met by the Israeli representative to the court of Muhammad Reza Shah Pahlavi. The diplomat led them to a small complex of buildings behind a tall wall close to the center of Teheran which had been the German embassy, soon to become the Israeli embassy.

The security team examined the buildings and prepared them for the Prime Minister and other attendees. They also called for the paratrooper company and the drone control truck to move into the compound.

The last step was for one of the security team members to visit the conference venue. The Soviets insisted that the conference be held at their sprawling compound. Churchill wasn't happy with this and the Israeli Prime Minster flatly refused. It took a week to negotiate an alternative venue.

The venue agreed upon was the former French embassy. It was smaller than the other embassies but adequate for the purpose. After the conference the Free French government was supposed to take possession of the building.

It was guarded by British and Soviet soldiers who now were joined by Israeli paratroopers. An Israeli security man walked through the building. He was followed none too politely by a Soviet NKVD agent and a curious MI6 one. The Israeli pretended not to understand Russian. The NKVD man spoke English fluently but with a strange accent and the Israeli pretended to have difficulty understanding him. The Israeli admired the furniture, the drapes and the general décor of the former French embassy. He managed to leave behind bugs without alerting the Soviet secret police officer. The NKVD as well as MI6 and Israeli security each swept the building for such invasive plants several times a day but only their own equipment showed the Israeli bugs.

✡✡✡

Jacob Hirshson tried to relax with a book on the couch in his living room. His house in Refidim was well lived in, the furniture used but in very good shape. It wasn't easy to find furniture in a country whose population had more than doubled in just over a year.

Jacob found himself spending less time in Beer Sheva at the university and more in Refidim. His uncle Chaim was running the surveying company, leaving Jacob free to study civil engineering, but he was distracted and restless. The idea of setting up a computer business looked more and more appealing.

After half an hour of trying to read the book, Jacob started, again, checking numbers in the latest version of his business plan. It looked good to him. There really was no need to procrastinate. It was time to take action.

The doorbell chimed and Jacob heard his mother greeting his friend and would-be partner Zalman Gurevich. Jacob had known Zalman for many years, since they were youngsters in Vilna before the war. Jacob trusted Zalman and told him about his idea to build and sell computer. Zalman was excited. His only experience in sales was at his small grocery store in Vilna, inherited from his father. Zalman believed he could sell anything. Computers seemed modern, exotic and exciting.

He came into the living room and threw himself onto one of the armchairs. “Jacob, I found just the guy we need. He’s from Vilna, used to be an electrical technician repairing radios there. He graduated from the Refidim College in computer engineering here and has a repair shop in a strip mall on Ben Gurion Avenue. He knows how to build computers and has the space for it. We can start with him running the building operation and opening a shop to sell them.”

“Wait a minute! Before we start building and selling we need money to finance the operation.”

“That should be easy,” Zalman responded. “I see no reason why Ze’ev won’t give you a loan. I will pitch in as well.”

“Yes, Ze’ev already offered but I don’t feel comfortable taking money from him. He helped me with my surveying business and I want to start this one on my own.

“Don’t worry, Zalman. I went to the bank yesterday and they will give me a loan that should be enough to start, if we don’t have to pay for a storefront. Let’s meet with your friend and discuss this with him. I want to set up a mail-order business. Do you know how those work?”

Zalman smiled a big smile. “How do you think I’m making such a nice living now? Not by competing against the big grocery chains. I buy specialty cheese all over the country and also import items and then sell them by mail. Haven’t you seen the weekly newspaper ads for the goodies at Z&G Stores?”

“Sure I have. I didn’t know that was your business. I thought that your little specialty food store in the strip mall was what kept you busy.

“Is the stuff you are importing kosher?”

“Some is and some isn’t. There is a significant market here for non-kosher foods. The truth is that both my mother and mother-in-law gave me a hard time about selling treif. My father was unhappy too. That's one reason I'm looking to hook up with you on the computer business. Not dealing with food will be a relief."

"Let's go meet your friend now. There's no point in wasting time."

✡✡✡

Ze'ev Hirshson was both bored and bothered. Things were going too smoothly. Whatever production problems popped up, his managers solved. Even the fledgling car assembly plant was taking shape nicely. There was very little for him to do except make strategic decisions and this was the problem: There weren't that many to be made. He was bored.

When he brought this problem up with his wife, Linda told him that he has to either become lazy and just enjoy life, which she knew wasn't in his nature, or do his normal thing and make trouble for everybody. He was now looking into making trouble and thought he found the perfect venue.

Ze'ev went to visit with Consolidated's Vice President for Research and Development on the floor below. "Omer, I want to look into more vertical integration of our activities.

"I think that we need to expand into mills. If we could make our own rolled steel stock and plate, it would hugely reduce our dependence on the Italians and Americans for our cars' material. We could also start making vehicles from high strength steel alloys, which is seventy years in the future. What do you think?"

Omer Toledano knew his boss and had figured that something like this was coming. "I would need to estimate the investment necessary and the income it would generate. Steel mills are not cheap. On the face of it our car operation doesn't justify an independent mill. If we also setup a forge next to it we could make ball bearings and other standard machine parts too."

Ze'ev nodded. "There are all kinds of ways to execute this idea. You'll be the lead on this. Get marketing and finance to help you. I would like to meet in a month or so to discuss this. If it's feasible we can go ahead almost immediately. We're sitting on a pile of cash and it needs to be put to work. If not this, we'll have to think of something else.

"How about widening our technology base? I was looking into electronics and such. The field is crowded except for flat screen displays. Israel has only one company that makes them and they are expensive. The high price is in part because these guys are used to making specialized military and scientific hardware and in part because they're slow in expanding production. What do you think of entering the field of consumer grade displays?"

Omer looked surprised. "I thought you were going to suggest a computer chip fabrication facility. At least there we have some foothold through our ceramics operation."

Ze'ev smiled. "Don't be shy then. Look into both. I may be wrong but it seems to me that both Intel and AMD have an advantage over us since they design the processors and already make them. If we get into this we will be only a contract manufacturer."

"There's a place for contract manufacturers in the current market, but what about our car operation? We might yet become one of the largest in the world and a car has a number of specialized processors that are different from what Intel would want to make. We're using a small company in Rehovot to make ours. Maybe we can buy it?"

"That's an idea. Ask the Finance VP to check it out. Tell him that I really like the idea if the price is reasonable."

✡✡✡

The Boeing 737 carried the Prime Minister, Foreign Minister, Chief of General Staff, other Israeli officials and staff. The jet landed and taxied next to the parked Hercules and Arava.

By now the Israelis had a little enclave not far from the control tower. The Soviets also had a couple of aircraft parked nearby, including a Lisunov Li-2 transport (a licensed copy of a DC-3) and several Lavochkin La-5 fighters. The British contingent was the largest, with a number of Spitfires. Prime Minister Churchill's Liberator was already parked among them.

The Israelis got into the waiting Sabra cars and, with a couple of armored military escorts, drove off to their embassy.

It didn't take them very long to settle in. Less than an hour later the ministers and generals were briefed by a security agent. "Gentlemen, the building is swept for bugs twice a day. We found a lot of listening devices. They were mostly of NKVD origin but we found several made in the USA, a standard FBI model that is powered by telephone lines, and one of British origin. They look quite old and might have been planted when the building served as the German embassy. According to instructions we left one room untouched and still bugged. It's clearly marked, so be careful what you say in that room and in the ones next to it."

✡✡✡

After the briefing a clerk settled behind a desk in the "dirty room". There was a knock on the door. "Ah, Oded, just in time. Do you have anything to report on the bugging of the Soviet Embassy?"

"No, but you can tell the boss that our agent there checked in. He will see that there are bugs in all the right places."

"I thought that he's too senior to plant bugs," said the first clerk.

"He is indeed very close to the top but he also knows how to do the little things. Don't worry - you'll have your information soon."

✡✡✡

The meeting with Churchill was held in a room clean of bugs.

"Prime Minister, I'm glad to finally meet you in person," Churchill began.

"Please call me Amos. I'm honored to meet you," Amos Nir responded. "I studied your career in school. In our time you are much admired for both your political skill and principled treatment of Nazi Germany."

"Call me Winston. It's a bit strange to be told you studied me in school, but I guess I'll get used to the concept.

"I wanted to further refine our approach to Stalin. We seem to agree on most things, but I'm sure that Stalin will do his best to surprise and divide us."

"I think that we must take the initiative, surprise him and keep pressing relentlessly. This is what I propose we do…"

✡✡✡

Stalin didn't like leaving Moscow and hated flying. He came to Teheran by plane and was angry – just a general anger to be released at the first opportunity.

Poskrebyshev stuck his head around a slightly open door. "They're here."

"Let them in then."

Molotov was the first to enter, followed by Voroshilov, Beria, Zhukov, Poskrebyshev and Nikolai Vlasik, head of Stalin's bodyguard detail.

After everyone was seated General Vlasic surprised them by being the first to speak. "I have a piece of information that has to be dealt with immediately. Yesterday one of our bugs at the Israeli embassy picked up a conversation of great interest. It seems that they have an agent very high in our government and this agent is present here in Teheran."

Stalin looked at Beria. "Lavrentiy, you have anything to add?"

Beria was rigid in his seat. "The intercept is correct. It took us a couple of hours to translate it – Hebrew speakers are not very common among us. We have no idea who the agent might be but we will find him."

Stalin put his empty pipe on the desk in front of him. His moustache was bristling with anger. He was silent for a long time. Finally he said very quietly, "Beria, you are an inept idiot. You didn't bother to have a staff of Hebrew translators at a conference where Israel is a major party? Idiot! You also have no clue who the traitor might be! I'm of a mind to order Vlasic to shoot you right here and now."

All present were looking at Beria. His lower lip was trembling slightly. It wouldn't be the first time that someone was dragged from such a meeting and shot.

Molotov spoke up. "I just received a packet from our new ambassador in Jerusalem. The most important information it contains is that Israel is not what we were led to believe it was." He looked pointedly at Beria.

"Go on," Stalin said picking up his pipe. Beria relaxed visibly – If the boss played with his pipe he was not likely to order an immediate execution.

Molotov continued, "Our ambassador, Aralov, reports that Israel is an extremely advanced country. He estimates their population is many more than the six or seven million we were told they have." He looked at Beria again.

"Devices unknown to us are common there. Aralov couldn't even name most of what he has seen, but advanced automobiles and glass skyscrapers are plentiful. I prepared an executive summary." He put several pages in front of Stalin and gave copies to everyone.

It took Stalin ten minutes to read the summary and then read it again. Finally, he nodded to Molotov. "You have had the most time to think about the implications. What is your opinion?"

Molotov was prepared – Here was a double opportunity. "Despite what comrade Beria led us to believe, I think Israel can be a valuable ally but a very, very dangerous adversary. We need to be careful not to alienate them and, above all, not to make them into an enemy. Some careful diplomacy will be necessary."

Beria saw the danger to himself. "I suggest calm for the moment. We shouldn't decide anything based on a report from a person who has been in the country for only a couple of days. We will have more information from Aralov and his team within a week and then have a much better understanding of what we are facing." This wasn't a solution to his problem but the proposition, if accepted, would give him at least a week's grace.

Voroshilov stirred in his seat. "It may sound strange, but I agree with both of you. We should be careful but there's no need to rush."

Stalin said nothing, smoking his pipe and thinking. Finally after a long silence he said, "We know exactly what we want from this conference. I want to achieve our goals no matter what. Molotov, devise a diplomatic approach. In tomorrow's meetings I will introduce our demands and you will keep up the diplomatic pressure to achieve them.

"Beria, your highest priority is to find the traitor. It shouldn't be very difficult. There are a limited number of top level people you need to check, so be quick about it."

✡✡✡

Alexander Comstock Kirk, the U.S. Ambassador to Israel, got off the Egyptian steamer Talodi at the port of Ashdod. A Foreign Ministry limousine took him, his secretary, and his chief of staff to Jerusalem.

Kirk settled at the King David hotel and started organizing the embassy. He explored the U.S. consulate building at 18 Agron Street, which the U.S. had owned since 1912, but decided it was too cramped and old to serve as an embassy. The building next to it, a Lazarist monastery, was also a U.S. holding, as was a modern building on 14 David Flusser Street . Kirk judged it too small for an embassy.

There was another problem: the consulate building on Agron Street served as the consul's residence and the former/future consul was still there.

Kirk was only slightly surprised by the Israel he found. He had been briefed on the possibility of time travel so was at least somewhat prepared.

Finally, after a long consultation with his assistant and chief of staff, as well as the former/future consul, he decided to seek advice from the Israeli Foreign Ministry.

The Foreign Minister was polite. "Ambassador Kirk, please take a seat. How can we help you?"

Kirk settled in the proffered armchair. "I examined the U.S. consular buildings here and frankly they are, in my opinion, inadequate for an embassy of the U.S."

The Foreign Minister nodded. “There’s actually only one building. The other two were leased by a future U.S. government in the 21st century. The leases are not valid and can’t be transferred to the current U.S. government.”

Kirk shrugged, “That’s arguable, but that’s not my point. Can I count on your office to assist us in finding a suitable location?”

“Certainly, Ambassador. My office will put you in touch with a reputable real estate agent and assist you with the legalities.

“May I suggest that you consider getting help from the staff of the embassy and consulate of the future we came from?”

“Thank you for the suggestion, Minister. I would appreciate very much a list of these people.”

The Foreign Minister pressed the intercom button and asked his secretary to bring the lists.

Kirk looked through the names on the way back to his hotel. He was surprised by how many of the senior staff were women. That would never do. He couldn’t employ a woman as a second secretary of the embassy or head of the consular department. This was most inconvenient.

Kirk set his secretary to call the senior employees, starting with the Ambassador, to invite them to a meeting with him one on one.

✡✡✡

Wolf Frumin spent the weekend at his parent’s home in Carmiel. His sister Esther joined them, although she was restless and planned on leaving at midday on Saturday. She had a date with Jacob in Beer Sheva.

At breakfast Wolf brought up the decision he was trying to make: to go to NCO school or become an instructor, and whether to go on to officers school, assuming he graduated from the NCO school. After explaining to his parents and sister the options, he wanted their opinion.

Tzila Frumin had a question: “How safe is NCO school and how safe is it to be a First Sergeant compared to an instructor?”

Wolf smiled. “There isn’t much of a difference. Armor units are small and everyone is protected equally well.”

“Or not,” Nachman Frumin interjected. “You were seriously injured in a tank, so it’s not perfectly safe. Combat is combat.”

Esther smiled at her brother. “I understand that the instructor’s job is only temporary so there’s not much point in discussing it.”

"No, it has to be weighed," her mother disagreed. "By the time Wolf would be done with that job the war might be over and he will be safe."

Esther nodded agreement. "True, but it's also important what Wolf wants in the long run. The NCO and officers schools will take a while, longer than six months, so the war may be over by the time he graduates." She looked at her brother. "The question is whether you want to stay in the professional army?"

Wolf hesitated. "I never really thought about it that way. I like army life and being a sergeant. I didn't consider making this a lifetime career, so there's more thinking to be done and more questions to be asked of the army."

Esther agreed. "Think some more, clarify to yourself what kind of future you want and only then decide." She got up. "I need to get going. Jacob is meeting me at the train station in Beer Sheva."

Tzila smiled. "Are you two going steady?"

Esther shrugged. "I don't know. We meet a lot, talk, go out to eat and to shows. Is this going steady?"

Nachman nodded. "I think so. Do you like him or is he just persistent and bothering you?"

"He's not bothering me. Jacob is very nice and I think he cares about me. Actually, I like talking to him." She looked at her watch, "I really have to run. I'll call you soon."

✡✡✡

Semyon Ivanovich Aralov, the Soviet Ambassador to Israel, spent a day being driven around Jerusalem in a taxi. The driver seemed knowledgeable and talkative, in fluent Russian. Aralov indulged his intelligence gathering instinct. He needed to know the environs he was supposed to operate in, but his time was limited by the need to gather as much information as possible as fast as possible.

One of his assistants was in the Hebrew University library discovering that it wasn't as easy as it seemed. There was the language barrier. Some here spoke Russian but not many of those wanted to help a Soviet official. There was also a problem of understanding most of the technical literature. Apparently the locals were so advanced that even when he found books in Russian, which he did with the help of a librarian, they seemed completely opaque. Finally he settled on researching history. This was both interesting and comprehensible but he wasn't sure what to do with the results of his research. They could cost him his life.

Another important find was a section of the library accessible only with a special pass, which he didn't have. An attempt to sneak in caused two security guards to appear and eject him from the library with a stern warning and a threat of diplomatic complaint.

After receiving his assistant's report Aralov decided that the time had come to write to his superiors and dispatch the message by diplomatic pouch. The problem was, of course, that such a message would be delivered too late to do any good during the Teheran conference. In the meantime he used his radio transmitter to send a short summary:

> The State of Israel is definitely from the future. No idea how far. They have observation platforms in space. Suspect that is how they obtain visual information. Also weapons we don't understand, planes powered by rockets that are faster than sound, and thinking machines like in science fiction. Israel has a large, well-equipped and well-trained military. Probably numbering in the millions. Details in pouch, more to follow.

After the message was sent Aralov called for a brainstorming session with his two assistants. They needed to set up an embassy but also to establish a network of spies and, most important, research the libraries.

The three decided that the best thing to do was to prioritize: a secure extraterritorial base of operations was most important, hence an embassy. The next most important was library research. This needed a team of experts. They decided on three or four to begin with, adding others as required, including experts fluent in Hebrew and English.

Aralov was especially interested in the historical data. His assistant had writen down some information which Aralov found fascinating. He was relieved to know that he would live to a ripe old age and die only in 1969, even though he realized that might change now. He decided to go to the library and research the history books himself. This kind of knowledge might be vital for his survival.

✡✡✡

Molotov read the decoded message, for the third time. The political and security situation was far worse than he expected. The State of Israel was extremely dangerous, but the situation also presented an opportunity. The clock on the wall of his suite in the embassy showed it was close to two in the morning. Stalin would be going to bed soon. Molotov made his decision and called Poskrebyshev. "Alexander Nikolaevich, I just received a message from Israel and I need to speak to the leader now."

"Wait." A minute later Poskrebyshev was back. "Come now."

Molotov climbed to the next floor, passed several guards, and knocked on a heavy, ornate door. It opened to admit him. The guard searched the People's Commissar for Foreign Affairs, found no weapons, and nodded to a second guard to open a door leading to Poskrebyshev's office. Poskrebyshev admitted him to Stalin's office and followed him in. An arrangement very similar to the one in Moscow.

Stalin was reading a document and, without looking up, pointed to chairs in front of his desk. Five minutes later he asked, "What's the earth shattering news, Vyacheslav Mikhailovich?"

Molotov extended the page with the decrypted note.

Stalin read it several times before looking up. "I don't see how this changes anything much."

Molotov hesitated. "First, we need to be very careful of Beria's assessments. I don't understand how he missed this story and why he tried to sell us on a small and helpless Jewish state. Regarding Israel, this changes only one thing: we've got a country that has to be reckoned with. Maybe we should rethink our approach to the negotiations."

Stalin nodded. "And what do you propose we change?"

"If they have demands, which I expect they will, we will have to consider them carefully. I don't know who the senior partner is in the alliance between Israel and Britain. I thought it was Britain but now I suspect it's Israel. If I'm correct, we will have to figure out how to satisfy their demands, whatever they may be."

"The only thing we can't sacrifice is our objective," Stalin replied. "When this war is over I want to control at least the territory we controlled in 1939 before the German attack. We need a buffer between us and Central Europe, particularly Germany. This means that we must retain control over the Baltic countries and at least part of Poland. We also need to control Bessarabia and Moldova."

✡✡✡

The Foreign Minister showed the others a translation of Aralov's message – Single use pads were useless against decrypting software and supercomputers. Amos Nir smiled after reading it. "He captured the essence but may be horrified by what he hasn't found out yet. In any case, I believe that this will make them somewhat more flexible. Let's go meet with Winston. We agreed on a breakfast."

When they arrived at the British embassy Churchill and several generals were waiting. The crowd filed into a large dining room where a buffet breakfast was served.

"Gentlemen, we have two separate sideboards," a majordomo announced. "One is the usual menu, the other is certified kosher. Please note that the service with the blue border is kosher."

The dining room was noisy. It was the first time second tier functionaries on both sides had met and everyone was talking.

Gad Yaari, the Israeli Chief of General Staff, sat, not accidentally, next to Field Marshal Viscount Alan Brooke, the Chief of the Imperial General Staff.

"My dear General," the Field Marshall started, "it's a great pleasure meeting you. I must say that I wasn't in agreement with the strategy you proposed, but it seems to have worked."

Yaari smiled. "Field Marshall, we had to devise a strategy to accommodate your army's relative inexperience with the new equipment and combined arms operations. I'm glad it worked as well as it did. It certainly reduced your losses.

"What approach do you think we need to take with the Soviets?"

Sir Alan Brooke looked quizzically at Yaari. "Are you anticipating a war with them?"

"Not if we are ready," Yaari responded. "But if we're not, we might get a nasty surprise. Stalin is generally cautious but he's also stubborn and has clear objectives. He will not hesitate if he sees an opportunity."

"Hear, hear." A third voice entered the conversation. Churchill, sitting opposite Yaari and next to Amos Nir, continued, "I keep telling my generals and Chiefs of Staff Committee that Stalin is dangerous. They seem to be skeptical."

Amos Nir carefully placed some lox on his cream cheese covered bagel. "We have a bit of new intelligence that just arrived. Stalin received a communication from his ambassador to Israel. He now knows that we came from the future. He will be more careful than he would have been otherwise. This doesn't preclude any future treachery, of course."

Churchill, who took an experimental bite of his bagel and lox, said, "The future is in the future. We need to stick to the tactics we discussed and see where that leads. Wouldn't you agree, Amos, that if we give Stalin a little finger he will try taking the whole arm?"

"True in principle. In practice he has few options. The Red Army isn't ready to take on the Germans by themselves. As we discussed earlier, we will see to it that the Polish and Czechoslovakian armies are reconstituted and equipped. This is not to say that Stalin won't try to undermine the Baltic countries and Poland.

"I would prefer to negotiate in good faith, especially as we have the means to check on the other side's conformity with the agreements.

"I agree with the Latin saying 'Si vis pacem, para bellum' – 'If you want peace, prepare for war'.

"We have lived by this rule for many years. It's one reason we survived."

✡✡✡

The three leaders sat around a large round table with enough room for their advisors. The foreign ministers and military advisors were in the first row behind the heads of state; the less senior personnel farther back.

Stalin was finishing his argument. "The Soviet Union fought the Hitlerites by itself for two years and we stopped them. We demand that this alliance agree that when Germany is defeated the Soviet Union will return to the starting positions it held before hostilities began in 1941."

Churchill responded, "Premier, we fought the Nazis starting in 1939. As soon as we defeated them in Northern Africa we attacked them in Europe. Without us drawing so many of their forces, who knows what would have happened in the first months after they attacked you. Our ally, Israel, has been providing vital intelligence that enabled you to stop the German advance and prepare for a counter-attack.

"Neither Britain nor Israel are going to demand territorial holdings in post-war Europe. The Soviet Union shouldn't either."

Amos Nir waited for the Russian translation to be finished before speaking. "Premier Stalin, we've had preliminary contacts with the new German government and will start formal negotiations soon. It is our intention that a Soviet representative participate as well, but only if we agree on a common position.

"We propose to return European borders to the positions of February, 1938, before the German-Austrian unification rather than the positions agreed to between you and Germany in the Molotov-Ribbentrop pact of 23 August 1939. There will be small changes. The old Polish-German border was untenable for Poland. We propose to move it west to the Oder–Neisse line. There will also be some border modification between France and Germany."

Stalin shrugged. "If this is your position, maybe we need to continue fighting the Germans and defeat them. When all of central Europe is in our hands I will be satisfied."

Churchill smiled a predatory smile. "Maybe you should do that. We will sign a peace agreement with Germany, assuming they agree to our terms. I doubt that you will enjoy fighting Germany alone."

Amos Nir added, "You will also have to manage without our assistance."

Stalin whispered to Molotov and then responded, "We will take a break to discuss this matter."

The other two leaders nodded and the meeting broke up.

✡✡✡

The mood in the room was tense. Stalin held his empty old pipe and inspected it thoughtfully. Finally he said, "I want opinions on just what happened and proposals for our next step."

None of those present was about to volunteer an opinion. That would be too dangerous if it contradicted what the leader thought. After a lengthy silence Stalin shifted in his seat, reached for his tobacco pouch and started filling the pipe. Everyone relaxed a little; this was a sign that the worst might be over.

"Molotov, what do you think?"

"Comrade Stalin, diplomatically the situation is difficult. I think that Churchill hates us enough to make peace with Germany and leave us fighting them alone. On the plus side, it will not be a win for Germany either. He looked at Voroshilov, "Maybe Marshall Voroshilov can elaborate."

Voroshilov nodded. "We're in the last stages of preparations for a big offensive against the Germans. As you all know, we pushed them back from Leningrad, breaking the blockade, and we will push them back on every other front. It will take them some time to transfer forces from the west to face us. It may be wise to attack now. We are ready."

Beria shrugged. "Not that I disagree with the esteemed Marshall, but what happens in, say, six months? The Germans will be stronger than they are now and getting stronger every day. With the Western Allies not attacking their industry or drawing their air force to defend the Fatherland, they will be very difficult to beat. But they will not be able to conquer the Soviet Union. Eventually we can arrive at a peace agreement with them."

Stalin looked at Beria without blinking, causing the chief of the NKVD and Marshall of the Soviet Union to visibly wilt. Finally the great leader pronounced, "Lavrentiy, surprisingly you make sense even though I disagree with you. We will eventually beat Germany. It will take a long time and a huge effort, but we will win this war.

"But Churchill and this Jew Amos Nir won't leave the Germans to their fate. We have no idea what capabilities the Israelis have. They might offer the Germans the same services they are giving us. In that case, we will have difficulties."

The room was quiet for a while. Stalin smoked his pipe and leaned heavily on his desk. Finally Molotov offered his opinion. "Maybe we should accept their proposal of going back to our old border. We can take control of the Baltic States later, after the capitalists dismantle their war machine. This will provide us with the minimal buffer we need. I'm sure they will compromise on all the other demands – reparations, war crime trials, repatriation of our prisoners of war."

Stalin surprised Molotov by standing up. "Yes, I agree. There's no point fighting now for something we can take later at our leisure."

The meeting was over.

✡✡✡

Ambassador Lapid and Ambassador Viscount Halifax shook hands and entered the Oval Office together. FDR rose from behind his desk and greeted them; Secretary of State Cordell Hull also shook hands with the ambassadors.

After everyone was seated FDR nodded to the two ambassadors. "Gentlemen, I'm pleased to see you both. What brings you here together?"

Halifax looked at Lapid who nodded. "We would like to update you on the latest developments. Both our governments are conducting preliminary peace talks with the new German government. We expect to have an agreement very soon, after the German civil war is over.

"As you know, our leaders are now meeting with the Soviet leadership in Teheran. They invited Mr. Stalin to participate in these negotiations. There is a slight difficulty. The Soviet leadership expects to gain control of European territories occupied after the Molotov-Ribbentrop pact. We are not agreeable to this. Mr. Stalin implied that he might try fighting Germany on his own if we sign a separate peace.

It would be helpful to disabuse Mr. Stalin of the notion that the U.S. is supporting his position, which he seems to think is the case."

Harry Hopkins, who sat to the side of the President's desk, spoke up. "The only thing that might give him such an impression is our supplies of war materiel to the Soviet Union. Are you asking us to stop lend-lease?"

"That would certainly be helpful," Ambassador Lapid said.

Hopkins said, inspecting his fingernails. “Such a move will, justifiably, upset the Soviets.”

“I have no doubt this is true, but why should the United States care?”

Halifax added, “It would please both our governments. That should balance out the ‘feelings’ scale.” He smiled.

FDR smiled in return. “I can see that, but I also have to weigh the consequences to us. We will certainly do nothing suddenly or without discussions with the Soviets.

“As it happens, in this case our interests diverge from yours. I am aware of Mr. Stalin’s desire for a buffer between the Soviet Union and Germany and find it reasonable, as is your governments’ position. I’m sure we can find a settlement agreeable to all of us.”

✡✡✡

The next meeting was two days later. Molotov opened with, “The Soviet Union conditionally accepts an agreement that will return all European borders to their state in March of 1938. We demand that the countries concerned, including Germany and its allies, have free elections within six months after the agreement with no parties barred from participation.”

The Israeli Foreign Minister responded, “Mr. Molotov, you surely don’t intend for the Nazi party to participate. We want them banned and their members banned from public service for life.”

“This goes without saying. We also demand that Germany pay reparations to the Soviet Union for all the damage they inflicted and that fifty thousand German officers be executed for war crimes,” Molotov said.

The Israeli Foreign Minister responded, “These are fair demands but justice should be carried out no matter who the criminal is. I assume that the Polish government will demand that all the participants and planners of the Katyn Forest massacre be executed.”

Both the Israeli and British delegations nodded in agreement.

Molotov looked surprised and Stalin furious. Finally Molotov shrugged. “We have no idea what you are talking about.”

“Approximately 22,000 Polish officers, enlisted men and civilians were shot by NKVD troops,” the Israeli Foreign Minister said. “This is a list of the participants in that massacre. We probably missed some but not many. If German army officers are going to be executed, then those on this list should be executed as well. And their higher ups need to stand trial for war crimes.”

Stalin slapped his hand on the table. “This is not going to happen.”

“In that case, forget about executing anybody without trial,” said Churchill.

Molotov looked at Stalin. “We agree. All German criminals will be tried.”

Amos Nir smiled. “I am glad we resolved this problem. In general we have no disagreements. I would also like to propose that we each station forces in Germany for ten years as a guarantee that they actually go through with the denazification program we discussed earlier. If the allies are not satisfied with the progress being made, they will be free to extend the presence of their troops indefinitely in one year increments. This will, of course, require the unanimous agreement of the three allied powers.”

Stalin smiled for the first time. “What size of an occupation force do you envision?”

Churchill bristled. “We are not proposing an occupation force. The purpose of this force – which can be quite small - will only be to insure that Germany is getting rid of Nazi influence. We were thinking on the order of about one hundred thousand men in total. Each of the allied powers to have equal representation divided into mixed units with equal numbers from each ally.”

Stalin nodded. “I can see how the Soviet Union and Great Britain are entitled to be part of this enterprise. I have doubts about Israel. They didn’t contribute much to the fighting and should, maybe, have symbolic representation only. We also propose a much larger force, on the order of four hundred thousand.”

Amos Nir smiled an unpleasant smile. “Mr. Stalin, you must have extremely incompetent people surrounding you if you think that Israel didn’t contribute to the fighting. Our offer stands. Feel free to reject it and have no representation in Germany.

“We thought that an international tribunal representing all allies, including France, should judge the Nazi war criminals but we can manage on our own.”

Stalin shrugged. “We thought that such a burden may be too much for a small country. I was just trying to be helpful.”

Amos Nir nodded. “I think that we have covered everything. If there are no other proposals, we will have a written copy of the agreement for the parties’ approval in a couple of hours.”

✡✡✡

Wolf Frumin remembered the good old days, only eight months ago, when he was listening to lectures and studying to be a tank commander. It all seemed so easy and trivial. Now he was dead tired, trying to listen carefully to what the instructor was saying. The course was named "Psychology of Command"; failing would wash him out of the NCO school.

Wolf was happy when the lecture was over and the class dispersed. He went to the cafeteria for lunch and a cup of coffee.

"Hi, Wolf! How is it going with you?"

Wolf looked up from his lunch; it was the commander of his class, a lieutenant. He motioned for Wolf to remain seated and sat opposite him.

"I'm doing fine," Wolf responded, "just tired like everyone else."

The lieutenant smiled. "That's how the course is designed. We get you tired for a week and then run some tests. You need to perform well tired and under pressure." He started on his own meal and ate in silence for a while. "I joined you here not to ruin your lunch but to present an opportunity. This is an informal conversation and won't influence anything."

Wolf looked at the officer and sipped his coffee in silence.

Finally the lieutenant said, "If I'm not mistaken you are considering joining the professional army. We think you are officer material and suggest that after you graduate from this course, you apply for officers school."

"Who is 'we'?" Wolf asked.

"Myself, the school commander, and the monitoring psychologist." The lieutenant smiled. "I hope that's enough?"

Wolf smiled. "Yes, that's enough. The problem is that I'm not sure I want to become a professional soldier. My medical profile is never going to be 97%. The doctors tell me I'm at about 85% now. It might improve but there are no guarantees. So even if I decided to become a professional, my advancement will probably be limited."

The lieutenant looked at Wolf carefully. "Being an officer requires no additional physical exertion over what you are already doing. You might have noticed that generals are overall less fit than sergeants. You studied our history and know that some of our senior commanders had missing body parts. Your injury will not hamper your promotion."

He was silent for a moment, sipping his soda. "I would advise you to become an officer even if you decide against a military career. We need good armor officers and you would be one. Just to be clear, there's no pressure. Take your time. This course will be over in three weeks so there's no reason you can't apply in a month or two. You will probably also want to discuss this with your family."

✡✡✡

Dan McKenzie, who had been the U.S. Ambassador to Israel, waited impatiently in the room Ambassador Kirk used as the foyer of his temporary embassy.

Finally the door opened and a secretary peeked out. "Mr. McKenzie, the Ambassador will see you now." Her expression was severe and not particularly welcoming.

Dan McKenzie followed her into the inner room. She pointed at a door and settled behind her desk. McKenzie noticed the implied slight bordering on rudeness but made no comment. He proceeded to open the door and enter the room. He was familiar with the general layout – this had been the American Consulate in Jerusalem and he had visited a number of times during his service.

The current Ambassador, Alexander Kirk, got up from his seat behind a modest desk and made a movement to extend his hand. It stopped in mid-motion. He pointed at a chair in front of the desk and sat down.

After a prolonged silence Kirk finally smiled a somewhat strained smile. "So you are the former U.S. Ambassador to Israel. I was hoping to learn from you."

"Ambassador, I am ready to assist you. Just tell me what you need to know."

Kirk hesitated. "Was Israel at the time an unimportant country?" He added to himself that this would explain a Negro having been assigned as Ambassador.

Dan McKenzie figured out what was behind the question. "Mr. Kirk, before I became the Ambassador to Israel I served in several other countries, including the United Kingdom - what you know as Great Britain - as well as in France and the United States had elected a Negro President before that. To answer your question: Israel was an ally of the U.S. in the Middle East."

Kirk considered the reply for a moment. "A Negro President? How interesting. I also understand that the Department of State had women employed as senior staff. Is that true?"

"Depends on what you call senior. We had several female Secretaries of State, including a Black, or Negro, one, and a large number of female Ambassadors."

Kirk's face was expressionless. "Do you have any questions for me?"

"Yes. Would I and the other U.S. citizens be admitted to the U.S. on our current passports?"

"According to the records I received from the Consul's office we're talking about approximately two hundred people?"

"No, we have more than two hundred with diplomatic passports but thousands of tourists got stuck here after the transition and thousands have been living here for years. Brigham Young University has a campus in Jerusalem, for instance, and most of their students are U.S. citizens."

Kirk was surprised. "In that case I will have to consult. Please contact my secretary from time to time about this."

✡✡✡

Stalin sat thinking. Finally, he pressed the intercom button and told his secretary, Poskrebyshev, to admit the head of security, who was waiting just outside the rail car compartment. The compartment of the special car was big, with a full-sized desk and a second room that served as a bedroom.

"Sit," Stalin pointed at a chair in front of his desk.

General Nikolai Vlasik sat, managing to stay at attention.

Stalin examined his empty pipe, thought some more, then said, "You never reported to me about any other intercepted conversations from the bug at the Israeli embassy in Teheran."

"Comrade Stalin, just before we left Teheran I was told that another conversation had been recorded that may be of importance. I received the translation only a couple of minutes ago." He extended several sheets of paper.

Stalin read the text carefully, then read it again. "Have you read it?"

"Yes, comrade Stalin."

"Your opinion?"

Vlasik hesitated. "I'm not entirely sure. They're clearly saying that they received the text of our Ambassador's message from the same high level agent but never mention a name."

Stalin looked at the typed pages again. "It says they got the information from a top security official. This would eliminate Molotov. Do you know what was in the message?"

Vlasik shook his head energetically. “No, comrade Stalin. I never even heard of any message. All I know is the line quoted there.” He pointed at the pages Stalin was holding.

Stalin nodded. “Good. Prepare a full list of all the senior security personnel that attended the meetings in Teheran, including your people. On your way out tell Molotov to come in.”

A minute later Molotov knocked on the door.

Stalin extended one of the typed pages to Molotov. “Do you have any idea who the traitor might be?” The page he gave Molotov held the quotation from the Ambassador’s message but not the fact that the Israelis got it from a security official.

Molotov carefully studied the text. “Only three people on my staff knew about the message: the radio operators in Moscow and Teheran and the person who did the decryption. The radio operators would have no idea about the content.”

Stalin smiled a little smile that caused Molotov to start sweating. “You neglected to mention that you also knew what was in the message.”

“Comrade Stalin, you surely don’t think I’m the traitor!”

“No, Vyacheslav, I don’t suspect you. I was just making sure that you know we have a traitor somewhere very close to us. Be careful.”

After Molotov left Stalin tried to order his thoughts. He knew that the leak must have come from the NKVD. Several senior NKVD personnel from Teheran were returning home on this train. None of them could know the content of the message. It had been presented by Molotov to him and Beria with no one else in the room. Well, Poskrebyshev was there as well, but he trusted Poskrebyshev and the man had no connection to security. The overheard conversation explicitly mentioned a top level security official. That left Beria. Stalin wasn’t happy. Beria was useful in a number of ways besides keeping the enemies of the state, and of Stalin, suppressed. He was responsible for all the special projects being developed in the GULAG system. There were research establishments that were probably known only to Beria and a handful of others.

The loss of Beria would be felt throughout the system but there was no way Stalin could let the traitor live. Beria’s deputy, Ivan Serov, could probably carry on as the top NKVD security man. Stalin would have to find a suitable replacement to manage the other projects. A simple arrest and execution as a spy or enemy of the state would undermine morale in the middle of a war. Better to have Beria die as a hero.

Chapter 14
February 1943

General Ephraim Hirshson was back in his headquarters in Udine, Italy, examining a map of the Balkans, trying to figure out a way to accelerate the fall of pro-Nazi regimes in the area.

The most egregious were the Ustashi in Croatia, closely followed by the Romanian regime of Ion Antonescu. The regime of Admiral Horty in Hungary wasn't good either but not as bad as the other two. Ephraim came to a decision.

The next day a mechanized Israeli force of about division size started moving from its base near Udine in the direction of Zagreb, the Croatian capital. At the same time several jets attacked Croatian airfields, systematically destroying the Croatian air force.

A message was sent to Josip Broz Tito, the leader of the largest partisan army in Yugoslavia, with an invitation to a meeting. General Hirshson thought, and the government in Jerusalem agreed, that Tito was the best bet to unify Yugoslavia and keep the peace, as he had in the original history. Both Hirshson and the General Staff in Israel were somewhat surprised at the almost complete lack of resistance from the Croatian government. It looked like the Ustashi and their leader Ante Pavelić knew what had happened to the German troops that tried to attack the Israeli positions in Austria. Possibly they just lost faith in their future when the German civil war started.

After a single violent encounter with a Ustashi unit in the suburbs of Zagreb, the capital was under Israeli control.

Tito was flown in from Serbia and met with Hirshson in Zagreb. The meeting was short. Israel offered the partisan leader support, mostly from the air, and weapons to unite and pacify the region. Tito accepted. He was only slightly surprised. Israel had dropped arms from the air to his troops several times before. Communications channels and procedures were established. Tito departed, after declaring his presence and intentions on Zagreb radio.

Meanwhile Tsar Boris III of Bulgaria had declared his country's neutrality and withdrawn troops from the neighboring countries.

That left the problem of Romania. After some consideration the allies decided to wait until after Germany surrendered. This would likely make overthrowing the Antonescu regime much easier. They were hopeful that King Michael would be able to accomplish this as he had in the original history and, if the Soviets didn't interference, stay in power.

✡✡✡

Ze'ev Hirshson finished reading his son Ephraim's email, printed it out and gave it to his wife Linda. "It seems like the boy has a future," Ze'ev said with a smile. "Go figure, a soldier becomes an international politician."

Linda nodded. "You doubted Ephraim had a brilliant future? When he retires he should run for Prime Minister. He'll make a good one."

"No, no, no," Ze'ev protested. "I want him to join the family business. I have serious plans to expand into another universe and we need his talents. I'll discuss it with him next time he's home."

The couple was relaxing in the library where they frequently spent 'quality time' after dinner. Linda was reading one of her favorite books. "You seem to be obsessed with this alternate universe. The fact that we can go there doesn't mean we should."

Ze'ev put aside the tablet he was using. "True, but look at the advantages. We have access to all the natural resources we need and all the land we need. Why not go there?"

"I don't know. How is the exploration going?"

"We have looked at most of the Middle East from Turkey to North Africa to the Persian Gulf. We found no signs of intelligent life but lots of water and everything is green. I like it a lot and would consider moving there, except there's no civilization and at our age doctors and hospitals are important."

"Yes, that's true. So can you claim this land now or do you have to prove that there's no intelligent life on the whole alternate Earth?"

"We could claim it now. The preliminary regulations that the government passed two months ago state that we can claim any land that is not occupied by intelligent life. I'm waiting partly because the regulations don't define what constitutes intelligent life. Personally I'm for a definition that relies on the use of language and self-awareness.

"In any case, only our company can make the gate boxes so we control the gateway to that universe. I'm trying to set up a conglomerate of private companies to develop the planet, with the government's involvement."

Linda looked at her husband in silence for a while. "Ze'ev, we have been married for a long time and I know you're not a megalomaniac. You are also quite lazy and before the event were planning to retire in a year or two. Is this new activity what I think it is?"

"If you're thinking of an escape hatch then it is."

"And what brought that on?" Linda asked.

"You did. Remember last year when I was all excited about our air force beating up the Nazis in North Africa and you said, 'Now they will really hate us.' I responded that the Nazis couldn't hate us any more than they already do. You said, 'Not the Nazis. The Brits.' I thought about it and concluded you were right. We are helping the Brits, the Soviets, the Americans and even the Germans. The result will be, I hope, a better world for everyone. Except the Jews. The anti-Semites will claim that we're evil and control the world. That's what they always say. The hate will grow stronger as Israel grows stronger, like always.

"The world accepts the Jew if he's weak and at their mercy. Then they kill some. The Holocaust was a first attempt at total extermination. After that, most of the perpetrators and collaborators, including most nations, felt guilty and treated the Jews with pity.

"It didn't take very long for the guilt to transform itself back into hatred and for people to decide that whatever the Jews had suffered it wasn't enough. The stronger Israel grew the more it was dehumanized and the more anti-Semitism grew. They found the Palestinians, a fake nation created only to destroy Israel, and decided those poor, oppressed Arabs were the true owners of our land. No matter how badly the 'Palestinians' behaved and how many they murdered, they were always supported.

"I believe that this pattern will repeat itself. We will be accused of imaginary crimes, ostracized, dehumanized, and eventually physically attacked. So why not create a safe haven completely inaccessible to any other nation?"

Linda thought about his long speech. "I agree. It's a worthwhile project. I'll help as much as I can. You need to discuss it with Amos Nir. If I am not mistaken, the Prime Minister will be sympathetic to the idea."

✡✡✡

The Israeli and Soviet ambassadors, General Wilson, and Jean Moulin, the representative of the Free French government, were discussing procedures when Wilson's secretary opened the door to announce, "Mr. Goerdeler is waiting."

Wilson nodded. "We are almost finished. I don't think it will be long now."

Ambassador Mizrahi smiled. "Gentlemen, we've covered everything, except the question of occupation and the exact composition of the occupying forces. If you agree, we can discuss that at a later date."

Ambassador Maisky nodded agreement, as did Wilson. Wilson, seeing that there were no more issues to discuss, pressed the intercom button. "George, please invite Mr. Goerdeler in."

Carl Goerdeler, the temporary chancellor of Germany, entered the conference room. Wilson pointed to a chair positioned separately from the others. "Chancellor, would you like tea or coffee?" Wilson asked.

Goerdeler smiled. "I'll take tea, thank you."

Wilson informed the secretary of the German's choice and continued, "The four of us present here are fully authorized by our respective governments to negotiate with Germany. Are you authorized by the German government to negotiate with us?"

"I am. Since I am not a dictator I will have to refer back to the full government before coming to an agreement."

The others nodded agreement and acceptance. Maisky said, "As you know, we joined the other allies and stopped military operations against German forces. We will resume such operations if the negotiations are stalled."

Ambassador Mizrahi added, "This statement is correct for all of us. We will negotiate only so long as these negotiations bear fruit. I hope that Germany has accepted that it lost the war and is in no position to pose any conditions. Our governments agreed to negotiate only with the view of saving lives, but this is a limited objective."

"We understand the situation," Goerdeler said quietly. "The military understands it very well. The civilian population is eager for peace. The bombing of our cities has led to terrible losses."

Wilson shrugged. "We didn't start that practice. You should blame Hitler and those of your compatriots who supported him. But that is neither here nor there.

"These are our terms." Wilson gave Goerdeler several typed pages, which the German started reading.

Goerdeler looked up. "Am I to understand that you want us to retreat to the Soviet border of 1938, stop there and, while the Soviet Army takes up positions in front of us, train and arm forces of the national armies of the Baltic countries and Poland?"

Wilson nodded.

"May I inquire why?" Goerdeler asked.

"Certainly. Germany attacked Poland in 1939 and dissolved the Polish state. It also caused the Baltic States to be dissolved and later occupied them. It is our view that Germany is responsible for restoring these states and their ability to defend themselves."

Mizrahi thought about the real reason for this demand: to create an obstacle for Stalin, who might be tempted to cross the old border if there were no organized entities on the other side. It would be a more difficult proposition if the Baltic States and Poland were reconstituted and rearmed.

Maisky fidgeted in his seat. "I wouldn't say that this is a rigid requirement. The Soviet Union is not going to protest if your soldiers just go all the way back to Germany."

Wilson smiled. "As you may have guessed there is a difference of opinion on the relative importance of the various paragraphs in the proposed agreement. It's enough that two of the three allies think that a paragraph is of vital importance."

Goerdeler was serious. "Is Germany supposed to pay for the arms and training it provides?"

"Oh yes. It will bear all the costs," Mizrahi responded, "which is only a minor part of the reparations that will have to be paid. Since you will not need most of the arms you have now, arming your neighbors to the East should not be difficult."

Goerdeler continued reading. "I'm not sure I can agree to move the border with Poland to the Oder-Neisse line. This is ceding a lot of territory to Poland."

"Mr. Chancellor, if you need the approval of your government we will wait a reasonable time for you to get it. Just as long as you understand that this is not negotiable," Wilson said.

Maisky added, "You can understand the legitimate concern for providing your neighbors with natural and defensible borders since you attacked them twice in a couple of decades."

The meeting ended several hours later and resumed the next day, this time with several experts present on both sides. Goerdeler was concerned about the demand that Germany pay reparations to the countries damaged during the war.

"France and Britain declared war on Germany so we should not be required to pay reparations. It was those countries' choice to make war on Germany."

Jean Moulin responded, this being his first contribution to the discussion. "Yes, I understand that Germany would have preferred that we ignore our obligations to Poland. It was Germany that started this war and Germany has to pay."

Mizrahi nodded at Goerdeler. "You have noticed that the amounts of the reparations are not stated. Those are subject to a separate agreement. We have no incentive to bankrupt Germany. The Versailles treaty was too one-sided. We all want to preserve a democratic and peaceful Germany. Abject poverty will not be conducive to this purpose."

Goerdeler shrugged. "It may make political sense for both the Allies and Germany to pay some reparations, as long as they are not ruinous."

Maisky responded, "Some of the things you did can't be repaid with money. Germany will have to cooperate in finding and severely punishing the criminals among you."

Goerdeler nodded. "We are already eliminating the Nazis. We have no choice if we want to survive."

"It's not only the Nazis. They had many willing collaborators. We all fully agree with Ambassador Maisky," said Jean Moulin.

✡✡✡

The books, in Russian, - *Stalin*, by Soviet journalist Edward Radzinsky, and *Stalin's Last Crime* by Jonathan Brent and Vladimir Naumov - arrived with the morning diplomatic pouch from Jerusalem. Molotov, after reading the ambassador's note and looking at the pertinent chapters, brought them to the leader. He told Stalin that the books came from a store in Israel and pointed out the chapters he had marked in each book.

Stalin dismissed Molotov and looked at the books. He was only mildly interested in what future corrupt capitalist historians thought about him and leafed quickly until he reached the bookmarks left by Molotov.

Stalin was slightly disappointed that he had only ten years left to live and was about to close the book when a short phrase caught his eye: 'It is not clear to what extent Poskrebyshev was complicit in Stalin's death. Beria's complicity is certain.' The great leader read the chapter again, very carefully.

Apparently his trust in his secretary and confidante was misplaced. But Stalin congratulated himself on his decision to liquidate Beria. He locked the books in a drawer of his desk and considered how to deal with his secretary and the head of the NKVD.

Stalin left the office early, at about two in the morning. On the way out to his Kremlin apartment he nodded to Poskrebyshev, who was still hard at work at his desk.

Poskrebyshev had been eagerly waiting for the boss to leave. Earlier in the evening Molotov had showed the secretary the books he brought with him. "I need to see the leader now," and added in a much quieter voice, "Chapter 22 in this one and 12 in the other one." Now Poskrebyshev unlocked the office door, went inside and unlocked the desk drawer with a duplicate key he had made in secret. He took out the books and looked at Chapter 22 and then Chapter 12 in the thinner book. It took him almost ten minutes of reading and re-reading the chapters to realize he was doomed. He also realized that he wasn't alone. Beria was doomed as well.

Poskrebyshev returned the books and went back to his desk. After hesitating for a couple of minutes, he made a call.

Beria took less than ten minutes to arrive. Poskrebyshev told him about the history books Stalin had been studying. The head of the NKVD wasn't a trusting man and demanded to see the books. After reading the pertinent chapters he thought for only a short time. "Alexander Nikolaevich, we are both dead men and it will be a very unpleasant death. Will you back me up? I promise that I will save both our lives if you do."

"Do I have a choice? Sure, I will back you up."

"Good." Beria displayed an unpleasant smile. "Tomorrow, when he asks for his tea, pour this liquid in it." He took a small vial from the inner pocket of his jacket, a vial he always had ready in case he was arrested. "But be sure to do it only after he asks you to taste it, assuming he does that."

Poskrebyshev took the vial. "I usually pour a glass for myself and one for him from the same kettle. I drink from my glass and he waits for ten minutes before touching his. I'll pour the liquid on the sugar cubes in the bowl. What does it do?"

"A very small amount of this will kill you. It's prussic acid, also known as cyanide. The liquid smells slightly of peaches. I hope that's not a problem."

"It shouldn't be. He always has some preserves served with the tea. As long as the smell isn't very strong…"

Beria shrugged. "It's slight. Just make sure that some of the preserves are peaches and we will be fine."

"Lavrentiy Pavlovich, I didn't realize you carried such stuff with you."

"One can never know," Beria responded and was gone.

✡✡✡

Lior Lapid was impatient. He had been waiting for almost forty minutes for a meeting with the President. It seemed to Lapid that after he and Halifax requested the cessation of lend lease to the Soviets, FDR was annoyed with both of them and displaying his annoyance in a petty way. Viscount Halifax, who sat next to him, didn't look happy but said nothing.

Finally the door opened and a military officer invited them in. For this meeting, at the two ambassadors' request, the Secretary of State was also present. Harry Hopkins was there as well.

"Gentlemen, it's a pleasure to see you again," FDR said in greeting. "I understand that you want to report on the talks in Teheran and discuss other issues."

Halifax explained to the Americans the basics of the agreement with the Soviet Union and Germany. He then continued, "Regarding a future world order. We understand that the U.S. is interested in reviving the League of Nations. Is this correct?"

Secretary Hull responded, "We wouldn't call it a League of Nations. Too much baggage is connected to that name. We prefer to call our initiative 'The United Nations'. It will be an organization different from the old League. Every nation on earth will be eligible to join and every nation will have an equal vote in the World Parliament or as we call it 'The General Assembly'."

Lapid nodded politely. "Do you envision an executive body with some power behind it?"

Cordell Hull smiled. "Of course we envision an executive body with coercive and even military power. We would also like to ensure that a world war never happens again. For this purpose the organization would have a World Security Council on which the current allies in the fight against Germany and Japan will have permanent seats."

Edward Wood, Viscount Halifax, smiled. "Am I correct in my assumption that every nation will be admitted to this organization with no constraints whatsoever?"

"That's what I said," Cordell Hull responded.

"This means that Hitler's Germany would also be admitted," Viscount Halifax stated.

"Hitler's Germany doesn't exist so why should we concern ourselves with it?" the President responded somewhat impatiently.

"But the U.S. would admit existing and future dictatorships into this organization?" Lior Lapid asked.

"We certainly would," the Secretary of State responded. "I'm not saying that we should but there are no dictatorships as vicious as the Nazis or Imperial Japan so the question is moot."

"Is that so?" Viscount Halifax asked. "You don't consider the Soviet Union to be as vicious as the Nazis?"

The President looked annoyed.

Harry Hopkins answered, "How can you compare a state where the people are the sovereign to Nazi Germany? I'll grant you that there are some excesses in the Soviet Union but their system is moving a very primitive country into the 20th century."

"Did you ever ask yourself at what cost they're advancing?" asked Lapid.

Hopkins just shrugged.

Viscount Halifax nodded. "In that case I can say with certainty that Great Britain will not join such an organization."

Lapid nodded, "Neither will Israel. Our governments will reconsider their position if the organization is open only to democracies or democratic republics. Actual democracies, not those in name only."

✡✡✡

Jacob Hirshson knocked on the door. Esther opened it almost instantly and invited him inside. Jacob was only slightly surprised to see his sister Sheina, who shared the apartment with Esther, and Esther's brother Wolf.

"Hi, everyone," Jacob pronounce cheerfully. "Are you guys joining us for dinner?"

Sheina smiled. "If we do, it might spoil the evening for you two love birds."

"Not more than it would spoil it for you two," Esther responded with a smile. She turned to Jacob, "Yes, they're joining us. Wolf has some news which none of us has heard yet."

"Good, let's go then. I found a very nice place a short drive away."

The restaurant was indeed nice, with white table coverings, flowers and candles on every table, and dim lighting.

After they settled in and placed their orders Wolf asked Jacob, "How's your new business venture going?"

“Apparently I can sell many more computers than I can make. We’re now negotiating with several parts suppliers and will start assembling our own machines.”

“I thought you were already assembling them,” Esther said.

“Well, we kind of did but not really. We bought standard parts on the open market and assembled them to customer specifications. There’s nothing special or unique about that. Anybody who has basic knowhow can do it. The margins are very slim. The business exists on the difference between wholesale prices and retail prices, with after sale services being a crucial part of profit. I’m establishing a different model: parts made to my specifications and branded accordingly. The next step will be to manufacture as much as I can in-house.”

Jacob turned to Wolf. “What’s the news you wanted to tell us?”

“Next week I’m going to graduate from the Armor NCO School. They already told me that I qualify for officer’s school and I’m thinking about going.” Wolf looked at Jacob. “What’s your opinion?”

Before Jacob could respond Sheina said, “I keep telling him that there’s no point in spending time and effort on officer training unless he wants to become a professional soldier.” Esther nodded agreement. She also didn’t like the idea of her brother being an officer. From what she learned during her time in wartime Russia, this was a much more dangerous position than a sergeant.

Jacob thought for a moment. “Are you thinking of a career in the army?”

Wolf shrugged. “I thought about it a lot but don’t have enough information to make a decision. I definitely would not like to become a professional if I’m not an officer. If I do become an officer, my options are open and can I decide later.”

He turned to his sister. “The stories we heard at home and you witnessed in Russia are not relevant to the Israeli army. True, we lead by example and the order is always ‘Follow me!’ but that applies equally to officers and noncoms. On the other hand, we’re speaking about armor. We have the best tanks in the world and officers are protected as well as sergeants and privates.”

“That’s true.” Jacob agreed. “In the battle I witnessed there was never any danger to anyone in tanks, officers or privates. You’re also right about having more opportunities as an officer. Just don’t forget that if you choose not to join the professional army you will have to serve two months every year as a reservist. As a noncom it will likely be between a month and six weeks.”

Sheina was surprised. “I didn’t know that officers serve so much longer every year. This is definitely a reason for you to stay a sergeant.”

Again, Esther nodded agreement. “I’m sure that our parents will not be happy with you gone two months every year.”

Wolf smiled. “Yes, I’ve heard that argument a thousand times. I’ll think about it.

“Just to add to your worries, both you and Sheina are exempt from service while studying, but after graduation, Esther, if you become a doctor, you’ll have to go to officers’ school and all these bad things will apply to you as well. Sheina, being smart, will be a computer specialist someplace safe and likely not called up for reserve duty at all.”

“Or we could get married. The IDF doesn’t take married women, unless they volunteer,” Jacob said with a smile.

“Am I hearing a proposal here?” Esther asked with a smile.

“Yes. Will you marry me?”

Esther’s smile widened. “I’ll have to think about it after you propose properly, with a ring, on one knee.”

✡✡✡

Ambassador Kirk finished reading the latest missive from the State Department. This was the fifth such document in the last several weeks. His question about restoring the citizenship of up-time Americans stranded in Israel had provoked a storm. The President got involved and messages were flying back and forth at a distressing rate.

The one he just finished reading said, “We rely on your judgment regarding citizenship in individual cases. The President as well as the Department of State oppose a blanket admission of former citizens into the country.”

Personally Kirk thought that this was a mistake and resented that the responsibility was left to him to admit these people. Up-timers had knowledge the current U.S. needed. Kirk was aware of the influence living in Israel was having on him and could understand that people in the U.S. didn’t see what was obvious to him. He also understood the position of the President: admitting large groups of blacks and Jews would cause serious problems for FDR. Especially among his strongest Democratic supporters in the Southern states. FDR appeased them, by segregating the armed forces for instance. Kirk could see how an influx of thousands of citizens brought up in an advanced society similar to the Israeli one would undermine the current American culture which he liked and approved of.

The Ambassador put aside the long message and turned to a summary of responses his secretary prepared for him. After he was instructed to admit individually approved citizens, Kirk had contacted all the Americans they could locate to ask them whether they would like to move to the U.S. Now he was looking at the results and was saddened.

Of the eight thousand Americans who responded less than a thousand expressed any desire to move, and most of them were associated with the Mormon university or other missionary groups. Apparently the whole long discussion within the establishment back home had been unnecessary. The few who would, maybe, go back would do no damage but also bring very little with them.

He went to his next assignment from home: buy and ship as many books as possible. The first on the list, by category, were history books, with engineering and science close behind. This was a large assignment but he had just the right person for it. Kirk picked up the phone, "Please ask the consul to come to my office."

The former consul was one of the few who expressed a possible desire to go back to the U.S. He was still on the staff and being paid a salary by the U.S.

✡✡✡

"Gentlemen, do I understand you correctly? Are you rejecting our conditions for a peace agreement?" Ambassador Mizrahi sounded incredible.

General Wilson, Ambassador Maisky and Ambassador Moulin sat next to him opposite the German delegation. This time Goerdeler brought with him two military officers: General Rommel, the Defense Minister of the new German Republic, and Field Marshall von Kluge, the new Chief of the German High Command, replacing Alfred Jodl.

"Not exactly." Chancellor Goerdeler shook his head vigorously. "We are only disputing two conditions: the new border along the Oder-Neisse line and the requirement to stop our withdrawal at the old USSR border.

"We feel that the instability caused by Premier Stalin's sudden demise makes it more likely that our forces will come under attack, so we would prefer them withdrawn directly to our border."

The Soviet Ambassador bristled. "Are you saying that you don't trust the Soviet Union to honor the agreements it signs?"

The two generals started nodding but Goerdeler quickly responded, "Not at all, but you will agree with me that there is no certainty about what is going on in Moscow. We know there is fighting between the Red Army and NKVD troops. We also know that there are uprisings in the

Caucuses. We definitely don't want to be involved in a brewing civil war."

General Wilson looked at his partners and seeing them nod said, "We all assure you that Germany will not be blamed for events it didn't cause. The allies, all of the allies, will guarantee the agreement. This is not negotiable.

"As to your second objection, the Polish border will be moved and Poland will have unhindered access to the Baltic Sea."

"But this is unfair," Rommel objected. "Germany is going to lose a large chunk of land which has always been German. Why should we agree to this?"

The French Ambassador smiled an unpleasant smile. "General Rommel, you may have forgotten but you lost a war that you initiated. Losing a war has a price and, in my opinion, Germany is getting off very lightly."

Rommel was indignant. "But it was a different Germany that started the war."

Wilson shrugged. "I fear that my memory misleads me. Aren't the Germans the same people who voted for Hitler and supported him in this war? The people are responsible for the actions of their government. You are a good example of this: Didn't you fight for the Third Reich under Hitler? Aren't you now the Defense Minister of the new Germany? I grant that you will not be able to participate in the upcoming elections, but explain to me how Germany isn't responsible for what was done under the Nazi regime? Would you prefer we demand an unconditional surrender, occupy Germany, and do as we wish?"

Rommel looked slightly embarrassed.

The Soviet Ambassador shrugged. "I agree with my British colleague. If Germany objects to losing a bit of land as the cost of an unprovoked attack on its neighbors, maybe you need a much tougher lesson."

Goerdeler intervened. "We accept both conditions. If a paragraph is added guaranteeing the integrity of our borders in case one of the allies reneges on the terms."

The four allied representatives looked at each other and nodded agreement.

Chapter 15

March 1943

Wolf Frumin knocked on the door and entered the office. The regiment's liaison officer nodded to him. "Congratulations on graduating from the NCO school. Have you made a decision about officers' school?"

"I still have a couple of questions. I'm not clear on my obligations if I graduate from officers' school. How long do I have to stay in the service beyond my regular conscription term?"

The young lieutenant brought up his record on her computer. "You have eighteen months left to serve. The officers' school is six months long. Those six months will not count towards your regular service so you will be free to return home twenty-four months from now instead eighteen."

"Will being an officer make a difference to the length of my yearly reserve service?"

"Everyone is worried about that, at least in the beginning. The answer is maybe. In times of tensions or war, like now, you will likely be called to serve two months. Some of it will be field service and some will be training and taking care of unit business. As a first sergeant you can expect about six weeks of service per year."

"I think I would like to try the officer training option, assuming I don't need to make a commitment to future professional service."

The lieutenant pulled a stack of forms from her desk. "Please read this, fill out the necessary information and sign."

✡✡✡

"Ladies and Gentlemen, let's start. The first and only item on our agenda is the demand by the Americans regarding technology." The Foreign Minister paused and looked around the conference table. "Our legal counsel will elaborate on the document in front of you."

The legal expert from the Foreign Ministry stood up and drew a diagram on the whiteboard. "The document we received from the U.S. embassy refers to three sources of technology: technology that belongs to the U.S. government and is part of the weapon systems that have been sold to Israel by the future U.S., technology that belongs to companies that now exist in the U.S., and technology that belongs to companies that do not yet exist but might exist in the future.

"The first category of technology transferred as part of weapon systems is more or less clear, although there are complications with items the U.S. government bought from private companies. The second category includes Israeli subsidiaries of American companies like IBM and others that exist now. The third is subsidiaries of American companies that do not exist now, like Microsoft, Intel, AMD.

"The U.S. government claims ownership of all three categories."

The legal expert from the Ministry of Industry was the first to respond. "Do they justify their claim? After all, the current U.S. government has given us nothing. Neither have IBM or Ford."

"Their position is simple: the U.S. government gave us weapons, therefore all the science and technology in those weapons belongs to the U.S. government, and since the current United States is the only one around it is the legal heir to the rights of the other, future U.S.," responded the Foreign Ministry lawyer. "The same reasoning applies to currently existing subsidiaries of U.S. companies. They claim that the U.S. government represents the interests of future shareholders of companies that do not yet exist."

A Justice Ministry representative responded, "There are, obviously, no precedents for any of this under law. Time travel has never happened before so nothing has dealt with it legally yet. But there is a simple approach that might resolve the problem with the property of private companies. Shortly after the time travel event, the Knesset, at the request of the Justice Minister, passed a law that only people currently living in Israel or Israeli corporations can own shares in Israeli companies. If IBM sues it will have no grounds since it owns no shares in any company here.

"All the subsidiaries of foreign companies in Israel are registered in Israel as publicly held entities. To take over such an entity, the potential new owner has to negotiate with the company and its shareholders. It is each company's decision whether to agree to sell themselves or give themselves away. The government of Israel has nothing to do with it. Of course the valuation of IBM Israel would currently exceed the valuation of IBM U.S. or IBM International by several hundreds of times. If I was on the board of IBM Israel I would suggest that we offer to buy all of IBM, U.S. and international."

The Ministry of Defense representative was next. "Regarding the U.S. government ownership of technology and science in the weapon systems we now own, the matter is not as simple as they claim. Here's an example: The F16 we are using is designated F16IL. It uses almost exclusively our home-made avionics and lots of other modifications we made, like missiles and radar. In addition, most of the original technology was developed for the U.S. by private companies, some in Israel. It's a tangle. Disclosing any of the details to a foreign government is against our law so in practice their claim is moot.

"There are items, such as our missile defense systems, that we developed with some U.S. funding. That wouldn't entitle them to full access even in the old timeline let alone now. My recommendation would be to deny this part of the request flat-out.

"As the Justice Ministry said, there is no precedent in law and we need to set one now and do so firmly. The current U.S. government owns no part of what a future U.S. government might pay for. The reason is simple. Obviously history will not repeat and the present U.S. will not pay a dime for all the science and technology they want from us for free.

"The Ministry of Defense would not object to selling them some weapon systems with prior approval of the Ministry."

The Foreign Ministry lawyer had a remark. "My colleagues haven't dealt with one issue: that of subsidiaries of companies that do not yet exist, like Intel. This is actually a simple issue and we can follow the advice of my colleague from the Justice Ministry. If the U.S. government proposes to buy the shares of these companies in the name of future American shareholders it needs to negotiate with the Israeli companies. Personally I think that they wouldn't be able to afford the price of even one company.

"It would probably be more convenient for everyone to resort to a free trade regime. That way they would have access to modern products without paying for the basic technology. It may also be worthwhile pointing out to the Americans a couple of facts they may not be aware of.

"First, a great number of patents on this 'modern' stuff are held by Israeli companies. This includes everything from cell phones to software to advanced materials. Then there is the question of how useful the technology would be to them. What could the U.S. do with an advanced computer chip? It will take about thirty years to get to the stage where they understand how it works and how to start making them. By that time their knowledge will be outdated and completely useless for industrial competition."

The Foreign Minister summarized. "Thank you. We will draft a response and let each one of you comment on it."

✡✡✡

Ze'ev Hirshson wasn't used to waiting for anybody and was getting impatient. He had been sitting for slightly over fifteen minutes, enough time to examine the mediocre artwork on the walls as well as drink a cup of coffee. He was about to open the door and ask the secretary how much longer he would have to wait when another door opened and the Prime Minister entered the room.

The two shook hands and Amos Nir smiled apologetically. "Sorry for the long wait. We have some problems that needed an immediate response. How can I help you?"

"As a matter of fact I am here to present an opportunity. An opportunity for the government and the State of Israel.

"As you know, Consolidated has been working on improving its trans-universe travel technology. We can now open a stable portal to another universe and transport both people and materiel back and forth. We even experimented, successfully, with power transmission."

The Prime Minister discreetly glanced at his watch. Ze'ev noticed and responded, "I will not take up much of your time and will get right to the reason I'm here.

"We are exploring an alternative Earth where, so far, we found no intelligent life and roughly the same natural resources we have here. Consolidated is negotiating with several companies to partner in the exploration and exploitation of these resources."

Amos Nir smiled. "I'm happy that you're doing something and that there are enough forward looking businesses in Israel to join with you but I see no role for the government in the venture."

"Neither did I at first. During the last several months I became convinced that we won't be welcome here for much longer. Jews have been hated for thousands of years. In the history we left behind Israel was being denied its right to exist. It seems that the guilt of the Holocaust turned easily into hatred and, as usually happened to us in the past, we were being blamed for our hater's behavior."

Amos shrugged. "True, but here we are one of the most powerful countries. We're also contributing and will continue to contribute to a more peaceful and equitable world."

Ze'ev smiled a sad smile. "Yes, we are building a better world, but isn't that what we were doing back in the time we came from? Our contributions to science, medicine and technology were hugely out of proportion to the size of our population. We were the only democracy in the Middle East and tried for many years to achieve peace with our neighbors. The result was hate. Not just from the Muslims but also from the Europeans. By the time we left, the hate infected South America and the U.S. as well.

“We found ourselves here because of a nuclear attack by Iran, a country that by all objective measures had an ideology as similar to the Nazis as to make no difference. Don’t forget that they could have acquired their bomb only with the acquiescence of the West, and the West knew what their first target would be and, as usual, didn’t care.”

“That may have been true then but we will not let it happen now. Not as long as I’m the Prime Minister.”

“I have no doubt of that, but how long do you expect to be in the driver’s seat?”

The two sat in silence for a while. Finally the Prime Minister asked, “So what do you propose?”

Ze’ev leaned back in his chair. “I propose we create an escape hatch, a refuge, where we can go if the situation requires it. The last time we inadvertently moved, the experience was somewhat disturbing and it was a close thing. I am proposing that we prepare a place where the whole country can move and where no one else can follow. To accomplish this we need much more than an industrial consortium. We need government support.”

“You’ve convinced me, although by now I know that you have your own ideas of what to do and how to do it and will argue every step of the way. I will need the agreement of the full government, as well as a serious budget, which will take some time to achieve.”

“We don’t need money yet, but it would be helpful to have some expert advice and specialized equipment. For example, we could finish our survey for intelligent life much faster if we had several long-range military planes with the right equipment.”

The Prime minister thought for a couple of minutes and finally said, “I have an idea how to fast track the whole thing through the government and maybe even the Knesset Foreign Affairs and Security committee. We don’t want this to become public knowledge yet.

“In the meantime I want to see how this portal works, and I want you to show it to the Defense Minster and to the Chief of General Staff. I will bring the cabinet for a visit.”

✡✡✡

“This is the office building where my company is located, on the fifth floor.” Jacob pointed the building out to Esther and led her to the entrance.

This was her first visit to Refidim since her arrival in Israel. Jacob was proudly showing her around. They started with lunch at the house he purchased for his mother, himself, and his sister. There his mother served a substantial lunch in the East European tradition. Esther asked for her goulash recipe and Sara was very pleased. So pleased, in fact, that she became genuinely friendly, surprising Jacob. He had been trying to think of a way to make his mother treat his girlfriend, and hopefully future wife, as nicely as possible and could find no way. His appreciation for Esther grew. She was not only beautiful and smart but had people skills that overcame his mother's natural wariness of a woman about to take away her boy.

They took the elevator to the fifth floor. The Hirshson Surveying and Design Company leased half the floor. After greeting the receptionist Jacob knocked on the door to one of the offices. Chaim Hirshson, Jacob's uncle, got up from behind his desk to greet them.

"Pleased to see you again," he said shaking Esther's hand. "Jacob warned me that you were coming to inspect our operations and instructed me to have everything ship-shape. I can't ignore his polite requests. If I get him too mad he might fire me." Chaim's smile got wider.

Ester returned the smile. "I doubt he'd fire you. From what I hear he thinks you are irreplaceable."

"I don't know about being irreplaceable, but Jacob definitely doesn't want me involved in the Hirshson Computer Corporation."

"Uncle, you're being unfair. You are doing an excellent job running the surveying business. It's growing like crazy. You are needed here. We have close to forty employees and without a full-time manager the company would fail."

He looked at Esther. "I offered Chaim 49% of the company and the title of President. I remain Chairman but don't participate in the daily management."

Esther nodded. "Chaim, I would offer an opinion but I have no idea what to say except that I trust Jacob."

"The problem is that I trust him as well. My managerial experience can be summed up in one paragraph: I used to own a small grocery store in Vilna. My education is also iffy, so I was surprised that the business has done so well.

"I have to add that I don't really resent Jacob excluding me from the computer business. Besides, he doesn't really. He keeps me up to date and pretends to listen to my advice.

"But enough of this. Let's go show you this grand company."

In addition to the executive offices there were two other private offices for managers. The rest of the staff had their desks in a large open room divided into cubicles. Next to that were a cafeteria, kitchen, and recreation room.

Jacob explained. “I was reading about how to run a company with an educated workforce and keep them happy. There were a number of articles about Google and other high-tech companies so I decided to try their methods. Then I discovered the practice was started in Israel much earlier. It works well. People are happy and it improves overall communications and performance.”

Chaim agreed. “That’s true. I was skeptical when Jacob proposed this loose organization and open office floor plan. But our people keep discussing work at lunch and during break time so information spreads much faster.

“The only serious problem we had was a shortage of computers, just one for every four employees. Now we have a computer for almost every employee, which makes a huge difference and is part of the secret of our success.”

“Exactly. That was what first gave me the idea to start building my own machines. Of course I ran into the scarcity of some parts and decided to either make them myself or, at least, have exclusive contracts with manufacturers.”

“And how is that working out?” Esther asked.

“I’ll show you.”

They said goodbye to Chaim and went outside. There was a bus stop across the street and a short wait. Twenty minutes later they were deposited at the edge of town in front of a large industrial building. A sign across its front proclaimed ‘Hirshson Computer Corporation’.

Inside, the building was brightly lit and air-conditioned. Jacob pointed to the rows of assembly tables. “We employ 105 people in assembly. The air here is heated or cooled as necessary and filtered to eliminate dust. There are more workers testing the assembled machines, installing operating systems, and preparing them for shipping.

“We still have difficulties with some parts. Monitors, especially large ones, are in short supply. There are only two manufacturers. I have contracts with both of them and am considering setting up my own manufacturing plant. For now it’s beyond my financial ability, but I hope to be able to do it soon.”

Esther was impressed. “You are a real entrepreneur. How do you get these ideas? I would never have thought about starting a business just because I had difficulty obtaining something.”

Jacob smiled. “I had to learn to adapt to changing circumstances. When my father died I had to take over his cabinet-making business and learned very quickly how to run it. Later, when the Soviets occupied Vilna I voluntarily nationalized the business. That saved us from being deported to Siberia for being rich but wouldn't have ended well if Israel hadn't come around to save us from the Germans."

They kept chatting on the way back to town and on the train to Beer Sheva. Just before the train arrived Jacob produced a small box, opened it and presented it to Esther. "Will you marry me?"

She looked at the engagement ring in the velvet box and smiled.

✡✡✡

"Quiet please!" The Prime Minister had to repeat it twice before the members of the government quieted down. This was a full government meeting and he was prepared to be rude, if necessary, to manage it effectively.

"Ladies and Gentlemen, we will first hear a report by the head of the Mossad."

An utterly unremarkable looking man reached for a remote control and turned on the overhead projector. "First, a report on the situation in Germany and Central Europe.

"As you all know the Germans accepted the terms we offered and signed the peace agreement. They have already withdrawn from France and the Low Countries and are in the process of evacuating their forces from Norway and Denmark. With our agreement they are keeping an armed presence in Austria. Their military there is busy hunting down senior Nazis. They promise that the operation will be finished in a couple of months."

The Minister for Transportation interrupted. "Is there any reason to believe them about hunting down Nazis? Weren't their armed forces complicit in what the Nazis did?"

"You are correct in that they were complicit, but since the overthrow of Hitler and the civil war they view the Nazis as a deadly enemy and the only serious threat to both the generals and the current government. They exterminated them quite ruthlessly in Germany and are doing a fair job in Austria.

"Now, to Eastern Europe. There things are a bit complicated. The Germans started their withdrawal just as fighting broke out in Moscow after Stalin's assassination. The German High Command was asked by a group of Ukrainian and Belorussian nationalists to slow down until they set up their own independent governments. The Germans asked the Allied Oversight Commission for instructions. The Commission instructed them to assist both the Ukrainians and Byelorussians on condition that there are no Nazi sympathizers among the proposed governing group. As of yesterday the German army continues its slow withdrawal from both areas, leaving behind some weapons for the new governments. They will reach the old Soviet border in another two weeks and, as per the agreement, entrench there for a while.

"Any questions?"

"Are we sure there are no Fascists or former Nazis in the new Byelorussian and Ukrainian governments?" asked the Tourism Minister.

"No, we're not sure at all," responded the head of the Mossad. "On the contrary, I'm quite sure that there are both, especially in the Ukraine. There's not much we can do about it and, frankly, I see no reason to intervene."

Since this seemed to be the only question, he continued. "The situation in the Soviet Union is somewhat murky. We have a fair idea of what happened but it's difficult to predict what is going to happen next.

"To sum up: Stalin was assassinated during the second week of February, several days after he returned from Teheran. He seems to have been poisoned by someone close to him. On the day he died Beria declared himself provisional General Secretary of the Communist Party as well as Premier. We are assuming that he was complicit in the murder and that his hand was forced since he started concentrating NKVD troops in Moscow but didn't have enough for a successful coup. It's also possible that it was a judgment error on his part.

"In any case, several members of the Politburo, including Khrushchev, Kaganovich and Molotov, managed to contact the red Army garrison of Moscow and ask them to intervene. Fighting between the NKVD and the Red Army lasted for several days. The final blow to the NKVD came from troops outside of the capital. Since the Germans started their retreat, the command of the Moscow front moved enough troops to the capital to finish off the NKVD forces.

"Beria was executed a week later and open season on the NKVD started a week after that. Several regions that have always been restive decided it was a good time to secede from the Soviet Union. Practically all of the Caucasus declared independence. This includes Georgia, Armenia, Azerbaijan and Chechnya.

"There is serious unrest in the central areas of Russia. The civil war triggered by the Bolshevik revolution ended only about twenty years ago and anti-Communist sentiment is strong in some areas. One thing that is eerily reminiscent of the breakup of the Soviet Union in our timeline: As soon as a region perceives some freedom to say what they want, the first words are 'Kill the Jews.'

"In a perverse sort of way that helps us since Soviet Jews who could fool themselves that the state eliminated anti-Semitism - and there was a surprising number that believed that canard - can now see the naked hatred. Immigration from the Soviet Union increased tenfold in the last month and is still growing. But lawlessness is not our friend and our Ministry of Defense is taking measures to prevent open pogroms."

Amos Nir looked around the long table. "If there are no more questions I suggest that we let the gentleman go and ask the Foreign Minister for an update."

The Foreign Minister leaned back in his seat, seemingly relaxed. "The analysis by the Mossad may have led you to believe that we have no direct problems except in Europe. This is not true. Both the Americans and the British are doing their best to endear themselves to Saudi Arabia and Iran. In Iran we have good contacts with the current Shah. This is the same ruler who was overthrown by the ayatollahs in our timeline and with whom we had a good relationship. The Brits tried to interfere with our access but stopped when they realized that we don't want to control Iran's oil.

"I expect that with some luck and a consistent policy we will be able to both democratize the Shah's rule and prevent the Islamists from overthrowing him. This will of course depend on the actions of our future governments and on the continuing cooperation of Britain and noninterference from the U.S.

"The situation is very different in Saudi Arabia. As of now the California-Arabian Oil Company is pumping not insignificant amounts of oil and is on its way to becoming ARAMCO. We know that the Saudis will become obscenely rich because of their oil and will use the money to support and spread their flavor of Islam: Wahhabism.

"We have good relations with King Abdullah of Jordan. He urged us to help him recover his 'heritage' from the house of Saud. The cabinet discussed this option a while ago and decided against it. We see no good reason for a conflict that may involve hostilities with U.S. backed interests."

The Minister Without Portfolio from the Labor party had a question: "Are you saying that there's nothing we can do to prevent the future rise of the Saudis?"

"No, that's not what I'm saying. I'll leave the rest to the Prime Minister," the Foreign Minister responded.

Amos Nir smiled. "We have plenty of options, all with unsavory baggage. We could, for example, encourage Abdullah, who just graduated from Emir to King of Jordan, to attack the Saudis and assassinate the Saud family. It probably could be done discreetly. The question is where do we stop? Do we assassinate every leader or ruler we don't like? It's easy to send a drone and kill someone, but what is the moral price? And what guarantee do we have that a worse replacement won't materialize? Or perhaps a vastly richer and more powerful Abdullah will start eying our territory.

"In addition, American interests will remain no matter who rules the countries. They will continue pumping money into these areas. Abdullah might be worse than Saud. We just don't know.

"Several days ago I was presented with a new option. Before I disclose it I need all present who haven't already signed the official Secrecy Act to do so now. Please read it carefully, it's only two pages long but breaching your promise carries a very long prison term. Those who choose not to sign will have to leave before we continue."

Some of the members of the government present started reading, some were objecting loudly, several signed immediately.

The Labor Minister, who was also the leader of the Labor party, got up. "This is a dictatorial requirement. You are depriving us of our right to free speech. I refuse to sign. We will leave the coalition."

The Prime Minister said quietly and with deceptive calm, "You are being deprived of your ability to disclose vital state secrets to our enemies. As opposed to other information that you keep leaking to the press, leaking what I'm about to disclose will land you in jail for a very long time. If you feel you have to, please feel free to leave the coalition."

The Labor Minister shook his head. "I don't understand why you insist I sign this document. We all swore allegiance to the state of Israel and promised to keep her secrets when we were sworn in as members of the Knesset and of the government. Why this document?"

Amos Nir smiled an unpleasant smile. "You would have understood if you read the document, but I'll explain. How well did you keep your oath? If I'm not mistaken, not very well. Everyone leaks what they want to the press and there's not much to be done since prosecution is complicated. After you sign the Act, anything you disclose that is covered by it, which is very narrow, will result in arrest and prosecution by a military tribunal, after a proper investigation by internal security of course."

The room was quiet for a while. In the end everyone signed and Amos continued. "Several days ago I was approached by a businessman who enlightened me to the existence of a technology allowing the opening of portals into other universes. Apparently there are uncountable versions of our Earth existing side by side. I actually went through a portal and visited an alternative Earth. It was very similar to our Earth but seems to have no sentient life. It does have a nice climate, somewhat cooler with more rain. A very crude and preliminary exploration done by this business shows oil and gas reserves in roughly the same places as on our Earth.

"I propose that we help private businesses explore for oil on this parallel Earth and develop the known fields. This will allow us to start selling oil at a price that will undercut the Saudis. The Western oil companies that are operating in the Middle East need a minimum profit margin to make exploration worthwhile. If we start selling oil at a low price their operations in the Arab countries become unviable. They can't lower their prices by much because of the risks they're taking. We can always help those who are friendly, like the Shah. Those who operate oil fields by themselves don't need such high profits since the risks they're taking don't include political risks and they don't need to share with a foreign government. Again, the Shah is a good example."

The Finance Minister nodded. "Controlling the price of oil is a blunt tool but it will work, at least for a while. Maybe a very long while, like seventy or eighty years, until fracking and horizontal drilling are invented."

When the time came to vote on the proposal Amos was surprised: two thirds of the government voted for it, including the two Labor Party ministers.

✡✡✡

After the government meeting, Amos Nir met with the Foreign and Trade Ministers and their legal counsels. The two ministers wanted to reach a decision on trade relations with the U.S.

The Foreign Minister began. "You all read the American ambassador's letter and our ambassador's report from Washington. It seems that the Americans want to take possession of whatever technological advantage we have. I need to instruct Ambassador Lapid on what to do."

Amos asked, "By 'Americans' do you mean their government or private entities?"

The Foreign Minister shrugged. "I wouldn't have worried about private entities. It's the government that worries me."

The Foreign Ministry's legal advisor nodded. "The claim they presented is that technology developed by American companies belongs to the developers. The government of the U.S. has the right to declare itself a legal trustee of this property."

Amos nodded. "I looked this up and asked a number of lawyers I know. They all agreed that under International Law any knowledge developed by an entity belongs to that entity. But there's a little snag here:

the International Law in question doesn't exist here and now. We need to look at our own laws and at American laws. It is obvious to me that our law takes precedence – this is true for any sovereign country. So what do our laws say?"

The lawyer from the Trade Ministry spoke up. "It's clear: either the developer or their designate owns whatever they've developed. It's best defined with patents. A patent is normally owned by whoever is the designated owner. This can be a researcher, their employer or a third party that has contractual ownership."

Amos smiled. "In that case everything is simple. I understand that everything we are discussing has been patented and has an Israeli patent number?"

"That's true, although sometimes our patent refers to a foreign patent."

"Which changes nothing," said Amos. "Every patent has an owner. We don't need to discuss what happens if a patent owner ceases to exist as this is not the case. According to my researchers all the patents in questions are owned by Israeli registered corporations or individuals. I think that this closes the legal question."

"What about shareholder rights?" asked the Trade Minister.

"What about them? The Israeli Microsoft Corporation used to be a fully-owned subsidiary of Microsoft USA. Microsoft USA doesn't exist anymore and except for a very small number of people we don't know who the shareholders were. But let's assume that we want to give the two largest share owners, Bill Gates and Steve Balmer, their shares. Neither individual has been born yet. Bill's father is about eighteen years old now. We have no idea whether he will have a son and whether the son will be identical to the Bill Gates we know. Balmer's maternal family moved to Israel a month ago. Whether they will have offspring named Steve is questionable, especially as his father was a Christian from Switzerland. Even if Bill and Steve are born, they obviously won't be the people we knew."

The Foreign Ministry lawyer nodded. "Put this way the only owners of record of any future technology that we brought with us are people and companies we brought with us. No one outside of Israel has any claims. This is a plausible, though novel, legal approach."

The Prime Minister smiled. "It certainly is novel. None of us has heard of any other country coming back from the future. This is a unique situation and the solution is ultimately political, not legal.

"So, politically, I propose that we present to the Americans our legal position and refuse to give them anything."

"This will anger the U.S. government," the Foreign Minister said.

"Do we have to respond to them?" the Trade Minister asked.

"No. Actually the next step is up to them. I don't even know what the President's position is on this."

Amos got up, signaling the end of the meeting. "I don't see them starting a trade war; it isn't in their interest. After consultations with their ambassador here they will see it as well."

✡✡✡

For the first time in a couple of months Ze'ev was hosting a family dinner. Wolf Frumin was at officers' school and couldn't get a weekend pass. Major General Ephraim Hirshson, Ze'ev's second son, flew in from Europe and attended with his wife. Their year old son was at home with a baby sitter and Ephraim's wife kept looking at her watch.

After Kiddush Ze'ev asked Jacob, "I hear that you have an announcement to make?"

Jacob smiled a big smile. "Yes, we were keeping it for this occasion. On Wednesday I asked Esther to marry me and she agreed. We are formally engaged."

Jacob's mother, Sara, and Esther's parents, Nachman and Tzila looked surprised. Nachman was the first to recover. "We expected something like this but not so soon. When are you kids planning on marrying? I hope it's not too soon. We need to make preparations."

"It will take a while," Esther responded. "I want to graduate before we tie the knot and Jacob plans on being a billionaire before he is a married man," she joked.

"No, I don't. I'm ready to get married tomorrow," Jacob protested as everyone laughed.

"I promise to let everyone know in plenty of time," Esther said.

Talk turned to other topics. Ephraim, seeing his brother-in-law Noam Shaviv for the first time since Noam had been injured, looked at him carefully. "How are you doing? I don't see any signs of an injury."

"I was lucky. I'm almost back to normal. Walking long distances is still difficult, but getting easier.

"I heard of your promotion and heroic leadership in Europe. How are *you* doing?"

Ephraim smiled. "There was nothing heroic on my part. The guys on the front lines, like Wolf, showed courage. Generals are not supposed to be heroic. They are supposed to prevent the necessity for others to become heroes. I did my best, which was adequate."

"I heard different but will not try to inflate your ego beyond bare necessity. I have a serious question though. Many here assumed our technological superiority would guarantee an easy and bloodless victory, so why all the casualties?"

"The technological difference provided us with a huge advantage," Ephraim said, "but it didn't guarantee a bloodless campaign. Both sides are using firearms, and ballistic projectiles, like mortars, can do serious damage, especially if tactical errors are made. I know of no commander who's immune to error, so there you go.

"By the way, how much do you know about this short campaign?"

"There was detailed reporting in the media so the general facts are public knowledge. Then I was called up for training and we were briefed on the tactics and strategy our side used."

"Good," Ephraim smiled. "In that case I can tell you why I did what I did. I figured that the only way to minimize our casualties was to make the Germans come to us. I provoked them and they responded as expected, at least while Hitler was in charge.

"You see, I learned a couple of things from observing them fight the Brits and the Russians. The Germans are tenacious, their field commanders are good and they don't run. We could have attacked them and destroyed them quickly, but at a cost I didn't want to pay. It was a gamble, although not a serious one, to fight from prepared positions instead of advancing. Our troops and commanders are trained to be aggressive and it took a lot of discipline not to do what they were trained to do. But it worked."

The other conversations around the table petered out with everyone listening to Ephraim.

"What do you think will happen now?" his mother Linda asked.

"We have a peace agreement with Germany, which they seem to be scrupulously observing," Ephraim responded. "Our forces are switching to observation and treaty-enforcement format. It means that the heavy weapons - armor, artillery and such - are going back home or to the base in Brindisi. We are deploying a much larger infantry force that will, in cooperation with the other allies, be stationed in Germany and Austria to oversee their denazification."

"And how's that going?" Sara asked.

"Surprisingly well," Ephraim answered. "The Nazis alienated most of the population during their civil war and the rest are afraid to say or do anything that will draw the ire of their army.

"On a different subject, I went to a computer store today to look for a tablet and found a Hirshson Computer laptop, although they had only the one on display. Is this another family business?" He looked at Ze'ev.

"Don't look at me. The culprit is sitting right next to you."

Jacob smiled. "Guilty as charged. Although I have to admit that my partner Zalman Gurevich is a bit too eager to sell. We don't have the merchandise in adequate quantities yet."

Ze'ev nodded. "I hope you'll rein him in. Otherwise he will just increase the demand and someone else will step in to fill it. By the time you're ready it may be too late: You will have a competitor or two and angry customers."

"Yes, I'm aware of the danger. I already told him to stop advertising and pushing stuff we don't have."

"So when *will* you have something to sell?" Ephraim asked. "I really need a good tablet or a small laptop."

"You want a Windows machine, a Linux, or an Android?" Jacob inquired.

"I would prefer Windows."

"You're in luck. I have a mini notebook with me. You can have it. It will go on sale by the end of next week. We already started shipping small numbers."

"How much?" Ephraim inquired.

"For you, it's free, but you have to promise to give me completely honest feedback about it."

Ephraim moved uncomfortably in his seat. "I would prefer to pay, especially as I can't promise feedback. I'll be very busy the next week or so and after that I go back to Europe."

"Somehow I expected that answer. But it's not really free. Think of it as my company hiring you to demonstrate our product. I can't take money from family, especially since your father helped me get started."

"Okay. But when people ask, what should I tell them it costs?"

"Retail is 400 shekels," Jacob responded.

"That's really inexpensive. I hope you make a profit."

"We will. This is a small machine, good for browsing the net, word processing, and not much else. Don't expect it to be a super computer."

"Sounds like just what I need."

After dinner Ephraim went into his father's study and signaled Ze'ev to follow.

"Dad, I suspect that what I'm going to say will come as no surprise to you. I'm hoping you'll clarify some things for me. Do you have 'Top Secret' access?"

"Sure. Go ahead."

"I was instructed to move some of my forces to our base near Venice. It's small but has a landing strip, fuel tanks, and other facilities. I was told to prepare to accept a combat engineer battalion for operations in a wilderness. Does this have anything to do with your alternate universe project?"

Ze'ev smiled. "I'm very reassured. Our Prime Minister is not a slouch and apparently things are moving at a reasonable pace. To answer your question: yes.

"It will not be a breach of secrecy to tell you now. You will know in a couple of days anyway. We have an operating portal into a parallel Earth. We call it, not terribly creatively, Earth 2. When the uses of this new Earth were discussed with your boss, the Chief of General Staff, he came up with an idea: we can move armed forces, or whatever, to Earth 2, and have them pop out anywhere on the globe. The only thing we have to do is move them into position on Earth 2, open a portal and there you are.

"Last Thursday we discussed the possibility of establishing several transport points to take in refugees from the Soviet Union. Transporting people long distances from the inner parts by train is becoming seriously dangerous. It's anarchy there and anti-Semites are popping up all over. We don't want to endanger our emissaries or the refugees.

"The solution your boss proposed was to set up several portals and take people in directly. The size of a personnel portal is about like a doorway so we could have them anywhere. The idea is to set up airstrips on Earth 2. People will walk through a portal in the Soviet Union, board a plane on the other side and fly to another air strip located in the Earth 2 location for Israel or Brindisi. From there they just step through a portal back to our Earth."

"Sounds good. Thanks for telling me. Now I will not sit with my mouth open like an idiot at the Sunday briefing. I may even have some suggestions of my own."

"We have been exploring the neighborhood on Earth 2 for a while and arrived at one important conclusion: We need to set up a communications network. Consolidated is maintaining an aerostat floating at 600 meters in the area of our main gate near Hertzlia. It serves as an antenna and broadcast/receive station. Very handy to communicate with the exploration teams in Sinai 2 and Kuwait 2. For the military it would probably be more economical to use satellites. A couple of geostationary communication birds would solve problems for everyone."

✡✡✡

"Dr. Salk, we appreciate you joining our research team. I sincerely hope you will be successful in whatever you decide to do." The Chairman of Teva paused for a moment looking at the young man sitting across the desk from him. "I trust that you are satisfied with your lab and personnel?"

"I'm very satisfied. I only hope that all the expenses will be justified. There is an inherent difficulty; I have to learn a lot before I know what I want to do."

"I understand. There are a number of cancers we can't cure. Maybe start there? But it's up to you. Take your time. There is another issue I wanted to bring up with you: the polio vaccine."

Salk smiled even wider. "Amazing what I would have done in ten years. I'll definitely have to find something new."

"Before you do, we need to settle the rights to the vaccine. Under our current law and regulations everything an inventor invents is theirs but they can't claim rights to inventions that they might have invented in the future. This means that legally you have no right to the vaccine, but since you are working for us we would like to show good will and reward you."

Jonas Salk shrugged. "I read my biography and will do what I did in your past. I don't want to profit from this vaccine."

"Good. Let's shake on this. We will start selling the vaccine at cost all over the world and give out the manufacturing formula."

✡✡✡

"Mr. Ambassador, I would like to thank your country for the latest insight into the Japanese situation. You knew the Japanese Empire was on the verge of collapse and needed only a small push to surrender. We acted on your information and told them them if they surrendered their Emperor could remain and not be touched. To our surprise they agreed. It seems that Japan was not only starving but also had no fuel to continue hostilities."

The Israeli ambassador bowed slightly in his seat. "This is what allies are for."

FDR continued, "Is there something else you wanted to discuss?"

"Yes. As you know we have a vaccine for polio, or, as it's better known here, Infantile Paralysis. Teva Pharmaceuticals decided that for the good of everyone they will sell the vaccine at cost and license the manufacturing process."

"This is very good news indeed. I'm sure the American people will appreciate this gesture of good will."

After the Ambassador left, Harry Hopkins, who had sat quietly through the meeting, said, "Mr. President, you showed a lot of good will in the past. Are you sure it was justified?"

FDR got up and slowly walked around the Oval Office. "Harry, I had no choice. I understand why Cordell pressed them for rights to technology. I don't particularly like uppity Jews either, but we either start a trade war or get as much as we can from dealing with them. I chose the latter."

"They are complicating our lives. Their ally in the Middle East, the King of Jordan, is gaining influence because of their support. If Abdullah starts a war with the house of Saud, we will have to intervene to protect our oil interests."

Roosevelt sat back behind his desk. "As you know the British Ambassador voiced a similar complaint. They're also wary of the Jews interfering with their interests. The thing is, the Brits don't have anything specific to complain about. They're just worried on general principle. The presence of a strong power in the Middle East challenges their primacy in the region. The strong power being Jewish only makes it worse. The Brits share the Nazi's view of Jews, as do most Americans.

"Right now I am worried about a different issue: the Soviet Union seems to be in trouble and I have no idea whether the new government, assuming there will be a stable one, will honor Stalin's obligations to us. We have invested a lot in them and the Republicans will make hay if they default on payments."

Hopkins brooded for a short time. "I'm sure this mess is also Israel's doing. I carefully read Ambassador Kirk's report. The press in Israel thinks that the disintegration of the Soviet Union is a good thing. I disagree."

The President shrugged. "We'll have to figure out what to do about that."

Chapter 16
October 1943

"Lieutenant, I need you to take a platoon and investigate a piece of information we have about mysterious activity in Hernals." Major Ivan Ivanovich Bobrov pointed to a far suburb of Vienna on the map spread between them.

"We have reason to believe that there might be a Nazi cell holed up in an industrial building. You are to investigate and take any measures necessary to resolve the situation."

Lieutenant Wolf Frumin examined the map. "Are the Austrian police aware of the situation?" The question was posed in Russian. Wolf was fluent in the language and both he and the major used it rather than English, the agreed upon language of the Alliance. Both knew enough English to communicate but neither was comfortable with it.

The major belonged to the Allied Treaty Control Forces, as did Wolf. The Allies participating in the treaty had changed in the last six months – the Soviet Union didn't exist anymore and was replaced by the Russian Federation, which assumed all the Soviet obligations under the peace treaty with Germany. The Allies were empowered to observe and enforce the denazification of Germany, Austria and other Axis allies. The enforcement powers were very wide and allowed the Allies almost unlimited operational freedom.

Ivan Bobrov was much calmer these days; the feared NKVD was gone and he expected to live to draw his military pension. He didn't particularly like the other members of the force under his command in Vienna but he respected them, including the Israeli contingent. Jews or not, they were very dangerous in a fight.

Bobrov considered the question. "You know that captain Angus Campbell was wounded last week. He was on a similar mission, also in Hernals. His force was ambushed. We coordinated with the Austrian police. It's my belief they have a leak and betrayed us. If you insist on notifying them, it's your funeral. I would tell them nothing until you're on the spot and decide what to do.

"I know that you guys have some advanced 'magic' tools. Feel free to use them. If you need more troops you can draw another platoon from whichever part of the force you like."

It took Wolf two days to prepare for the mission. The building in question was about five miles from the Allied headquarters - an abandoned warehouse with a partly glazed roof that had suffered some bomb damage during the war. Wolf had the intelligence company send a drone to land on the roof and look inside. The glass was broken in several places, but even with some dirty windows in the way it was clear that the building was partly occupied. The people inside made lame attempts at concealment but a fire during the cold night betrayed them. The images from the drone showed close to twenty individuals coming and going. Superficial surveillance also showed that several of the occupants visited a nearby abandoned office building on a daily basis, in the early evening.

Wolf informed Lieutenant Rabinovitz of the Russian Army that he needed his platoon to join in the operation. Wolf had become friendly with the Jewish lieutenant, communicating with him in both Yiddish and Russian. The locals were afraid of the Russians who were, sometimes, brutal and not above looting or beating the Austrians. The fear could be used to advantage in this operation.

The joint Allied force left for Hernals at three in the morning. By four, the building was surrounded and a section of the Golani platoon was detached to take a look at the office building visited by the occupants of the factory. The corporal leading that section reported twenty minutes later that they found a large stash of preserved food in the basement. That explained the frequent trips. Wolf scheduled a couple of trucks to come later to pick up the supplies.

His next step was to have the Austrian police liaison use a loudspeaker to inform the people inside the warehouse that they were surrounded. Lieutenant Rabinovitz encouraged his troops to yell in Russian, which they did enthusiastically. Shortly thereafter the people in the building were told to surrender or else. The 'else' wasn't specified but that and the presence of Russians scared some of them enough to come out with their hands over their heads.

Wolf counted eight men. "Where are the rest?" He waited for the liaison's translation and the reply. "There are only the eight of us."

"Start deploying tear gas," Wolf ordered. Ten minutes later three more men came out. Then two squads of Golani fighters wearing gas masks entered the building. It took them close to a quarter of an hour to determine that the building was empty. By then there was enough light to see by, so Wolf ordered a thorough search. He also asked the prisoners. "I know there were twenty two of you. Where are the rest?"

"There are only eleven of us," responded the Austrian.

A Russian sergeant standing nearby shot the Austrian, shattering his hip. Wolf gestured for two Golani soldiers to disarm the Russian and handcuff him. The Russian didn't try to fight or protest.

Lieutenant Rabinovitz arrived on the scene a minute later. "Sergeant, are you crazy? The penalty for what you did is a shooting squad. Why did you fire?"

"Comrade Lieutenant, I recognize this man. He's an SS noncom who commanded the unit that burned down my village in 1941. I barely escaped with my life. My family wasn't so lucky. He deserves to be killed but I knew you'd want information from him."

Wolf, as the commanding officer of the small force, took control of the situation. "Release the sergeant," he told the Israeli soldiers, "and give him back his weapon." He turned to the Austrian liaison, who stared at the scene, sweating despite the cold weather. "Get us another prisoner."

The first man was still shrieking and bleeding on the ground. The second man brought before Wolf looked visibly shaken and when asked about the whereabouts of his co-conspirators kept looking at the rapidly growing pool of blood.

"Will you talk or shall I leave you to the Russians?" asked Wolf.

He talked. Apparently the group found a basement under the warehouse and the rest were hiding there.

"Are they armed?" was the next question.

"They have guns, mostly pistols and a couple grenades."

The prisoner, who was a member of the Nazi group the Allied force had come to investigate, showed the soldiers the entry to the basement hidden behind a pillar and under a thick layer of debris. The ones who had surrendered piled the debris over the entrance before coming out, in hope of protecting the rest of the group.

Wolf consulted with Rabinovitz and decided not to endanger the lives of his soldiers. According to the radar sensor the Israelis brought, the trap door was almost three inches thick. It also clearly showed a flight of stairs going down and some movement at the bottom.

The soldiers placed a charge on the door, blowing it off its hinges. Thick smoke started billowing from the basement. It took only seconds for the first man to come up the stairs. He was bleeding from his nose. "We have several injured that need help," he said loudly.

Wolf had a message that the liaison yelled downstairs: "Everyone that can walk should come out now with their hands on their heads. You can carry those who can't walk."

The soldiers moved about forty feet from the opening to prevent a sudden attack but none came. The rest of the group came up carrying two men that were bleeding from various wounds. Ambulances were waiting.

A search of the basement and warehouse and recovery of firearms and an explosives stash completed the operation.

On the way back to their base Wolf had a short conversation with Lieutenant Rabinovitz. “How reliable is that sergeant of yours? Will he talk?”

Rabinovitz smiled. “He is not crazy and not stupid. The penalty for what he did, if a court martial were called, is a firing squad. He’ll be as quiet as a fish.”

“Good. There’s really nothing special to report, just wounding three Nazis. This was to be expected in a firefight. Now it’s in the hands of the Allied War Crimes Commission. I’m sure they will demand an explanation from the Austrians why a large group of Nazis wasn’t prosecuted. I hope that the Russian representatives won’t accept the normal Austrian excuse that they were just as much victims of the Nazis as everyone else.

“We need to look very closely at the Austrian police. They enabled those Nazis to ambush the British unit of Captain Campbell and then let them escape.”

Wolf looked at Rabinovitz. “Tell me, Lieutenant, why are you still in the Russian Army? Don’t you want to move to Israel?”

“I still have six months to serve. After my enlistment term is over I’ll go back to Bobruisk for my family and then we’ll leave.”

✡✡✡

Hans Paulus reflected on how much his attitude had changed in only two years. He had been working for Siemens when he was stranded in Israel after the time displacement incident. At first he was upset but also grateful for being in Israel and not in Germany. The Nazi regime did not appeal to him; he held Hitler personally responsible for his great uncle’s fate. The great uncle in question was Field Marshal von Paulus of the 6th Army, famous for being the only Field Marshal to surrender instead of commit suicide after a defeat.

Hans wasn’t any more enamored of the Nazis now than he was then, but his attitude toward contemporary Germany had changed. His great uncle was one of the men that defeated the Nazis. Hans was eager to meet him. And Paulus was bothered by the fact that the Jewish state was one of the world powers dictating terms to Germany. If only Germany had the bomb. Hans developed a plan to get the necessary information but didn't know to whom or how to transfer it.

In the meantime Hans went to the University library where he was sure he could find all the information he needed. It took him less than half an hour to determine that all technical texts relating to nuclear technology had been removed from the library's computerized catalog. He remembered clearly having seen a research paper on the vulnerability of Siemens industrial controllers to specific viruses in the context of nuclear enrichment plants. The paper was old and referred to the Stuxnet virus and the disruption of Iranian uranium enrichment; now it was missing from the catalog. Hans went home and thought some more. By the next day he had a plan.

The information he needed was obviously still in the library but not accessible to just any visitor. He had noticed people approaching one of the librarians and, after showing ID, being admitted to a separate room. Hans approached one of the librarians, whom he chose because she was young and seemed nice, and asked to see the paper on virus vulnerability.

"I will need your ID and the reason you need to see the paper."

Hans presented his ID card. "I work for Siemens Israel and the paper describes some problems with one of our controllers. I need to review it."

The librarian smiled. "Just let me scan your card. You should have clearance by tomorrow."

"Is this a general clearance or is it going to be specific for this paper?"

"I can request a general one for material at the same level so you won't have to apply every time you want to see something," the nice girl responded.

"Good. Let's do that."

On the way out Hans noticed a well-dressed man intently looking at him. He assumed the man was part of Israeli security and nodded to him. Hans Paulus wasn't worried. After all, he had done nothing illegal, yet.

When he arrived at the library the next day the librarian smiled at him from afar and motioned for him to come over. "Mr. Paulus, I have the clearance you requested. Please feel free to enter the special reading room."

On the way to the special reading room Hans noticed that the man from yesterday was again observing him.

The man was there when Hans left the reading room two hours later. He stopped by the librarian's desk. "I would like to copy a couple of pages to review in my office."

The librarian smiled her usual wide smile. "No problem. Leave whatever you want copied with me. Mark the pages. Copies will be ready tomorrow and cost you one shekel for every five pages."

Hans was slowly walking through the campus when the man from the library approached him. "Hans Paulus?"

"Yes?" Hans replied carefully.

"I'm Rudolf Gerzitz from the German embassy. We met about two years ago." The man looked hopefully at Hans.

"Ah." Hans smiled with relief. "That's why you looked familiar. I mistook you for a security agent."

"No no, I'm the third secretary at the German embassy. As you know, diplomatic relations were re-established after Germany surrendered. The German government decided to use the services of the up-timers who were already here.

"But back to the business at hand, I got interested in you after Germany surrendered. You are the great nephew of General Paulus, yes?"

"That's a widely known fact. What is it to you?" Hans was slightly impatient.

Gerzitz looked around and said in a quiet voice, "Since you gained access to the restricted part of the library I am assuming that you may not be happy with Germany's position in the world. Please correct me if I'm wrong and you will never hear from me again."

Hans said nothing for a while. They continued their slow progress through the university campus. Finally Hans responded, "You are not wrong. I think Germany needs to be much stronger and more respected than it is."

Gerzitz nodded. "Possession of nuclear weapons might do it."

Hans stopped. "Assuming that's correct and assuming I may be able to collect the necessary information, there's no way to give it to someone outside of Israel."

Gerzitz resumed the slow walk. "There may be a way. Would you entrust the information to me if I assured you that it would get into the right hands?"

Hans hesitated. "Yes, as long as it isn't going to the Nazis."

Gerzitz was surprised. "What does it matter who gets it as long as Germany benefits? I can tell you that there's only one entity in Germany that would be able to make use of this information. The group is headed by a former Nazi, but please remember that the Nazis are no longer in power. Whatever this entity develops will benefit the German state."

Hans Paulus said nothing for a long time. They left the campus and walked in the general direction of the Siemens plant, though it would take hours to get there on foot.

Finally he said, "It is true that the Nazis are no longer in control. I do want Germany to be one of the great world powers, so I will give you the information. We need to work out a system so the Israeli security services do not catch us."

Gerzitz smiled. "That's simple. You know what a dead drop is?"

✡✡✡

The Prime Minister started the Cabinet meeting with formal introductions. "You all know Dr. Ze'ev Hirshson or at least have heard about him. I propose that we let him make a presentation which we will discuss later."

Ze'ev began by explaining why he thought that Israel would be wise to prepare an escape hatch in case things go sideways and how his technology of opening a portal to a parallel Earth could provide a safety valve.

He continued, "We have the means to move the whole country to Earth 2 but if there's no prepared base we will find ourselves in a bad situation - We need sources of food, energy, and raw materials. We can't wait for these resources to be developed on Earth 2 after an abrupt more. Our reserves would run out too soon. I propose setting up an agricultural and industrial infrastructure and settling enough of our population on Earth 2 so that if the time comes we could all move with no great shocks to the system."

The Finance Minister asked, "I assume that you expect the government to finance you?"

"Not at all." Ze'ev smiled at the surprised expressions around the table. "We might need some loans but no direct financing. The oil companies received government guaranteed loans. We would be satisfied with similar terms."

"I can see how the oil companies will make a nice profit selling their oil in order to repay loans. How will you?" the Infrastructure Minister asked.

"We expect to profit in a number of ways. The technology necessary to open the gates is ours. The government declared it a 'National Security asset' and controls its use but we are still paid for traffic that passes through the gates. We also expect to acquire some real estate on Earth 2. As you know, we received approval to move some of our plants there and have already started doing so. This will significantly reduce our costs.

"In addition, Consolidated applied for the right to extract some mineral resources necessary for our industrial endeavors. Approval of this application will also increase our profits. Any industrial company moving to Earth 2 will be in a position to realize future profits. I could go on and on but you get the general idea."

The Justice Minister nodded. "I'm not an economist but you seem to make sense. My expectation is that your plan will eventually be approved. It will require some thinking and fine tuning. We will probably have to pass new laws, or at least new regulations, to account for the different conditions."

Ze'ev smiled. "Minister, the government doesn't have to approve a 'Grand Plan' all at once. Parts of it are already being executed. The oil companies are working at breakneck speed. Consolidated is also working as fast as we can, and construction is moving ahead on auxiliary services and housing for workers. As long as you approve the essential parts of our application and start working on the master plan we are going to be fine. Just don't let the bureaucracy take over and extend the timetable.

"The only reason I'm here is to offer the State of Israel an escape hatch. This I do not for profit or any other gain. I am a child of Holocaust survivors and it is my sincere estimation that sooner or later the world will again gang up on the Jewish people. I'm preparing an alternative to fighting an unwinnable and bloody war. I'll do it with or without your support, although I very much hope that you will agree to help.

"In the meantime the resources of this alternative Earth will, hopefully, postpone the need to escape. It may even eliminate it completely. Still, it's better to prepare for the worst."

The Defense Minister shook his head. "What do you mean by 'do it with or without' our support?"

"I mean that we don't need the government involved at all beyond authorizing the use of our technology for this project. If loan guarantees are not forthcoming we can still manage. At a slower pace, but we will do it. Don't misunderstand me. I would prefer the support of the government. My company would benefit from it, as would Israel."

The Foreign Minister nodded. "I have some concerns, which I voiced when we were discussing the original permission for the oil companies. What do we do if information of the ability to go to alternative universes leaks and foreign governments ask to participate?"

Ze'ev responded, "I have a partial solution. Every person that knows about this project has signed the Official Secrets Act form. This will not prevent the secret from leaking eventually but will buy us some time. At present the gates are operated by Consolidated with government inspectors present and are protected by IDF troops.

"We can change the whole structure. We can form a new company. Call it the Gate Corporation, a fully owned subsidiary of Consolidated. This company could own and operate the gates under an exclusive contract with the government. The contract doesn't need to be published and can, in fact, be protected under the Official Secrets Act.

"The Gate Corporation would be responsible for security, using a government-approved contract to sign up others for the project. In case the government is approached by a foreign entity you can refer them to us and not get involved directly."

The Prime Minister nodded. "This is a good first draft of the idea. We will discuss it and, if we approve, let our experts work out the details." He looked at Ze'ev. "It will not take long. I'm as aware as you are of the dangers. Most members of the Cabinet agree as well."

✡✡✡

The Security Service agent who authorized Hans Paulus' access to the special section of the library set up surveillance and notified the Mossad.

A couple of days later the agent met with his Mossad counterpart and heard the news. "I'm glad that someone finally showed interest in nuclear affairs," the Mossad agent said. "We're conducting an operation in Europe and this fits in."

"What is the European operation about?" the agent asked.

"I won't give you details, but it's important. Someone is discreetly financing nuclear research. As soon as we became aware of it we concluded that they had a chance only if they could steal information from us. This is the first sign that someone is trying. I'm telling you this just so you know how important your catch is."

"Good," the Security agent smiled. "We will take care of this on the domestic side. Any special requests?"

The Mossad agent nodded. "Yes, one. We need to feed them false information. I will deliver packets to you to be fed to Hans. We will also need to know how they smuggle it out of the country."

✡✡✡

"Ladies and gentlemen, every one of you will have to agree to this basic contract. If you don't agree you won't get access. If you breach any of the conditions you will lose access and be liable under the Official Secrets Act." Ze'ev Hirshson paused to let his assistants hand out printed copies of the contract.

The meeting was being held in the brand new auditorium on the grounds of Consolidated's headquarters in Hertzlia. The auditorium had no windows. It did have two sets of doors, one on each side of the large room. Everyone entered through the doors on the east side.

After every participant had a printout of the contract Ze'ev continued. "As you see, the contract is only two pages long. These are the most important points:

"1. The environmental laws of the State of Israel apply in all of the new domain.

"2. The Labor laws also apply, except as explained in the addendum.

"3. The criminal and civil code of the State of Israel will serve as a guideline for the new domain but it will be up to the community to decide which rules to enforce and how to enforce them. There are two exceptions: the death penalty is reinstated for certain crimes, and everyone is free to carry any weapon they desire.

"You will also note that every applicant to enter the domain will have to pass a thorough background check as well as a medical exam. We will not allow criminals, even those convicted of petty crimes, or carriers of infectious diseases to enter.

"Any questions?"

The room was quiet at first. About fifty people were in attendance, which left the auditorium more than three quarters empty. The attendees were business people, including heads of oil companies, food processors, agricultural exporters and a representative of the power company.

The deputy manager of the Israel Electric Corporation was the first to speak up. "I can see why the oil and gas industry may be interested but why do you think we would want to operate there?"

"Actually, I'm sure that when your management team digests the information they will be the first to rush in. As of now you are making a modest profit but it's mostly the result of no longer having to supply free power to the Palestinians. Your margins are low because of the cost of fuel and the interest you're paying on capital investments. Even when the supply of natural gas from the platforms on top of the Leviathan field is resumed your costs will be higher than if the power generation was done in Iraq or Kuwait, right on top of gas sources on solid ground.

"You're using emergency gas turbines to keep up with demand. It's both wasteful and expensive. Our population is growing and will reach close to twenty million in a couple of years. You will have to build new power stations very soon. The question is where? It will be much more efficient to have power transmission lines going from Iraq than ship the fuel to stations in Israel."

"But we have no option to build power stations in Iraq!" The representative exclaimed.

"I apologize for not being clear. I was talking about Iraq 2. The equivalent place in our new domain."

"But how do we transfer power between universes?"

Ze'ev smiled. "The same way you transfer it now: by cable. The same way we are powering this auditorium."

The auditorium exploded with noise as everyone began talking. Finally Ze'ev used his mike to quiet them down. "I see that you're surprised. Please take a look." He gestured and one of his assistants opened the doors on the west side of the room. The view was a green plain gently sloping towards the Mediterranean.

The CEO of a food processing business asked, "Apparently the climate there is not as hot and dry as here?"

"Generally, that is correct but the reality is a bit more complicated than is apparent just looking out these doors. For reasons that will be explained to those of you who sign the contract and the secrecy agreement, settlements will be built outside the borders of the current State of Israel. The best close place for agricultural communities in this domain is in Mesopotamia – in other words Iraq. There's plenty of water from the Tigris and Euphrates rivers, the soil is fertile and unspoiled by thousands of years of primitive agriculture. The agronomists who examined the area told us that several thousand farmers can feed more people than we expect to be living in Israel for the next thirty years. Provided of course that they use modern techniques and machinery. Combine this with all the auxiliary services they will need and position them close enough to the oil fields and we have the makings of a large settlement."

"How soon can we start moving people there?" asked a petite redhead. She was the Secretary General of a kibbutz in the Negev that had been scratching out a meager living from the desert for many years. By now the kibbutz had several successful industrial ventures but a sizeable percentage of members would be happy to revert to agriculture.

Ze'ev yielded the lectern to the CEO of Second Domain Oil. "We have been drilling in the area for three months and have several operational oil and gas wells. Our partners are laying a pipe line to a terminal on the Israeli border as fast as they can. We're also working on the construction of our first refinery. The infrastructure is being developed very fast, mainly to support our own operations although it's suitable for other uses. Maybe I'll let our main construction subcontractor explain."

Another man came to the lectern and switched on an overhead projector with maps and aerial photographs. "Our company will be ready to start construction of villages, roads, and other infrastructure in about six to nine months, assuming everything goes according to plan. We will construct wherever our customers want. All work will have to be paid for by the customers, although I understand that there are government guaranteed loans available to both individuals and groups."

"Do we have to use your services?" the kibbutz secretary asked.

Ze'ev came back to the lectern to answer the question. "You can use any construction company you like, provided they sign our contract."

The president of a large furniture maker had a question. "I am familiar with the concept that an armed society guarantees freedom but isn't it going too far to remove all limits on gun ownership?"

Ze'ev expected a question like that. "The short answer is no, it's not going too far. As it is now we have very wide gun ownership, including all the people serving in the reserves who bring their weapons home on leave. Here we will have a society of people that have been carefully screened. I see no downside. There is a significant upside. You will be crossing into a world that has a lot of wildlife, mostly identical to ours and with lots of predators. You remember the Biblical stories, like Samson killing a lion? Well, there are plenty of lions, tigers, wild boar and other predators. They are much more dangerous than they were here in Biblical times. They have never encountered a human being and don't have an ingrained fear of us. To a lion you just look like a tasty morsel. If you're not armed your life expectancy may be very short. This is not to say that you'll see lions coming into a factory, but, like in some areas of the U.S. and Russia where bears come into settlements, you might encounter a lion or tiger on a street."

✡✡✡

Sir Thomas Harvey, the British ambassador to Israel, was patiently waiting to be invited into the Foreign Minister's inner office. Two years ago he would have fumed and complained but now he just sat and waited. Britain was an ally of Israel and he had come to understand that it would be extremely foolish to alienate this ally.

Finally the receptionist said, "Mr. Ambassador, the Foreign Minister can see you now."

The Foreign Minister shook hands with Harvey and invited him to sit on a couch in the corner of his office. "Would you like something to drink?"

Harvey used this question to mildly hint at the twenty minute wait. "Thank you, but I already had two cups of tea."

The Foreign Minister ignored the dig. “I’m glad that my staff took care of you while I was busy. What can I do for you today?”

“I would like to clarify a couple of questions for His Majesty’s Government. We understand that you offered King Abdullah of Jordan military assistance. What are your aims?”

“I wasn’t aware that we are required to explain the aims and means of our foreign policy. According to your agreements with King Abdullah he was obligated to inform you. Didn’t he do so?”

“He did, but his report was vague. Whether it was so on purpose or just the result of his not knowing all the details is uncertain. Can you shed more light on this?”

“Let me start from the beginning so we have some context. As you know the Arab Legion - which is another name for the Jordanian armed forces - was organized, armed, and trained by Britain starting in 1920. By 1939 it was a force of more than 6000 troops, including armored cars, mortars and artillery. John Bagot Glubb commanded the force beginning in 1939. He was also their commander during our war of Independence in 1948-49. Under British command and with British encouragement the Arab Legion burned Jewish villages, executed some of the Jews living there, destroyed every Jewish synagogue in the old city of Jerusalem and either killed or expelled the Jewish population in a number of areas. Britain also turned over its forts and police stations to the Arabs in contravention to its obligations under the Mandate for Palestine.”

“Yes, Minister. I know the history, although there’s always another side to the story.”

The Foreign Minister leaned towards the British Ambassador and said, “Mr. Harvey, murder is murder. The modern term for what the Arab Legion did, with British support, is ‘ethnic cleansing’.

“But let me continue. We found Mr. Glubb in command of the Arab Legion here and now. We could not condone the force being trained and groomed for anti-Jewish activity. We asked the British Foreign Office to remove him and other like-minded officers and to initiate a training program that would result in a literate armed force less likely to commit mindless acts of genocide. You know of these communications since some of them went through you and you were copied on the rest.”

“That’s true. But Britain is a sovereign country and is free to act as it chooses in its domains.”

The Foreign Minister smiled a humorless smile. “That is true indeed but Britain is also an ally of Israel, which is also a sovereign country free to act as it chooses.

"Since your government chose not to act, we decided to defend our vital interests in the region. You recognized Abdullah as King of Jordan so he is free to sign agreements with foreign powers. We offered him a deal: we will arm and train his army and personal bodyguard. In return he agreed to get rid of the British trainers and accept our methods.

"For some reason" - the Foreign Minister's voice carried clear irony – "the king believed we would be both a more reliable and a much stronger ally than Britain. You see, he also read some of the future history books. Not being stupid he realized we had a great interest in keeping his kingdom safe and stable and the ability to do so, which could not be said for Britain.

"The Royal Jordanian Army we are creating will not be inherently hostile to us and will be able to defend Jordan from foreign threats. Does His Majesty's Government have a problem with that?"

"I can't answer that question. I will transmit your remarks to my government. They will certainly appreciate the clarification.

"Could you elaborate on your plans - the weapons you are giving Abdullah or anything else that might be of interest?"

"No, I don't think that we need to keep you informed on our plans and progress. I'm sure that His Majesty's Government has its own means of finding out what it needs to know.

"Are there any other matters you wished to discuss?"

"As you know, the price of oil has been dropping for the past month or so. This is becoming a problem for our oil companies. If the price drops by more than an additional 10%, they will start losing money. According to our information the drop in price is caused by two of your companies selling oil below costs. His Majesty's Government would like to arrive at an agreement regarding this issue."

"I understand the problem your oil producers are experiencing but I see no reason to involve our governments. Maybe your oil producers should talk to ours directly to find out how they can improve their efficiency. As far as my government is concerned this is a private business matter."

✡✡✡

Hans Paulus walked slowly along one of the paved trails in the Australian Soldiers Park of Beer Sheva - a nice place to take a stroll and mostly empty this time of day. He took a seat on one of the benches in the center of the park and, after carefully looking around, placed a plastic bag with some papers in a trashcan to his right. He sat there for another minute, got up, put a pebble on the bench and walked back to his apartment.

Hans was relived. This was his last delivery, marked as such on the front cover. He had copied more than a hundred pages for Rudolph Gerzitz. Hopefully they were delivered to the right people. His job was done.

A couple of minutes after Hans left, a casually dressed older man walked by the trash can. He extracted Hans's package and replaced it with a similar looking one, also containing printed pages.

Half an hour later the Third Secretary of the German Embassy walked by. On seeing the pebble he approached the trash can and removed the plastic bag with its papers. He also placed the stone back on the ground.

✡✡✡

"Hi, Jacob. Haven't seen you in a long time. How are things going?" Ze'ev looked around the spacious, sparsely furnished office.

"Things are both better and worse than I expected. We are selling computers at a rate that exceeds our ability to assemble them. That's our problem."

"Your company is doing well. 'Hirshson Computers' is among the largest computer manufacturers and still growing. So what specifically is bothering you?"

"Will you accompany me for a quick tour of the facility?" Jacob responded.

Half an hour later they were back in Jacob's office.

"You have seen my problem," Jacob said. "We're assembling computers not making them. Because of our size we get some customized parts from manufacturers and our name is on all components but we don't make them."

"How much vertical integration do you want? Do you want to make your own processors? Motherboards?"

"I would *like* to be able to make my own processors, but that would be stupid. I can't compete with the likes of Intel and AMD. It is also impractical to make our own memory chips. It *would* be advantageous to design and make our own motherboards - expanding into memory for solid state drives at some point - and displays and printers."

Ze'ev smiled. "Be careful and don't overreach. That leads to disaster.

"So what is preventing you from setting up a motherboard manufacture?"

Jacob fidgeted uncomfortably. "The problem is capital. I started this business with a couple of loans. Most of the money came from a bank and some from friends. I paid off the bank loan and still owe some money to a couple of old time friends. I can't do the same with a motherboard assembly plant. The equipment is expensive and requires a significant investment up front."

It finally dawned on Ze'ev why Jacob had invited him. "I think that I can convince the board of Consolidated to either loan you the funds directly or guarantee such a loan." He saw Jacob start shaking his head. "But it will not be free."

Jacob stopped the negative head shake and looked thoughtful. "What would be your terms?"

"How much money do you need to set up this factory?"

Jacob pulled out a spreadsheet. "The assembly line and prep equipment cost about five million shekels. We can lease the rest of this building and install the air filtration equipment. Because of the dusty conditions the cost of that will be approximately four million shekels."

"There are several ways to do this. I estimate that your company will be worth about fifty million in five years. I'm also sure that you are underestimating your startup costs. In any case, I think that Consolidated will make a good deal buying 10% of your company now for five million. Just so you know, I own all of Consolidated and on my death Chaim gets 51% equity, with the rest equally divided between my other children.

"I could also arrange to give you a loan or guarantee a bank loan. The disadvantage of that is loans have to be paid off on schedule, with interest. You'd be in a much better position with Consolidated as a 10% partner."

"Only if I can buy back my shares at any time," Jacob responded. "What bothers me is interference from my partner."

"Not for 10% of fifty or even a hundred million. Consolidated has sales of about 500 million shekels and it will be ten times as much in a couple of years. I could just give you the money but I know you won't accept a handout."

"That's true. Okay. I will sell you 10% of my company. I'll tell my lawyer to prepare the papers. Thank you very much. Maybe now Esther will agree to set a date for our wedding."

Ze'ev didn't even try to suppress the laugh. "Good luck. She's very stubborn and I doubt that the state of your finances will influence her decision. But keep trying. In my past you out-stubborned her.

"To change the subject, I am setting up a new company, the Portal Corporation. It will develop, manufacture, set up, and manage portals to alternate universes. I would like you to be on the board, possibly an executive board member, time allowing."

"Chaim mentioned this portal business a while ago, as did Omer Toledano, your chief of research, but I thought this was all theory. I know nothing about it and doubt that I can be of any use."

"You will be surprised what you can do. You have the distinction of being a successful business owner, a family member, and intimately familiar with the psychology of the here and now as well as with modern technology and thinking. Your input would be important and on some issues critical."

✡✡✡

The chief of the European desk assembled his senior staff for an urgent meeting. The Mossad needed to act quickly.

"Several weeks ago we discovered a Nazi plot to develop a nuclear bomb in Switzerland, of all places. We have two agents inside the facility. We're feeding the scientists there false data. We need to stop this activity once and for all. The only way to do this is to shut down their funding and eliminate the source.

"Our people know that the money is transferred to a private bank in Zug, Switzerland. We need to discover where it's coming from. Any ideas?"

The communications expert raised his hand. "It will be easy to tap into their phone and telex lines. That way we can catch the next wire transfer. Assuming we can decrypt it."

One of the cryptologists smiled. "That's easy. Give me the telex or teletype and I'll decrypt it in five minutes on my laptop."

The chief raised an eyebrow. "It can't be that easy. The Swiss banks are supposed to be secure."

"So they are," the cryptologist responded, "but we know the algorithm they're using. If I know the date of the transmission and have access to our historical archives I may be able to do it in less than a minute."

The historian of the team had been busy on his laptop. Now he spoke up. "According to the records the Beerli bank accepted a shipment of gold in 1942 - a small shipment from Goering. At that time in our timeline Goering wasn't in a great hurry to move his stolen riches to Switzerland. He might have transferred more in this timeline."

The chief nodded. “That may be very useful. Can we find out the amounts, the account number and the password for the account?”

“In our original timeline the shipment was accompanied by Goering’s assistant, one Dr. Friedrich Goernnert. I would assume that he was also the one to do it this time. We find him, we find all the information.”

The meeting went on for several hours of planning and assigning tasks. The teams left for Europe several days later. None of them carried Israeli passports.

Chapter 17
January 1944

According to the records of the German border patrol, one Fritz Goernnert had indeed escorted a truck into Switzerland in March of 1942. The IDF Captain representing the Allied Oversight Forces requested the German Ministry of the Interior find where Fritz Goernnert was resided now. It was surprisingly easy. Apparently Goernnert didn't feel guilty and lived openly in Berlin on a small pension. He also worked as an aviation consultant to the German Ministry of Defense.

On a snowy and cold morning in the first week of January two Mossad agents visited Goernnert at his apartment. A week earlier, the agents and their boss debated whether the visit to Goernnert should be by German police or something else. They settled on a compromise.

The apartment building was on a street close to the center of the city. It looked like it was newly renovated; judging by the adjacent buildings the neighborhood had been hit by at least one bombing raid.

The two men entered the lobby. There was a doorman and a receptionist. This was an expensive building; Goernnert either made a lot of money as a consultant or had other sources of income.

The doorman was polite but followed closely behind the two as they approached the receptionist. "We need to see Dr. Goernnert," the older man said.

"Is he expecting you?"

"No, and you will not notify him," the older man said, flashing his fake German KRIPO (Criminal Police) badge.

The receptionist nodded to the doorman who pressed a button to summon an elevator and opened the door for them.

As soon as the door closed the older man opened it. The receptionist was on the intercom.

"I told you not to notify him. Is it really worth spending a couple of years in the slammer for interfering with a police investigation?" He jerked the receiver from the receptionist, replacing it in its cradle.

The receptionist was a big man and started to get up from his seat. He quickly sat down at the sight of the second agent's gun. The older agent pulled the telephone's cord out of its wall socket; it would take a technician to reconnect it. "I wouldn't like you to be tempted," he said with an unpleasant smile.

The man who opened the door of the fourth floor apartment was cautious but not hostile. "How can I help you?" he asked through the door, opened a crack and held by a security chain.

"Dr. Goernnert, my name is Heinz Kimmel. This is my colleague Rudi Alprecht. We would like to ask you a couple of questions." The older agent showed his police ID to Goernnert.

Goernnert hesitated. "It's very early and I will have to go to my office soon."

Heinz smiled. "We could take you to the precinct but that would be a hassle and it's not really necessary. You should be able to make it to your office in plenty of time."

Goernnert made a decision, removed the chain, and opened the door.

After they were seated in the living room Goernnert said, "Please go ahead but try to be quiet. My wife is still asleep and I wouldn't like to wake her."

"No problem. We have only a couple of simple questions. Some facts first: On June 25, 1942, only a few days before Reichsmashall Hermann Goering was assassinated, you arrived at the Beerli bank in Zug, Switzerland, with a truckload of gold. Tell me the account number and access code you used."

"You are mistaken. I never left Germany during the war."

Heinz nodded to his partner, who opened his briefcase and pulled out two pieces of paper. The first was a page from the border post at Konstanz listing Goernnert as escorting a truck into Switzerland; the second was an authorization letter signed by Goering.

"Dr. Goernnert, please don't underestimate us. We know everything there is to know about you." Heinz smiled a predatory smile. "I really would like to finish this business quickly. On the other hand, I'm not against Rudi having some fun with you."

"You're not from the police, are you?"

"Not on this assignment. We are part of your old organization and, as you know, will stop at nothing to get information. We really don't care what it costs you. Your wife and two kids are less than pawns in this game."

"Please, not my wife or kids. They know nothing of this matter. I will tell you everything."

"Good. Just don't lie. The bank opens in an hour and a half and our comrades will present your information then. If it's correct you will never hear from us again. If you lie, we will know as soon as the bank opens and you will regret it."

Goernnert hesitated and then gave them two numbers. Rudi picked up the phone on a little stand in the foyer, dialed, and recited the two numbers.

Now they waited. Soon there were noises from the other end of the apartment and a woman called out, "Darling, where are you?"

Goernnert looked at Heinz, who nodded. "I have business visitors. We are in the study. Can you please keep the kids out of here?"

At five minutes past nine the telephone rang. Rudi picked up. "The sun is shining," said a voice on the other end.

Rudi nodded to Heinz who got up. "Dr. Goernnert, it was a pleasure doing business with you. Remember that if you mention this to anyone, you and your family will pay the price."

After the two agents were gone Goernnert congratulated his foresight in putting aside enough loot to make him and his family comfortable for a long, long time.

On the drive to the airport Heinz Frankel, a German Jew from Frankfurt who volunteered to work for the Mossad in 1941, said to his partner, "I was afraid for a moment that he might carefully examine the Goering letter. After all we don't know whether our up time copy is identical to what Goering wrote this time."

Rudi Cohen, also from Frankfurt, responded, "Nah, he was under pressure and seriously scared. After all, he knows what his friends are capable of."

✡✡✡

"General, according to the information we have..." Hans Kammler interrupted the speaker with an energetic gesture. "No generals here. Remember where we are. You might endanger the whole operation and our lives. Just 'Hans' will do. You were saying?"

Dr. Karl-Heinz Höcker nodded. "My apologies, Hans. According to the information we obtained from your source, it is not too complicated to make a uranium bomb. But there are several very tall obstacles to overcome. The most difficult is obtaining highly enriched uranium."

Dr. Wilhelm Hanle agreed. “We need enormous industrial resources to achieve this goal.”

SS General Hans Kammler, former commander of the Nazi underground weapons development complex near Gusen Mauthousen, shrugged. “Gentlemen, we will have plenty of resources once we show our sponsors that we know what we’re doing. They’ve already allocated a significant amount - this building, for example.”

The scientists looked around the nicely furnished office. Finally Dr. Hanle ventured a comment. “It would be useful for us to take a look around and see exactly what we have here.”

Both scientists had been part of the Nazi Uranium group disbanded in 1942 after the notorious Diebner incident. They went back to teaching and research at their universities but were more than happy participate in this exciting new venture.

Kammler got up from behind his desk. “Good. Let’s go for a walk. We will not be able to see everything. The Swiss Industrial research Institute is quite large. We will see the main labs on the top four floors.”

After the tour Höcker asked, “Can we count on more detailed technical information from your source?”

“I’m not sure. My source can look up information and answer questions. You will need to ask the right questions.”

“How much technical staff will we have here?” Hanle wanted to know.

“I’m assuming that you want well-trained and qualified German engineers and technicians,” Kammler responded. “We have close to three hundred here now and can recruit many more. Don’t worry about this.

“ You do have to be very careful not to let anyone outside this project even suspect what we’re doing here. As far as the locals are concerned the Institute is doing industrial research for Swiss companies, mostly connected to manufacturing improvements of watches and such. Just a bunch of Germans working for Swiss industry.”

Höcker raised his eyebrows. “So the Swiss know we’re here?”

“The Swiss are quite well-organized and informed. They know that a group of Germans is working at this place for the benefit of Swiss and German industries.”

He picked up the telephone. “Karl, can you please come in and meet some new people?”

A minute later the door opened and a man around thirty entered the room. He was slightly over six feet tall, athletic, with blonde hair and blue eyes – the embodiment of the Aryan ideal.

"Gentlemen, pleasure to meet you. I'm Lieutenant Karl Merkel, late of the SS Death Head Division." He clicked his heels.

"Karl is our quartermaster. He will show you to your rooms and provide all the necessities. If you need any equipment just let him know."

Both scientists nodded and shook hands with Karl.

Kammler smiled and got up, signaling the end of the meeting. "I am available most of the time. Please keep me up to date on your progress."

✡✡✡

Amos Nir relaxed. The election results were coming in and there was a marked movement to the "right" by the electorate. He had hoped for this but hadn't counted on it and so had campaigned very hard for several months. It looked like a majority of the newcomers, who now constituted the great majority of Israel's population, were not particularly receptive to the social justice and pacifist message of the left. The booming economy presented too many opportunities.

The American immigrants didn't see how pacifism would make them safer, especially in view of the war just won, and wealth redistribution had only a limited appeal for them. The millions rescued from Europe were even more skeptical about a peaceful approach, although more than half of them had supported left-leaning parties in their old countries. Apparently they viewed the economic success of Israel as proof enough that the current government was best. Most of those who escaped the Soviet Union didn't want to see or hear anything about socialism or communism.

The Prime Minister's secretary opened the door and looked in. "Amos, the Ministers and the head of the Mossad are here."

"Let them in." Amos got up and welcomed the three men.

After everyone was seated around the conference table he said, "I invited you to hear an update from the Mossad. I heard some of it – It's intriguing." He nodded to the head of the Mossad.

"I will make this story as short as possible, so please don't hesitate to ask questions if I miss any details. I also have to warn you that at this time some details must remain hazy to protect the operation and our operatives.

"About a year ago, when the war in Europe was winding down and the civil war in Germany was at the top of its intensity we received some strange information from Austria. The essence of it was that an SS General by the name of Hans Kammler was assembling a team of engineers and scientists. He was also recruiting former SS officers. This was highly unusual activity in the middle of a civil war. We decided to keep tabs on him. He disappeared for several months and then popped up as the head of an industrial research institute in Mauthousen."

The Defense Minister waved his hand. "You said Mauthousen? Like the infamous concentration camp?"

"Yes, it's also the name of the town nearby. The institute is in the town, not the camp.

"He didn't stay there for very long. It became clear to him that the Nazis were going to lose, so he disappeared again. We got lucky last month. An allied force became aware of a group of Nazis in a Vienna suburb and, after a minor shootout, they were taken into custody. The officer that commanded the raid, an IDF lieutenant, reported to headquarters that the Nazis seemed unusually reticent under interrogation. Since we're copied on all such reports we sent a team to Vienna.

"Our interrogation team managed to extract most, or maybe even all, of the information from members of the group. They were on their way to Switzerland. Apparently they were waiting for someone to take them to their final destination. This person was supposed to come a week after we captured them. Since the incident wasn't reported publicly, we found an operative who fit the physical description of one of the SS officers. He met with the guide and was taken to Hans Kammler in Zug, Switzerland.

"That's how we found out about Kammler's new position. He's the head of the Swiss Industrial Research Institute, in a nice area with some light industry. We also used a female operative to infiltrate the operation. She's now the secretary for one of the scientists."

The Foreign Minister interrupted. "Why are we so interested in this guy Kammler?"

"It started just as a matter of routine. Since in our timeline Kammler was responsible for nuclear research and since his signature was, and still is, on all sorts of technical documents - like the plans for the Auschwitz gas chambers - we consider him a person of interest. After our operative started working at the facility in Switzerland it became clear that they're trying to develop a nuclear weapon."

The Defense Minister asked, "What are their chances of success? They would need enormous resources to develop all the technologies needed."

"True, but they don't know it. And if they can steal all the information from us, the necessary resources will be significantly reduced.

"This brings me to the really interesting information. We know that a person in Israel tried to gain access to nuclear design details. His attempt triggered our alert system and we followed him very carefully. Now we know where the information - or rather, the misinformation we fed him - went. What remains to find out is how it was smuggled to Switzerland and where the Institute is getting its funds."

✡✡✡

Jacob looked at his friend Zalman Gurevich. "Why don't you want to file a claim?"

Zalman shrugged. "The store they took from me in Lithuania wasn't worth that much and I hate wasting time on claims and litigation."

"My friend, you have obviously not read the government announcement very carefully. According to the terms of the peace treaty with Germany, the Germans are obligated to compensate everyone who suffered a loss of property due to their actions in the war. The only thing you need to do is file a claim. *And* you can do that online in five minutes."

"Right. Sounds easy, but how do I prove that the store was taken? They made me sign a bill of sale to that Lithuanian. It was for one Reichsmark but it's still a legitimate bill of sale."

"I'll tell you how. I spoke to Esther's father, Nachman. He abandoned his property. We went online and started filling out the forms. As soon as we submitted them the site came up with a list. Nachman's house and the warehouse where he stored his grain was there.

"The only thing he had to do was to mark the correct property and sign a declaration that he was indeed who he claimed to be. That was all. The government will present these claims with documentation they have from uptime archives and demand payment from the Germans. So don't be stupid and submit your claim. Just don't try cheating. If they catch you claiming property that isn't yours, you'll get in trouble with the police here."

"Okay, I'll try it.

"So how is it going with Esther? Will I get an invitation to your wedding anytime soon?"

"If it was up to me we would have been married a long time ago, but she's stubborn and wants to finish her medical studies first. I'm working on convincing her otherwise. I promise not to forget your invitation."

✡✡✡

The Mossad team met in their Bern hotel room. The communication specialist started. "Last week we intercepted two transfers into the

Institute's bank account. One was from the Essen, Germany, branch of the Dresdner Bank. The other transfer was from a branch of the Deutsche Bank in Mannheim. We ascertained that the account in Essen belongs to a Krupp family foundation and is, most likely, controlled by Alfried Krupp. The account in Mannheim belongs to a law office. We think that it actually disburses funds for a group of Daimler-Benz executives."

A second operative took up the tale. "We also have the account number and pass phrase for a Nazi gold account at the Beerli bank. Our man just checked with a teller. The account is still there and the pass phrase is correct."

The head of the team asked, "Does anyone have ideas how to proceed before I contact the home office?"

"We know that Beerli holds some funds that have been deposited by Jews. We also know that the Nazi account is big, probably close to 40% of the bank's capital. We can use that as leverage to take over the bank. After we control the bank, we can repatriate the Jewish funds to their rightful owners even if the current owner of the bank objects. And we can cut off the Institute's funding. We will also have copies of all the transfers to the Institute's account and so will know with certainty who has been funding them and for what amounts."

"You're correct, except for who's funding them. We already know the account numbers and banks the money comes from. The source of the money in Mannheim is still uncertain since we don't know who controls the account there. I think that we can nail Alfried Krupp though."

"If we have access to all the records of Beerli Bank we might also find the information we need on the Mannheim source."

The head of the team got up. "We will meet here in three hours. I'll speak to the main office and, if they agree, we'll devise an operational plan."

✡✡✡

"It's not going to be a simple undertaking." The Finance Minister paused to check her counterparts' reactions. The Foreign Minister nodded but clearly didn't really understand. The intelligence representative looked openly puzzled.

"Restitution of real property or businesses confiscated by the Nazis or with their support is relatively simple. We have records for the overwhelming majority. The only difficulty will be in determining the value of what has been taken. We're speaking of a lot of money since the properties range from a little hole in the wall store to enterprises like

Leica. There's also confiscated art and other private property, not all of which are in our uptime databases or can be located now."

The intelligence official interrupted. "We know where a lot of that is. For instance, we know where the massive amount of art Goering stole is stored and who it belonged to. Not a simple task to return it but possible, especially since the owners are alive and with us. We will have real difficulties with property that was converted to gold and deposited outside of Germany. Swiss banks hold most of it and I don't think they will be happy to give it up."

"We can apply diplomatic pressure but it will go only so far with the Swiss," the Foreign Minister added.

The intelligence official nodded. "We have a current operation going in Switzerland and, if I get your permission, we may be able to kill a number of birds with a single stone." He went on to explain, with no details, the search for the source of funding of the Swiss Industrial Research Institute. "So we will be speaking to Swiss bankers and, unlike the Foreign Ministry, we can and will if necessary use force to persuade them."

The Finance Minister smiled. "Feel free and we will thank you for the service, as long as you don't involve the state and don't sully our name." The Foreign minister said nothing, just nodded in agreement.

✡✡✡

Franz Beerli was generally a happy man. He was the chairman, general manager, and majority owner of the Beerli Bank. Not a big bank but a very successful one with world renowned firms among its customers and discreet and personal service. Secrecy was its key operating principle.

Franz was a little curious about the visitor who had inquired about his largest account, presenting the correct pass phrase. The inquiry had been routinely reported to him. Nothing happened for a full week so he forgot about it. Now his secretary announced a visitor who gave his account number instead of his name (not an unusual practice) and asked to see the chairman.

The man who entered his office was well-groomed and expensively dressed. He extended his hand. "Heinz," he said with a smile. "That should be enough for the moment."

Franz Beerli shook the offered hand and led his visitor to a coffee table and two armchairs in the corner of his spacious office. "Would you like coffee, tea or something stronger?"

"Coffee would be nice."

Beerli waited for the coffee to be served. “How can I help you?”

Heinz leisurely sipped his coffee. Finally he said, “Mr. Beerli, I would like to make a withdrawal.” He extended a piece of paper with a number and a passphrase.

Beerli glanced at the paper. “When do you want the funds?”

“Right now.” Heinz smiled. “A bank draft would be nice.”

“This is a very large amount. I would need some time to have your funds ready.”

“I understand, Mr. Beerli. How long?”

“I could give you a banker’s draft for about 10% right now and the rest in 10% increments every two weeks. Would that be satisfactory?”

“No, that is not satisfactory at all. My associates want the whole amount within the next three days.”

Beerli smiled a somewhat supercilious smile. “That’s impossible. I offered you the best I can do.”

“I understand. I will report to my associates. I have to warn you that the consequences will be extremely unpleasant. I hope you have your will ready.”

Beerli wasn’t smiling anymore. “The deposit agreement allows ‘a reasonable amount of time’ to arrange for withdrawal. I don’t keep the money here. It’s invested and I need time to retrieve it.”

“Of course. I have a copy of the agreement right here. It says clearly that the funds should be available within not more than three days of the depositor requesting them unless the depositor agrees to an extension. It also states that no problems are foreseen by the depositor in extending the time. Well, depositor doesn’t agree to an extension.

“But I see your problem. This particular deposit comprises close to 40% of your bank’s equity. Removing that amount will undermine the bank’s stability and might even cause it to close. If you prefer, my company can take a majority share in your bank in return for leaving the money deposited. You get your shares back as soon as you repay all the funds. It’s a very generous offer.”

“You want a controlling interest in the bank for 40% of its equity?”

“No, I want 60% of the bank for not bankrupting it right now.”

“I need to think about this. Can we meet tomorrow afternoon to finish this discussion?”

“Certainly.” Heinz got up and left.

He went directly back to his hotel, Hotel Löwen am See. Once in his suite he took a small radio out of his briefcase and keyed in a frequency. "Josh, what's new from the bank?"

"Your guy made two calls as soon as you left. One was to the Research Institute. A short conversation. He informed Hans Kammler of your visit and said that he's sure that the German authorities are on to him.

"His second call was long distance. It took a while but he eventually got through to Alfried Krupp. He told Krupp about your request to cash out the deposit and asked for help. Krupp offered a loan to tie him over. He also informed Krupp that the German authorities might be on to the transfers to Kammler."

"Did you report to Center?"

"Yes, I did. Their instructions are to liquidate the Institute and take care of Krupp. With extreme prejudice. I notified Karl, Michella and the rest of our team. The operation in Essen is probably on its way."

"Good. I'm going to rest for a while and later play tourist and see the city. I'll be meeting with Beerli tomorrow."

✡✡✡

"Hi, Michella. I have some papers for Dr. Hanle to sign." Karl Merkel went into an explanation about the documents as he discretely handed Michella a piece of paper. The message was: "Need to finish everything now. On my way to do Kammler. You take care of both doctors. Meet me in Storeroom 5 in fifteen minutes."

Michella nodded and thanked him aloud.

After Karl was gone she knocked on the inner office door and entered without waiting. Dr. Hanle, who heard Karl's loud explanation, was waiting to sign the papers. She shot him twice in the head with her silenced .22 Beretta. A relatively slow small caliber bullet will make a complete mess of the brain. If it doesn't have enough energy to exit the scull it bounces around inside, causing instantaneous death.

When Dr. Hanle was 'done', Michella locked the door, descended one floor, and entered the office suite of Dr. Höcker. His secretary looked up from the letter she was typing. "A bunch of papers for the doctor to sign," Michella announced. She shot the secretary once through an eye and continued to the inner office. The doctor was surprised to see her but accepted the explanation and was reaching out for the papers when she shot him in the face and the forehead. He died instantly.

Karl was late. While waiting for him she went ahead with the preparations, opening two 50 liter containers that had "Caution! Flammable!" stenciled on them. They contained ammonium nitrate mixed with hydrazine. The resulting clear liquid is a powerful explosive, several times that of TNT. Michella attached detonators to the inside of the two caps and screwed them back onto the containers. Everything was ready for an encoded radio signal to explode the bombs. An explosion equivalent to several hundred kilograms of TNT, in addition to the conflagration caused by the solvents stored in the room, was certain to destroy the building.

Karl entered the room five minutes after she was done. He was slightly stressed. "The damn Nazi disappeared. His secretary said that he receive a phone call from the banker and immediately went somewhere. He's certainly not in the building."

"We have to go ahead with the final stage. He's not likely to come back here, that is assuming the banker warned him about Heinz."

"Are the doctors done?" Karl inquired.

"Yes. I also locked both office suites, but it won't take long for someone to get suspicious. We need to go now."

The couple went out the front door of the Institute holding hands – the guards, and everyone else, knew that they were dating and were not surprised.

"See you after lunch." Michella waved to the head of the guard detail, who waved back.

Half an hour later a huge explosion shook the calm air of the far western suburb of Zug. The Institute for Industrial Research was no more.

On board a train to Lugano, Michella said to Karl, "I still feel uncomfortable killing everyone at the Institute. There probably were innocents there."

"What innocents? They may have looked like nice people but all were handpicked by General SS Kammler and you know what kind of monster he is. They were all members of the SS, the Gestapo, or some other Nazi organization. Some, like the head of the guard detail that liked you so much, had a lot of blood on their hands. That guy was SS and killed prisoners of war in Poland and in the Balkans. I know that one of the secretaries was very proud of her service to the Fatherland, in Dachau.

"The civilians were no better. All of them knew what they were trying to build and had no problem handing the Nazis a nuclear weapon. I'm sorry you had to take care of the two doctors personally but they were good scientists and eager to do Kammler's bidding. Too dangerous to leave them to chance."

Michella smiled at Karl. “Thank you, that helps. But I’m not sure I want to continue in this business.”

✡✡✡

Ze’ev looked at the landscape unfolding below the helicopter. They were flying several hundred meters above the green, wooded landscape. The chopper was on Earth 2 bearing southeast, from where Herzliya would be to Red Sea 2. The new oil terminal and refinery were in Aqaba 2. In this universe the land was mostly empty, except for animals panicked by their noisy passage.

They arrived at the refinery location several hours later, landing on the pad by the brand new office building.

“Welcome to the Delek refinery.”

The man that greeted Ze’ev was dressed casually and smiling. They shook hands and proceeded into the office building. Inside the light wasn’t as glaring as it was outside. The glass walls were darkly tinted.

After settling in the operating manager’s office and getting the obligatory coffee and cookies, Ze’ev said, “I see that you’re mostly done here. When will you start deliveries?”

“We started already. Only test batches. We will be at full production within five months, if everything works out according to plan. Which it probably will not.”

“Sounds good. As much as I enjoy chatting with you I still need to catch a flight.”

“The plane is almost ready to go. We’re finishing loading cargo. There are several other passengers, although you are the guest of honor. They will call when they’re ready for you. You’re scheduled to be in Baghdad 2 before sundown.”

“It’s a really silly situation. I have a small airstrip by my office in Herzliya but the Environmental Agency told me to stop using my jet. They think it scares the wildlife. Do they mess with you a lot?”

The manager shrugged. “They’re enforcing the same standards as in Israel. Here we’re really close to the border in our universe so it kind of makes sense. In alternate Iraq it makes less sense but we’re not objecting. Our families live not too far away from the oil.”

Ze’ev main purpose on this trip was tourism of a kind. He wanted to see how the alternate universe settlement and industry were developing. To do that he needed to actually see and smell what was happening.

He was impressed by what had been done in less than a year. On their approach to the little airport - which had a proper control tower, three runways, and a terminal building - Ze'ev could see a medium-sized settlement. He noticed a number of smaller agricultural villages on the way in. He knew that the whole area supported close to twenty-five thousand people and imported no basic foodstuffs. In fact, it was scheduled to start exporting food by the middle of the year.

Ze'ev enjoyed his short vacation. He decided that the time was ripe for Consolidated to expand its operations and start mining the raw materials it needed instead of buying them abroad.

Chapter 18
February 1944

The Prime Minister gestured to the Head of the Mossad to sit at the conference table with the rest of the Cabinet. Amos Nir invited the chief spy to start his presentation.

"I have mostly good news. As you know from my previous updates we discovered a Nazi-led operation attempting to build a nuclear weapon using information stolen from us. In fact, the Nazi general that started it all, SS General Hans Kammler, tried to organize a research facility in Austria. He disappeared as the German civil war was ending. Apparently he was contacted months later by someone from the German Foreign Ministry and told that information from the future on how to build a bomb might become available.

"It took us some time but we unraveled the mystery of who was the source in Israel. The Security Service notified us months ago that a German national who arrived here just before the time travel event, one Hans Paulus, wanted access to the recently classified area of a university library. We took over from there.

"Apparently Mr. Paulus is an electrical engineer who used to work for Siemens and is now employed by Siemens Israel. He discovered that his great uncle, General Paulus of Stalingrad fame, was alive and well in this timeline and a member of the German temporary government. This somehow ignited his patriotic instinct. He decided to steal information he thought would be useful to Germany.

"The current German government decided, as you all know, to keep their up-time staff here. Over the last several months senior members travelled to Germany. They were supposed to be updated on the current situation and the objectives and policies of the government. We kept an eye on some of them, especially the Third Secretary of the embassy. He used to be rabidly anti-Israel, supporting Hamas and any other enemy organization he could find. We also knew that he held far left views, so far left that he was really a fascist. Our surveillance paid off: while in Germany he contacted a Nazi in their Foreign Ministry. This wasn't difficult since he had all the historical records and could reliably contact a Nazi even though the man was hiding his loyalties. Apparently they arrived at an understanding and the Third Secretary started looking for ways to transfer uptime scientific information to this person. He followed Hans Paulus for a while and finally contacted him after Paulus was admitted to the secure part of the BGU library. Apparently he thought that Paulus was a good candidate because he is a German national, an engineer working for Siemens and, most importantly, a member of the famous Paulus family.

"Paulus was to leave nuclear information at a dead drop for the Third Secretary to pick up. We replaced those documents with our own version - all dead ends leading to costly failures. We discovered later that General Hans Kammler did receive the information and gave it to the scientists cooperating with him.

"In a separate operation we discovered the location of Kammler's research facility in Zug, Switzerland, and planted two agents inside. Zohar Kimmel, known to the Germans as SS Lieutenant Karl Merkel, and Michella Stern of the Mussolini operation fame. We monitored the Institute's work with the view of eventually destroying it but in the meantime letting it attract pro-Nazi scientists and engineers so we could identify them. We also wanted to find and shut off their funding sources. Hans Kammler was also a primary target and marked for liquidation."

The Defense Minister interrupted. "Why not destroy the Institute immediately? It seems to me that you took an unreasonable risk. What if they actually learned something valuable and transmitted it to a third party?"

"We considered that possibility and actually rigged the whole building for complete demolition as soon as our people got there. We carefully monitored their communications and found it a useful honey trap for Nazi nuclear scientists and engineers. There was also the question of funding. If we destroyed the Institute before we found their financial supporters we would likely never have found them.

"In any case, a couple of week ago we found the banks and accounts in Germany that were feeding the Institute's Swiss account. We also found that the private bank where the account was located held gold deposited there by Goering just before he was killed. At that point we made a mistake: our agent tried to pressure the owner of the bank into giving us control.

"This would have had a number of advantages but our attempt failed. Not only did the banker refuse but he also warned Kammler that something fishy was going on. Kammler disappeared. We destroyed the Institute the same day so he was the only person to escape. I believe that he took with him records of all the work that had been done by the Institute. This is not necessarily a bad thing. It could mislead them into spending lots of resources on dead ends.

"We were successful on the financial end. Approximately 60% of the funding was provided by Alfried Krupp. He is a known Nazi sympathizer, very rich and influential, enough so that the current German government was reluctant to touch him. We didn't bother them with the information. Mr. Krupp had the bad luck to die of a heart attack at his mansion in Essen.

"Just a reminder: In our timeline, after the end of WWII Krupp was tried and convicted of crimes against humanity. He served three years in prison, was pardoned, and died in 1967.

"The rest of the funding came from an account owned by a foundation. Our information pointed to a group of Daimler executives controlling it. We gave this information to the German authorities. They seized the opportunity to take down this group of people who had supported their enemies. The Third Secretary of the German embassy was expelled and immediately arrested in Germany as an accessory to Nazi activities. We arrested Hans Paulus and he will be tried for espionage. The German government agreed not to ask for his extradition. I'm sure they're eager to lay their hands on our nuclear secrets but are reluctant to anger us and so cooperate, at least for the time being.

"We continue to look for Hans Kammler but I have to warn all present that we will have to continuously guard our nuclear secrets.

"The Swiss banker who refused to cooperate with us agreed to do so after the Institute exploded. He's still running the bank but we have full access and will use it to repatriate all the assets taken from Jews."

✡✡✡

Yaron Weizmann, the Israeli Ambassador to the Kingdom of Jordan, was seated in an overstuffed armchair opposite the King. He sipped from his cup of coffee. "Your Majesty, we realize that your neighbor Ibn Saud is in a bit of trouble. He lost huge amounts of money when oil prices collapsed and he can't pay his army. But this is not a reason for you to attack him."

"On the contrary. I think this is a perfect time. I have no idea how long the oil slump will last, and in the meantime he's defenseless against the Royal Jordanian Army. The Americans have barely a presence there and the whole kingdom will be easy pickings."

"True, but are you prepared for a prolonged war and possible American involvement? Our intelligence is that while you could defeat the Saudi army quite handily, after that you will have to contend with uprisings by his client tribes. Your army isn't large enough to intimidate them into submission."

"You're absolutely correct, Ambassador. The thing is that I don't need to intimidate them or even conquer them. If I topple Ibn Saud, take the holy cities of Mecca and Medina and a swatch of land between my current border and the two cities, I will be the ruler of the most important part of Arabia. In time I will pacify the rest of it."

Ambassador Yaron Weizmann thought for a long while. Finally he said, "I know that my government is wary of military adventures of the kind you're proposing. There may be a better way. What do you think of putting your son Prince Naif bin Al-Abdullah on the Syrian throne?"

Abdullah eyebrows climbed up. "Is this possible? Won't it entail a war even worse than if I try to take over the Arabian Peninsula?"

"It could get complicated but it may be possible to arrange for it to happen. The republican factions in Syria are fighting each other. They are superficially united to get the British and French out. That will end as soon as the colonial powers leave, which the French are already preparing to do. We know all the players, both minor and major, and dislike them all. We can persuade one of the large Syrian factions to support a friendly ruler as king. They are open to the idea of a constitutional monarchy."

Abdullah was silent for several minutes. Finally he said, "What is your interest in this?"

"It's really very simple. As I said, we know the Syrian factions. They will end up fighting each other. In our time, a dictator won out and attacked us."

"What do you care? You can defeat them without lifting a finger. So destroy them if they attack."

"Would you have us kill all Syrians?"

"You don't have to kill them all, just the leadership."

"And how long would it take new leaders to take revenge on us? There would be no end. Arranging for Syria to have leadership that is friendly to us and slowly getting the population used to the idea of being friends with Jews seems like a much better idea.

"By the way, we already see some changes in your kingdom. With religious leaders not spewing venom against us, relations should stay on an even keel for many years to come."

"This is to my advantage also, but I will need more assistance to make the people peaceful. I am worried about the British and French machinations and the Americans' influence in the Arabian Peninsula."

"We're also watchful of the colonial powers. All three are interested in the Middle East only because of its oil reserves. If the price of oil falls low enough they will lose interest. Left to our own devices we will manage just fine."

"True, but how do you drop the price of oil?"

"We already have. Our oil companies discovered huge reserves. We are exporting oil at a price that neither the British nor the Americans can match. Our output is growing and in a couple of years will be more than the combined output of the British and American interests in this region. I expect that they will try pressuring us to raise the price."

"And will you?" Abdullah inquired.

"I don't think so. We are negotiating to supply oil to them so they will become our allies. Our aims are political, not economic. We want them to leave us in peace and leave this region to its inhabitants. Of course, there's a strategic aspect to oil. Countries want a secure source to supply their energy needs. We'll see how this develops. Hopefully with a cheap, steady and secure supply no one will worry about strategic problems. At least not for a long time."

✡✡✡

"Gentlemen, I have some bad news and some good news." Nitzan Liebler, the Defense Minister paused. "I guess I'll give you the bad news first: We decided to scale back our tank manufacturing program. We will go back to our original one tank per week schedule."

The bosses of the big companies looked at each other. Ze'ev Hirshson of Consolidated and Itamar Herz of the Israel Aircraft Industries said nothing. The Chairman of the Military Industries looked upset. The commander of the Engineering Corps said nothing.

The Defense Minister continued. "Now the good news. We need large numbers of four wheel drive vehicles. We'll also start building our own helicopters and transport planes and restart the development of our own jet fighter.

"The companies represented here have some knowhow in most of these areas but will need partners. We will distribute basic specifications for the equipment we need and give you a couple of months to respond."

Itamar Herz, president of IAI, raised his hand. "Jets and cargo planes we know. It will take us a while but we can restart the Arye fighter program. We can copy cargo and passenger jets. I have doubts about helicopters. Our knowhow is limited to maintenance. How soon do you want a working model?"

"As soon as you can make one. We have no set timetable.

“Maybe I should explain where the need is. We are expanding into a parallel Earth - call it Earth 2. It is mostly identical to our Earth with the keyword being ‘mostly’. We need to explore it and be able to move quickly. The government will lay claim to some areas and leave the rest to private enterprise.”

Herz nodded. “Dr. Hirshson and I were discussing this before the meeting. I think that Israel Aircraft Industries would be interested in setting up facilities on Earth 2. We have a surveying party out and they will, hopefully, find an appropriate site. We might partner with Consolidated in developing the area.”

The Israel Military Industries’ chairman perked up. “I’ll have to obtain my board’s approval, but we will likely want to join you.”

The Defense Minister smiled. “You have this Board member’s vote.”

Ze’ev nodded. “This is all well and good, but we have a problem. The government decided at an early stage that Israel 2 has to be kept empty so that we can move there in a hurry if the need arises. That creates a hardship. We build on sites outside our current borders. This means a long commute over undeveloped land. Building on Earth 2 next to our current locations in Israel it would make everything so much easier.”

Nitzan Liebler smiled. “I’m sure you have an idea that will solve both the need for a short commute and the government’s restrictions.”

“Yes, it’s simple. We open up Earth 3 and reserve it for the state. We develop the industries that need more space on Earth 2. Completely private, no government investment at all. If the state has move to Earth 3, Earth 2 will be ready to support it. We will soon have massive amounts of goods flowing through the gates from Earth 2. This traffic can easily go to Earth 3, solving our emergency supply problems.”

Liebler nodded. “I’ll bring it up at the next cabinet meeting. I doubt you will get a private planet all to yourself. The State of Israel will probably retain control.”

Chapter 19
April 1944

"Wolf, what plans do you have for after your army service?" Ze'ev smiled. "Did you think of taking a job?"

"My army service will end in six months. Afterwards I want to go to college."

They were sitting in Ze'ev's study at home, after a family Sabbath dinner.

"Yes, college is a good idea. What do you plan on studying?"

"I'm undecided between electrical or mechanical engineering."

"Engineering is good. Plenty of interesting jobs. The Technion offers a degree in industrial management. Have you consider that?"

Wolf shook his head. "I didn't. I have some 'management' experience as an officer but never thought of it as a career."

"Yes, I know how that works. Which engineering schools are you considering?"

"A year ago I thought I'd like to attend the Technion. Now things are more complicated. We haven't announced it yet, but Sheina and I are going to get married as soon as I'm out of the army. As you know, she's studying computer science at BGU in Beer Sheva. She's agreeable to transfer to the Technion, which might work out, although there are difficulties."

"Yes, my alma mater is difficult to get into. They have high admission standards and make it hard to transfer credits from other schools even if you are accepted. Difficult but not impossible, especially for students that are at the top of their class.

"Excuse me for the direct question - How do you plan on paying for college?"

"You're not the first one in the family to ask this question. My parents offered to help. I plan on getting a part-time job to pay the rest."

"Unless you're a lot more gifted than most people, you will have problems working during the first two years. At the Technion they keep you extremely busy and if you screw up you're out.

"What about Sheina? She's graduating next year, isn't she?"

"Yes, but we want to start a family."

Sheina entered the room at that point. "Mind if I join you, or are you two discussing secrets?"

Ze'ev smiled. "Please, come in. I was just going to look for you anyway. We were discussing what you and Wolf are planning.

"I have a proposition that might make life easier for you. Last year Consolidated started a scholarship program funding studies at the Technion, including tuition and living expenses. The company needs engineers and managers. Your grades must be in the top half of your class and you have to sign up for four years of employment with us after graduation."

"What if we decide to stay in Beer Sheva, next to family?" Sheina asked.

"We will think of something," Ze'ev responded.

✡✡✡

The Prime Minister opened the weekly Cabinet meeting by summarizing the agenda.

"As you all know we approved several government-owned corporations expanding their facilities on Earth 2. Since the approval, many private companies have joined in and we now have a sizeable industrial infrastructure in close proximity to Israel 2. The Israel Electric Corporation concluded that a Mediterranean to Dead Sea canal to generate hydroelectric power is feasible there. Israel Chemicals objects because it might elevate the level of the Dead Sea and reduce their profits. Our experts disagree. I recommend that we allow the construction of a second hydroelectric plant on Earth 2. The project will be funded by private investors and will sell electricity on every Earth."

The Foreign Minister waved a hand. "How should we respond to questions from foreign governments about Earth 2?"

The Defense Minister responded, "The same way we respond to questions about nuclear weapons."

"But no one asked about nuclear weapons," the Foreign Minister responded.

“Exactly. The only way a foreign government will become aware of the other Earth is by spying and I doubt that they will ask questions,” responded the Defense Minister.

The Prime Minister added, “If they do ask, we should, in my opinion, ask for clarifications. For the time being the whole thing is classified. There are several thousand people who know the truth and eventually, with the growth of employment there, the secret will leak out. We will deal with it when it does.

“Going back to my summary, our relations with the big powers are reasonably good. Both the Americans and the British are complaining about the low price of oil. There are others who are quite happy about the low price, including all the other European countries.

“We hinted to both the British and French that it may be to their advantage to clear out of the Middle East. The French are likely to get out of Syria very soon. The British say they will leave but are dragging their feet. They don’t want to abandon their empire.”

The Infrastructure Minister asked, “Can you update us on the situation in Russia?”

The Foreign Minister responded, “Lots of things are happening there. Nothing we haven’t seen before. Ukraine and Belarus declared independence, as did most of the republics that don’t belong to the Russian Federation.

“Up to this point the Soviet Union has fractured along the same stress lines as in our timeline. One difference seems to be that the NKVD and the Communists are much less popular here and now. In our timeline the people got used to them whereas here their rule was much shorter and people remember both Stalin’s atrocities and the relative freedom of Kerensky’s government. There’s still fighting so it’s difficult to say how it will settle out.

“The Russian situation has repercussions in China. In our timeline Mao received help - arms and military advice – from the Soviets. Mao parted ways with Stalin quickly, but in this timeline Stalin disappeared before the Chinese Communists received much assistance. The Nationalists are still being supported by the U.S. We will see how this develops.

“One thing that didn’t happen here is the French attempt to re-take Indochina. They probably read some of the uptime history books and decided against it. So no U.S. involvement and no Vietnam War in the future. On the other hand, without Soviet or Chinese support there may be no Communist Vietnam to fight.”

“We started supplying Jordan with water from Earth 2 and are building a desalination plant in Aqaba. This should strengthen Abdullah and make our alliance stronger. If the Brits and Americans get out of the region, we hope to build stable alliances and avoid most of the grief in our timeline."

✡✡✡

Michella spent the last week mostly on the beach in Tel Aviv with her friend, and maybe future husband, Zohar Kimmel, known to the Germans and Swiss as Karl Merkel.

"Michella, do you want me to re-apply your sunscreen?" Zohar asked. "If not can you re-apply mine."

Michella knelt beside Zohar with a tube of sunscreen. "I was meaning to tell you that I'm not going back to the office. I was offered a job that is very interesting and decided to take it."

Zohar turned his head trying to see her from his belly down position on the sand. "What kind of job?"

"Head of intelligence for the Portal Corporation. I can't wait to start. Exploring a new planet and maybe eventually settling in the wilderness on Earth 2."

Zohar rolled over on his back. "Must be a well-paying job for you to abandon all the excitement of the service."

Michella Stern smiled. "It does pay very well, and I'm getting tired of the kind of excitement we get at the office. Aren't you?"

She got down on the blanket and snuggled up to Zohar.

"Will we continue dating?" Zohar asked.

"If we want to. I'll be spending most of my time just twenty steps from the gate in Herzliya, so nothing will change unless you move far away."

"So you're planning to go exploring the wilderness on the other side?" Zohar inquired.

"That's one of the perks of the job. I will also be able to claim some land as my own. I'm going there tomorrow and will take a week to travel and see the sights. Want to join me?"

Chapter 20

August 1948

Jacob Hirshson woke with a start. It was very early; the light outside was grey. He took a couple of seconds to orient himself, and finally figured out that the baby was crying. Jacob promised Esther that he would take care of the second child so it was his turn to get up and see what was wrong. He extricated himself from his wife's embrace, careful not to wake her, and went to the next room. The baby was sound asleep - a false alarm of his imagination. Since he was up already Jacob checked on their toddler daughter. She was also asleep.

By now he was wide awake and decided to do some work. There was a lot to do. Uncle Chaim was still running the surveying company and had ideas of expanding into construction. Jacob had doubts but needed to review the business plan before deciding. His main business, Hirshson Computers, was prospering but needed a lot of attention. A major issue was quality control. Hirshson Computers commanded an above average price that was justified by performance and quality. His other concern was marketing, or rather not doing too much of it. Hirshson was the largest personal computer company in the world and he had to be careful not to sell more than he could deliver.

At 6:30 a.m. Jacob heard the alarm clock go off in the master bedroom. Esther emerged a little later.

"How early did you get up?" she asked.

"At five. Leo woke me but went right back to sleep."

Esther nodded. "Yes, Mira used to do that too sometimes. Well, I'll get ready to go." She was a year away from graduating from the Ben Gurion University Medical School in Refidim and was busy.

Jacob got up from his desk. "I'll start getting ready as well. Gina should be here soon."

Gina was their baby-sitter/housekeeper. She took care of the children and supervised the cleaning lady and cook. Esther's parents considered her family - She had been their next door neighbor in the old country. Now in her mid-sixties, with grown children living in Refidim, she enjoyed being their housekeeper.

As he was leaving the house Jacob's cell phone rang. It was his mother. "Come to Sabbath dinner at our place, with the kids. Sheina and Wolf and their children will be here as well."

"Okay. I'll check with Esther. Unless she has a night shift at the hospital we will be there."

"Good. Avram and I will be happy to see you. It's our anniversary. But no presents, please."

His mother had married Avram Soloveichik in 1947. Jacob remembered him from Vilna, where he was a furniture merchant and customer of Jacob's father. A nice, gentle man, widowed in 1941. The newlyweds lived in Jacob's old house, which he left to his mother after he married Esther.

Wolf and Sheina also lived in Refidim. Wolf had gotten a loan from Ze'ev to cover his first year of tuition and expenses at the Technion but decided it was best to stay near Sheina's family instead of moving to Haifa. Wolf enrolled in the new Refidim branch of Ben Gurion University, majoring in electrical engineering, and Sheina started working at her brother's computer company.

For a while Wolf took a part-time job as a teacher at a local high school to pay for school, but he didn't like teaching. During his third year at the university he accepted Jacob's job offer to refine a design for a new motherboard using a chipset just announced by Intel. Now they lived, with their three children, in a nice house not far from Jacob and Esther.

✡✡✡

The Prime Minister took the time to shake hands with every Cabinet member. Yoram Keinan was new to this job, elected only a week ago. Amos Nir had decided not to run for reelection. He claimed that he needed a rest and didn't deny that he might run again. The right-wing ruling party was still firmly in the saddle and the coalition was stable.

Yoram Keinan invited everyone to sit. "Since this is our first formal meeting, I would like to stick to the agenda. First, we have a presentation by the new head of the Mossad and new head of the Security Services."

The Security Services man stood. "Not much to report. Our local Arab population is content. There have been a few subversive activities on the far left and on the far right, but nothing serious.

"After the Knesset allowed the death penalty for certain offenses we saw a significant drop in espionage attempts. Since the incident four years ago with the Secretary of the German embassy we have had no more such cases. There are, of course, the normal attempts of industrial espionage and also attempts to steal military technology. As far as we know none have been successful."

The head of the Mossad began her presentation. "The situation is slightly more complicated outside our borders. We noticed that there was less interest in advanced arms and more interest in quantum mechanics and, of all things, magic. This doesn't mean that arms are not high on the list, only that something else is higher.

"Apparently, some information about our ability to open gates to other universes has leaked so a number of countries are trying to get into the game. We know that the U.S., Britain, Russia, Germany, and France are all investing resources in quantum research. Of course it's not easy to accomplish what we did without the necessary background. They will likely get there eventually, maybe sixty or seventy years. Then there are institutions investing in the research of magic. Maybe they will also come up with something interesting. In the meantime we seem to be secure and we know of no plots against us. Unlike the timeline we left, this one is friendly to us. Mostly it's the absence of a forum like the old UN that gave a voice to various anti-Semites."

The Foreign Minister raised his hand. "Our embassies in several countries have been approached, discreetly, with questions about alternate universes. We follow the script we devised a while ago: ask whether the inquirer was referring to a science fiction story. This usually terminates the inquiry. They either decide that the whole thing was a misunderstanding of a science fiction fable, or that we're not welcoming these questions. A Secretary at our embassy in Japan mentioned an occult reference. Maybe they believed him."

After the two spymasters left, the Prime Minister asked the Foreign Minister for an update.

"As we expected, Abdullah's son isn't fit to rule, so his father is the regent for Syria. He's not a bad ruler and, somewhat to our surprise, instituted a relatively liberal constitutional monarchy. His rule seems to be stable and both Jordan and Syria are prospering, with some help from us.

"Egypt is a different story. King Faruq is weak and corrupt, as is his bureaucracy. We anticipate a revolt sooner or later, as happened in our original timeline. We tried all we could think of to correct the situation but neither the king nor his British supporters see a problem.

"Speaking of the British: their empire is starting to unravel. India is restless and their Southeast Asian possessions are making independence noises as well. Singapore and Malaya in particular are demanding autonomy. The Brits read our history books and are introducing reforms. How successful they'll be is uncertain.

“China is still fighting a civil war, although it seems that a coalition led by the Nationalists – with American support - is slowly winning. They are cleaning up their government and gradually gaining more popular support. It might take decades before we see a stable government in China.”

The meeting went on for a while. There were no Earth-shattering revelations or dangers that had to be urgently acted upon.

The End

Made in the USA
Middletown, DE
15 December 2016